QD
QG
QF
QA

Kate Furnivall was born in Wales and studied English at London University. She worked in publishing and then moved to TV advertising, where she met her husband.

In 2000, Kate decided to write her mother's extraordinary story of growing up in Russia, China and India, and this became *The Russian Concubine*, which was a *New York Times* bestseller. All her books since then have had an exotic setting and Kate has travelled widely for her research. She now has two sons and lives with her husband by the sea in Devon.

Visit Kate's website at www.katefurnivall.com

The GUARDIAN *of* LIES

KATE FURNIVALL

**SIMON &
SCHUSTER**

London · New York · Sydney · Toronto · New Delhi

A CBS COMPANY

First published in Great Britain by Simon & Schuster UK Ltd, 2019
A CBS COMPANY

Copyright © Kate Furnivall, 2019

The right of Kate Furnivall to be identified as author
of this work has been asserted in accordance with the
Copyright, Designs and Patents Act, 1988.

1 3 5 7 9 10 8 6 4 2

Simon & Schuster UK Ltd
1st Floor
222 Gray's Inn Road
London WC1X 8HB

Simon & Schuster Australia, Sydney
Simon & Schuster India, New Delhi

www.simonandschuster.co.uk
www.simonandschuster.com.au
www.simonandschuster.co.in

A CIP catalogue record for this book
is available from the British Library

Hardback ISBN: 978-1-4711-7231-1
Trade Paperback ISBN: 978-1-4711-7232-8
eBook ISBN: 978-1-4711-7233-5
Audio ISBN: 978-1-4711-8087-3

Typeset in the UK by M Rules
Printed and bound by CPI Group (UK) Ltd, Croydon, CR0 4YY

For Lilli, April and Pete
with all my love

The
GUARDIAN
of LIES

CHAPTER ONE

Paris, France, 1953

It started right here. In Paris. In the Eighth Arrondissement. The night that ripped my life apart. It was a night when the wind was sharp and the scent of the river strong. I was seated in the dark in my cranky old Renault on a dull street outside a dreary five-storey building you wouldn't look at twice. But I knew that behind its ordinary black door and beneath its innocuous grey zinc roof it was anything but dull. I wanted to be inside that building so bad it choked me.

It was late evening. I had been waiting for three hours, hands clamped on the steering wheel, sweat crawling between my shoulder blades, and every ten minutes I wiped my palms on my coat. Cars droned past. Headlights chased each other through the night down towards Boulevard de Clichy, where I could hear heavy traffic grinding past, ignoring me. An old lady, black as a cockroach in her widow's weeds, leaned out of a brightly lit upper window and studied me with suspicion. I swore, sank down in my seat and burrowed into my scarf. I'd swept my long dark hair up out of sight under an unmemorable felt hat and my navy coat collar was pulled up around my ears. I was well trained.

When the black door finally jerked open, the overhead fanlight showed me a man who flew down the three front steps in one stride. I studied his face, seeking signs. He was tall, alert, fast. He moved with authority and focus as he hurried to my car. His name was André Caussade and he was my brother.

'Drive,' he ordered.

I prodded the engine into life. He threw himself into the front passenger seat and slammed the door with such force I felt its old bones grind against each other. He smelled of polished boot leather.

'Drive, Eloïse.'

Not a shout. No panic. But the urgency of his words left me in no doubt. I threw the gear lever into first and the car skidded away from the kerb. I forced a path through the darkness into the incessant flow of Paris traffic, elbowing my way in behind a wheezing truck. This was why I was here – to help my brother. The Caussades together. But Parisian drivers are like Stalin's army – they take no prisoners. Horns blared. My mother's moral status was loudly called into question by a driver who nearly took my bumper home with him. It was ten o'clock at night, and no Frenchman in his right mind thinks of anything after that hour except a glass in front of him and a warm thigh under his hand.

André offered no explanation. He was a man who used words sparsely and those he did use were often shaped into lies. To distract. To make you look in the wrong direction. He was good at that.

My brother worked for the CIA, the American Intelligence agency. I don't say that lightly. I say it with reverence. It was the job I yearned for, in vain. To follow in my brother's footsteps. I wanted to be part of those who help keep France safe in these dangerous times, and yes, I know it sounds over-dramatic, but the life of a field agent can be dangerous, André kept assuring me. I was learning the truth of that myself right now.

André had spent his whole childhood being both mother and father to me – far more than Papa had ever been. So when the telephone rang this evening and it was André's voice telling me to be in my car outside a certain house on a certain street, I was there within a heartbeat.

Whoever was chasing André's tail didn't stand a chance. He was too quick, too smart. André was … I want to say invincible. But it is the wrong word. My brother was the kind of man who, if you were hanging by a slippery thread, dangling over a raging pit of hellfire, you'd want him there.

Believe me, you would. You'd want him and his cool certainty that he could outwit all the hard-eyed bastards that the Kremlin could throw at him. As children growing up in the wide marsh delta of the Camargue, he taught me the delights of creating codes and the thrills of the dead letter drop, and later in Paris he took me to secret meetings in places my father would skin the hide off me for setting foot in. Paris, you must understand, was not a city in 1953. It was a cesspit. It rotted the soul. It was the devil's own vile hairy arsehole, according to Papa. I'd learned from him already that bulls and horses mattered more than motherless children, and that up in the towering mountains God rumbled his disapproval each time I went skinny-dipping in the sweet pools of the River Rhône.

My father looked like Abraham in my children's Bible. Long beard. Ebony staff. And like Abraham, my father performed a sacrifice to God once a year up among the rugged sun-bleached cliffs of Les Beaux de Provence. Not of his son; of course not. No, even Abraham was spared that.

But every Easter my father led one of his beloved black bull calves up into the wilds of nowhere and slit the poor creature's throat. I always watched for his return, clinging to the top rail of our fence and to the desperate hope that this Joseph – or whatever Old Testament name I had bestowed on the condemned animal – would return this time. But no. My father stumbled down the mountain alone, hands steeped in blood.

I never knew what he was atoning for and I never asked. He had named his younger son Isaac, though we were not Jewish. It meant something. Like the blood meant something.

But I didn't know what.

But even with Papa's curses ringing in my ears I'd come to Paris and now I could smell danger on André. Sour as cat's piss, and I was frightened for him. Beside me he swivelled in his seat to study the traffic behind us, but all that was visible was a blur of headlights. The darkness curled around us and white fingers of fog rose up from the River Seine, ready to snatch away familiar landmarks.

Soviet Intelligence had a liking for the use of black cars and there were plenty of those in the city. Hairs prickled on the back of my neck as I drove. André glanced across at me – did he sense my nerves? – and in the flicker of the sulphur-yellow light from a streetlamp, I caught one of his rare smiles, his long jaw softening. His skin and his hair were the colour of sand, his jacket too. He claimed it made him harder to pick out in a crowd. But I could spot him anywhere.

'Lose them,' he whispered.

Who *them* were, I didn't know. But I knew Paris and its secret places. I had learned every one of them. I swung the wheel hard and my car mounted the pavement, scattering pedestrians like confetti, narrowly missing a domed pissoir with an alarmed occupant. On Rue de Richelieu with its coin shops and formal grey façades I squeezed the car between the narrow walls of a side alleyway meant for nothing more ambitious than a cat and my offside wing squealed in protest as a layer of its skin was peeled off. I knew the city's byways the way a spider knows its own web. From the grand thoroughfares of the Champs-Élysées to the cobbled mean streets of Montmartre up on its hill and the nooks and crannies of the Latin Quarter's bars and cafés on the Left Bank, I had walked them all in my sleep.

I spotted the tail the moment I hit Boulevard de Sébastopol. The boulevard was a broad four-lane highway flanked by large five-storey buildings and bare-limbed trees that threw spiky black shadows across our path. It sliced through the Second and Third Arrondissements, and I was weaving between lanes, dodging in and out. It took only seconds to pick out the car swerving behind me – a dark sleek Renault Frégate. Faster than mine, but my 4CV could corner on a centime. I watched the glare of its headlamps draw closer.

Who were they?

What were they after?

They must be working a three-car net around me to still be in touch. The buildings were grander here, the roads wider, and beside me André held a small but silent High Standard HDM/S pistol on his knee, his hand rock-steady. My heart was hammering, my own fingers ice-cold but I concentrated on the road ahead. I waited till the last moment, then flipped off to the right. Zipped past the dark looming arches of Les Halles market, and immediately sharp left. The Renault behind me reacted too late and overshot. I released my breath. André uttered a grunt of approval and I made a dash for the Pont Neuf.

We shot across the oldest bridge in Paris, its ranks of tall lampposts throwing a shroud of amber over the fog that was rising from the Seine and swirling around us like layers of old lace. The wide stone bridge was not busy at this late hour, though a ramshackle lorry trundling along ahead of me slowed me down, so I was trapped when a motorbike suddenly roared out of nowhere. I was acutely aware of its single eye fixed on us in the darkness, its rider hidden inside his balaclava. It was swerving up on my passenger side, its engine roaring in my ears when I saw André raise his pistol. Instantly I twitched the steering wheel. Just enough so that my rear wheel clipped the bike. We felt the impact judder through the car, and heard a screech of metal but I didn't look back. I didn't care to see the rider sprawled across the pavement or hear the Russian curses he was throwing after me.

I rolled down my window a crack, I needed more air but the fog crept in, carrying the stink of the river with it. I glanced across at André and saw a smile spreading across his face.

'Well done,' he said. 'Turn left here.'

'No.' I shook my head. 'I know a place, a safe place.'

I veered right and plunged us into the maze of narrow roads that riddled the Left Bank district, turning and twisting past brightly lit bars and brothels until I was absolutely certain no headlights were following us. Finally, in a mean passageway with only two streetlamps still functioning, the beam of my headlights picked out a small brick archway and I drove through it with relief. It opened into a courtyard, cobwebbed with iron staircases and a row of lock-up garages. I cut the lights, jumped out of the car and unlocked one of the garage doors. Before André could blink, I'd reversed the car in and locked the doors behind us.

At last my head grew quiet. The grind and growl inside it ceased, and the blood flowed back to my fingertips.

We sat in the car, André and I, in silence, just the ticking of the engine as it cooled. The darkness was solid and smothering, sticking to my skin.

'What is this place?' André asked. 'How do you know about it?'

'It belongs to the father of a friend of mine whom I met while I've been working in the detective agency here. You know that I know Paris streets backwards, all the alleyways and backstreets that my work takes me to. Normally he stores bicycles here, probably stolen ones, I suspect. But he let me borrow it because he's in prison at the moment.'

'Why would you want to borrow it?' He shifted round to peer at me in the gloomy interior.

'In case I ever need a safe place.'

He smiled. 'That's good thinking, Eloïse.'

His praise mattered to me more than I let him see. 'And what were those chasers after?' I asked.

'Me, of course.'

'Why?'

'Oh, Eloïse, the less you know, the safer it is for you. You know that's how it is. I'm sorry.' He squeezed my hand hard. 'Thank you.'

'For what?'

'For protecting me in your safe hideout.'

'I don't want thanks. I want information.'

'My little sister, will you never give up?' But he laughed.

No, I don't give up. When you are raised in a family of tough men and tougher bulls, you learn not to give up. I'm not that kind of person.

I had kept him safe, hadn't I?

How was I to know what waited outside?

CHAPTER TWO

I heard André's breath in the darkness, slipping in and out of his broad chest. Slow. Unhurried. As if we were not cooped up in this garage, rank with rat droppings. As if we were not hiding from men with thick necks and names like Volkov and Zazlavsky.

'These men kill,' he'd once said to me. At the time it had sent a shudder through me and I thought I'd understood. I'd worked with wild bulls on my father's farm, hadn't I? And I'd seen them kill a man, so I knew what that meant. That's what I thought in my innocence. But I was wrong. Only now did I understand what those three words really meant: *These men kill.* And it sent a streak of fear through me that chilled the blood in my veins.

I released my grip on the steering wheel and peeled my fingers off one at a time. I didn't want André to see my fear, but nevertheless he put out a hand and briefly touched mine. He possessed long square-tipped fingers and the hands of a man accustomed to years of hard physical labour in his boyhood, but now his skin had grown smooth. His nails were groomed Parisian-style, instead of cracked and grimy. Sometimes it worried me. I felt as though the brother I'd known and loved all my life was abandoning me.

'Are you okay?' I asked lightly.

'I'm okay.'

His smile by the faint gleam of the streetlamp that crept under the door was slow in coming, but it was worth the wait. In repose his face was long and serious, his eyes watchful. Years ago he used to have the wild looks of a pirate with long unruly golden locks, riding bareback through the Camargue on a vile-tempered white horse called Charlemagne. But these days you would mistake him for a lawyer. The suit sharp-edged. Hair clipped. Mouth tight. Briefcase under his arm.

My disguise, he called it.

Your tamed soul, I teased him.

'You've done well,' he told me. 'Really well. I couldn't have driven better myself. We are secure here. I'm lucky you found it.' He uttered a soft laugh that caught me unawares. 'What have you got planned next?' he asked. 'We stay locked up here in this garage for a week?'

'Sit back,' I said. 'Trust me.'

My brother stared hard at me through the gloom. 'I trust you,' he said.

I jumped out of the car, threw open the garage doors, eager to get out of there, and let the lamplight invade the blackness. Sometimes I lost my bearings in the shadows of

André's dark world and couldn't tell which way was up and which way was down. I saw André frown as I slid back into the driving seat and started the engine.

'Is that wise?' he asked.

'They will be long gone,' I assured him, so bright and so sure of myself. 'We've been here well over an hour and they'll have scuttled away back to the holes they came from. You'll see.'

The noise of the engine resounded off the old brick walls, shaking apart the silence of the last hour in the grubby lock-up. I flicked into gear and eased the car out into the cobbled courtyard. A one-eared greyhound on the end of a chain sat up on its haunches and barked at us, but no one else took a blind bit of notice.

'Trust me, André.'

I drove slowly, cautiously, through the archway that led out on to the road. Headlights flared, carving holes in the dark streets. Cars rushed past. Even at night Paris traffic gave no quarter. Beside me I could sense André alert, his eyes scanning the dim corners of the street, checking the shadowy doorways and the glowing cigarette ends that peppered the darkness, his mind assessing the danger points.

I whispered, 'It looks all clear.'

André nodded.

I spotted a gap and swung the big steering wheel, slotting into the flow. That was when the massive grey truck reared up off the pavement, its huge headlights blinding me. I wrenched hard at the wheel, muscles tearing. Too late. The truck slammed its steel bumper into the passenger side of my car and tossed us, spinning us through the air.

Oddly, I heard nothing. No sound. No impact. No noise of any kind. Silence swelled inside my head.

Was I already dead?

No, I could taste blood as my teeth clamped through my tongue. I was hurtling upside-down in a trembling bubble of steel that was not built to fly. Splinters of glass sliced into my skin. The engine was racing, the wheels spinning frantically as they whirled above me in the Paris night, but I heard no scream, though my mouth was open and I felt air rushing out of my lungs.

No pain.

I felt, rather than saw, the blood. Scarlet streamers of it. Twisting and turning through the air, sweeping into my face. Was it my blood? Or André's?

I didn't know.

I saw his hand. Reaching for me through the red veil within the car. Or was the veil inside my eyes? Reaching to hold me. To keep me safe.

Then my car smashed down on to the ground and my world broke into a million pieces.

CHAPTER THREE

I woke in a strange bed.

Whiteness was filling my head. At first I thought it was still the shapeless fog from the Pont Neuf, but this was more solid, much heavier. And it was crushing me.

I opened my eyes a crack and took a squint at a thin slice of a hospital ward with a woman in the bed opposite mine reading a letter and chuckling to herself. My eyes travelled from her bandaged head to the white plaster on my left arm. I blinked with surprise and belatedly became aware of pain punching on every heartbeat. But alongside the pain came memory. It slunk back in like a thief and I was gripped by an overwhelming terror for my brother.

I had turned right, when André said, 'Turn left.'

I had opened the garage door when André asked, 'Is that wise?'

The whiteness in my head was not fog. It was guilt.

*

I forced myself out of my hospital bed.

I shuffled and I stared at my feet in slippers I'd never seen before. Every ten paces I leaned against the wall and I couldn't work out whether the swaying was the wall or me. The hospital corridor stretched ahead, shiny and impossibly long. Too full of light. My eyes hurt. I pushed myself off the wall and jerked one foot forward. The strange slipper came with it.

'What on earth are you doing here, mademoiselle?'

'I'm looking for my brother.' My words stuck to each other.

'You should be in bed, my dear.'

The voice sounded kind. She was a blur of white, one of the nursing nuns, and I forced my gaze into focus on her. She was looking at me with soft grey eyes, creased with concern. 'What is your brother's name?'

'André Caussade,' I said. 'I need to know is he . . .?'

Alive? Is he? Is he alive? I couldn't say it.

She tucked her arm under mine to give me support and set off down the corridor at an urgent pace.

The figure in the grey metal hospital bed looked dead. He didn't need me. He needed a miracle.

Who is this person lying so still on the bed, he does not look like my brother? Face bruised, features blackened, swollen and distorted. Nose smashed. Swaddled in bandages. The metal-cage contraption over his legs scared me. It was hidden under blankets but my heart churned in my chest each time I looked at the small mountain it created.

15

'André,' I called softly. 'Can you hear me?'

No response. Not a flicker from his sandy eyelashes. I hadn't kept him safe.

The hospital ward was not unpleasant, long, white, bloodless and busy, but it brought bile to my throat because under the lingering crisp aroma of disinfectant, it smelled the way our barns smelled the year our bulls got the fever. Of meat going bad while still on the hoof.

'André, stay with me,' I whispered to him.

I clutched his hand in mine and sat at his bedside all that day and all night, wrapped in my grey hospital gown. I watched shadows touch his face where his left cheekbone and eye socket were broken, while a needlepoint of moonlight threaded its way through one of the tall windows and turned his skin to pewter. I wanted to wrap my arms around him and nurse him back to health the way I'd done with so many puppies and kittens or injured calves and foals since I was old enough to hold a bottle for them.

I laid my head on his hand, my own limbs trembling. I thought about the massive steel bumper grinding against my brother's poor bones. Somewhere behind those blinding headlights had sat a driver, foot stamping on the accelerator.

'Eloïse.'

It was barely a whisper. Did I imagine it? My head shot up. I had dozed off. A nurse had drifted silently to the bedside to check on my brother earlier and had pronounced, 'No change. His condition is still critical.'

A ruptured spleen. Broken bones. A smashed sternum. Internal bleeding. His life on a thread. Yet his amber eyes were staring at me. Thin slits, bloodshot and battered. But open.

'André,' I tried to whisper, but it came out as a moan.

It was light now. I could hear the rattle of a breakfast trolley, as well as early-morning coughs and the protests of old bedsprings. I leaned close.

'You're safe here. The doctors are—'

'No.'

His lip split open and a trail of scarlet trickled along his chin. It glistened on his morning stubble.

'I won't leave your side,' I promised. 'I'll make sure you're safe.'

'I know.' His fingers tightened on mine. 'Thank you, Eloï . . .' A spasm of pain shook him.

'Don't speak,' I begged.

Our eyes held and I knew what he needed. He didn't have to tell me.

'Who shall I contact?' I asked.

His eyes slid painfully to one side to indicate the tiny bedside cabinet. I pulled open the drawer. Inside lay his black leather wallet and his watch. I lifted up both because I knew he needed to leave no trace of himself. I'd been an attentive pupil. I tucked them under my hospital dressing gown.

'A telephone number?' I asked.

He closed his eyes. After a full three minutes, during which I watched the pulse in his throat flicker, he murmured a number. A Paris number. I nodded and committed it to memory.

'And you?' His narrow gaze skimmed my face. 'You don't look good.' I had a rich assortment of cuts and bruises, my cheek swathed in a bandage and a plaster cast on my arm.

I smiled at him. 'A damn sight better than you.'

His breath was making a noise like a bird, high-pitched and unbearable. I kissed his swollen cheek.

'I'm sorry, André.' Tears fell from my cheeks to his. 'I am so sorry that I turned the wrong way.'

'No,' he whispered.

'I'll make the call.'

'Be quick.'

I stood up. The walls shifted around me but then stayed where they were meant to be.

'Eloïse.'

'Hush now.' The effort of speaking was killing him.

'Be careful.'

I nodded.

'Go to the Hôtel d'Emilie. On the Île Saint-Louis. Make the call . . . from their . . . lobby.'

I didn't ask why. If he had asked me to make the call from the moon, I'd have done it.

'May I help you, mademoiselle?'

'Thank you. I need to make a telephone call.'

The hotel manager blocking my path was as elegant and as attractive as the foyer we were standing in. The façade of

Hôtel d'Emilie may be classic eighteenth century, decorated with stone *mascarons* and ornate ironwork outside, but the interior was all 1953 pale wood panelling and seats in primary colours. Money had been invested in this place.

The manager regarded me with concerned eyes, taking in the sodden dressing on my face, the disintegrating slippers on my feet and the stolen nurse's woollen cape I was clinging to. He did not turn me away, so perhaps I was not the first to wind up on his doorstep in this state. He gestured to the two telephone booths at the back of the foyer, but his gaze stayed on me.

'Are you all right, mademoiselle? Can I get you ...?' He paused, wondering which to pick of all the things I so obviously needed. 'A drink?' he offered.

'*Non, merci.*'

I hurried to the telephone booths, as fast as my battered knee would allow.

I dialled the number.

It rang and was picked up immediately. A wave of relief hit me, and I pictured someone at the other end hunched over the phone all day, waiting for voices in distress.

'Who is it?' a man's voice demanded.

'I have a package.'

'What is the label on the package?'

'Caussade.'

Silence. Other than the thudding of my heart, I could hear nothing.

'Don't hang up,' I said.

'I'm here.' The voice was smooth. Deliberately calming. 'Where is the package?'

I hesitated. 'Who am I talking to?'

'My name is Victor. Where is the package? You were told to ring this number, so trust us.'

I had no choice. 'At the Hôpital de Sainte Marie-Thérèse.'

'Listen carefully, mademoiselle. I am going to confer with someone. Stay on the line. I will be back shortly.'

I counted the seconds.

Six and a half minutes passed according to the star-shaped clock on the foyer wall. I spent it leaning my back against the booth for support, willing André's broken chest to keep rising and falling.

'Hello?'

'I'm here,' I said.

'Who are you?'

'A friend.'

He gave a soft snort. 'The sister?'

How the hell did he know that? I looked around me quickly but I could see no one taking any interest in me. I made no comment.

The voice continued calmly. 'Remain where you are.'

'What are you planning to do? He is in danger and needs—'

The line went dead.

My finger shook as I dialled the number again. And again. And again.

No answer. I stood there. Like a fool. Minute after minute

ticked past before I realised the quiet voice was not going to ring me back. Nor was he coming to get me. *Remain where you are*, he said. Not to keep me safe. To keep me out of the way.

I pulled the hood of the cape tight over my head and forced my legs to start running for the door.

CHAPTER FOUR

'Where is he?'

'Who?'

I leaned over the old man in the hospital bed, so he would see me clearly, see what lay in my eyes. He was all bones and thin wisps of hair. 'The patient who was in the next bed,' I said. 'He has gone.'

'Yes, they took him.'

'Who took him? Nurses?'

'Two orderlies. In white coats.'

'How? In a wheelchair?'

'No, my dear, on a trolley.'

'What did the orderlies look like?'

The thin bones shrugged under the sheet. 'Ordinary men, brown hair, ordinary nose, mouth and eyes. Nothing to remember.' His papery face creased into a smile.

'Did they speak?'

'To the man in the bed, yes.'

'Did they speak in French?'

'Yes. But in low voices. My old ears aren't as good as they used to be. Shouldn't you be in bed, young lady? You look worse than I feel.'

I conjured up a smile and stuck it on my face. 'I'm okay, thanks. Did the man in the bed go willingly?'

'Oh, yes.'

Air rushed out of me with relief. I stepped over to the empty bed and I placed my hand on the pillow, where my brother's damaged head had lain, seeking even a trace of him, the faintest echo. I had made an unforgivable mistake. I had turned right instead of left. And now he was paying for it. I laid my head on the pillow and waited.

When they came I was seated on a chair at the old man's bedside, reading to him from *Le Monde* newspaper. An article about our latest victory in the Indochina War in Vietnam. News of a victory always went down well, especially when the government was in a frantic tail-spin.

I saw the doors to the ward swing open and the suits enter. Two of them. They looked as out of place as elephants in a birdcage. Big, broad, hard-muscled men who walked in, chest-first, as if they owned the place. The old man took one look at them and closed his eyes. They approached the vacant bed, muttered something to each other and turned to inspect me, taking in my hospital gown, my plaster and the wound dressing on my face.

'Where is the man who was in this bed?'

I shrugged. 'I don't know. He was already gone when I arrived. Try asking the nurses.'

'The old man? Did he see anything?'

'He's been asleep.'

The suit studied me for a long moment and I felt a thin trickle of dread that he would associate my damaged face with a car crash. I rose to my feet. He towered over me as I committed each feature of his square face to memory. Grey eyes, cold as stone. Large nose, black spiky hair and spiky eyebrows in a dead-straight line that met in the middle.

'Who are you?' I asked. 'His family?'

'Keep your nose out of my business, bitch.'

The pulse in my temple under the dressing was pounding like a jackhammer.

The other suit frowned and muttered, 'Draw the curtain.'

He was thinner, with the eyes of a man who liked to give orders. Dark trim moustache. Efficient and precise in his movements. A deep cleft in his chin.

They drew the privacy curtains around the bed with a dismissive flick of the wrist and I heard them rummaging behind it. The bed had already been stripped and I counted to twenty in my head, then reached out and grabbed a handful of curtain. I yanked it open. One suit had the empty drawer of the cabinet dangling from his fist, the other had propped the mattress up on its edge and was examining the underside of it. Like vultures picking at bones. If it was André's wallet they were searching for, it was not there.

'If he comes back,' I said helpfully, 'who shall I say was looking for him?'

'Fuck off.'

'That's not polite, monsieur.'

'Neither is this,' said the suit with stone eyes.

He came close to me and hooked his thick fingers into the bulky dressing on my face. I very nearly jerked my head away but I could see how much he wanted to rip off the white gauze, so I stood still.

'How did you get this?' He grinned at me.

'I was in a fire.'

'Shall I take a look?'

I gripped his hand and he didn't shake me off.

'For Christ's sake, Piquet,' the moustache suit snapped. 'Enough of this shit.'

That was it. They walked out without another word, thumping the doors so hard that they continued to swing on their hinges long after the suits had gone. My knees buckled on me and I slumped into a chair, my cheek on fire. My anger was stretched taut and my need to find my brother gnawed at me, but I allowed myself a small ripple of pleasure. I had discovered three things in the last hour.

First, the men sent to kill my brother were French, not Russian. Though that didn't mean they were not in the pay of Soviet masters.

Second, the people I'd phoned who had taken André had acted fast and efficiently and he went with them willingly. I just hoped they were as fast and efficient with medical treatment.

Third, I had a name: Piquet.

It was a start.

Hospital bathrooms are the worst of places. Their tiled walls have absorbed so much pain and have seen the private tears of so many diseased patients that the room feels weighted with sadness.

This one was green with a white border at waist height and the taps were old-fashioned heavy ones that were stiff to turn. But I locked the door and washed my hands in the basin for far too long, soaping each finger over and over, taking care not to wet my plaster, delaying the moment when I had to look in the mirror. I rinsed them. Dried them. And raised my eyes.

The face wasn't mine. I blinked, expecting it to change, but it didn't, so I lifted a finger and touched the glass as though there might be another person hiding behind it. All I found was a flat distorted version of myself, but I knew it must be me because of the eyes. They were dark oak-brown. My father's eyes. But where was the happiness that lived inside them?

It wasn't just the bruises or the cuts and nicks and the swollen side of my jaw that robbed me of me. It was also the huge white dressing that covered my face from my temple to my chin, and that was what I was here to make right. I needed to see me. To know I was still there.

With care I picked at the adhesive strips one by one, sliding my nail under the sticky tape. I winced but that made it worse, so I sped up and with just two left to go, I tore it off.

It was bad. I couldn't pretend it wasn't. But not as bad as I'd feared. A neat sickle-shaped scar ran from in front of my ear to my chin, red and angry and swollen with spidery stitches criss-crossing it, and blackened with dried blood at the top. I looked in the mirror and managed a very small smile.

'Hello,' I said.

The girl in the mirror mouthed it back at me; her eyes looked frightened.

'Don't be afraid,' I said, brushing my hair back from my face.

She flicked hers back too, long dense dark waves that needed a wash to rid it of blood. Her face was a different shape from mine. Mine was slender-cheeked with clear skin and a straight strong nose, too strong for my face. But hers was lumpy with an odd shape to her lips and terrible skin.

I leaned over the washbasin, pushing my face very close to hers. 'Don't worry,' I said. 'I'll take care of you.'

Two tears started to roll down her cheeks.

I waited.

I waited day and night. Week after week. I waited through March and April while the clouds of lacy cherry blossom burst into life in the Jardin des Plantes and while the pavement cafés where I lived in Montparnasse teemed with lovers from morning to night. I waited for some word from André.

I was not good at waiting but he had taught me persistence and I wore out my finger dialling the telephone number he'd given me to ring from Hôtel d'Emilie. Never any answer. Then one day the line went dead and it was like losing him all over again.

I worked hard at trying to trace the vehicle that had transported him from the hospital, but it seemed to have vanished into thin air. A green split-screen Citroën H van had hung around briefly that day, I learned. But that was all. A dead end.

And do you know how many Piquets there are in the Paris telephone directory? Enough to keep me walking the city streets day after day till my arm had almost healed, but none of them possessed the stone eyes of the one I sought. Each morning I stood at the window of my fifth-floor room at dawn, a dull ache pulsing in my head. I gazed out across the neat grey roofs of Paris, to the spiny wrought-iron lattice work of the Eiffel Tower, and imagined André doing the same. He had never been a sleeper. Always restless. Always on the move. Dawn had always been the time when we used to throw ourselves on the sturdy white backs of our Camargue horses and race them through the marshes, their glamorous manes flying, shimmering in that first light. The gaudy flamingos dipping their long matchstick legs in the languid lagoons.

I leaned my forehead on the cold pane of the window.

Why? André, why haven't you contacted me? So many possible answers. Is your battered body too damaged to put

28

pen to paper? Or are you still too angry with me? Disowning your sister? Leaving her unforgiven for the mistake she made. Or have you forgotten me? Is that it?

But always hovering in the shadow was the big question, the one I turned my gaze away from. The one that drove hot pokers through me at night.

Are you dead?

CHAPTER FIVE

I went back to work in May when my arm had finally healed. I had rent to pay. The city slid eagerly into summer, embracing the delights of longer lazy days, each breath warm and fragrant, while a colourful riot of scarlets and golds burst into bloom in the parks. So full of life it made me ache inside.

Still no word.

Even when, on the 1 August, the city emptied as Parisians trekked south for their summer exodus, I didn't leave. I stayed. Each evening I trailed through bars he'd taken me to and along the quayside promenades because I was convinced, absolutely convinced that I would find him.

I didn't know then how easy it is to fool oneself.

One of the things that André had taught me was how to pick a lock, a brotherly gift to me. How to use a set of fine points, to feel for the pressure, fingers as precise and delicate as a surgeon's. He'd shown me the way to do it and I admit I enjoyed it. I relished each challenge to be conquered, whether it was a curtained lever lock or a simple cylinder one. So I was disappointed on the evening that I worked on a brass lock and found it too easy.

I pushed open the door. The office lay in darkness, the kind of darkness you can stick a needle in. That suited me. Without a sound I entered, closed the door behind me and drew breath. The air smelled bad. Over-hot. Something festering. But I'd smelled worse. I flicked on the pinpoint beam of my torch and whipped it around the room across the bare floorboards, leaping into corners, checking that the fat bastard who owned this office wasn't sleeping one off under his desk.

No, no one here. I breathed out.

Shadows were swarming up and down the walls, as though they'd been waiting for me in the darkness. I shot the torch beam at them and they vanished, the way dreams evaporate when you try to grab them by the throat.

I headed over to the coffin-size filing cabinet propped against one wall, but the smell was getting to me. It was coming from the desk. I walked over and inspected its surface. It was a mess with piles of folders and unsteady heaps of paperwork jumbled together, but my torch picked out in the middle of the pale blotter a lacy item of female underwear. It was stained dark red. Whether from wine or blood, I couldn't tell, but flies had dipped their feet in the stain and trailed it across the blotter. I bundled the underwear inside a sheet of paper from one of the piles, wrapped it up and dropped it into my satchel.

My torch beam flared off the murky tumbler and wine

bottle that stood within easy reach of the chair but I moved over to the filing cabinet. The lock on it was child's play. I heard the pick's telltale click and slid open each drawer in turn. Where was the heavy-duty security that a photographer – even a shoddy one like this – was meant to have in place?

I heard a noise. A soft tapping. I froze. Listened hard. But it was no more than a sudden squall of rain brushing against the shutters. My fingers skimmed rapidly over the contents of the filing cabinet, and the brown envelope I sought was hiding in the third drawer. I lifted out the whole folder, dropped it into the satchel on my shoulder and quietly closed the drawers once more. I was ready to leave, but first I walked back over to the bottle on the desk. I clipped it smartly with the metal casing of my torch. Glass and wine exploded over his shit-heap of papers.

Why am I here, rifling through an office?

Because this is what I do for a living.

I let the large brown envelope drop on the desk of Clarisse Favre and she looked at me with a bright scarlet smile. The desk was as immaculately groomed as its owner, polished and sleek, the kind of desk you only see in magazines. However early I came into the office of 'The Favre Detective Agency, Private Investigator & Associate' – the Associate was me – she was always in ahead of me and stayed long after I crawled home at midnight. She could be sharp as a razor or soft as her Dior powder puff, I never knew which Clarisse I would get.

'*Ma chère* Eloïse,' Clarisse beamed at me, 'you are the Favre Agency's secret weapon.'

She laughed, a warm sound that always drew me in and made me want to hear it again. Her light-brown hair was swept up in an effortlessly elegant chignon and she was wearing the same dove-grey dress she had on the first time I saw her. She had taken me on in her chic Saint-Germain office exactly a year before when I was fresh out of the Sorbonne and found that neither the French Intelligence service nor the American CIA were remotely interested in making use of my talents.

So how did I end up here? It was one of those strokes of luck that you can never plan for. I was seated at a pavement café with my friend Nicole from university, hunched over a small round table with a metal ashtray spilling out discarded cigarette butts. We were smoking like hardened Parisians and consuming too much coffee, both of us edgy and frustrated by our lack of success in finding jobs we wanted, now that we had finished university. Nicole was a scientist with curly auburn hair and a shining determination to become one of France's leading physicists.

I was in the opposite camp, a language graduate. Thin, broke and depressed. Being rejected by the CIA despite my fluent Russian and English had knocked me off-balance. I'd been so sure that my future lay alongside my brother's that I felt as though I'd stepped on a patch of ice, my feet skidding from under me. Nicole and I were moaning to each other as we watched the struggling street artists painting in the hustle of the Place du Tertre and vaguely I was aware of an elegant female who smelled nice taking a seat at the table next to us. After ten minutes she removed her sunglasses, leaned over and tapped my arm with the corner of her business card.

'Here,' she said and dropped the card on our table. 'I couldn't help overhearing. If you're serious about looking for a job, ring my office. Make an appointment. I have a position that might interest a bright kid like you.'

Surprised, I inspected my benefactress. A perfect heart-shaped face, flawless make-up, a wide mouth curved into a warm smile, and green eyes as intense as emeralds.

I nodded, trying to disguise my enthusiasm. I picked up the card. 'Why me?' I asked.

'Because you're a prickly young arsehole who sounds ready for a bit of excitement.'

I laughed. She had me with the words arsehole and excitement.

'Why study Russian?' she had asked when I came knocking on her door that first rainy morning.

'I thought it might come in useful,' I'd said.

I didn't tell her that the Cyrillic alphabet was to me an irresistible code to unlock Russian words. But she must have spotted something that made her think I had the makings of a private investigator because she took me on and sent me on a two-week course in Neuilly-sur-Seine. Running around learning about foot surveillance techniques or handling different cameras for photographic surveillance set me up with the skills for the job, it seems. And I was good at it. When I told André about it, I was all puffed up with pride and he'd laughed and cracked open a bottle of champagne to celebrate.

Now Clarisse slipped a finely buffed nail under the flap of the envelope I'd presented her with and slid the contents on to her desk in front of her. A clutch of photographs. Five of them, glossy black-and-white, eight by ten. Plus – more importantly – the strip of film negative that I had 'liberated'. Her face pulled a moue of distaste and, after briefly studying the pictures, she tucked them back out of sight in their envelope. Her face was expressive, always mobile and interested, with strong features and eyes that could lead you to believe you knew what she was thinking. But you would be wrong. No one knew what Clarisse was thinking. Sometimes I caught her looking at me. I had no idea why.

She held the strip of negative film up to the light and squinted at it. 'Where did you get this piece of filth?'

'In the bastard's office.'

She nodded approval. No questions about how I got in.

The *bastard* was the photographer. A nasty creep who made a habit of taking compromising snaps of the sixteen-year-old daughters of wealthy public figures, daughters who had gone off the rails and were running head-first down black holes. This was the 1950s. Every one of us believed that the bad times were behind us. We were all desperate for the good times to come rolling in, but drugs and drink and the nuclear threat of instant extinction kept black-eyed sharks circling. The country was on edge and Clarisse's services were much in demand.

We worked for an hour discussing two new clients who had brought her their problems to solve – one a blackmail case, the other a suspected fraud – and I was taking down details in my notebook when I became aware of her silence. I glanced up. Clarisse was sitting very still, studying me. For no obvious reason I felt a twitch of fear.

'What is it?' I asked.

She leaned her elbows on the desk. 'Tell me, Eloïse, have you heard anything?'

Her tone was soft, so soft it scared me. We both knew what *anything* meant.

'No.'

'No news of your brother?'

'No.'

Her gaze flicked to the scar on my face. Clarisse had been good to me after the crash, allowing me time off to recover and breezing into my cramped apartment every few days with a box of glossy patisseries or a racy book or the latest *Vogue*. I valued her friendship, she'd make me feel almost human again, but now her eyes had narrowed to green slits, as bright and as hard as the king-size emerald nestled on her finger.

'You have to let it go, Eloïse.'

'Let what go?'

'The guilt.'

'What guilt?'

I stared right back at her, refusing to let her feel sorry for me, but she stretched out an arm and peeled back my fingers from their grip on the curved edge of her desk. Her hand was gentle. Silence crept into the room and all I could hear was our breathing in the quiet office with its Eames chair and modern colourful coat stand. My head hummed with darkness.

'What is it?' I asked. 'What is it that you're not saying?'

Clarisse sat back in her chair, tapped her nails on her desk, then opened a drawer and withdrew a piece of paper from inside it. She placed it in front of me.

'For you,' she announced.

A telegram. I saw it had been opened though it was addressed to me. From my father. I felt a pain at the back of my eyeballs so sharp I couldn't read. There was only one reason my father would send me a telegram.

André was dead.

My eyes blurred. The world turned a smoky grey.

'I opened it,' Clarisse said quietly. 'You'd given the agency address to him and so I opened it. Read it.'

I blinked, forcing my eyes to focus. There were only two words. *Come Now.*

CHAPTER SIX

I drove. South. Straight south.

I drove my flimsy 2CV so hard and so fast that it moaned and rattled and expelled fumes in my face that smelled of overheated wiring, but I did not take my foot off the pedal for a second except to refuel. I cursed the grey tin-can's lack of pace a thousand times. It may have been fine for around the city, but a top speed of 65kpm was not exactly greased lightning with a journey of 750 kilometres to drive.

The South was pulling at me. I could feel it. Drawing me to it like a magnet, as though there was something hard and metallic lodged inside me that was powerless to resist and yet I felt a softening of my sinews, a loosening of my bones as the hours crawled past. The sun played hide-and-seek with the ladybird-shaped shadow of my car on the N6 and I passed the towns of Auxerre and Avallon, barely aware of them. The tedium of the pancake-flat landscape lulled me into a false sense of passivity where too many memories from the past could sneak in, such as André's arm tight around me when he told me goodbye and to be strong, as he departed for Paris. I was twelve years old, he was eighteen. Losing him was like having my right arm ripped off.

My father's face had turned a strange shade of grey that wasn't grey because it was also purple. I knew then it was the colour of an anger so deep it burned away the words *I'm sorry*. Their words were hurled at each other like grenades.

'He'll be back,' Papa had growled into his beard, as André strode off down the gravelled track to the road with no more than a small pack on his back.

Papa's hand lay heavy on my bony shoulder, holding me there in a grip of iron. I longed for André to turn and wave but he kept his sandy eyes fixed on the road to freedom.

'He'll come back,' Papa reiterated, 'because this farm is in his blood.' His fingers dug deeper. 'I tell you, Eloïse, Mas Caussade is in that boy's soul whether he wants it there or not.'

But he didn't. He never came back.

The trees told me I was nearly home. They were the first. Instead of shady avenues of the pale trunks of plane trees peeling like lepers at the roadside and the silvery shimmering poplars, there were bold stands of dark cypress trees and pines stretching tall to the sky. Vineyards with a haze of green shoots started to spill around me on both sides of the road, worker-bees humming, as I rubbed shoulders with the mighty Rhône. All I had to do was hurry down its broad valley and I'd be in Arles. I had grown up with the Rhône river, it flowed in my blood. I'd learned to swim in it before I could walk, dived for catfish in it, paddled a homemade raft on it. Almost drowned in it more than once, and I still heard the sound of its dark waters coursing through my dreams at night.

The heat hit me. I had grown soft. Four years in Paris and I had forgotten what a humid August in the Camargue felt like and how monster mosquitoes set your bare skin on fire.

I pulled over and climbed out of the car, stretching my limbs, and drew great lungfuls of the breeze that smelled like nowhere else on earth. It carried in it the salty earth of the Camargue, the wide delta of the Rhône, the rustle of the tall reeds and the warm musky scent of the hides of the wild bulls and horses that roamed the landscape here. I gazed out across the flat marshy fields and watched a pair of white egrets rise into the crystal-clear air, weightless as ghosts, as they drifted south towards the salt lagoons. I felt my heartbeat slow. It knew it had come home, even while my mind insisted I was now a hardened Parisian, here for one purpose only: to find my brother and the person who tried to kill him, and to put my family back together again.

I heard a noisy snort and a sturdy white stallion emerged from the shade of a cluster of tamarisk trees, while his harem of eight mares hung back in the shadows. He tossed his cream mane at me, pawing the ground with his wide front hoof, designed to thrive on marshland.

I started to cry. Silent relentless tears because of what I'd done and what I'd not done. In this familiar landscape my failure lay all around me, because in every tree, every velvety stretch of grassland and in every splash of sunlight on the glassy surface of the cool ponds I saw the pale ghosts of us children. Flitting in and out of sight. I caught glimpses of my brothers everywhere. When the crying was over I climbed back into the car and drove to the Mas Caussade.

Nothing had changed while I'd been gone. I'd turned my back on the Camargue and it hadn't even noticed.

The house hadn't changed. It stared back at me. Square, solid, part of the landscape. It stood in the middle of nowhere, flanked by my father's fields that stretched out of sight in every direction.

I drove up the long dirt drive in a cloud of dust, chest tight, heart racing, terrified of what news awaited me. It was a traditional Camarguais *mas* or farmhouse, built of local stone, two storeys, facing south. Its back was squarely facing north to offer protection from the cold ferocious blasts of the mistral wind that could rip your roof off if it put its mind to it. No windows on that side of the house, just a blank wall to keep out the danger.

Was I a danger?

Did the house need a blank wall between its occupants and me?

The Mas Caussade farm was arranged as three sides of a rectangle around a central cobbled yard. One side was formed by the farmhouse itself and the other two by the thatched stables and long sleepy barns where the hens liked to annoy the farm cat dozing in the straw. All around, as far as the eye could see, lay the wide-open pastureland owned by my father, green and glossy, except where the bright emerald carpet of glasswort had adopted its scarlet summer colours, soaking up the sun. The constantly high level of the underlying water-table made the plant-life rich and vibrant. A thousand different greens tumbled over each other and shimmered with papery butterflies and gaudy tree frogs.

I never tired of this landscape. It stirred things in me that got lost and trampled in the city's daily hustle and bustle, but which I could feel coming alive again. Squeezing their way into my heart once more.

With a roar, a fighter aircraft streaked low overhead, shattering the peace as I skewed my car to a halt in front of the bull-yard and raced to the house, but someone was there before me. Outside the front door stood a car, its chrome gleaming in the bright sunlight, its black wings bulbous and glossy. My heart tripped over itself. We all knew who used black Citroën Traction Avants.

The police.

I knocked. I could have lifted the latch and walked in, but I didn't. I knocked. I heard one of the dogs barking in the yard at the back – it sounded like old Lyonette – and I felt childhood memories brush against me, making my skin prickle, like walking into cobwebs.

The door swung open and my father filled the doorway. It was hard not to reach out a hand to him, but I kept it tight at my side. He was not that kind of father. Aristide Caussade was not a tall man but he was built of solid muscle like his bulls. His hair and beard had turned white years ago but his bushy eyebrows and his deep-set eyes were still as dark as old oak.

'Hello, Papa.'

He nodded and his stern gaze fixed on my cheek. He showed no flicker of emotion. 'Come in, Eloïse.'

As he moved back to allow me entry, I didn't let the moment slip by, and before he could stride away down the hallway and vanish into one of the rooms, I seized his arm. It was like seizing a tree trunk. He looked at me, surprised.

'Is he here, Papa, is he? Tell me quickly. Is he alive? Have you heard from him? How is he? Where is he? I've been sick with not knowing or hearing.'

'André is alive, if that's what you mean.'

A low gut-wrenching sob broke loose from me and relief coursed through me with such force that my knees buckled and only my grip on my father kept me upright. I clamped my other hand over my mouth to stop the sounds that threatened to come out of it. I didn't realise that the pain inside me had to come out somewhere and it flooded out in my hold on my father's arm. My fingers sank deep into his muscles, digging in between his tendons, gripping with all my strength until our Caussade flesh for that brief moment merged together again.

'Eloïse,' Papa said and I could hear an odd hitch in his deep voice.

I forced my fingers to release him. Somehow I stayed on my feet. 'Is he here?' I asked.

'He is.'

I pushed past my father in the hallway, running for the stairs, but he halted me with an abrupt, 'André is not in his room.'

'Where then?'

He walked away into the living room. I followed him, impatient, into the room where the ancient sideboard had stood on the same spot for three generations and where the floor tiles were the exact same colour as my father's eyes.

'Papa,' I started, but halted.

A figure rose politely from one of the chairs and I became aware of his dark uniform and gun holster on his hip. A gendarme. What were the police doing here?

My father gestured at the officer. 'You remember Captain Roussel.'

But I didn't hear the name. Instead my eyes were fixed on my father's hand. It was covered in dried blood.

'*Bonjour,* Eloïse.'

I regarded the police officer with surprise. 'Of course, Léon Roussel.' I held out my hand. 'I apologise for not recognising you. You look different in uniform.'

He smiled and I noticed that he didn't fight to keep his eyes off my scar the way most people did. He looked at it openly but without pity and I liked him for that. Léon

Roussel and I had been at school together, though he'd been in André's class six years ahead of me. I was surprised to see him in uniform now, as he had always been something of a hell-raiser. He was tall with brown hair clipped short like a GI and calm eyes, not exactly good-looking, but there was something about his face that held my attention. A quiet authority that had certainly not been there the day he set fire to our geography teacher's desk.

'I'm here about the attack,' he said.

'What attack?' I swung round to my father. 'On André?'

To my horror, his eyes filled with unshed tears. I had never seen my father cry, not once in my whole life. Not even when my mother died giving birth to Isaac. He snatched up a porcelain statue of Saint Genesius, the patron saint of Arles, which had stood on the sideboard eyeing us sternly for as long as I could remember, and hurled it with a bellow of rage at the tiled floor. Without a word he strode out of the room, slamming the door so hard that the plaster on the wall cracked.

'What is it?' I said urgently to Léon Roussel. 'What has happened? Is André worse?'

His expression had grown sombre, his police captain face firmly in place.

'Goliath,' he said, 'has been hacked to death.'

CHAPTER SEVEN

LÉON ROUSSEL

Captain Léon Roussel moved quickly into the cobbled yard, because he didn't want the Caussade girl running headlong into what lay in the barn. He'd been there. Seen it. Smelled it. The stench still clung to his nostrils. He stepped in front of her slender figure as she took off towards the largest of the old barns and placed a restraining hand on her arm. Her bare skin was cold.

'Steady, don't rush. It's not going anywhere,' he said.

She jerked to a halt. Shock changes people. He'd witnessed it time and again in his work in the police force. When it hits hard, really hard, some people freeze. Some scream. Some shake or weep their hearts out. Others seem to lose their bones, they crumple, eyes glazed. With Eloïse Caussade, shock stole her tongue.

They stood awkwardly in silence while he gave her time, aware of the scar on her face pulsing bone-white. He'd heard

rumours. That she'd almost killed her brother in a car accident – you can't keep that sort of thing quiet in a small town
like Serriac. The last time he'd laid eyes on Eloïse Caussade
she'd been a scrawny fifteen-year-old who'd possessed the
wildness of the marshes in her. All elbows and knees, gal-
loping her horse through a rainbow of sea-spray across the
wetlands, long black hair streaming loose behind her like
river-reeds.

Now look at her.

Eight years later, a Parisian to her polished fingertips,
she was wearing a sleeveless blue shirtwaister, the colour
of the wild irises among the glasswort, with a full skirt and
cinched tiny waist. She obviously hadn't come to ride horses.
Her patent leather shoes were out of place in a bull-yard
but she was like her father. They had the same capacity for
silence, and the same bloodless lips today. Léon turned his
face away, giving her a moment of privacy. A fitful breeze
from the south carried the tangy scent of the sea and the sun
hovered low on the vast horizon as though reluctant to leave
the scene.

The fields were low-lying and stretched out in the hazy
distance with long alleyways of willows and silvery white
poplars that fringed the numerous narrow waterways that
cut through the salty earth. Léon kept an eye out for anyone
approaching on the single-track road that ran past the
Caussade farm but it remained empty, yet he had an uneasy
sense of being watched. He glanced at the farmhouse windows upstairs but saw no one.

Léon nodded towards the barn. 'The bull is in there.'

'Who did it?' She'd found her tongue. 'Goliath *is* the farm. He *is* Mas Caussade. Who killed him?'

'We don't know yet.'

'Who do you suspect? Who *might* be guilty?'

'That's what I'm here to find out,' Léon said. 'Most probably the attackers are people who object to what your father is doing. There appears to be a forceful group of them working together.'

'Against my father?'

'Yes.'

She took that in, lungs pumping hard, then she strode towards the barn, her feet kicking up the dust. Under the Parisian poise Léon recognised the energy and the determination that had driven her as a child to undertake the impossible.

'Goliath.'

Léon heard the name whisper out of Eloïse as she dropped to her knees on the soiled straw. He wanted to snatch her away from the blood and the gore of the mutilated black carcass of the Caussade farm's prize bull. Camargue bulls were small compared to the massive bulk of their Spanish cousins, but even so, it dwarfed her slight figure. The air in the barn was dim and dusty. It caught in his throat, and the stench turned his stomach. Eloïse placed the palm of her hand on the creature's bloody black hide and leaned close.

'Goodbye, my friend,' she whispered to the animal lying on its side in front of her.

Its horns had been broken into jagged stumps, its ears, tail and genitals hacked off. It was a vicious, violent slaying that appalled Léon in its brutality. Gaping axe wounds split open the muscles of the beast's powerful back and its throat was sliced from chest to jawbone in a raw slash that was a seething carpet of flies.

'Goliath and I were born on the same day,' she said. 'Twenty-three years ago.' She made an attempt at a smile. 'He was my hero.'

'He was magnificent,' Léon acknowledged. 'The strongest and the fastest of the bulls in the Arles arena.'

He had seen the prize bull a hundred times charging across the golden sand of the Arles and Serriac arenas, a black tornado in pursuit of the local young *razeteurs* who dared to try to steal the cockade from its horns. Himself included. The cockades were a symbol of manhood that tempted young men to risk their lives, because in the *course Camarguaise*, unlike the *corridas* of Spain, no blood is shed. The true star of the show is the bull, not a matador. The bull's name and its *manade*, the farm from which it comes, gain great fame and respect. For years Goliath was a magnificent celebrity and could draw an audience from all over Provence.

'I'll wait outside,' he said quietly, 'until you're ready.'

'Ready for what?'

'I've already interviewed your father and brother. I need to ask you a few questions too.'

For the first time her gaze left the animal and she studied his uniform thoughtfully as if she had forgotten the job he was here to do. 'What did my father do?'

She stopped. Léon saw her eyes fix on something behind him. He turned and in the gloom at the far end of the barn beside what looked like grey bins of livestock feed there was a shape, indistinct and unmoving.

'André!' Eloïse leaped to her feet.

Léon looked closer. She had good eyes. It was indeed her older brother, seated in a wicker chair with a pair of wooden crutches lying on the floor beside him. Across his knees lay a hunting rifle. Léon felt the hairs rise on the back of his neck, but André gave him a reassuring nod. His sandy hair had grown down over his collar during the last few months and he was wearing a soft checked shirt that had been scrubbed too often, as if he were trying to pretend he was a simple country boy again. But his eyes said otherwise.

'I'm keeping watch,' André said softly.

He had always been good at that, Léon recalled. Taking you by surprise. He and Léon had been through school together and too many teachers had been caught out by his slouching shoulders and soft voice.

'I thought you were resting in your room,' Léon commented, eyeing the rifle.

'I changed my mind.'

'André!' Eloïse cried out again.

She saw the crutches splayed out on the dirty straw, his right leg below the knee encased in a metal leg-iron, and her cheeks flushed a dull crimson. She darted towards her brother and dropped on one knee in front of him, so he wouldn't have to look up at her. Something about her position of supplication jarred with Léon and he wanted to raise her to her feet. She used to hang around as a child on the edge of André's gang of unruly boys and even then Léon had been the one to swing her up on to the first branch of any tree they were climbing, while her brother sat at the top urging her on to greater effort. But by fifteen she could outride and outshoot the lot of them. Everything they did, she strove to do better, but it was never good enough. Not for André.

'Why didn't you tell me you were at the farm?' she demanded. 'I thought you were dead. Why didn't you tell me?' Her hand reached out to his knee but stopped just short of touching it. 'How are you now?' she asked. Her voice was shaking.

'How do you think?' He rested his hand on the stock of the rifle. 'They would not have dared touch Goliath if I had not been a cripple.'

It was worse than a slap. Léon watched the dark blood drain from her cheek. André was blaming her for the prize bull's death. Léon feared tears from her, but he was wrong. Underneath the Parisian gloss of silky black hair and the stylish dress with an animal's blood on its skirt, the old Eloïse still stalked. He saw it in the speed with which she shot to her feet, in the straightness of her spine as she stared down at her brother.

'What happened here? Why would anyone want to slaughter Goliath? What have you done?'

'It's not what I've done. It's what our father has done.'

She turned to Léon. 'Is it true?'

'It's true, Eloïse.'

'What has Papa done? Tell me.'

Léon was aware of the dense humming of the flies in the sudden silence. 'He is selling part of his land to the United States Air Force to expand their nuclear air base here at Dumoulin.'

'No,' she insisted. 'Papa would rather chop off his right hand than sell Caussade land.'

André gave her a hard tight smile. 'It might yet come to that.'

CHAPTER EIGHT

I stood in the bull-yard and watched a monstrous silver bomber dip one long wing as it banked towards the east with a roar, its wing-lights flashing against the sky darkening behind it. It seemed to flatten the trees and punch a hole in the evening. So this was it. This was what my father wanted to inflict on Mas Caussade.

Why? It didn't make sense.

I had intended to go straight from the barn to the house to question my father, but instead I headed in the direction of the stables. I was wound so tight, I couldn't trust myself. The wrong words might come out to Papa. What better way to calm down than a nuzzle with one of the Caussade white horses?

The second reason was Léon Roussel. I'd seen him heading in the direction of the stables after he'd walked out of the barn. He had left André and me to our privacy, to brother and sister talk inside the barn, except, of course, at first there was no talk. Just silence, solid as a wall. Each brick in it seemed unbreachable.

I'd said, 'I'm happy to see you are walking again, André.'

'Is that what you call it? Walking.'

My brother lifted one of the crutches from the floor and held it aloft for me to admire. It was beautifully handmade – undoubtedly my father's work – with a strong black leather pad to fit under his armpit.

'My legs,' he said. 'Very handsome, don't you think?'

'Yes.' The word caught in my throat. 'Why didn't you tell me you were alive, André? I've been worried out of my mind, not knowing whether you were dead or alive. How long have you been back here?'

'Only a month.'

'A whole month and neither you nor Papa thought to tell me.'

'I didn't want you informed of where I was, either here or in Paris. Because I knew you would come and I didn't want you near me. Go back to Paris, Eloïse.'

I kept breathing. I don't know how, but I made the air go in and out of my lungs. I didn't blame him. If I were him, I wouldn't want me near either.

'You should talk to Papa, Eloïse.'

'I will.'

'I mean now.'

That was it. He didn't want me here. I walked out of the barn and straight into the sound of the aircraft blasting across the sky.

*

It was a different sound that greeted me in the stables. The high-pitched welcoming whinny that I knew so well, though I hadn't heard it for a long time. It belonged to Cosette, my fine Camarguais mare, twelve years old, who even now recognised my footsteps and huffed a greeting through her broad nostrils.

Léon Roussel was standing at the half-door of her stall in the stable. He was talking to her with the kind of easy smile on his face that whisked me back to the carefree days before the war came, when we all laughed just with the pleasure of being alive. I recalled that he had always been good with horses, never riding them too hard or driving them over jumps that were too dangerous for them. As I approached, Cosette pawed at the wooden door with her hoof and leaned out to nuzzle my neck and breathe moist air into my face. I was glad the light in the stable was dim because her delight in my return home brought me to tears that I had managed to avoid in front of anyone till now. I ran a hand down her short muscular neck and gently scratched her velvety muzzle. She smelled wonderful.

My father owned about a hundred and fifty Camargue horses that roamed across the landscape in small white herds – though officially termed grey – each one bossed by an unruly handsome stallion. I'd wanted to be one of those stallions as a child, to roam free, to toss my hair and stamp the ground if anyone so much as looked at me the wrong way. They lived semi-wild in the marshland and even gave birth out there. Only the working ones were kept in the stable for the *gardians* to ride when herding the bulls – even the females were called bulls. Papa possessed more than three hundred black Camargue bulls, but never any Spanish ones like some neighbouring *manades*. The barking sounds that were uttered by their deep chests and the special musky bull-smell that rose from their dusty hides had formed the backbone of my childhood.

'Do you still ride?' I asked Léon. It was like slipping back in time to the days before we forgot how to laugh.

'No.' He shook his head with a disparaging smile. 'I'm a town dweller. I ride a motorcycle instead of a horse.' He ruffled a hand over one of Cosette's pricked ears, an elegant snowy white curve with a smoky inner shell. 'But handlebars don't sit as well in the hands as a pair of well-used reins.' He glanced down at my hands, still moving over the horse. 'And you? I don't expect there's much scope for bareback-riding down the Champs-Élysées.'

I gave a token laugh. 'I didn't think you'd end up in the *gendarmerie*, Léon.'

'And I didn't think you'd end up a Parisian, Eloïse.'

I nodded. 'We both have our reasons.' I tickled Cosette's chin and she batted her long white eyelashes at me. I stepped back and focused on the policeman in the forbiddingly dark uniform. It seemed to have swallowed him. Devoured him. The bold young boy I used to know was gone. Grey eyes still clear and alert, still on the lookout for trouble, but where was the fizzing grin with teeth too large for his mouth? And the honking laugh? Now was not the time or place for either of them, I admit, but even so, I missed them. The strong features of his face were clothed in stillness and a seriousness that felt alien. I wondered whether he pulled them on with the dark-blue serge uniform each morning, or whether they were imprinted permanently on his skin like a tattoo.

'Please tell me,' I said, 'the reason for what's going on here.'

'You should ask your father.'

'I'm asking you.'

The lines of his face sharpened. 'Why not your father?'

'My father may choose not to tell me.'

He did not challenge that.

As the last rays of the sun slipped through the doorway and painted a dusty golden rectangle on the cobbles of the stables, I walked over to the windowsill where a riot of small rosy apples overflowed a reed basket. I took three, one for each of us. Cosette whickered her thanks prettily.

Léon took a bite of his. 'I've come to ask questions, Mademoiselle Caussade,' he said formally, 'not to answer them.' But he smiled. A genuine one, not a polite one, and for the first time that day I felt the tight band around my chest loosen enough for me to breathe freely.

'There's no point asking me anything,' I pointed out. 'I know nothing about the killing of Goliath. I came because my father asked me to but I don't have any idea what is going on here.'

'You know about the American plan to construct eleven air bases in France?'

'Of course. There have been mass protests in Paris against the idea.'

'The United States Air Force – USAF – as part of NATO, is putting together a defence strategy against the threat from the Soviet Union's build-up of forces.'

'But I thought the air base sites were all going to be on France's north-eastern border, not down here in the south. Why us?'

'They are proposing for this one to be a back-up base. They've taken over Dumoulin airfield and have expanded it. But now they want to extend the runways much further and that's why they need your father's land.'

'So the new runways will be . . .' I couldn't finish.

Léon frowned and waited for me to complete the sentence. I didn't. So finally he voiced the words himself. 'Right next to your father's *manade* on its western edge.'

A *manade* is the Camargue word for a farm. The Americans were setting up camp right on our Caussade doorstep.

'Will there be nuclear weapons stored there?'

'Of course. In readiness to strike back in case of an attack. The Americans' – Léon was feeding his apple core to Cosette – 'are the only ones with sufficient money and firepower to confront the Soviets. Europe is teetering on the brink.'

A chill touched my spine despite the warmth of the evening. I looked out through the stable doorway to where the barn stood hunched and shadowy in the last dying rays of daylight. Inside sat my brother.

'Léon.'

The apple-scented breath of Cosette shifted the musty air in the stables.

'Do you ever visit my brother now?' I asked. 'You used to be his friend.'

'I tried.'

'He turned you away too?'

'He's in a dark place right now. He needs to be alone.'

A rifle across his knees. As if he knew what was coming. I didn't attempt to speak. I had no voice and the silence deepened along with the shadows but Léon made no attempt to brush it aside. It was only when one of the *gardians* who worked on my father's *manade* rode in on Pépé, a muscular high-stepping horse, that the stables came back to life with the rattle of hooves and the creak of warm leather.

'*Bonsoir*, Mademoiselle Eloïse.'

'*Bonsoir*, Louis, *ça va?*'

The rider's mouth pulled down in a grimace and he gestured towards the barn where Goliath's body lay, hacked to death. He glanced at the police uniform at my side, wiped the back of his gloved hand across his mouth as though ridding his lips of the words that rose to them, and moved off to the far end stall. Police were never welcome. They always meant trouble. I nodded goodbye to Léon and walked towards the wide doorway. It was time to speak with my father.

'Eloïse.'

I halted. Léon was barely visible in the gloom. 'What is it?'

'If you are going into town, into Serriac or even to Arles, take care.'

'Take care?' A pulse kicked in my throat. 'Why?'

'Because a lot of people know you are the daughter of Aristide Caussade.'

'Léon, understand this: I am proud to be the daughter of Aristide Caussade.'

He nodded. 'Of course you are.' I could hear the smile in his voice rather than see it on his face.

I moved closer. 'Do you think there could be some other reason for the brutal death of my father's prize bull? Other than the air base land?'

'Do you know of one?'

'No.'

'Are you sure?'

'Yes.'

I wasn't certain he believed me. I started to return to the house, but I heard his policeman's boots just behind me.

'Eloïse, I am sorry about what happened to your face.'

Most people daren't mention it. Daren't look at it. As if it might contaminate them. He came to stand in front of me and for a long moment he studied my face. 'It makes no difference,' he said in a low voice. 'You are who you are. Still the Eloïse Caussade who leaped from the top of a tree into the Rhône river to show her brother how tough she was.'

He reached out and ran the ball of his thumb along the length of the ridge of my scar from eyebrow to chin. He had no idea how that hard shiny lump of tissue craved human touch. I felt it come alive. It throbbed. It breathed. When he removed his hand, I walked rapidly away into the darkening yard, my own hand cupped over the scar to hold in the warmth of his thumb.

'Thank you,' I called blindly behind me.

'For what?'

'For the warning.'

CHAPTER NINE

The farmhouse was empty. The rooms were dark. The walls and floors and ancient doors lay silent and I had a sense that the house had died too. No buzz of heat-heavy flies or creak of boards contracting as the day cooled. I turned on the lights and inspected every room.

Nothing. Nobody. Not even the old dog Juno curled up on my father's bed. The house was deserted, except for its memories. They were there, hanging from every beam, stretched from table to chair like cobwebs, brushing against my skin, clinging to my hair.

Where was Papa?

Outside. That's where he'd be. Stalking his land, hunting rifle in the crook of his arm, dogs at his heels, seeking out any intruder who might try to take advantage of a moonless night. I would not want to be one of the shadows that crossed his path. His feet knew every patch of grass, each channel of water, the exact placing of each dyke and tree and fence. In his head my father carried an intimate map of every square metre of his land, and yet even he could not know what was out there.

I worried for him.

I entered André's bedroom. He was still in the barn. I felt like an intruder. Nothing had changed in my brother's room and I poked and prodded into the few cupboards. I discovered a handsome wristwatch in the drawer of his bedside cabinet, with a black leather strap and gold case in art deco style. A Bulova. An American watch I'd never seen before.

It made me wonder what visitors André had received down here in his hideaway while I was running around Paris waiting and waiting to hear from him. I rummaged through his shelves and under a stack of *Les Ailes* aircraft magazines I came across his old copy of *Les Misérables* that matched mine and under it a Bible. Both well-thumbed. The touch of them triggered the memory of the Île Saint-Louis in Paris and the sound of the calm voice on the end of the telephone in Hôtel d'Emilie telling me to wait where I was.

Talk to me, André.

How can I protect you when I am in the dark?

I looked under his pillow and I felt no shame. If he would not help me help him, I must help him myself. A hymn book. I found a hymn book tucked under the neatly smoothed white cotton pillowcase. It was a dark-blue book with gold trim, its corners soft from years of handling. Years of being loved.

By my brother?

Surely not. André had no time for what he called primitive superstition. Yet here it was, where he could reach for it in the darkest holes of the night, when pain and despair engulfed him, robbing him of the man he believed himself to be, so that he turned to the soft holy hymnal for comfort.

My hand started to shake when I thought about his pain and the small navy-blue book between my fingers blurred. I replaced it where I'd found it and returned downstairs, where I made a thick soup from home-grown potatoes and white onions. I threw in fat garlic cloves and a handful of thyme and when it was ready I carried a bowl of it out to the barn, steam coiling up into the night air.

To my surprise André accepted the soup. 'Thank you, Eloïse. It's kind of you.'

So polite. So polite it broke my heart.

'Go and get some rest in the house, André. I'll sit here with Goliath.' I glanced at the black mound. The air felt stiff with the smell of flesh.

'Thank you for the offer, but no. I'll remain.'

His politeness and his stubbornness sent a spike of anger through me.

'What is the point?' I asked. 'Whoever did this could return, we both know that. It is dangerous and pointless to sit here all night alone.'

His face was hidden in darkness but I saw his shoulders jerk forward. 'Have you forgotten what the bulls mean to us, Eloïse? Has Paris turned your head so quickly?'

'Can you not see? To put yourself in danger for no reason is senseless.'

'It is my legs that are damaged, not my mind.'

I was not sure about that. 'Then I will sit here too.'

'No, Eloïse.' His tone was sharp now. 'This is not a game that I can let you join in, the way I did when we were children. Leave me alone. I want you to go away.'

Go away. From the barn? Or from the farm? I didn't ask. I knew the answer.

Without a word I walked away, out into the night where the air was silky soft on my skin and carried the salty scent of the marshes and the high-pitched whine of mosquitoes. I left my brother alone in the barn. With his hunting rifle. With the stench of death in every breath he took.

I lay awake all night. Hour after hour. Ears alert to the slightest sound, the faintest whisper, expecting the roar of a rifle at every moment. The night was long and oppressively hot. I lay naked in bed, legs tangled in the sheet, arms flung wide, and when my thoughts grew too heavy to hold inside my head I stood at the window and peered out into the blackness. Seeing shadows within shadows, imagining movement where there was none. I needed facts not phantoms so, despite Léon's warning, I would head into town when it was light.

An hour before dawn I heard men's voices outside, low and secretive, the words too tight together for me to catch, but I recognised them as belonging to my father and my brother, and felt a hefty kick of relief in my chest. They were safe. Both safe. Below me in the kitchen their voices rumbled for a few minutes, then I heard noises on the stairs. Unfamiliar sounds. I was slow to make sense of them, my mind sluggish with exhaustion, but the sound was slow, laborious, full of effort; a dragging, scraping, arduous sound. It was my brother hauling his damaged body up the stairs. I tried not to picture it, but failed.

I pulled on a light robe, stood close to the old oak door and didn't breathe. I could hear his grunts of pain. The curses under his breath. I matched them with my own, curse for curse. Finally he reached the landing and the tap of his crutches on the floorboards came nearer. Tap, slide; tap, slide; tap, slide, until he was outside my door, where he halted. For four minutes he stood there in silence, no more than a hand's breadth from me and when I could bear it no longer I swung open the door. It was a mistake. André must have been leaning against it, gathering his strength after the climb, because he stumbled into my room and would have fallen to the floor if I hadn't wrapped my arms around him and held him on his feet.

'I apologise,' he said awkwardly. 'I didn't mean to disturb you.'

I continued to hold him close as he manoeuvred the crutches back under his armpits. For this moment, while I supported his weight and smelled the farm on his skin, he was my brother again. I was his sister. I let my cheek brush his, and for no more than a heartbeat I felt his body sag against mine, before he pushed himself upright and slid from my grasp.

'André, who is Piquet?'

His eyes widened and his lips pulled back, baring his strong white teeth.

'He came to the hospital in Paris,' I continued. 'Looking for you. Eyes of stone and an attitude that needed a lesson in manners.'

He almost smiled. 'Did you give it to him?'

'I was tempted.'

He nodded. Looked at my scar. 'He didn't hurt you?'

'No. He wanted to, but his sidekick stopped him.'

His face hardened. 'Have you seen him around here?'

'No.'

'Let me know if you do. Don't go anywhere near him.'

'Who is he?'

'A nobody,' he replied, and swung himself on his crutches in the direction of his room.

I noticed how strong his arm muscles had grown, bulging under his shirtsleeves to compensate for the damage to his legs. I let him go and shut the door but an ice finger touched my throat in the darkness. Piquet was not a *nobody*. And he could be here.

Tomorrow I would put a strong bolt on my door.

'My Eloïse, *ma chérie*, you have come home.'

A kiss was stamped on each of my cheeks by my father's tiny housekeeper, Mathilde. She was a small wiry woman in her mid-fifties, as skinny and fussy as one of our hens. She plonked a bowl of coffee on the kitchen table in front of me and I could smell the familiar lavender water she always sprayed on her short iron-grey curls. Alongside the coffee sat a *tartine* gleaming with her homemade apricot jam. The warmth of this woman could melt an iceberg. She wore a chin-to-toe cotton apron bright with sunflowers printed over it and her hair was bound up in a sunflower-yellow scarf. She brought sunshine into the dark corners of the house and I gave her the set of lavender soaps I'd brought for her from Paris. They were in fact made in a lavender distillery just up the road from here in Avignon, but I knew their fancy Galeries Lafayette box would please her.

She had been a vital part of this family ever since my mother died. My father employed her as a housekeeper, but she was far more than that to us. She bound our wounds, made us sing the 'Marseillaise' and above all cradled us in a love we found nowhere else. But she had her own family of four strapping lads to care for, so after two o'clock each day the child-rearing duties fell on the reluctant shoulders of our father. Had we been bulls or horses, it would have been different. As it was we either ran wild, went hungry, or worked as field-hands till we dropped.

'Bad times here,' she muttered, 'I'm glad you've come, Eloïse.' Her rough hand tapped my cheek. 'Poor little one.'

'I'm fine.'

She nodded, prepared to take my word for it. 'They need you.'

'Where is André?'

'In his room.'

'How is he?' I asked.

'Do you mean does he hate you?'

I nodded.

'He says little,' she said. 'He reads, great mountains of books on things I've never heard of.' She paused and wiped her hands vigorously on her apron. 'When the pain allows him to, that is.'

'Does he have visitors?'

'Some. Not often.'

'Who are they?'

'I don't know.' She stepped forward and lifted the empty coffee bowl from my hand. 'Why don't you go upstairs and ask him yourself?'

CHAPTER TEN

I tapped on André's bedroom door but there was no answer. I waited two minutes, then tapped again. Still no answer, and I was suddenly worried for him. With barely a sound I opened his door a crack and peered in. He was there, lying in bed flat on his back, eyes closed, and I could not resist the temptation to enter the room.

I stood beside his bed, the light dim with the shutters half-closed. I studied his face on the pillow and saw it had changed. One cheekbone sat at a different angle and there was a thickness of tissue across the bridge of his long nose that hadn't been there before, as well as scars zigzagging through one eyebrow and along his hairline. But that's not what I mean. Something had gone from his face. Even in repose. Like in a room when the electricity is switched off and shadows are all you're left with. I wanted to hold his hand in mine but it was tucked under the quilt where no one could touch it. His hair was longer, no trips to the barber, and his

70

skin was paler, no sitting out in the afternoon sun. No life that he would call a life.

I lowered my head in my hands and fought to make no sound as time ticked past and the ache inside me circled relentlessly. During the half-hour I stood there, André lay still as the grave, not even a flutter of an eyelid or a flicker of muscle. He could be drugged. Or he could be in a far-off place in his head. But not for one moment did I believe he was asleep.

He chose not to speak to me.

'André, do you remember my birthday in the Chat Noir?'

I had moved over to the window in his room, snatching a glimpse of my father's land as it dozed in the morning sun. The shutters blocked all but a thin strip of the view. I leaned my forehead against the glass, drinking in the thousand different greens that beckoned to me, out there in the wide-open spaces where wild spinach grew and the vibrant stalks of samphire spread in abundance underfoot. In Paris the cobblestones were hard and unforgiving, and my feet itched now to race through the cordgrasses of the Camargue.

'Do you remember?' I asked again, my eyes focused on Papa, whom I could see striding through the yard outside with one of his *gardians*. 'In Paris? We were both drunk on Bollinger cocktails and I was wearing my first ever evening gown. Emerald silk. Remember, André?'

I waited. Just long enough for Papa and the *gardian* to move out of sight.

André's life in Paris was a closed book. I knew nothing about it. Not where he lived, what he did all day, who his friends were. Not even what his job was, at first. Though he'd claimed to work in some vague capacity for the Ministry of Defence. We would meet up for coffee or a drink about once a month, and last year he took me to the Chat Noir to celebrate my birthday.

I had no telephone number for him, no address. I used to contact him by using a DLD, a dead letter drop, the way we did as children, a secret place where you leave a message or a package when communicating covertly with someone. A method dearly loved by Intelligence agents.

In the distance I could make out the salt meadow and the emerald tips of the rice fields rippling in the breeze off the Rhône. Out there everything moved. In here all was still. The bedroom was sparsely furnished, a single bed, a rush-seat chair, a homemade rug, a heavy wardrobe. It gave nothing away. Even the display of twenty or more aeroplanes had gone, the ones André had carved out of wood during his hours of hanging round the nearby airfield during the war. He was good with his hands even back then. In Paris they liked to pick locks and fiddle with a tiny subminiature spy-camera instead. He had shown it to me in the Chat Noir.

'Do you remember that night, André? When I asked you what it was that came between you and Papa and made you leave.' I breathed noisily on the glass pane of the window. 'You pinched my nose between your fingers and laughed.

You told me to keep out of Papa's business. I shouted that I was his daughter and had a right to know more, but you just released my nose and sighed from somewhere deep in your boots. "I'm his son," you muttered, and slurred something about finding a photograph of Papa. That was it. I was no wiser.'

The silence in the room was thick and suffocating.

'Do you remember?' I whispered.

'I remember.'

I spun around. André's eyes were open and he was watching me, but his eyes were all wrong. The shining amber colour had gone and in its place was a dirty mud shade, tense with pain and exhaustion. I returned to his bedside.

'André, how are you?'

'What are you doing here, Eloïse?'

Answer a question with a question. He was good at that.

'I came because Papa summoned me,' I said, keeping my voice steady. 'And because I've been so worried about you.'

'I'm all right. You've seen me. Now leave.'

'Leave?'

'Yes, go back to Paris. You are not wanted here.'

'I want to look after you, André, to make sure you—'

'I don't need you to look after me. I have Mathilde. So go. Now.'

He closed his eyes, thick sandy lashes on his thin cheeks, shutting me out. I rested my hand on the quilt on top of his arm.

'Hear me out first, André. Please. Listen to what I have

to say.' I rushed on before he had a chance to say no. 'First, I am sorry. Desperately sorry. I am to blame for . . .' I gestured at the bed, 'for this, but—'

'Stop. Stop it, Eloïse. I don't want your *sorry*.'

I removed my hand from his arm.

'Second,' I continued, and sat down on the chair, going nowhere, 'I am frightened that whoever did this to you will track you down to finish it. You need someone to guard you.'

'You?'

'Yes. Day and night. Till you are better. I saw no guards outside. I have your High Standard gun in my bag and can keep you safe. If you don't wish to see me – which I understand – I will remain downstairs at all times. You won't know I'm here.'

He made a faint sound. Whether it was disgust or anger, I couldn't tell. I watched the large tendon in his neck tighten.

'Third,' I continued quietly, 'tell me who these people are who tried to murder you. Why did they do it?'

'I cannot tell you that.'

'André, you're the one who taught me that knowledge is power. With that information I can help you. I can protect you better. I can even find the person behind the wheel of the van that—'

'Eloïse, I trusted you before. Look what happened. Why would I trust you now?' He turned his face to the wall.

The air suddenly became too heavy to breathe. The shadows deepened and what little light was in the room seemed to seep out under the door. I sat there in silence, but my lungs betrayed me, pumping as fast as if I'd been running. Minute after minute ticked past until finally I rose to my feet and walked to the door, but before I could open it, André spoke.

'Do you have my wallet?'

'Your wallet?'

'You took it away from the hospital.'

'Yes. I have it.'

I had ransacked the wallet a hundred times looking for clues.

'Burn it,' he ordered.

I nodded and walked out.

CHAPTER ELEVEN

The reason I knew André was a spy was that one day I saw him in action. I saw him execute a brush-pass in the street. It was soon after I'd gone to Paris, a stifling summer day, and André and I had enjoyed a drink in a bar on Rue Gabrielle. When he left I tried to follow him to discover where he lived – I'd tried before but he'd always lost me. This time he was distracted. The pavements were busy and I was getting better at it, so he didn't spot me.

I saw him suddenly slow his pace. His shoulders dropped, his arms hung loose at his sides, the fingers of one hand folded over. Instantly I knew what was coming. I'd seen it a thousand times. We used to do brush-passes all the time as children, first when we played at being spies and then for real when we helped the Resistance pass messages under the noses of the Nazis during the war.

But there on the streets of Paris on Rue de la Goutte d'Or, I was stunned. I watched his hand brush innocently against the hand of a tall fair-haired man wearing a pale linen suit and spectacles. Neither looked at the other or broke their stride. If I hadn't been watching for it, I'd never have spotted it. Blink and I'd have missed it. This time it wasn't a game. I knew my brother worked in the Ministry of Defence and I couldn't help wondering why he would be passing information in such a secretive manner.

'Are you a spy?' I asked outright the next time we met.

'What makes you think that?'

'I saw you do a brush-pass.'

André was shocked and annoyed to be caught out by his little sister, but he didn't deny it. In the end, after I applied thumbscrews, he admitted he worked undercover for the CIA – the American Central Intelligence Agency – to help save France from falling under Communist domination.

'France is sleep-walking right into the Soviet Union's open arms,' he warned me. 'Our country needs to wake up. *Vite.* And the only ones who have the firepower to protect the whole of Europe from the Communist threat are the Americans.'

What I'd seen him do on the street that day was pass information on a new Soviet sleeper about whom he had suspicions to another CIA agent. When I asked the obvious – 'Why don't you just hand it to him over a drink at Maxime's?' – he'd just laughed and told me I had a lot to learn.

'So teach me,' I'd said.

That's when I learned to pick locks, work a daylight and night-time trace on foot and on wheels, to decipher different kinds of codes and to use a spy camera. By the time I left the Sorbonne, I was a cherry waiting to be picked.

After leaving André's room, I went straight to mine and pulled my suitcase from under my bed. I opened it and from the bottom I dug out his wallet.

Why burn it?

I had scoured every inch of its black leather and discovered no hidden messages. What was it he wanted destroyed, what secret did it hold? I removed the banknotes – about one hundred thousand francs in various denominations. Since the war our money had gone crazy with the devaluation of the franc, so a hundred thousand francs sounds far more than it actually was – in real money it was a bit less than one hundred British pounds, or around three hundred American dollars.

That was still a lot to carry around. Don't think I hadn't already examined every one of the banknotes with a magnifying glass, because I had. Nothing. Just banknotes. Also in the case sat a roll of black felt, bound with tape. I removed it and unrolled it on the floor. Nestled within were my tools. I picked up the scalpel which lay beside the lock-pick, and sat down on the floor with the wallet. Neatly and carefully, the scalpel blade sliced open every stitch and prised apart the areas glued together. When it was all in pieces I examined the leather spread out in front of me and at first I saw nothing. I fingered the raw underside of the dark leather that I'd not seen before until my fingertip suddenly found the slightest of indentations. I peered closer. Something. What was it?

Then I spotted it. Numbers in black ink. Three of them. I fetched a torch.

511609

271314

901906

It was a code. This was a message from André to someone.

But to whom?

To me? No, he had no need to send a message to me because I was right there at his side on the day of the crash.

Part of a telephone number?

A security box access code?

I knew of course that it was neither. On my bedside table lay my copy of Victor Hugo's *Les Misérables*. It was old and dog-eared, its pages well-thumbed and soft as peach-skin. I sat cross-legged on the bed with it on my lap, as I had hundreds of times before as a child, and opened its pages.

The first number on the raw leather of the wallet was 511609. I split it up into pairs and turned quickly to page 51. Line 16. The ninth word. It was TAKE.

The second number was 271314. My fingers retraced their steps to page 27. I counted down to line 13. Across to the fourteenth word. It was ME.

TAKE ME.

Take me where?

When André and I were children, *Les Misérables* had been our cipher book. André had taught me how to use a simple cipher code and we had left secret messages for each other all over the house and barns. To say where we were hiding. Where we were going. What mood we were in. The key to it all had been *Les Misérables.* Now he had used it again with someone else. Old habits die hard.

901906 was the third number.

I skipped forward to page 90. Familiar names flashing past my eyes – Jean Valjean, Madeleine, Javert, Fantine. A powerful tale that examines the nature of good and evil. As a child I was screwed up in knots by it but I'd clung to its final offer of redemption like a life raft. Now I clung to its pages again. Page 90. Line 19. Sixth word.

OUT. The word was *out.*

Take. Me. Out.

Who was the message meant for and what did it mean? It had been written before his stay in hospital when he was well, I reminded myself. Was the message incomplete?

Take me out – but out of where?

I walked over to the window and focused my attention on the yard, on the white horses being saddled up for their day's work. I thought about the person who had driven the van that smashed into my brother. Was he preparing for his day's work? I tried to conjure up a picture of him. Are you lazing in bed, curled around your wife's warm buttocks, no thought in your head for the man whose life you ruined? Or sipping your first coffee? Smoking a cigarette? Walking your dog through the cool morning shadows of the statuary in the Tuileries Garden?

You think you are safe.

But you are wrong. Wherever you are hiding, whatever plans you are hatching, I promise you this. I will find you.

I could hear men's voices, a deep rumble, low and respectful. I found Papa outside the barn handing out large purposeful shovels to five of his *gardians*, each one of whom wore a black neckerchief around his throat in memory of the butchered bull. All of the *gardians* had known Goliath like an old cantankerous friend and at some time each of them had been one of the local *razeteurs* who had risked the animal's wrath by snatching cockades from his horns in the ring.

A string of crows sat on the barn ridge and watched us in the thin morning light. The day was just beginning to heat up and the sky now stretched white as a shroud over us and the flat landscape shimmered silver instead of green. All colour had drained from my father's *manade*, the way it does from a corpse. I too was dressed in a black sheath dress, my dark hair tied back from my face by a black silk ribbon, sleek as a seal. In Paris it would look chic. Here it looked like I was treading in the footsteps of death.

'Eloïse,' my father called out.

Everyone turned to watch me approach, even the crows. In the past I had ridden many times with these men, herding the bulls to new pastures on my father's farm, swatting at the dense clouds of black flies, each of us with a guiding pole in one hand, reins in the other, a black felt-brimmed hat on our head to keep off the sun. Yet now, I looked at their eyes, and I could see that I was a stranger to them in my Rue Saint-Honoré dress. Worse. I was a stranger who had crippled their *patron*'s eldest son.

I smiled broadly at them. '*Bonjour, mes amis.*'

Only Louis smiled back, the one who had been in the stable last night. A wide smile crossed his leathery cheeks and he touched the brim of his hat. '*Bonjour,* Mademoiselle Eloïse.'

The others said nothing. My father was wearing his brown work cords and a grey collarless shirt. His white beard was in need of a trim, a task I used to perform every fourth Sunday when I lived at home, and his dark eyes were in need of comfort. Neither job was I fit for now.

'Here,' my father said, and held out a spare shovel to me. The sinews under the skin of his arm were thick as serpents, muscles that could bring down a bull by the horns.

I looked at the proffered shovel and I knew what it was intended for. Goliath would be granted an honourable resting place; he deserved such respect.

'No, Papa, you and Goliath don't need me for that. I am driving into town to do my own kind of digging.'

CHAPTER TWELVE

Serriac was the kind of town that threw a net over you the moment you set foot on its dusty main street. An invisible net, but still a net. A net of watchful eyes. Don't expect to escape it, because you won't. You can't. So when I climbed out of my car, I paused, stared boldly at the windows along the tree-lined thoroughfare and smiled back at them. It is the same as when you face a bull. Show fear and you will be trampled.

Serriac was a pretty town. Tubs of geraniums and zinnias splashed scarlet and buttery yellow over the ancient stone buildings, with their wrought-iron balconies and roofs the colour of freckles in the sun. Cafés and bars spilled on to the pavements, where old men in caps sat and smoked with yellow fingers. Off behind the single main road, narrow streets darted and dived in unexpected directions to confuse the unwary.

Above it all soared the imposing bell tower of L'Église Saint-Joseph. It was a church built in the Romanesque style so beloved by medieval France, with sturdy pillars, massive rounded arches and barrel vaults. It was a church you didn't argue with. I knew. I'd tried.

Ahead of me lay the Hôtel de Ville. The town hall. It looked old and lazy with a pockmarked façade, dozing in the morning sunshine, eyes half shuttered. I wasn't fooled.

'I wish to speak to Monsieur le Maire, please.'

'The mayor is occupied at the moment.'

The middle-aged secretary behind the desk tapped the end of her pen on the form she was filling out and raised her gaze to me at a snail's pace that was designed to irritate. I was half inclined to lean across the desk and snatch her pen away to ensure her full attention, but I had no need. The moment she caught sight of my face, I had her full attention. I saw the pity flow into her pretty blue eyes and turn her cheeks a dusky pink, but I was used to it. Pity and I were old friends these days.

'When will Mayor Durand be free?'

She dragged her gaze off my face and made a fuss of consulting the large maroon leather diary on her side of the desk. 'In forty-five minutes,' she announced precisely, looking up at the ornate clock on the wall. It had no scars. Its face was unblemished.

'I'll wait. My name is Eloïse Caussade.'

She made a note of the fact on a sheet of paper that already contained a long list of names. I retreated to join other supplicants on a row of seats along one wall of the echoing space of marble and pillars that was the reception area of the town hall. The clock ticked away while we waited on the mayor's convenience. Men in important positions often like to play games with time, and I hoped Monsieur le Maire was not one of them or I could be here all day. I pictured my father's *gardians* digging down into the black earth while I sat staring at my white sandals.

But in exactly forty-five minutes the secretary walked over, the heels of her brown pre-war shoes tapping on the veined marble floor and, without actually looking at me, led me to a pair of large double doors. An official crest at the top and a doorknob that looked more like a cannonball announced the importance of the man behind the oak panels. The secretary knocked discreetly.

'Enter,' came a man's voice.

She opened the door. I entered and she shut the door silently behind me. I was in a beautiful room, the kind of room that makes your thoughts grow into something bigger than you expected, with its high ceiling, cornices and gilded curlicues, and tall elegant windows of perfect proportions. No wonder they put the mayor in it. He certainly needed his thoughts to be big and elegant and in proportion. But it pained me that the furniture was so ugly.

'*Bonjour*, Eloïse.'

The man behind the black desk rose to his feet, strode across the room with arm outstretched and shook my hand with sufficient force to impress on me how important he had become since I'd last seen him.

'*Bonjour*, Monsieur le Maire.'

There. His full title. He could release my hand now. Under the cover of smiles, we studied each other. He was still a handsome man, in his fifties now, but lean and upright with a bearing that hinted at a military background. His hair was dark with silvery threads but a little too carefully groomed for my liking. His smile was a politician's, broad and welcoming, but could not erase the permanent crease of irritation that crossed his high forehead. His suit was exquisite.

He paid my scar no more attention than he would a bramble scratch. I asked myself why he had agreed to see me, this busy man, with a queue of people outside his office waiting for his attention. The answer came easily – it was because I was the daughter of Aristide Caussade.

What did he want from me?

He stepped back with a light laugh. 'I remember a time when you ran round in grubby riding trousers and a black *gardian* hat, but now look at you. *Très chic.*'

He took my elbow, steered me to the seat in front of his desk and resumed his own chair behind it, sitting back as if relaxed, but I could feel the sharp point of his attention like a needle tip at my forehead. I had known Charles Durand since I was eight years old. He was the father of my best friend at school, though he was one of those fathers who breezed in and out, rarely around, always preoccupied with his property business and his part-ownership of the local newspaper, *La Voix de la Camargue*.

'So,' he said, 'what can I do for you, Eloïse?'

'I'm sure you know why I'm here.'

'The death of the bull.'

'The brutal butchery of the Caussade champion bull, Goliath, yes.'

He released a sigh. That is how men like Charles Durand deal with difficult women. They sigh. And when the sighing doesn't work, they laugh. To tell you that you are wrong. But he didn't laugh. Not yet. He gave me a serious regretful frown and shook his head without dislodging a hair.

'I am sorry, Eloïse. Please convey my regret to your father.'

'Monsieur le Maire, we want more than regret.'

In the silence that followed, we both counted to ten.

'It is in the hands of the police,' he pointed out.

'No one knows this town like you do, monsieur,' I said quietly. 'You have eyes and ears on every street corner.'

'What is it you want?'

'I need your help.'

'I agreed to see you today because your family is going through a bad time at the moment, as we all know. Your father is a respected member of our community and I wish to offer him my sympathy.'

'Why tell me? Why not tell him?'

The mayor flashed me an elegant shrug. 'Aristide Caussade and I have not always seen eye to eye.' He reached for a cigarette from the silver casket on the desk and offered me one. I shook my head. He lit his own, and I wondered why he'd felt the need to gain himself some time. 'The loss of land to the

United States Air Force, the violent death of your bull, the sad state of your brother, your own injury – these must have hit your father hard. I am pleased to see you have returned home to pull your weight in the family.'

'Pull my weight?'

'Yes. Instead of deserting them.'

He had no right. No right to say that. I felt a flush of anger rise to my cheeks. Even if it was true, it was not his business to voice such a comment.

'Now, Eloïse,' he said soothingly, 'tell me what it is you want.'

Oh, he was good. I felt my feet slipping, as if he had pulled away the polished floorboards beneath my seat, and I conjured up a memory of him down in the dirt in front of my horse Cosette after she had barged him to the ground when I was fifteen. Cosette never tolerated anyone shouting at me, even if I was in the wrong. That moment of fear had bleached the skin around his eyes as white as paper. I remembered that.

He regarded me now through a flimsy veil of cigarette smoke and I wondered if he remembered it too.

'Will you explain, please, Monsieur le Maire, what is going on in this town? What makes the people of Serriac turn into a bunch of murderers, instead of a peaceful community that discusses problems over a civilised glass of wine?'

'Murderers?' He gave a snort of dismissal. 'That's too strong.'

'They murdered Goliath.'

'Now, Eloïse, be careful of your tongue.'

I studied his pale blue eyes, committing each detail of their colour and shape to memory, so that I would know in future when he was lying.

'So what are they, if not murderers?'

He exhaled a skein of smoke and his eyes narrowed. Was it the smoke? Or was a lie coming?

'Most likely it was a foolish group of two or three drunken youths at night trying to prove how macho they are.' He gestured with his hands, as if he would smack one of the youths' cheeks, but it was done with amusement. 'Taking on the biggest and best bull in the whole of the Camargue. I can imagine them driving out in the darkness to . . . No' – he smiled – 'probably on bicycles, eager to become men.'

A lie then.

I sat forward. 'If a group of drunken youths had approached Goliath in a field in the dark, he would have trampled them to the ground and gored them to death.'

He considered my words. 'You are of course right, Eloïse. I had not looked at it like that.'

'So who was it?'

'The men in this town are angry that your father has sold a large tract of his land to the American military.'

Sold?

The word went off like a grenade in my head. I had not realised. The sale was already settled. Why had Papa not said?

'But the men of Serriac,' Durand continued, 'would not take the law into their own hands, I assure you.'

'Who would?'

He smiled patiently. 'That is for Captain Roussel to find out.'

'Monsieur, we all know that factions within Maurice Thorez's Communist Party are causing trouble for Prime Minister Laniel up and down the country over the nuclear arms issue. The presence of nuclear weapons in the Camargue is going to stir up a huge swell of anger. Do you have in your possession the names of any Communist agitators in Serriac?'

'Your brother is the person you should be asking that question.'

'What? André?'

'No. Your younger brother, Isaac. The one in Marseille.'

Smooth as silk. He poured hot oil in my ear, smooth as silk. I shot to my feet. I had to get out of there.

'I have taken up enough of your time, monsieur.'

But he was ahead of me. He strode across his grand room and reached for the ornate brass handle, but paused. 'How is your brother?' he asked me. 'How is André?'

There was something in the way he said it, in the deliberate lightness of his words. I had the odd feeling that *this* – this question – was why I was here. This was the reason I had been allowed into his inner sanctum.

'André is not well,' I told him flatly. No need for more.

'I hear that his legs are bad.'

I said nothing.

'And severe pain in the head, they say,' he added.

'Who are *they*?'

'Just the town gossips.'

'Old men warming their wine in the sun.'

'Is your brother able to walk better now?'

He was taking too much interest. I put out a hand to open the door and he smiled courteously. 'Will you tell him something from me, Eloïse? Tell André that as Mayor of Serriac I send him my best wishes for a total recovery very soon. Before the accident we used to see him regularly in the town's bars, most weekends. We miss him.'

I took three quick breaths. 'I will pass on your message, Monsieur le Maire.'

My fingers uncurled from the fist they had formed, I opened the door and walked out. It took an effort of will not to run into the blinding sunlight that drenched the street outside, as far away from Charles Durand as I could get.

In the town's bars. Most weekends.

While living in Paris? Someone was lying to my face. Was it Charles Durand?

Or André?

CHAPTER THIRTEEN

Serriac is a town that does not believe in change. In the four years I'd been gone, it had scarcely blinked. I knew this town like I knew each creamy strand in my Cosette's mane. I knew the glow of Serriac's peach-tinged pantiles and its ancient olive shutters shedding flakes like sunburned skin. I had roamed each street and alleyway. Learned its hidden corners and its hairpin bends, climbed over its twisted stone steps and its Roman archway. I knew this town.

I walked through it now in the placid heat, and I was greeted as if I'd never left by women who were shelling peas or washing babies on the doorstep with gentle hands, and by men fixing unidentifiable pieces of machinery. I stopped, exchanged words and smiles. Time and again the same question arose: *How is your brother André?*

Captain Léon Roussel was right. They know I am the daughter of Aristide Caussade. That is why no one referred to the American air base, though as I walked, a flight of three bomber aircraft passed overhead. No one referred to the massacre of Goliath either and that scared me. As if they thought it a subject too dangerous to mention, as if the stench of our champion bull's blood clung to my skirts. Even the town's idle dogs chose to hole up in the cool patches of shade rather than sniff at my ankles or growl at my approach.

I made my way to Thiery's Bar down Rue des Lavandières where years ago the washerwomen performed their work under the municipal water pumps in the town square. The *patron*, Monsieur Thiery, paraded in his trademark purple apron, laughed and kissed only one of my cheeks, the good one. I ordered coffee and a glass of iced water, and I sat outside under the lacy branches of a plane tree, observing the small square with its smooth cobbles and its two cafés facing each other, like bulls in a stand-off. Nothing much stirred. I made a mental note of the few cars that were parked around the edges of the square. It was safer that way. So that I would know if one followed me home.

Time passed. Shadows started to shrink as the sun climbed higher in a naked blue sky and I waited to see who would come. I sipped my water and picked over the bones of my meeting with Serriac's mayor. Why would he protect those who committed the crime against my father? He might be standing with those in the town who were opposed to the air base expansion, but as mayor he should not be condoning violent behaviour in any form. Still ringing in my head like a church bell on Sunday was his comment: *In the town's bars. Most weekends.* Followed by the cosy, *We miss him.*

André never said a word to me in Paris about any trips

home. Not a word. Why keep it from me? Why, André? Why? Didn't you trust me? Even then. *Trust*. The word spiked in my mind and wouldn't go away. The more it sounded in my head, the louder rang the lies.

A shadow spilled on to my table. I had heard no footsteps and I looked up quickly, one hand shading my eyes to see who had come to poke a stick in my cage.

'*Bonjour*, Eloïse. Enjoying Serriac again?'

'Good morning to you, Léon.' I smiled up at him. He looked bigger than yesterday, as though Serriac broadened his shoulders; his uniform looked darker, his grey eyes less friendly here in town. Something about his polite smile made me feel an outsider.

'Any progress?' I asked.

'We are questioning people.' So noncommittal.

'You'll let me know if you discover something?'

'Of course.'

He was patient. The way he'd been with me when we were children, and I was grateful. I wanted to invite him to join me for coffee but he had on his policeman's face that said he was busy doing whatever it was that policemen did in this quiet law-abiding town.

'Who are the people you're questioning?'

'Eloïse, I can't tell you that.'

'Are they local? People I know?'

Léon laughed and the warmth of it melted the edges of the cool politeness. 'You were never one to give up, were you, Eloïse?'

I stood up, face to face. 'No,' I said softly.

'Leave this to me. Please don't get involved. Whoever killed your bull has demonstrated the kind of violence they are capable of and I don't want you,' he lightly took hold of my wrist, 'caught up in the middle of it.'

'Violence works both ways,' I said.

He gave me a hard stare, a professional police stare, but a memory suddenly cartwheeled into my head of Léon Roussel skinny-dipping at twilight in one of the lagoons in the marshes, his naked buttocks as pink as the flamingos in the light of the setting sun. He must have been around twelve or thirteen years old at the time, lean as a hunting hound and unaware of the seven-year-old wide eyes watching him from among the reeds. I couldn't help but laugh now, surprising him. He took a pace back, but I followed him.

'Léon, why didn't you tell me yesterday that André used to come down to Serriac at weekends before the crash?'

Even now, that word – *crash* – cut like glass on my tongue.

He frowned. 'I thought you knew.'

'You know I didn't know.'

I nodded a polite farewell and walked away across the warm sunlit square.

I am no fool, Léon. Remember that.

'Where are the Americans?'

I was holding a delicate unicorn on the palm of my hand. I'd been hugged, kissed, my scar fussed over, inspected and I'd been kissed once more. I didn't realise how much I'd missed Marianne until I saw her again. My friend, Marianne Durand, daughter of Monsieur le Maire. She was large where he was lean, she wore floating flamboyant dresses while his suits were tailored and tasteful. *That* Marianne.

She was a gifted glass-maker and ran a small but fancy business from a shop in Rue des Dindes where she sold her own superb animal designs. I could have watched her all day long working her alchemy, wielding her shears and hairpin jacks. Snipping and tweaking on the steel marver. In a matter of minutes she could turn a lumpen cone of fiery glass into something exquisite that lived and breathed, with a whisker here, a tail there, a raised hoof pawing at the air.

Marianne and I had laughed and cried our way through our childhood together, and when the sunlight flickered through the magical glass creature I was holding, turning it into a rainbow in my hand, I had to ask myself why on earth I'd left in the first place.

'The Americans?' I asked again. 'Where are they?'

Marianne looped her arm through mine. 'They travel in gaggles,' she laughed. 'Like geese.'

They are different. American men. I sat in Gasparin's Bar and observed them the way I would a sea lion in my living room and listened to the strange noises they made. There was a casualness to the way they sat and stood, an expansiveness that was in sharp contrast to the Frenchmen hunched over their Gauloises, nursing their glasses of wine.

American airmen spread their legs and puffed out their chests. They laughed as if it were a competition and drifted from one crowded table to another, slapping shoulders, always touching one another the way children do. Using up our French air as if they owned it. Yet there was something about these healthy young men from the wide-open spaces of the prairies, something guileless, yet beguiling. Their smiles made me smile. As I sat at a table with Marianne watching the airmen in their shirtsleeves drinking their beer and smoking their Lucky Strikes or dealing a hand of cards, I tried to work out why they seemed so much freer. Easier in their skins. Happier to be alive. The French locals appeared so serious, so eager to discuss and dispute with solemn faces.

Is that what I looked like? As if the war had drained all the fun out of me? Out of France?

Maybe so.

A street-player was squeezing out a shaky rendition of 'La Vie en Rose' on his accordion while his bright-eyed little *gosse* dodged between tables, rattling a tin to collect a few francs. I saw more than one of the men in uniform toss in a handful of coins. Americans were generous, it seemed, or perhaps just liked kids. Either way, it was nice to see.

'So this is where they come to hang out in town,' I said to Marianne after we had ordered our wine. It was the kind of bar I liked, no frills or fancy flounces. It hadn't yet thought of trying to be modern. Just comfortable rough-plastered

walls, the whitewash of the ceiling tinged amber by dec-
ades of nicotine, round scrubbed pine tables, and rows of
dusty wine bottles lined up behind the counter that any bar
in Marseille would envy. It was no wonder the Americans
congregated here.

'Is there ever any trouble with the locals?' I asked.

'*Mon Dieu*, of course, there are always fights over girls.' She
laughed and waved to one of the Americans she knew and
he loped over, his friend in tow. They pulled up chairs and
offered cigarettes. Both looked as if they'd stepped right off
a farm, all straw and freckles, but I'd got it wrong.

'Eloïse, this is Mickey.'

'Hello, Mickey.'

'He's a mechanic from Chicago, and this handsome fellow
here is Calvin. He was one of those tough lumberjacks out
West before he joined up.' She smiled, flicked her dazzlingly
sleek blonde hair at him and accepted a light for her Lucky
Strike. She raised an eyebrow speculatively at me and at
Mickey. Mickey shifted his chair closer to mine and I saw
his gaze linger on my scar.

'Hello, Eloïse.'

I didn't look away. I didn't shrug a dark wing of my hair
over it. I hadn't dated anyone since the crash and I feared
that the hard defensive ridge of scar tissue might not just be
on the outside, but on the inside as well. I drank my glass
of smoky red wine, while I listened to Mickey in his crisp
khaki uniform telling me about the skyscrapers that literally
scraped the sky in Chicago. And then I leaned my elbows

on the little table, my chin cupped in my hand, my breasts pushing against my black dress.

'Tell me, Mickey from Chicago, do you ever hold dances on that American air base of yours?'

His eyes lit up as if I'd put a match to them and his smile was wide enough to swallow Serriac whole. 'There's one on Saturday night.'

CHAPTER FOURTEEN

Someone was messing with my car. A man with a pale shirt and dark hat. I could only see his back because he was bent over my 2CV's windscreen and I shouted out. Broke into a run.

'You!'

A horse-drawn cart piled high with crates of chickens, their yellow beaks panting in the afternoon heat, nudged its way between me and the corner where my car was parked. By the time it had trundled past, the man was gone. I scanned the car and spotted nothing amiss, but a piece of folded paper was tucked under the wiper-blade. I snatched it up.

I flicked it open. Three lines, handwritten, printed in capital letters.

YOU WANT ME TO KILL YOU?
LIKE GOLIATH. ALONE. IN THE DARK.
GO BACK TO PARIS. NOW.

Quickly, I spun on the spot where I stood and inspected every inch of the town square, but too late, far too late. There was no pale shirt nor dark hat on view in the doorway of the pharmacy, closed for the afternoon behind a metal grille. Nor behind the pockmarked limestone columns of the tiny concert hall. Nor tucked away among the scarlets and lavenders of the flower stall where the pigeons were chasing each other in the shade.

The note-leaver had vanished. I felt utterly out of my depth and my instinct was to flee. Not to Paris. To flee home to Mas Caussade like a whipped dog with my tail between my legs, to search out André and lay it all in his lap for him to make right, the way I used to as a child. But I was no longer a child, I was a grown woman.

Should I report it to the police? No, no, going to the police was not an option. Too dangerous, because it would mean explaining why I might be in danger and that would involve André in it. How could I consider for even one fleeting moment adding to the weight of pain my brother carried each day, the pain I'd created?

As I unlocked the car and climbed inside, a fat blowfly stumbled inside with me and began to batter itself insanely against the windscreen. It was how I felt, battering myself against something invisible. I knew I couldn't tell André about the note. I started the engine, took one final look around the square, and drove away with my guilt firmly settled on the back seat.

*

On the drive home, I focused more on the grimy rectangle of the rear-view mirror than I did on the bleached road in front of me. It was mid-afternoon, still hot and humid, the sun leaching the moisture out of me and making me squint.

No car behind me stayed there for long and there were none of the ones I'd memorised from the town square, though I admit that one black Citroën looks much like another. I was about halfway home and the road was empty, travelling straight as a bull-pole through the broad flat landscape I loved, edged by purple drifts of sea-lavender and raised up above the surrounding fields. The expansion of the vivid green rice crop, fed by a network of water channels, was made possible by finance from the post-war Marshall Plan. I could smell the familiar fragrance of it through my open window. It calmed me.

I was totally alone. In every direction I could see to the shimmering horizon. No houses, not even one of the old traditional thatched huts used by the *gardians* on this stretch. I liked being alone. It opened up my senses. I was able to see and hear more clearly, my thoughts came to me pin-sharp.

Just when I was starting to relax and think things through, a speck appeared in my rear-view mirror and grew larger at a startling speed until I could see it was a motorcycle. Its low-pitched growl reached me, setting the hairs on my neck on edge, but it hung back at around five hundred metres and came no closer. I sped up, pushing the 2CV's engine to its limit, but the motorcycle kept pace easily.

What did it want?

It was too far away for me to make out any details of the bike or rider.

I was almost home when suddenly I pulled over. I could hear the throb of the motorcycle engine as I reached into a canvas bag under my seat and drew out André's gun, his High Standard pistol. I had never fired a gun in anger, only on a practice range, so I was surprised to see my grip on it so steady. I swivelled quickly in my seat and peered out of the rear window to see that the motorcycle had also stopped on the side of the road, about five hundred metres behind me. I aimed the gun.

Stalemate.

For a full minute we remained like that, staring at each other. My finger tightened on the trigger. It desperately wanted to pull it. Another minute crawled past and then, without warning, the motorcycle abruptly gunned its engine harshly, spun on one wheel to face the opposite direction and shot off back the way it had come in a cloud of dust. It became a speck once more, then vanished.

I held on tight to the relief. This is what it did to you when someone threatened to kill you, it filtered out all else. Everything except that one thought grew fuzzy and faded.

Did the person on the motorcycle write the threatening note? But why turn and run? It didn't make sense, and my mind became a blur of questions groping their way towards answers. I threw the car into gear and with knuckles white on the steering wheel I drove in the direction of Mas Caussade. I needed to speak with my brother.

CHAPTER FIFTEEN

LÉON ROUSSEL

Léon Roussel was hiding in plain sight. Wearing a black suit, freshly pressed out of respect. No police uniform, not here. Not today. He didn't want to remind the mourners of the real reason he was in attendance.

He had to admit that Aristide Caussade had chosen a good spot, though it couldn't have been easy digging so deep in this waterlogged terrain. Léon knew that the water always got you in the end here, whether it was the river, or the thousands of canals, or one of the *étangs*, the salty lagoons, or even the water butt that caught the run-off from your roof. A man in Serriac had drowned in his own giant water-butt last week, head first, trying to rescue his cat from the bottom of it. The coroner had declared a verdict of death by misadventure.

Léon was not so sure. The thing about water is that it hides too many traces, fingerprints float away. So if a wife threw a cat into a water butt and then tipped her husband in there too, locking the lid down on him, who's to know? Especially if that woman is a barge-hauler by trade with muscles as thick as one of Caussade's bulls. Even when you are safe in your grave the waters of the Camargue can still come for you when the drainage pumps jam and the water-table rises unchecked.

The bull's grave lay in the shade of a grove of white pop-lars in the field at the back of the Caussade farmhouse where the roots would hold the soil firm. Over the years the tree branches had been stretched and elongated sideways by the relentless fingers of the mistral, the way a baker lengthens his dough. The mistral is the wind that shapes the landscape of the Camargue, forms its dunes, moulds the banks of its lagoons and scours its plains raw. Sometimes Léon thought the mistral had shaped him too. He could hear it at odd times blowing deep in his blood when the winds whipped up the soil and threw it in their face.

Word about the funeral had spread fast around Serriac. For Léon, that worked in his favour. Well over three hundred mourners had gathered around the large black gash in the ground, and it was surprising to him that so many people from all over the region would come to pay their last respects to a bull.

A bull?

It was a rare event to honour a bull with a burial ceremony even down here, but Goliath had been champion bull almost as long as Léon could remember. He looked around the faces circling the grave, mostly *gardians* with cheeks as creased as their saddles, but many were just enthusiastic spectators of the bull arena, unable to resist their favourite's last performance. Léon nodded to those he knew, but they were cautious. A crime had been committed and he was a policeman, in or out of uniform.

Aristide Caussade looked like a bull himself at the head of the grave, standing there in his funeral suit and tie, the wind whipping his white hair into horns. Léon could feel the man's grief like a dark storm over the field. He was not an easy man to be around, but Léon had always had respect for him. This farm had been a magical place when Léon was young; working the bulls with André had been a fascinating and terrifying way to spend summers for the son of a postman who was accustomed to negotiating the lanes on a humble bicycle.

He had learned to race through the marshes on a white horse with the wind tearing his lungs out, bringing danger charging into his neatly arranged ambitions, and it changed his life. Because Léon found he was good at danger. He had a calm head for it. He discovered a new Léon Roussel tucked away behind an unopened door inside the old Léon, and for this he had to thank Aristide Caussade, a man with such passion for his bulls and his horses that he swept others up into it.

He was doing so now, his voice loud and bold, encircling his listeners the way he encircled his bulls. He was relating stories of Goliath's glory in the arena, delighting those who had come to mourn but found themselves laughing instead. Many of them were remembering a brush or two with the champion bull during the weekly *course Provençal*. As reckless *razeteurs*, they had attempted to steal the ribbons from Goliath's lethal horns. Did the bull ever kill anybody? Yes, he did. In fact most of them bore scars to remember him by, Léon included.

Léon moved unobtrusively through the crowd. Watching faces, studying smiles. Listening. But he could detect no gloating at the disaster that had hit the Caussades. Oddly, unexpectedly, the gathering started to sing, softly at first but growing louder, reaching out to the edges of the field. It was a familiar old folk song that the *gardians* would sing around the campfire under the stars, giving praise to the prowess and speed of the Camargue bulls in contrast to the slower, more stupid Spanish bulls. These were bull people. They would never slaughter a champion.

But there were two men present who weren't.

Outsiders. They might think that in their dark suits and black ties they blended in with the other mourners, but they were mistaken. They stood out like white wolves in a black bull pen. Léon manoeuvred through the crowd until he stood shoulder to shoulder with the taller one of them.

'An interesting occasion, don't you think?' Léon commented in English.

'Hell, yes. Never seen the like.'

'Driven over from the air base for it, have you?'

'We have. It is impressive, the respect you have for animals here. I grew up on a ranch in Texas and I've never seen any-thing like this. It is powerful, isn't it, Matt?'

'Sure is. That old guy at the graveside is quite something, isn't he?' said the one called Matt.

'How did you hear of the bull's funeral?' Léon enquired casually.

They laughed. Of course they laughed. This was just local entertainment for them. Or was that what they wanted him to think?

'We have a damn efficient set of jungle drums at the camp,' Matt laughed again. 'Nothing gets past them.'

'I can believe that.'

'Or past us,' the other American added.

His eyes were fixed on Eloïse.

Léon had tried not to look at her too much. Something was wrong with her, something that had not been there when he'd spoken to her in the bar in Serriac this afternoon. She was standing beside her father, too stiff and too hidden under her black felt hat, its brim pulled down low over her eyes, her hair worn long, masking her face. She looked like one of the forest animals that he'd seen her father carve out of wood. She had cast aside her finery and was wearing oak-brown riding trousers and a plain black shirt, but she looked ready to flee.

'Who's the girl?' the taller one asked.

But at that moment two fighter jets streaked across the sky and both Americans tipped their heads back to track them with keen interest.

'Republic Thunderjets,' said the tall one.

'On patrol.'

Léon turned his back and moved away into the crowd. He exchanged a greeting with Father Jerome, who was looking hot and uncomfortable in his long black soutane. Whether from the sun's rays or from a distinct awkwardness at attending a bull's funeral was a question Léon found debatable. There was no sign of the vociferous groups of Serriac men who made a habit of hanging around the town's bars in denim overalls with hands still covered in axle grease. To make a point. They were the workers. The ones forging the trade unions and fighting for workers' rights, the ones the government feared. The ones who were aggressively anti-American. They didn't actually wear Communist Party lapel badges, but they might as well have. They had stayed away.

Interesting.

Léon prowled impatiently at the back of the crowd who had now all lined up to drop a snippet of coloured ribbon into Goliath's open grave, a token to acknowledge the cockades that he had worn so boldly in life. Léon was impatient to talk to André. His friend. Yet he barely seemed a friend anymore. When they were together, it felt like they were two strangers. André Caussade was dutifully positioned at his father's side, the three of them – father, son and daughter – presenting a wall of Caussade solidarity, but his injured friend was in a wheelchair.

The sight of it had come as a shock. There was even a rug, draped over André's immobile legs despite the heat, and it was the final straw. The enormity of the sadness was written all over André's face and Léon noticed the way people's eyes skittered away from him, the spectre coming too close.

Even for Léon it was hard, hard to look at him without pity. Was the companion of his youth still buried somewhere inside that broken body? Léon was seeing no sign of it. Neither André nor Eloïse raised their gaze from the rectangle of raw soil or from the canvas sheet that covered the animal's ravaged carcass as each well-wisher filed past.

'André,' Léon murmured when he drew near.

Again it was like reaching out to a stranger. To someone else whose name just happened to be André too. The eyes that flicked up to his were narrowed to slits, bristling with suspicion, no longer the gleaming amber that had urged Léon as a boy to be far more than he ever thought possible. Now they were the dull mud colour that you find on the soles of your boots after rain.

'André, they will not get away with it, I promise you.'

André gave an odd cracked sort of smile. He drew breath to say something, but at that moment the shade and the sunlight in the field were torn apart by the shrill and terrified scream of a horse.

Dense grey smoke poured up into the sky. Flames leaped from one end of the stable's thatched roof to the other, sparks spiralling on the wind and catching in hair and clothes. Shouts and cries echoed through the yard.

Somewhere someone was yelling, 'Quick! More water here, you bastards!'

Lungs were choking. Hooves lashed out. A voice shrieked a warning as a roof-beam burned through and thundered down on those beneath. Bridles were seized, but panic turned tamed animals into wild creatures once more.

The roar of blazing timbers and the reek of scorched horse-hair filled the air as the stables became an inferno. Léon was attempting to prevent people from hurling themselves inside the burning building to rescue the animals, but it was impossible. These were horse people. There were at least twenty horses in there. Probably more. Many of the mourners had arrived in the saddle.

He worked to help the *gardians* save as many horses as they could. Blinded by smoke, they beat off with bare hands the burning debris that clung to the white hides and though the terrified animals reared and kicked and rolled their huge eyes in panic, they led them out to a paddock where they were safe. But Léon could see neither Eloïse nor Cosette in the paddock. He darted one more time back to the flames.

'Eloïse,' he bellowed.

Timbers were crashing down around him.

'Eloïse!' He cursed the thick smoke.

A hand seized his sleeve. He whirled round but the roar of flames swallowed any words. Dimly through the wall of smoke he made out two grey shapes. One was a person bent double, the other larger one was a horse stumbling and shuddering and almost on its knees. Both were covered in blood.

He took a firm hold of them and together they forced a way towards the burning entrance.

CHAPTER SIXTEEN

My hands were covered in blood, as thick and glossy as scarlet satin. Not mine. *Mon Dieu*, I wish it were mine. It was Cosette's.

Have you ever seen a white horse covered in blood, the dense hairs glistening bright red? It twisted my heart. My Cosette's breath was coming in deep tormented gasps and my own matched hers, but I spoke calmly to her as I bathed the terrible gash. It ran from her withers at the base of the ridge of her mane, across the muscular left shoulder, right round to the front of her chest in a back-to-front C-shape. It was the mirror image of the one on my own cheek.

I'd tethered her in the barn and wrapped my arms around her. She placed her heavy head on my shoulder, her skin trembling and muscles quivering, breath blowing hard, whiskers twitching. A terrified sound was coming from deep in her throat.

'My poor Cosette,' I murmured, and hurried to fetch water and bandages from the house.

Outside was ordered chaos. *Gardians* know how to deal with fire and had formed a line to cart buckets of water and to handle a hose from the pump, but it was too little, too late. The flames had won. Wounded horses and people were receiving attention, Mathilde flitting between them with salve and sheets torn into strips.

I saw Léon directing cars and lorries to block the entrance to the farm. No one could leave or enter. It jolted me into the realisation that this was now a crime scene and he was doing his job. But I wanted everyone to go, to leave, to get off our land. Léon would call for a support team and there would be questions. More and more questions.

I craved quiet.

My hands swept over Cosette's heaving chest. I didn't know whether I was soothing her or she was soothing me, as the tremors pulsed inside both of us. The veterinary surgeon was sewing together the raw and splintered edges of her wound and she proved herself as brave as any bull, though the black-rimmed sockets of her eyes were pale with shock. He had injected her with a sedative and when he looked at me he'd laughed and asked if I wanted one too.

I nearly said yes.

People came and went. I spoke to no one. My hand never left my horse. Inside my head the sound of screams and the crackle of flames kept crashing into the question of who had set the fire?

Why?

First Goliath. Now the horses.

The same person? Or a different person?

I was caressing Cosette's hot neck when my father walked into the barn, his heavy features set hard, and I stepped back from my horse to let him examine her. When his great hands ran over her, he murmured soft loving words, and I was jealous. I had never received such words from him. He looked deep into her anxious brown eyes, then checked that each of her legs and fetlocks was sound despite the wound. He examined the burns on her flank and swept a hand up over her prominent white cheekbones and down the jugular groove. Satisfied, he leaned his broad forehead against hers with such devotion that she whickered gently in response.

When he finally turned and inspected me, he looked surprised. I didn't care to think what I must look like. I was alone with him for once and would not waste my chance to learn more.

'Papa, is it true you've already signed the contract to sell our land to the United States Air Force?'

I couldn't keep my anger out of my voice. I tried.

'Yes, it's true.'

'Why did you agree to it?'

'I had no choice.'

'That's not what Mayor Durand says.'

'Then Mayor Durand is lying.'

Lying. Which one was lying to me? Which one had reason to lie?

'Was it a Compulsory Purchase order?'

'No.'

'So why sell?'

'My reasons are my own.'

I knew better than to ask what those reasons were. 'First Goliath. Now the horses, Papa. What next? Your children?'

His face shut down and he started to leave.

'Papa, who are they, these people who kill our livestock? Do you know?'

He gripped his blood-streaked beard in the way he did when trying to control his anger. 'They are Communist trash.'

'Have they demanded anything from you? Like insisting you rescind the sale?'

'Too many questions, girl.' His straggly eyebrows descended in a deep V as he frowned at me. 'I have enough to deal with out there without you making—'

'Why did you ask me to come here from Paris? What was your purpose?'

'When the Caussades are in trouble, they stand together, shoulder to shoulder. You know that.' His mouth, large and broad-lipped, softened a fraction. 'It's why you came.'

It wasn't why I came. I came because I thought André was dead. But yes, he'd summoned me and I'd come.

'If the Caussades stand together,' I said, 'where is my brother Isaac?'

Papa turned his head and spat on the straw. 'The Communists are bastard traitors, every one of them. Driving this country to civil war. They're in every workplace, in every factory, twisting the minds of fools till we are on the verge of a general strike and that wet rag of a prime minister Joseph Laniel has no idea how to prevent it tearing our country apart. They think they are the ones with the clever intellectual ideas when really they are all empty-headed puppets being made to dance to the tune of the violent puppet-masters in the Kremlin. How the evil bastards must be laughing to themselves and rubbing their hands. France will come crashing down while the Red Army is waiting just over the border. Do you think we fought a war against one dictator just to hand our country over to another? Do you?'

His words halted. But his rage didn't. It had filled every corner of the barn. Even Cosette felt it. She was shifting from foot to foot and watching him with ears pricked and eyes wide, white eyelashes flicking anxiously.

I had never heard my father speak like that. He rarely said more than a dozen words to me. And never talked politics to me. For a full minute we watched each other, caught up inside our own heads.

'Papa,' I kept the word quiet, so that it would not snap the fragile thread between us, 'do you know who this person is who is killing our animals?'

I could hear my heart thudding and thought it was his.

'No,' he said at last. And walked out of the barn.

When Mathilde trotted nimbly into the barn carrying a tray, I was filling up hay nets for Cosette and the four other injured horses that had joined us.

'*Voilà,*' Mathilde said cheerfully. 'You'll need this, *chérie*, and then you must take a bath. You look terrible.'

On the tray sat a plate of hot *gardiane de taureau* with a bottle of my father's tart red wine and a glass. It was late afternoon and Mathilde should have been off to her own home long ago, but it was typical of her kindness to the Caussade family that she had remained to help.

'Thank you,' I said, and propped the tray on top of a barrel. 'Any news?'

'The police are still here, making a nuisance of themselves.'

'So I hear.'

'That Captain Roussel, as Léon now calls himself, questions everyone.'

'Have you seen my brother?'

'André? I think he's in his room. I've not seen him but when I was in the kitchen I heard the poor lamb. On the stairs.'

We exchanged a look. Both of us knew the painful laborious sound she was referring to.

When she'd gone, one of my father's young hunting hounds, Demeter, brindled and blue-eyed, slunk in and curled up beside me on the straw, his bony frame warm and comforting. I fed him the food from the tray while I poured the wine down my own throat straight from the bottle.

Enough, André. Enough, I tell you.

The moment Cosette finally fell into a deep sleep, I eased Demeter's head off my lap and I slunk out as silently as the dog had slunk in. I reached the house and hurried up the stairs, my fingers still wrapped around the neck of the wine bottle. It was half empty now, but I'd saved the rest for André. He'd need it.

Mon Dieu, he'd need it.

I walked into his bedroom without knocking. Instantly a gun was in my face.

In my face.

'Nice welcome,' I said.

'You fool. You could have been ...'

He flicked the safety on the gun, tucked it into his waistband and slumped his back against the wall, but I didn't let him escape so easily. I placed the wine bottle on the floor and stepped up close to my brother. I grabbed two handfuls of the front of his shirt, and I shook him. I shook him and I shook him. Thumping him against the wall till there must have been no breath left in his lungs.

He didn't try to stop me.

When I was finally done, I released his shirt and wiped my palms on my trousers as if there was something bad on them. There was fierce colour in André's cheeks and his gaze was sharp, but he said nothing. He knew I hadn't finished.

'Tell me, André. Tell me right now.' I tried to keep my voice low, but it came out bitter and angry. 'I will not tolerate your silence any longer. Who will be next on the death list? Me? You?' I swallowed hard. 'Papa?'

'Don't, Eloïse. Don't. You know I can say nothing. Don't ask.'

I hated the calmness in his voice, the control.

'I *am* asking, André. And I want an answer or I will walk straight to those policemen down there in the yard and tell them everything I know about you and who you work for.'

'No.'

'Yes. I will do it, André. Believe me.'

'If you do, you will be signing my death warrant.'

'The choice is yours.'

So harsh. So unforgiving. It frightened me.

Something in his face changed, something slipped. I saw it in his tawny eyes. That sense of having your feet skid from under you on a sheet of ice. It would be so easy to reach out to him, so tempting to withdraw the verbal knife I had slid under his ribs, but I pinned my hands to my sides, kept my mouth shut, my eyes flat. He had to believe me, even if I didn't believe myself.

For a long moment we glared at each other.

'Who is trying to kill you?' I asked. 'Names.'

He gave the laziest of shrugs. 'I might as well shoot myself.' He smiled and put two fingers as a gun barrel to his temple. 'It will make it easier for you all.'

I marched over to where his hunting rifle was propped in a corner of the room and picked it up. 'If you don't tell me some names right now, I'll shoot you myself, André Caussade.'

He laughed. Where the hell did he dredge that up from?

'I do believe you would.'

'Sit down,' I said.

He limped the few steps to the bed and sat down awkwardly on the patchwork cover that my mother had made. I replaced the rifle and sat myself in the chair beside the bed. I didn't dare sit closer. I might remember that he was my brother.

'Names,' I said. 'Give me names.'

He had withdrawn now, back behind his shell. Inspecting me. 'Do you know how bad you look?'

I glanced at the blood and the burns. My sleeve was more holes than fabric and I could see shiny blisters underneath. My hair smelled like singed wool.

'This is nothing,' I said, 'compared to what your friends will do to me, we both know that.'

'You always did exaggerate.' He tried a smile of sorts but it didn't sit well. He leaned forward and took the fingers of my hand in his. 'Go home, Eloïse, go back to Paris,' he said quietly. 'You are not wanted here. We can manage well without you.'

I removed my hand from his and rose to my feet so that I stood over him. 'No, André, no, you can't. From the neck down you are useless, you can do nothing to sort out this mess. You need me, you know you do. I can be your eyes and ears, I can be your ...' we both glanced down at the immaculate trousers of his funeral suit, 'your legs. You need me,' I whispered.

Saying the brutal words took all my strength.

I watched him die a little inside. Outside, the evening air was sultry and windless, and a pearly grey mist had crept on its belly from the fields, so that the light in the room was almost translucent.

'Yes, you have every reason to be angry with me,' I said, 'for what I did to you in Paris, to rant and rage at me. I do it myself every night. Yes, you can banish me back to Paris, but first let us hunt down the killers who tried to destroy you and who are now stalking this farm. And whoever wrote this note.'

From my pocket I drew out the anonymous square of paper that I'd found tucked under my windscreen wiper in Serriac. André took it, unfolded it, and read it with a face that gave nothing away. Yet when he looked up at me, for one bright flash, he was my brother again, his eyes burning with a feeling that I'd thought was lost between us. He slipped a hand into his trouser pocket and came out with the blood-red Victorinox Swiss Army pen knife he had carried around since he was a boy. He flicked open the blade and I knew what was coming. He cut a nick in the ball of his thumb, and when I held out mine, he did the same to it, then we pressed the two together. It was a childhood ritual, the blood of the Caussades.

'If you retreat to Paris,' he murmured, 'they will only come after you. It's what they're trained to do.'

At that moment two gunshots rang out from the yard and I dived to the window. Two of the injured horses hadn't made it. Grief churned in my chest as I sat down once more on the rush seat.

'Names,' I repeated. 'I need names.'

CHAPTER SEVENTEEN

'The death-threat letter changes everything,' André said. 'You have to realise that we are living in a peace that is no peace.'

My brother was talking to me. Sharing wine with me, swig for swig. It dawned on me that he had missed this as much as I had, our talks. 'I have no close friend,' he once told me in Paris. 'I keep them at arm's length. Friends are a risk I cannot afford, a luxury that is too dangerous. Friends come with curiosity and questions. Instead I travel light. Instead I have acquaintances.'

I loved the way his face came alive. The death-mask had vanished and his passion turned him once more into the lion I remembered.

'The war is over but we are still at war, Eloïse, a permanent war.'

'The Cold War,' I acknowledged. 'I thought it would all end. When Stalin died last March, I believed it would die with him.'

'Quite the reverse. It intensified. Malenkov seized Stalin's titles but he is locked in a vicious power-battle against Nikita Khrushchev. I warn you, Eloïse, these men are seriously dangerous. Committed to taking over not only the Soviet Union and Eastern Europe, but the whole world. They are determined to spread Communism like a plague across the globe. Whatever the cost.'

The room felt too small for such big statements.

André was still seated on his bed, but he had swung his legs up on top of the quilt, using his hands to do so, and arranged them straight, the way you do cutlery. He no longer wore the brace. He reached for a cigarette from a packet on the bedside table.

'In America,' I pointed out, accepting a cigarette not because I wanted one but because he'd offered it, 'Edgar Hoover and Joe McCarthy are yelling blue murder about reds under the bed, but that's not far off what is happening here too. Is that what you think?'

'Exactly. We must be so careful. There is a desire for change in France. We are a country on the edge. Governed by constantly changing coalitions. Nothing is stable. Look at the violent demonstrations in the Champs-Élysées demanding independence for Algeria from France.'

'You don't think it's scare-mongering?'

He turned his head sharply to look at me in the chair. 'Do you?'

I shook my head. 'You think Russia is trying to destabilise France?'

'Trust me, Eloïse. I know for a fact that the First Main Directorate of the MGB – that is the Soviet Intelligence agency – maintains a network of surveillance over sensitive positions in society and is infiltrating foreign governments and businesses. They are expert at insinuating themselves into industrial plants, as well as taking up posts in educational institutions to assert control over young minds. I tell you, it is happening all over France right now.'

'Laniel's government should be putting a stop to it.'

'The man who should be leading us is General Charles de Gaulle. His day will come again, and when it does, things will change.'

'André, why didn't you tell me that you used to come down to Serriac at weekends?'

The question caught us both by surprise.

He exhaled a grey skein of smoke to hide behind.

'Was there a girl?' I pressed him. 'Someone special you came to see?'

'No.'

'Why then? If I am to help you, André, I need to know what is going on.'

He lay back against the pillows, staring up at the ceiling. 'The American airmen like to come into town on a Saturday night.' His words were slow to emerge. 'I used to come down from Paris to mix with them, play poker to get them drunk. They are discouraged from coming into town by their senior officers because trouble has a tendency to flare up.'

The light in the room was drifting away, the way the haze

drifts over the marshes. A fat mosquito was buzzing against the window.

'Do you have a girl in Paris, André?'

'No.'

'Too dangerous to allow anyone close?'

'No, in Paris their blood is too thin. Their hearts are too small. Not like down here. Here blood runs deep.'

'It is such a dangerous job and you have to give up so much for it. Maybe it's a good thing the CIA turned me down. Why, André? Tell me why you do it.'

He sat up straight, as if I had lit a touchpaper.

'It is an incredibly complicated business, Eloïse,' he said in a solemn voice, 'that is becoming more difficult all the time. Intelligence work means you operate without recognition. Your failures are known, your successes are not.'

'But you live for your work. You love it, don't you?'

'Yes,' he answered, smiling reluctantly. 'I do.'

I smiled at him fondly. 'Tell me why.'

'I'm not sure I can explain it. All I can say is that it is about finding the truth. Though we deal every day in lies. But the sense of purpose . . . the sense of accomplishment . . . the incredible sense of pride and privilege that comes from serving my country. This far outweighs anything else. I am a lucky man.'

'Who is it who wants to kill me?' I asked flatly.

'I don't know.'

I held my tongue. I rose to my feet and walked to the window from where I could see the *gardian* Louis in the yard, his face in his hands. Léon Roussel's arm lay across his shoulder, and the dog Demeter was standing nearby. The tension on the farm was raising everyone's hackles. In the far distant sky I spotted a bomber cruising past. I waited for André to speak.

'A Soviet Intelligence operative,' he said at last. He retreated into his professional shell once more, cool and controlled.

'Why would he want to force me back to Paris?'

'Because you are going round asking questions. Stirring up things that people don't want stirred up.'

'Maybe Mayor Durand is right. It's just a bunch of Communist hotheads. Activists who are part of the movement of industrial unrest that is sweeping through the country. They are vehemently opposed to the Americans marching their boots into France again and bringing their nuclear bombs with them. So not personal to me. They just turn on anyone who assists the USAF forces.' I let my breath out slowly. 'It's possible.'

He threw his cigarette stub in the ashtray at his bedside. 'For God's sake, will they never see that America is the only one who can save us? They have the bombs, the equipment and the desire to stand firm against the Soviet threat. France will end up as a Soviet puppet state like East Germany if we blink for even a moment.'

I stood with my back to the window. 'I don't intend to blink, André.'

'Keep your eyes open and your door bolted.'

'Give me names. Who is Piquet? The bruiser at the hospital.'

'Maurice Piquet. He is an Intelligence operative who works as one of their heavies. He's a cleaner. He deals in the dirty work, the dirtier the better. Watch out for him. He likes to hurt.'

'He works in Paris?'

'Usually, yes.'

'Not always?'

'No. Wherever there are dirt and lies to be found, he could turn up. So yes, if necessary he could be sent to *clean* down here.'

'His friend?'

'Gilles Bertin.'

'The one with a prissy thin moustache and a chin that looks as though someone took a meat-cleaver to it.'

'That's him.' André's lips gave a half-smile. 'He makes scum like Piquet seem like a pussycat. He's the brains. He doesn't often deign to get his fingers bloodied. He collects information. But he favours the good life on the Champs-Élysées, so rarely leaves Paris. But if you ever spot him,' his voice was stern, 'don't hang around. Just run like crazy. Got that?'

I nodded. It was enough.

'The only reason I am agreeing to you working with me on this operation is because of the note left on your car. They won't leave it at that, and I don't want you blundering in blindly.'

I kept my face calm.

'The air base is where we start,' he announced. 'You will be my eyes and ears. My legs. To gather information.'

'Well, that's fortunate, because I have arranged to go there tomorrow evening.'

'How the hell did—?'

'To a dance. I was invited. By one of the airmen.'

His sandy eyebrows shot up. 'That didn't take long.'

A knock at the door startled us both.

'Come in.'

Mathilde's grey head popped around the door. 'Telephone call for you, Eloïse. From Paris.'

'Who is it?'

'Clarisse Favre.'

My boss.

'Is he alive?'

'Hello, Clarisse.'

'Your brother. Is he alive?'

'Yes.'

'I'm happy for you, *chérie*,' she said. 'So what are you up to down there in your dreary wilderness? Having fun?'

I laughed and the sound of it was odd in the gloomy hall of my father's house. 'What can I do for you, Clarisse?'

'When are you coming back? Paris needs you.'

'Paris?'

'*Merde*, all right, I'm the one who needs you.'

'What's going on? Are you on a new case?'

'Yes, I've been hired by a wealthy father whose son is caught up in an illegal gambling syndicate.'

'Tell me.'

We spent the next ten minutes discussing the case. I suggested several options of action and I could feel the purr of satisfaction in her voice.

'Are you able to come back to Paris just for a week or two to oil the wheels on this case?'

'Sorry, Clarisse, I can't.'

'C'mon, Eloïse. There's more to life than horses and bulls and bloody brothers. You need some fun in your life again. Pop back to Paris.'

'No time, sorry.'

'Can't I tempt you? I'm off to a party tomorrow night at Les Danseuses.'

'Well, I'm off to a party myself tomorrow night. A dance at the American air base.' I paused.

'What is it, *chérie*?' Clarisse's voice was soft and smoky. 'What's the matter?'

'I need to ask a favour of you, boss.'

She let loose a short surprised whistle that shot down the line. 'Now that's a first. What do you want?'

'I need information on two men. They both live in Paris, but they work in Intelligence so they are good at being invisible. Both big, both in suits, both French. Their names are Gilles Bertin and Maurice Piquet. Bertin has a pencil moustache and keeps his hands clean. The other one, Piquet, is pure beef muscle.'

'And why are you searching for information on these men?'

I said nothing.

'Okay,' Clarisse muttered. She sighed elaborately.

'They are dangerous, so take care,' I warned her. 'They are what our American friends call tough cookies.'

'So am I.'

Clarisse hung up.

CHAPTER EIGHTEEN

Americans do not dance as well as Frenchmen. I learned that much.

They stepped on my feet with as little finesse as America stepping on France. But they did it with such broad smiles and with so much laughter that I put aside all my fury and fear, and I laughed with them. They proved to be an unexpected combination of bold teeth and respectful hands, of tall stories and secret confidences. And they called me 'ma'am' — yes ma'am, no ma'am, would you care to dance, ma'am? Which made me want to kiss them. They didn't seem to give a damn about my face scar either. But maybe when you have hundreds of men from the United States Air Force on a base and only a handful of women, some in uniform, some not, well, what's a little scar between friends?

I drank beer, something I would normally never touch. But this wasn't normal, was it? This felt like a bite out of the future, a quick taste of what was coming our way. The evening in the recreation hall was buzzing with its bright yellow chairs on chrome legs and lamps that looked more like space rockets, its pulsing music and its young men convinced they could kick down worlds and rebuild them with their chewing gum, their Hershey bars and their big cars.

It sent a tremor through me, so strong the beer in my glass rippled. I wasn't sure if it was from excitement at this tidal wave of energy and American can-do attitude or fear of losing all that was dear to me in my beloved France. I knew that Prime Minister Laniel would just roll over and let the Americans take whatever they demanded, despite the unease about it in France. André was right about that. We needed them. Or we would soon be singing the state anthem of the Soviet Union over our morning coffee.

'Are you enjoying yourself?'

It was Mickey who asked, my attentive mechanic from Chicago, who had this evening told me more about the internal combustion engine than I expected ever to need in a lifetime.

'We're having a great time, aren't we, Eloïse?' Marianne answered for me.

My friend snuggled closer to her handsome lumberjack, Calvin, and treated me to a pointed look in case I complained about the Budweiser beer or the ear-splitting volume of the music. But she was wrong about that. I didn't object to them at all. The only thing I objected to was the double chain-link fence that stood between me and the business-end of the air base.

I had picked up Marianne from her apartment above her

glass shop in Serriac, and was knocked out by her Marilyn Monroe-style figure-hugging dress.

'Since when?' I asked.

'Since the Yanks hauled into town,' she'd grinned.

I'd driven us out to the air base with one eye on my rear-view mirror. At the gates we were met by Mickey and Calvin in smart khaki uniforms and greeted by two heavily armed guards who wanted to see passes. The base looked to me like a concrete fortress with a double stretch of chain-link fence and barbed wire around it. The sort of place where things went on you didn't want to know. But I wanted to know so bad, that I was happy to sit through a whole damn day of learning how to fix a carburettor if that's what it took.

Mickey must have noticed my eyes glazing over because when he heard Big Mama Thornton's 'Hound Dog' come on the jukebox, he wrapped his strong mechanic's hand around mine and said, 'C'mon, another jive?' But I had no more jives left in me, no more kicks and flicks or joyous bounces. I was all out of joy.

It was Calvin who rescued me. 'Give the girl a break, Mickey. French girls are more ...' He studied me for a moment, his eyes as brown and steadfast as one of my father's dogs. '... more refined than girls back home. You gotta give them time to breathe. Time to think.' He smiled at me. 'Ask her what she wants to do.'

'Thank you, Calvin.'

'You're welcome, ma'am.'

'So what would you like to do now? Another beer?' Mickey asked, still keeping hold of my hand, while his other arm slipped around my waist.

'I'd like some fresh air. Outside. It's very hot in here.'

He beamed at me. 'Sure.'

Outside were the planes. We started for the door.

'Good evening, Mademoiselle Caussade,' a voice said behind me.

I spun round fast. Too jumpy. *Calm down.*

In front of me stood a United States Air Force officer. Immaculate uniform, impressive insignia and dark hair parted ruler-straight on one side. One glance and I knew he was the kind of man I'd want defending my country. Well-muscled with dark intelligent eyes that knew exactly how to create order out of disorder, and a bearing that I could see would inspire men to follow him. I'd guess he was in his thirties, but he had a look about him that was older, as though he'd seen more than any man in his thirties had a right to.

I nodded politely, but suspicion ran over my skin like ants. How did this stranger know my name?

'I am Major Dirke. I'm sorry to disturb your evening but I saw you walking past my office window earlier.'

Beside me Mickey had jumped to attention.

'As you were,' the major told him. 'I just want a word with Mademoiselle Caussade.' He softened the lines of his face with a smile for me. He had a nice smile. 'If I may?' he said.

'Of course, Major,' I responded. 'Outside would be better. It's quieter.'

'Singin' in the Rain' was now belting out of the jukebox, but I shot out of there with more haste than was decent.

I could feel the menace outside. Hard and sharp-edged. I felt it in the bitter taste at the back of my throat. No amount of upbeat music drifting out from the recreation hall could pretend otherwise, however persistently it tried. This was a place dedicated to death.

'I apologise for breaking into your evening of enjoyment,' the major said with an easy Southern charm and long silky vowels.

'That's no problem. I'm happy to take a break and get some fresh air.'

Except the air was not fresh. It smelled of engine oil and aircraft fuel and male testosterone in equal measures. The darkness was not real here. Security lights all over the air base kept the night at bay, the same way its weapons were designed to keep the Soviet Union at bay. A creamy half-moon hung in the bull-black sky directly above the main runway and shadows shifted between the buildings each time the warm night breezes nudged against them.

I turned to face Major Dirke straight on.

'What can I do for you, Major, and how do you know me?'

'I want to speak to you about what happened yesterday.'

'A lot happened yesterday. What do you have in mind?'

'I was at the funeral for Goliath at your father's farm.'

I tried not to show my astonishment. 'I didn't see you.'

'You weren't looking.'

'True.'

'I saw you at your father's side, then running into the flames, and I was concerned. When I noticed you walk past my office window this evening, I decided to check that you're all right.' He gave me another easy smile. 'You certainly look more than all right.'

I was wearing a long-sleeved blouse. My blisters didn't show.

'Thank you for your concern, Major.' I let a silence linger for a moment in the sultry air, while I tried to work out what was going on, and my eyes strayed to the massive barrel of the heavy anti-aircraft gun on its raised platform at the edge of the nearest runway. Others were dotted about in the semi-darkness like giant fingers pointing the way to hell. It was hard not to stare at them. On the far side was a large floodlit area with men in white playing a game of some sort.

'Baseball?' I queried.

He nodded with a grin. 'An American camp would not be an American camp without a baseball diamond.'

'Is that a fact?'

'It may seem bizarre to a French person, but never underestimate the power of baseball, Miss Caussade.'

'Tell me, please, why did you attend Goliath's funeral?'

It struck me as odd.

We were strolling slowly along a concrete pathway at the edge of the road that ran in front of the row of recreation buildings, with Major Dirke making no effort to get to the point. A guard with a German shepherd dog on a leash saluted as he patrolled past us.

'It seemed courteous,' the major commented at last. 'Given that your father has surrendered a large parcel of his land for the expansion of our air base. I wanted to inspect the well of feeling on the ground for myself.'

In the semi-darkness I could just make out the concrete apron with at least twenty aircraft of varying shapes and sizes lined up on it. Like strange animals in a zoo. I wanted to go over for a closer look but a second chain-link fence had other ideas.

'You saw the reaction,' I said. 'How strongly people feel against the expansion – against the air base altogether.' I glanced up at his shadowy profile. 'Strong enough to set fire to my father's stables, strong enough to kill,' I added quietly.

His long stride slowed and came to a halt. 'Miss Caussade, it took the State Department, at the direction of the Joint Chiefs, years of negotiation to come to an agreement with the French General Staff for these air bases to be constructed. As well as to cost out the whole project.'

'Our country is contributing two billion francs towards the total cost,' I pointed out.

'You are well informed.'

'In France we all need to be well informed on this subject. The stationing of foreign troops on our soil again so soon after the war is like pouring salt on a raw wound. We all remember the feel of the Nazi jackboot on our neck.'

He nodded and swatted away a mosquito into the damp night air. 'It was why I was in civvies at the bull's funeral. But our new American president, General Dwight Eisenhower, has more military experience and expertise than any president since Ulysses Grant. He understands the impact of US troops on a foreign country and is trying to minimise the political damage that the USAF and our Seventh Army are doing in France right now. But we have a job to do, Miss Caussade. Russian forces could come marching straight through Germany like a blade through hog-fat and into your country any day now. We are *that* close to war.'

He held up his thumb and forefinger scarcely a hair's breadth apart.

'*That* close. We are on a knife edge. So tell your family and friends in Serriac, tell all the Communist Party hotheads stirring up trouble in the factories, tell them that they need American aircraft patrolling their skies, they need our nuclear warheads. It is the *only* guarantee of peace. For France. For the Western world.'

I wanted to wrap an arm around the major's stiff military neck in gratitude and weep. Men like this and men like André were laying their lives on the line for France while the rest of us sipped our *vin rouge* and went dancing. Even men like Mickey and Calvin were risking their lives for us, when I thought about it like that. They weren't *taking* my father's land. They were *giving* us safety.

'Thank you, Major Dirke, on behalf of my family.'

In the gloom I saw his face register surprise. Maybe these airmen were not accustomed to thanks from the French. He gave me a small formal bow of his head and smiled. 'Let's return you to your dance partner. I'll walk you back there.'

'No need. I can easily find my way, thanks.'

We had walked in a straight line under a bright moon and military-strength security lights, for heaven's sake. I was hardly likely to get lost. But he set off back the way we'd come.

'This path is rough in places,' he said. 'We don't want you to come to any harm.'

I didn't break stride. I didn't stumble. I made no sound.

Come to any harm.

Was it a threat?

Or was this charming American just demonstrating old Southern courtesy? I couldn't tell. The ground under my feet was shifting and cracking like Marianne's glass when she fired it wrong. Strangely, I had a sudden desire to have Léon Roussel at my side, inspecting the path and inspecting Major Dirke's face. He would know a lie when he heard one. His policeman's ear was fine-tuned to deceit.

'Two of the horses in our stables had to be shot,' I told him, but as the words came out of my mouth, I knew he would not understand what a horse means to a Camarguais.

'I'm sorry. My brother and I were raised on a ranch with mustangs, so I know how bad you must be feeling. I've exchanged horses for B-50s, but I miss them.'

'My own horse was . . .'

The dull drone of an aircraft's engines reverberated out of the night sky. I glanced up and as it came closer I saw the ghostly silhouette of a twin-engined plane. Its landing lights blinded me for a second before it skimmed down low and landed smoothly. This heavy-bodied shape was one I was already becoming familiar with, because they criss-crossed the skies throughout the day. The noise it made was a low-pitched growl rather than the high scream of the jet-engined fighters.

'That's our workhorse,' Major Dirke commented. 'A Douglas C-47 Skytrain. It's our transport aircraft and ferries in supplies for . . .'

His sentence lay unfinished. A car had pulled up alongside us out of the night, its headlights carving yellow craters in the shadows. It was one of the big American showy saloons with white roof and green body, flashing what looked like gleaming chrome teeth across the front. A Chevy. Even their cars made us feel small. Its door opened and the driver emerged wearing a dark suit.

I knew him like I knew the smell of a hospital ward.

It was Gilles Bertin.

It is important to know your limits. Shaking hands with Gilles Bertin, the man involved in the violent attempt to murder my brother, was beyond my limit. It was that simple.

I did not even attempt it.

'I'm sorry, I can't,' I said when he offered his hand in greeting. Same cold eyes. Same thin moustache. Same way of looking as if he intended to shape the world. 'My fingers were burned in a fire yesterday.' I hid my hand at my side.

'I'm sorry to hear that.'

Was he sorry? For what he had done. Did he ever give it

a thought? Was he the one who ordered the match to be lit yesterday? What the hell was he doing here on an American air base? Did Major Dirke not know Bertin worked for the MGB, the Soviet Union's Intelligence unit? Obviously not. They had greeted each other with smiles and handshakes, while I let my hair fall forward over the damaged half of my face and stepped further into the shadows. The three of us were standing on the path in the semi-darkness and I made sure I stood with my back to the nearest lamp, certain of one thing. Gilles Bertin did not know me. There was not a spark of recognition in his eyes.

Why should there be? I was nobody to him.

'I wasn't expecting you today, Gilles,' the major said. 'Let me introduce you to . . .'

'Eloïse,' I said, and left it at that.

Bertin inspected me with fleeting interest, clearly focused on getting down to the purpose of his visit, whatever it might be, and turned immediately back to Dirke. 'We don't have long, Joel, so I'll head on over to the office to get cracking. Follow as soon as you can.'

'Don't mind me,' I said at once. 'Goodnight.' And I walked briskly in the direction of the dance hall, the gentle throb of a drumbeat stirring up the heat of the night.

He had no idea. None at all.

CHAPTER NINETEEN

Did you think I would flee?

Did you think I had learned nothing from my brother?

If you did, you were mistaken.

I sat in my car half a kilometre out from the air base in the pitch dark. No headlights to betray my position and no moon. It had slumped down behind a heavy bank of cloud, and the countryside was now so dark that you would only see my tiny Citroën behind the clump of dogwood if you fell over it. I'd worked fast. I'd entered the recreation hall, found Marianne in a slow smooch on the dance floor, scooped her up and whisked her away with no more than a farewell wave for Calvin and Mickey. I bundled her into my car.

'Eloïse, slow down, what's going on?'

'We're going to chase a car.'

'In this tin can?' She laughed the way only someone who has enjoyed a few beers can laugh. 'You mean you're not leaving me on my own with five hundred airmen?'

'No, I'm not. They wouldn't stand a chance.'

She laughed again and watched in astonishment while I changed into a black shirt and trousers from the boot of my car and looped a black scarf around my head. I then discarded my red dancing pumps for a pair of sturdy boots. In a small backpack I carried a torch, the High Standard gun and a camera. I didn't show Marianne the gun because I didn't want to panic her, and anyway, I didn't for one moment think I'd need it. I wasn't going to shoot anybody. Not tonight.

We'd been waiting in the dark for an hour, Marianne in a doze, by the time I spotted the headlights leave the camp and spike their way towards me. The terrain in this part of the wide Rhône valley was as flat as the major's baseball diamond, so I had no trouble watching the car's approach.

It was the right one. As it swept past my dogwood hiding place I recognised its green and white colour scheme and when it was half a kilometre down the road to Arles, I started my engine.

I hung back most of the time, letting the Chevy get away. There was only one road cutting through the countryside, so he wasn't going anywhere but straight ahead. At times I lost sight of him, at times I put my foot down and hitched up closer, but he didn't drive fast as if he were trying to lose me. When the moon popped out and skimmed the fields with a silver sheen, I switched off my headlamps and drove half-blind. That was when I clouted a rock on the side of the road and jolted Marianne awake.

'*Merde*,' she muttered, 'where's the car you're after?'

I pointed to the pinpricks of tail-lights far ahead in the dark bowl of the night.

She leaned her head forward with a pretty frown of concentration. 'Who is he?'

'A bastard.'

She accepted that, too sleepy to push for details, and we drove in comfortable silence, each bound up in our own speculations. As we approached the Serriac turn-off I crept up closer but the Chevrolet didn't take the side road. It shot straight on.

Arles it was, then.

The streets of Arles defy logic.

Imagine if you picked up a box of straws, threw them in the air and let them fall at your feet. Criss-cross, higgledy-piggledy, no rhyme nor reason. Designed to confuse. That is the town of Arles.

It does not have streets built for cars.

Arles is one of the oldest and loveliest towns in all France, bristling with ancient Roman architecture and medieval stone walls that rob you of all sense of scale. They have been here forever and will be here for another forever, its creamy timeworn houses huddled on top of each other like old friends. The streets are narrow, no wider than you can spit, so that they can cosset every scrap of shade during the humid summer when the sun can suck the life out of your skin, if you give it the chance.

But at this time of night the town was quiet. The milky

river mist was seeping up around the amphitheatre, and in the pavement café the last drinkers were murmuring in low voices and watching the town cats sneak through the darkness in search of scraps. I tracked the Chevy past the black bulk of the monolithic town walls and eventually into the Boulevard des Lices, one of the wider thoroughfares that divide the new town from the old. I kept a shield of three cars between me and the big American saloon at all times as we trailed through the town.

I was careful. So careful. I was acutely aware of how my last car chase had ended.

Marianne asked, 'Where's he off to?'

'He's heading into the old town. That car is so wide it will have to crawl.' I took a risk and swung right too. Already I could see his brake lights on, gleaming red as he edged his way into the Place de la République.

'Listen to me, Marianne. At this hour I reckon he's heading for his hotel.' I pulled my 2CV up on to a pavement and tucked it tight against a wall, out of reach of the square's streetlamps. 'In these tight streets, I can run faster than he can drive. Wait here for me.' I leaned over, kissed her cheek and opened my door.

'No, Eloïse. I don't know who this guy is or what you want with him, but I don't want you to—'

'Lock your door,' I said, and climbed out of the car. From my bag I removed the gun. I placed it on the driver's seat. 'That's the safety catch,' I pointed out. 'If anyone tries to get in the car, shoot them.'

She stared at me, appalled.

'It's okay,' I whispered. 'No one will come.'

I closed the driver's door and locked it. From outside I watched her pick up the gun.

I ran, swift and soft-footed. Always in deep shadow, brushing past ancient walls and dark doorways. If he was taking this route, most likely he was heading over to the Place du Forum, where two hotels were to be found. The Place de la République lay empty, a large slice of darkness dominated by the elaborate town hall at one end and by a Roman obelisk at its centre, like a needle in its heart, but no American car. I felt a stab of panic. Had I lost him?

In my car I'd have been too conspicuous in these narrow rat-runs, but on foot I was part of the fabric of the night. I stopped and listened. I could hear the heavy note of its engine rumbling off the wall somewhere ahead of me, so I took a breath and raced across the stone steps of the Church of Saint-Trophime. Ducking down the next alleyway, I doubted if he'd have any paintwork left if he came through here.

I entered the Place du Forum, blood pumping in my ears. The Forum is the heart of the town, just as it was in Roman times and in the days when Vincent Van Gogh set up his easel here. A couple of bars were still open, their soft light spilling into the pretty square and turning the green paint on a car purple. It was the Chevy. Manoeuvring with delicacy around the bronze statue of Frédéric Mistral, our Nobel Prize winner, I expected the driver to park and enter the Hôtel du Forum at the southern end of the square. I leaned against the mottled trunk of one of the plane trees to obscure my outline, catching my breath and smacking at the wretched mosquitoes drawn to the sweat on my skin.

But the Chevy had no intention of stopping. As it slipped away out the other side of the square, I realised I was going to need a bigger breath. I started to run.

I followed the sound of the engine like a dog through the maze of streets between the Forum and the river. The streetlamps were poor here, the smell of the Rhône more invasive and the mist thicker as it lapped at my ankles and muted sounds, so that the engine seemed to whisper.

I was moving at a steady pace along one of the wider streets that ran downhill towards the river when suddenly the brake lights popped on. I dodged into a nearby doorway. I watched the Chevrolet slowly pull to a halt maybe ten or twelve houses further down and park on a patch of dirt where once another house must have stood. The engine uttered a growl and then stopped.

The sudden silence tweaked my nerves. I tucked myself deep into my shallow doorway till I could feel a doorknob indenting itself into my back. I reminded myself that I had done surveillance work before in Paris for Clarisse Favre, this was no different, no need for the sour taste in my mouth.

But no. This *was* different. This wasn't a headmaster cheating on his wife with one of his pupils, or a woman frittering away her accountant husband's hard-earned cash on the horses at Longchamp racecourse in the Bois de Boulogne every Saturday. No, this *was* different. This was a man who had tried to kill the brother I loved. Was he here in Arles to finish the job he'd started? Or was he spying on the USAF air base as a Soviet operative, and if so, what did his friendship with Major Dirke imply?

I had no answers. Not yet. In the silence I heard the click of the car door lock and I stopped breathing. The car was parked near the only lamp in the street and its light picked out the man who emerged from the driver's seat. He had his back to me and stood still, listening. Then, apparently satisfied, he turned.

It was Gilles Bertin.

Gilles Bertin crossed the road, moving quickly as though suddenly in a hurry, and by the light of the streetlamp I could make out that he was carrying a briefcase in one hand. He unlocked the door of a house on the opposite side of the road that I was on, but about ten houses further down. The houses along this stretch were all attached to each other, cheek by jowl, and their front doors opened straight on to the road.

The streetlamp's muted triangle of light didn't reach as far as my doorway, nevertheless I didn't move a muscle, didn't take a breath. Didn't risk a heartbeat. I watched as Bertin opened the door, placed his briefcase inside, then turned and walked back to the car. But before he reached it, I heard another heavy click, the sound of a car door. To my surprise the Chevy's front passenger door swung open and slowly a man's head and shoulders appeared. A hand grabbed the car's roof rim and the figure straightened up, his gaze immediately scanning the street.

It was André.

My brother.

In Gilles Bertin's car.

I had a sense of dread like a living thing caught inside me. I blinked, as if I could change what I was seeing in this dark backstreet, as if I could wipe it clean like a blackboard and start again.

Bertin opened the rear door, removed two crutches from the back seat and handed them to André. Everything about their movements was relaxed, their voices a low murmur that I couldn't catch. In my mind the only explanation was that somehow the MGB agent had kidnapped my brother, but my eyes told me otherwise. This was no kidnap. This was my brother's choice, to be in that car, to walk into that house, to be with this man. His battle for control of his legs as he crossed the road, forcing one foot in front of the other, stumbling on the cobbles, was agony to watch. He leaned heavily on the crutches and my instinct was to run and help, but my instinct could get me killed.

André shuffled his way inside the house, but Bertin paused, checked the street once more and drew a gun from a holster under his suit jacket. I crushed myself even tighter into my tiny pocket of blackness, but he didn't linger in my direction. Instead he glanced up at the streetlamp, took aim and fired. A silencer reduced the sound to a dull thwack, followed by the brittle crack of shattered glass. The light went out. The door shut.

I was in the dark.

I heard a sound. So faint I thought it was the thump of my own pulse, but it came again. And again. A footfall?

'Eloïse?' A whisper. Barely a word at all.

My palm was slick with sweat.

'Eloïse?'

I gave no reply.

The soft footfalls were closer now. The darkness swallowed them and I couldn't tell from which direction they were coming. A minute ticked past, two minutes. I listened harder and turned my attention to my right, where I heard the brush of a sleeve on a wall. A hand seized mine.

'Eloïse, it's me.' A murmur against my cheek.

'Léon!'

It was Léon Roussel, though it was so dark now that all we could see of each other was a black outline. How he knew it was me, I don't know.

'Eloïse, what the hell are you doing here?' he whispered.

'I could ask you the same question.'

It dawned on me then that for him to know what doorway I was concealed in, he must have seen me arrive before the streetlamp was shot out. It felt absurdly reassuring to know he'd been here all that time without my knowing. He stepped off the street and joined me in the shelter of my doorway.

'Why are you here?' I kept my voice low.

But he asked, 'Did you see André?'

'Yes, I saw him. It was a shock.'

'And the man he was with? Do you know him?'

I shook my head, though it was pointless to do so in the pitch dark.

'Do you know what's going on here?'

He spoke so softly I had to strain to hear. Again I shook my head. How could I tell him the truth when I didn't know it myself? The knowledge that my brother had deceived me seethed inside.

'Listen to me, Eloïse.'

I listened. I listened intently. I wanted him to give me a reason why this was happening. Léon was a policeman and this was his territory. There were things he knew that I didn't. His shoulder pressed against mine as he leaned close.

'Go home, Eloïse. Right now. Leave this to me. Go home and stay there until your brother comes home. I will continue to watch here and will telephone you the moment he leaves.'

'Léon, I am no longer that child who got stuck up a tree. I am leaving for five minutes, but I will be back. I need to give my car keys to Marianne.'

I took a long look at the house that my brother had chosen to enter, but it was no more than a blurred shape in the mist and darkness. On soundless feet I ran out into the black night.

CHAPTER TWENTY

LÉON ROUSSEL

Léon cursed under his breath. He tried to snatch at her but she was gone. That strange elusive creature who was so hard to pin down, so determined never to be caught in a net, driven by so many demons. Like her brother. His demons had always been ones that fed on risks to life and limb, zip-wiring from the topmost branch or tightrope-walking along the ridge of a barn. Now this. But this was not something that a sticking plaster and a rosy apple from the orchard could sort out. Yet again André had dragged Eloïse to the mouth of hell.

That's why Léon had come here tonight, but he hadn't expected company. Not André, and certainly not Eloïse, looking ready for trouble in her black garb with her jet-black hair pulled tight off her face. It made her look tough in the same way he knew his police uniform made him look tough, though he'd learned that outward appearances were, more often than not, false.

He'd learned to peel appearances away. That's what he'd wanted to do tonight, but the arrival of the Caussade brother and sister had put a stop to it. His eyes never left the spot where the front door lay barely visible behind the clammy night air. The man in that house calling himself Gilles Bertin did not realise the way things were down here. The loyalties. The blood feuds. The vast expanse of Camargue marsh wilderness where bodies might not be found for months, sometimes never if a wild boar got to them first.

It was too dark to see the dial on his watch, so Léon counted off the minutes in his head. Two minutes, three minutes. At four minutes he was tempted to slow his count but didn't. At five minutes Eloïse was back, as he knew she would be. As good as her word.

'Anything?' she murmured, tucking herself in beside him. Her hair smelled of sea mist.

'No, nothing.'

'We wait?'

'Yes.'

She touched her fingers to the back of his hand. 'We can't talk now,' she whispered. 'It's dangerous.'

'When this is done.'

He felt rather than saw her nod.

'Is Marianne here in Arles too?' he asked.

'Not anymore. I just gave her my car keys to drive home.'

'Good. I will take you home. Maybe André too?'

She didn't reply, but he felt the heat of her and for a

moment she leaned her weight against his shoulder. After that, they kept vigil in silence.

Headlights swept into the street at the far end, picking out a rib-thin dog slinking along one wall. The noise of the engine rattled off the walls, rowdy after the hour of silence to which Léon's ears had grown accustomed. He pulled his jacket over his face and Eloïse hid hers against his shoulder when the car slid past, and for two beats of his heart he forgot about the car.

'A taxi,' he whispered into her hair.

She lifted her head, her lips almost touching his and only the faint gleam of her eyes visible, and she seemed about to say something. But instead she turned her head to observe the taxi pulling to a halt in front of the house they'd been watching. The front door snapped open. Had the occupants been standing on the other side of it? Léon could see André silhouetted on his crutches against the light. The urge to go over and speak to the man who had been his friend was strong, to offer him a lift home, to make a connection, but Eloïse's words still chimed in his mind. *It's dangerous.*

Dangerous for whom?

André manoeuvred himself and his crutches inside the taxi. The man in the doorway offered no help. He watched the taxi drive away and turn left at the far corner, before he stepped back and shut the door.

Léon exhaled. Eloïse could not drag her gaze from where the ruby tail-light of the car had been.

*

Léon drove fast. He had scant hope of catching up with the taxi because they had remained at their post in the doorway for another half-hour before accepting that no one else would be leaving that house tonight. It was almost one o'clock in the morning. Sane people had taken to their beds long ago.

'What happened back there, Eloïse? What went on with André and that man in the Chevrolet?'

'I wish I knew.'

She was huddled on the front passenger seat in his black Citroën saloon, her knees tucked under her chin, her arms wrapped around her shins. She held herself tight. As if she was frightened that something might fall out that she was trying to hold inside.

'You were wrong, Eloïse, to go there.'

A baby-faced deer leaped out into his headlights on the road, all spindly legs and eyes like torchlights. Léon swore and braked hard, missed it by a tail-whisker.

'Bloody fool.'

Did he mean the deer? Or her?

'You knew,' he continued as he drove on, 'that the situation back there was dangerous but still you walked into it. You were wrong. André would tell you the same and maybe you would listen to him.'

A full minute flicked by.

'You don't know André,' she whispered. 'Neither do I.'

'Oh, Eloïse,' he said gently, 'you are not your brother's guardian.'

'Of course I am. I put him on those crutches.'

'Did you know he would be in the car tonight?'

'Of course not.'

'Who was the other man in the car?'

'Someone you should stay away from, even you, Monsieur le Capitaine.'

The use of his police title jarred, making Léon glance across. She was sitting with her cheek on her knee and was looking at him. The darkness outside had trickled into the car and all strength seemed to have drained from her. Léon felt a wave of sorrow for her.

'Whatever the hell it is you're doing,' he said, 'I'll help you.'

'Thank you. I am grateful for the lift.'

'I don't mean the stupid lift.'

'Léon, I meant what I said before. I am not a child anymore. I don't need to be hoisted up to the next branch of the tree.'

'I know.'

She paused. The ghost of a barn owl swooped low in front of the car, startling them both. 'Do you recall,' she asked, 'the day our little band of wildlings built the hut out by the *étang*?'

'Yes.'

'Do you recall the snake?'

'Yes.'

He recalled it all right. An asp viper. A nine-year-old skinny girl made to stand by their campfire with a forty-centimetre venomous viper held by a grip behind its flat triangular head. It was trying to escape and had coiled its sinuous body around her bony wrist, its dark zigzag pattern looking as if someone had run a charcoal stick down its back. Its jowls were open. The girl was muddy and scratched by brambles, her eyes on fire, her hand steady.

Yes, he recalled the snake.

'Do you know why André made me hold that snake?'

Léon sighed with annoyance. 'To test you. To forge you through fear. That was what he believed he could do with all of us. Make us stronger.'

'No, Léon, you've got it wrong. That day he was proving my courage. Not to me. To the rest of you, you older boys who thought I was a weed because I was younger and a girl.'

'Eloïse, not for one second did we ever think you a weed.'

'That day I earned the respect of all of you.'

'You always had my respect.'

'At the time I didn't understand why he did it, but I do now. What if he is doing it again? Making me hold a snake, even though I don't understand why.'

Léon stamped on the brake pedal and hauled the car over to the side of the road on the edge of an olive grove. The moon threw shadows of the tree branches at them like pointing fingers. He rolled down his window, deaf to the hum of mosquitoes, and spat his anger out on the black soil.

'Are you angry with me, Léon?'

'Yes. André is your brother, but he is not Superman. He is just like the rest of us. He makes mistakes, he gets things wrong, he has regrets, and yes, he lies at times. When he's cornered.'

Eloïse made a strange little sound and slid her feet to the floor of the car. 'I know that. I know he's not infallible, but he works tirelessly for the good of our country. Just as you do. I tried to help but . . . failed.'

She rolled down her window and the faintest of breezes off the wide-open fields blew warm sticky air through the car as if it would carry away her words.

'You haven't *failed*, Eloïse. But how can I help you if you won't tell me what's going on? Is it connected with the nuclear weapons on the air base?'

Her head whipped round to face him.

'And,' Léon continued, 'who was the other man in the American car? Tell me.'

'I can't.'

'You can. It's your choice. Not André's.'

She pushed down on the door handle and climbed out of the car, but she left the door open, a narrow bridge between them. Léon knew very well the power of silence. He had used it many times in interrogations and though he wanted to go out there after her, he made himself sit and wait.

Five minutes passed.

'Léon.'

He couldn't see her. She was leaning back against the car, staring out at the moonlight rippling over furrows in a field, leaving a film of silver over the earth.

'Léon, why were you in the street in Arles tonight?'

'I was looking for a man called Gilles Bertin. I believe he was the man in the car with André.'

'Why were you searching for him?'

'He's been drifting around the bars and cafés of Serriac asking questions. He doesn't realise what kind of community we have here, where everybody knows everybody. A stranger sticks in our craw like a thistle.'

'What questions?'

'Questions about you.'

Her head ducked down to peer inside the car. With the moon behind her it was too dark to see her expression, but he could hear her breath as harsh as one of her beloved bulls.

'Tell me.'

'Sit down,' he said quietly.

She sat on the passenger seat, with her feet on the ground outside, her back to him. Through the open door, the chirring of the crickets sounded like a dentist's drill.

'Word spreads fast in Serriac, a town so bored it thinks watching toenails grow is entertaining. Its tom-tom drums are second to none and as police chief I make certain I am always tuned into them. Often it means I can stop trouble before it begins. That's why I warned you to be careful if you ventured into town. Because of your father's land-sale.'

He felt her shudder.

'Did anything happen?' he asked quietly.

She shook her head. He didn't believe her.

'When I heard that someone was making enquiries about you, I was concerned.'

Concerned. More like shit-scared she would be on the receiving end of the same treatment as Goliath.

'So I found out a name – Gilles Bertin – and I checked it against every hotel and rental room in the area, which is how I ended up outside that house after I finished my work-shift. But I didn't expect to see you turn up.'

'Léon.' Just his name. Nothing more.

He reached out and rested the palm of his hand on the curve of her back. The tremor inside her was still there.

'Thank you, Léon.' Abruptly she straightened her spine, swung her feet back into the car and pulled the door closed. 'Let's drive.'

He started the Citroën, slid into gear and they continued on the road to Serriac.

'André told me about Gilles Bertin. He said he works for Soviet Intelligence, the MGB.' She was calm now, factual and precise. 'I saw him in Paris just after the crash, but I don't think he recognises me. I was a mess back then.'

He imagined the mess. The blood. The flesh torn off her face.

'I traced the car's owner through its plates,' he told her. 'It's registered to an address in Paris.'

'It seemed at first that he had come to finish the job he started,' she said. 'But now I am not so sure.'

'By *job*, you mean André?'

'Yes.'

Cool and unemotional.

'And now?'

'Now, after tonight, I think he has come for me.'

'*Merde*, Eloïse, why would you think that? According to you, this Bertin man from Paris doesn't even know you.'

'That's true.' She sat very still as the road unwound ahead of them. 'You tell me he has been asking about me in Serriac and . . .' she exhaled slowly, as if it hurt, 'I received a death-threat note when I was in town.'

'What?'

'It was a note tucked under my car wiper.'

'Why didn't you bring it to me at once?'

But she offered no explanation, and when he looked across at her he could see even in the darkness that her eyes were closed.

'What did it say?' The policeman in him was taking control.

'That I would be killed if I didn't go back to Paris.'

'Do you still have it?'

'Yes, of course. It's at home. I'll bring it to you in Serriac tomorrow.'

She talked as if they were discussing a book he wanted to borrow.

'André warned me,' she said, her dark eyes flicking open and flying to his, 'that this man is dangerous.'

Léon took one hand off the wheel and wrapped it tight around hers. 'The question is, can we believe what André says?'

CHAPTER TWENTY-ONE

I lay in bed. I couldn't unclench my teeth. I couldn't close my ears. The sound of the crutches marching back and forth across the wooden floor of André's room was relentless.

I couldn't confront him, not yet. If I burst in there now I might tear his lying tongue out. I turned everything over in my mind all night and I asked myself the same questions again and again. They raged and gnawed at me and curdled in the pit of my stomach.

Why is André spending time with a Soviet MGB agent in secret?

Why did he warn me off Gilles Bertin, saying he was too dangerous to approach?

Why did he say he didn't know where Bertin was?

If the MGB were still trying to finish off the job of killing my brother, why didn't Bertin do so? André was in no state to defend himself.

Was he still in danger?

Was I in danger?

Or Papa?

I stood at the window and wanted to rip my skin off. It was too tight. Too hot. The stink of the burned stables still hung in my nostrils after I'd checked on Cosette's wound. We'd make a good pair, the two of us, with our matching scars. I stared up at the moon, bloated in the grave-black night, and I was frightened for Léon. I was fearful that while investigating the stable fire he would run slap into the brute fist of the MGB.

Thak, thak thak.

The sound of the crutches ate into my mind.

Silence.

After two solid hours the noise of the crutches finally ceased. It was three-thirty in the morning, still another three hours till sunrise, but I gave André no respite. I wanted him exhausted. I wanted his defences low, his ability to lie to me at its weakest ebb.

I opened the door to his room.

I was carrying a glass of wine in my hand. The light was on and the two wooden crutches lay discarded on the floor. My brother was sprawled on the bed face-down, arms spread, legs trailing to the floor. He was lying just the way he'd fallen, too weary to move a muscle, and his shirt was clinging to his back with sweat. I wanted to go to him, to rip the sweat-stained shirt from his back and make him comfortable on the bed, but I didn't allow either of us that luxury.

I placed the wine beside his bed and touched his shoulder.

He spun over on to his back, his hand sweeping a gun from under his pillow, its muzzle directed at me.

'Put it down, please, André.'

'I'm sorry. I was asleep. I didn't know it was you.'

I took the gun from his hand and placed it on his bedside table beside the wine. I dropped down into the chair and waited while he arranged himself on the bed, half-sitting, his pale hair as dark as sand when the tide has come in.

'What is it you want, Eloïse? It's the middle of the blasted night. Can't it wait?'

'No, I'm sorry, it can't.'

His face looked grey and haunted by pain, but I didn't let myself look away.

'I saw you with Gilles Bertin last night,' I stated.

His eyes widened. My words had punched a hole in the air between us, so big I could put my fist through it, but he was quick to recover.

'You couldn't have.'

'Believe me, I did.'

'Where?'

'In Arles. What were you doing with an MGB agent?'

'Oh, my little sister, I should have known better than to underestimate you.'

He smiled, the warm big-brother smile I remembered from our childhood. I loved that smile but I wasn't a child now.

'Make me understand,' I said quietly.

'It isn't easy. Because you have to accept that in the world of Intelligence nothing is as it seems. It is all smoke and mirrors, and layers behind layers, secrets hiding secrets.'

'Tell me clearly, André. Why were you in the Chevrolet with Gilles Bertin last night? It can't be hard.'

I heard his sigh. 'I was in the car with Gilles because when I worked at the Ministry of Defence in Paris before the crash, Gilles was my colleague. He worked on the floor below me. At Hôtel de Brienne under General Charles Léchères. He is down here to conduct military business with Major Dirke at the USAF air base. He came to see me after you left for the dance while Papa was out on his rounds on the farm. He asked me to join their meeting. To discuss the arrival of the next shipment of B-50 planes from Boeing in America.'

He paused, studying my stunned expression. 'You see, my dear sister,' his tone was soothing, 'nothing is as simple or straightforward as it seems.'

I opened my mouth, but I didn't know which of the questions crowding on my tongue to choose.

'Everything you told me about Gilles Bertin before ...' I started.

'Is true.'

'He is a spy for the MGB in Russia.'

'Yes.'

'You know this, yet he is still employed at the Ministry of Defence?'

'He is employed at a low-grade level with no access to top-secret information. We use him to feed misinformation back to his Soviet masters.'

'Throwing in a few snippets of juicy truth to keep them believing it, I presume.'

'Exactly.'

'Are there many like him?'

'Not all have his talent for violence. But yes, you have to realise that every government department in France is infiltrated by Russian agents. Riddled with them. Not only in government, but in industry too. Every factory and every laboratory is subject to industrial espionage on a huge scale as the Russians struggle to compete with our developments in the West.'

I could hear the anger, like a rising tide in his voice.

'The Cold War is a war conducted on many fronts, Eloïse, unseen and unheard, but it is a war nonetheless. People are dying in it every day. Quietly and discreetly. Buried in cold earth. With no battle honours. So do not for one second think there is no danger because you cannot see bloodied uniforms or hear the boom of artillery guns. It is there. Right under your nose.'

'Oh, André, why didn't you tell me all this about Gilles Bertin before? Why keep me in the dark?'

'My clever little sister, why do you think? You are my sister. I didn't want you involved. I didn't want you hurt again. That's why I kept pushing you back to Paris. Don't you know that?'

I laughed, not a happy laugh but the best I could find. 'So does that mean you are not in danger? Not from Bertin. You were with him at the house last night, I saw you, but when did you get in his car?'

André nodded. 'I saw you too at the air base with Major Dirke.'

'How?'

'I was riding in the back of the Chevrolet. I ducked down on the seat in the dark when I saw you standing there with him. I thought you were meant to be dancing,' he laughed. It was no happier than mine.

'Is the farm in danger? The killing of Goliath, the burning of the stables, was that the work of the MGB? Will the farmhouse be next?'

'Gilles Bertin says no. He claims it was the work of angry anti-American, anti-nuclear locals.'

'Do you believe him?'

'No.'

'So are you in danger? Tell me the truth, André.'

I kept it low-key. I stopped myself reaching forward and shaking an answer out of him.

'Anyone in my business is always in danger, Eloïse.'

There it was again. An answer that wasn't an answer.

'I thought you'd finished with that *business*,' I said.

He reacted as if I'd poked a stick at him. He sat upright and, using his hands, he swung his damaged legs over the side of the bed, feet on the floor. He sat there, shirt still clinging to his muscular frame, and studied me in silence. Just the mention of his *business* seemed to have brought him back to life, eyes glittering and focused. His hair was drying, bushing out in thick waves around his head. Once more he was a lion on the hunt.

He picked up the glass of red wine and drank half of it in one go. He handed it to me. I drank the other half.

'You need rest,' I said soothingly. 'I shouldn't have woken you, but I wanted the truth from you.'

'You want honesty,' he said, 'I'll give you honesty. Gilles Bertin turned up here last night to put a bullet in my brain, but I convinced him I was more valuable to him alive. But he won't give me long.'

I locked my eyes on his. All I saw was hunger.

'Eloïse, I have work for you.'

CHAPTER TWENTY-TWO

LÉON ROUSSEL

In the Boulevard des Tanneurs a tractor had clouted a cart hauling hundreds of cabbages and traffic had ground to a halt in Serriac. The upturned cart and the disgorged vegetables, rolling around on the road like human heads, had resulted in chaos that it took Léon a good hour to sort out. Henri, the tractor driver, with a mouth as broad as his belly, refused to remove his brand new Latil tractor.

'Not until that bastard turnip-head, Jean-Baptiste, admits he's an arsehole and agrees to pay for the damage to my tractor. Look what his shit-heap has done to my radiator.'

A crowd gathered to watch the dispute. Any free-rolling cabbages were discreetly scooped into shopping bags and under shawls. With a curse Léon set one of his officers on cabbage duty and another to keep onlookers moving, while he banged the drivers' heads together and organised the removal of the obstructing vehicles.

Overnight the weather had changed. Heavy bruised clouds had swept in on a stiff wind and threatened rain, but at least it meant the sight and sound of the aircraft patrols would be less intrusive. A sudden downpour would empty the streets and ease the oppressive heat. Léon was acutely aware of the ever-growing mountain of paperwork on his desk, crying out for attention.

But that wasn't the reason he was in such a hurry to get back there.

She strolled into Léon's office mid-morning and placed a small reed-basket of fresh eggs on top of his desk. She glanced round the obsessively neat room, then eyed the forms he was filling out and said, 'You're busy.'

'Lovely-looking eggs, Eloïse. How kind of you.'

'They are a thank you for last night,' she said with a smile.

He noticed that a smile emphasised her scar. The skin around it puckered up and he felt the taut shiny line of it when he greeted her with a kiss on both cheeks. He liked the fact she didn't seem to care. He also liked that she was in a simple cotton frock today, none of her Parisian chic about it, and wore her long dark hair loose around her shoulders. Her face was scrubbed clean of make-up. All he needed now was to see her astride her horse, racing through the marshes, water-spray flying in rainbows around her. Then he'd be happy.

'Léon.'

He concentrated on the piece of paper she was handing him. 'Please sit down,' he said.

They sat either side of the desk and studied the bold printed words on the page.

YOU WANT ME TO KILL YOU?
LIKE GOLIATH. ALONE. IN THE DARK.
GO BACK TO PARIS. NOW.

He sat very still, then tipped his chair on to its back legs. A bad habit of his when rattled.

'Well, first, this is not the work of a professional, so I think we can rule out our MGB Intelligence friend from last night.'

She gave him a sideways look. 'Are you sure?'

'No. Not certain. But it smells of amateur work to me. A professional criminal would not have picked up a pen to scrawl such a note. The ink and the handwriting style are far too traceable. A professional would use a typewriter or preferably words and letters cut from newspapers.'

He nudged it further away from him, barely having touched more than a corner of the offending article.

'I'll bet you one of my nice new eggs that the paper is dripping with fingerprints.'

'Oh.' She stared down at her own fingertips.

'Don't worry. We'll take your fingerprints while you're here and eliminate them.'

She nodded. 'So who do you suspect?'

'An angry local. Scared witless by the arrival of nuclear weapons on your father's land.'

'Just as dangerous though.'

'I doubt it. A toothless threat, I suspect.'

She looked tired. There was a greyness around her mouth and her eyes had sunk deeper into her head, but he saw the effect of his words. Her shoulders came down from under her ears and the half-smile she gave him reached her eyes.

'I hope you're right,' she said, 'Monsieur le Capitaine.'

'To be sure of being safe, you could always do as the note instructs, you know. Return to Paris.' He said it casually, as if it wouldn't tear a hole in him.

'No. But thanks for the suggestion.'

'Did you speak to André about last night?'

'Yes, I did. It seems he knows Gilles Bertin better than I thought. They worked together in Paris. Before.'

She didn't say before what. There was no need.

'You're telling me that André worked with a Soviet Intelligence agent? And you're not worried? Seriously?'

'No. I'm sorry I can't tell you more, Léon. But it was a required part of his job.'

'His job.' Léon shrugged, but it didn't come across as carelessly as he intended. 'Always his job. Eloïse, I know what he does because a couple of years ago he tried to recruit me into his nefarious world of espionage.'

Her dark eyes grew darker. 'Did you accept?'

'No. I declined.'

'Why?'

'My life as a police officer is plenty dangerous enough, thank you. Only this morning I had an argument with fat old Henri Laurent on his tractor.'

He wiped imaginary sweat off his brow with exaggerated relief and saw he'd made her smile. He picked up one of her eggs from the straw-filled basket and cradled it in his hand, so delicate, yet so strong. As pale as her Parisian skin. Its shell was as smooth as the lie he was about to tell her.

'I've been going through the statements,' he tapped one of the paper piles on his desk, 'given by all the people who attended Goliath's burial ceremony. Not one of them saw anything suspicious.'

'Surely someone must have seen something.'

'No.' He moved on quickly. 'The fire was started at the rear of the stables while everyone was watching the ceremony, their back to the stables.'

'So any of them could have done it.'

'True.'

'A person who sets fire to horses should be shot.'

Léon was not going to argue with that. 'I am looking into their political affiliations. It might narrow the field down. Checking if any have a history of anti-American or anti-nuclear activities.'

'Can you do that?'

'We have lists.'

'I don't know whether to be thankful or scared.'

'Try impressed.'

That made her smile. She nodded. 'I hope I'm not on your list.'

'No, but your brother is.'

'André?' She frowned. 'He's not anti-American.'

'No, not André.'

'Isaac?'

He watched her mouth form her younger brother's name, as if she were biting on a tooth that hurt. He pulled a sheet of paper from a drawer and spread it in front of her.

'I'd like you to read through this list of names of attendees at the burial ceremony and tell me which ones you know. Or, more to the point, which ones you don't know.'

'Shouldn't you be asking my father this?'

'I have already done so.'

She cocked her head at him. Exactly like when she was twelve. 'Covering all angles?'

'Looking for holes,' he said.

He handed her a pen. She started skimming through them, ticking the ones she knew with rapid little flicks of the nib. At one point she glanced up at him and found him watching her, but it was when she paused a second time, her forehead wrinkled in an effort of recall, that he smelled a scrap of something meaty. He was about to ask which name had niggled at her, but the door burst open without the customary knock and the moment was lost.

'Can't you see, Travert, that I am busy?'

'Captain, all bloody hell is about to break loose.'

Travert was his sergeant, a man with a penchant for languidness. Not one to panic, not unless he had to, and right now, his cheeks were an odd florid colour. Léon rose to his feet.

'Excuse me a moment, Eloïse.'

But before he could exit the office, Travert started to spill the emergency news.

'They're coming. In coaches,' he blurted out. 'Coming here. To demonstrate in Serriac against the air base. Hundreds of the Commie trade union bastards being shipped here, maybe thousands. They're on their way right now, charging up from the coast and Marseille. They've reached Saint-Martin-de-Crau already and—'

'Enough! Silence, Travert.'

Léon rushed to the door and yelled down the hallway, 'Get me Monsieur le Maire on the phone. Now!' He swung back inside the room. 'Travert, see Mademoiselle Caussade out.'

CHAPTER TWENTY-THREE

The town of Serriac was choking. Crowded. Cracking at the seams. Shouts and anti-nuclear placards and raised fists disrupted the sleepy air that was accustomed to nothing more than the barking of dogs and the jangled notes of toothless old Fabron's accordion.

'Americans out!'

'Hiroshima never again!'

'No to nuclear weapons.'

'Yanks go home!'

'No USA air base here!'

I felt the hatred growing, as uncontrollable and as destructive as the fire in my father's stables. I feared for my town. I saw a woman with a baby strapped to her chest and she was brandishing a placard that stated in blood-red paint: I WANT A FUTURE FOR MY CHILD. I feared for her child.

I perched myself on the fountain near the church and watched Léon positioning his men, quick and decisive. On corners. In pairs. He was young to be in such a senior position of command, but the war had snatched so many of Serriac's men that it opened up opportunities for those who were left. I noticed the way his men treated him with respect, even those who were older than he was. He studied the huge crowd of protesters with quick eyes, picking out troublemakers. They moved the way a shoal of fish moves, tight together, jostling shoulders. Safety in numbers. Their rage so intense that all it needed was a match to set it on fire. I could see that Léon was determined there would be no match.

A van full of officers came racing in from Arles with police reinforcements to block off side streets and help keep the peace. They formed a human barrier between the demonstrators and the locals who resented this unwelcome intrusion. Insults were hurled. Tempers rose. Few residents of Serriac could stomach the air base because they knew it made them a target for a Soviet nuclear attack, so I couldn't blame them even though I knew they were wrong. But at the same time they didn't want this invading army marching through their town.

'Eloïse Caussade,' a woman's stern voice shouted out as she marched past me, swept along by the tidal force of the crowd, 'you and your father should be ashamed of yourselves for selling your land – French land – to the capitalist overlords from America. You are traitors to your country.'

It only took me a second to find the owner of the familiar voice and I felt my cheeks burn the way they had always done when she used to reprimand me when I was young. It was Madeleine Caron, the headmistress from the school I used to attend, tall and unforgiving. But before I could respond she was gone. Is that how the town thought of me? Of Papa? It saddened me and the urge to explain was strong, but how could I explain when I didn't understand myself?

I saw a hand in the crowd rise as a tall man reached up above the heads around him, and my heart tightened. His fist was wrapped around a chunk of rock. It swung back and then with explosive force shot forward. A shop window shattered.

One of Léon's police officers dived into the crowd, seized the culprit and hauled him out into the back of a police van parked across one of the side streets. But another hand went up, another rock. Violence erupting. The quiet world of Serriac was fraying at the edges.

The protesters were surging down towards the town hall, where I could already see Mayor Durand standing on the steps, waiting for his moment in the sun. The largest audience he could wish for was heading his way and I hoped he had the right words on his silver tongue. I jumped down off the edge of the fountain and ran to the police van that I'd seen blocking the side street.

It stood unguarded.

Its rear door was held closed by a metal strut that hinged across it and it was the work of a second to flip it up, releasing the door. I swung it open in search of the hooligan who had thrown the first rock. He was seated on a metal bench in the gloomy interior but leaped for the door, all long limbs and blazing eyes. He stopped dead on the step when he saw me.

'Isaac,' I shouted at him, 'you bloody fool.'

*

We sat at the back of the empty church and kept our voices low. The Church of Saint-Joseph was too grand for Serriac. Its rose-coloured marble floors too splendid, its marble columns too lofty, its vaulted ceiling too gloriously intricate to grace a plain-spoken rural town that had trouble raising enough money even to keep its library open more than two days a week.

I loved to sit in this church, though I rarely did so. Every time it made my heart swell because it smelled of my childhood. I remembered sitting on one of these pews with my mother. She wore a lavender frock and white gloves. A loving smile directed at me. Her belly swollen. The building had been gifted to the town in medieval times by a wealthy Parisian baron, Henri-Jacques de Montfer. It was to offer thanks to God for a Serriac fisherman saving the life of the baron's sister when she almost drowned in the Rhône.

A brother and sister. The bond was strong.

'Your face,' Isaac murmured. 'I'm sorry.'

'Don't bother about it. I don't.'

It was a lie of course, but I didn't want my little brother's pity. Not that he was exactly little anymore. Only nineteen, but taller than my father or André. and whippet-thin. A handsome face with a shaggy mop of wheat-coloured hair that had the coarse texture of Cosette's mane. Of all of us, he was the one most like my mother and possessed the identical round blue eyes which, like hers, opened straight into his soul. I saw into it now, burning with belief.

'What the hell are you doing here, Isaac? Arriving with rocks. Looking for trouble.'

'Trouble is already here, Eloïse.'

'We don't need more.'

'Trouble is staring us in the face in the shape of American nuclear bombs located in what they call a direct line of communications across France.'

His hands were jabbing at the air. He was seeing in his head the eleven sites chosen across the country where the American military bases were being constructed, picturing the nuclear arsenal piling up in storage silos on our doorstep. I knew. I'd seen them inside my own head.

'For heaven's sake, Isaac, see sense. The Soviet Union has installed Communist governments in all the countries of Eastern Europe and if it thinks it can get away with it, it will invade and crush Western Europe, as it tried to do when it blockaded West Berlin in 1948. The American nuclear threat is all that keeps them from our door.' I waved a hand towards the huge arched door behind us. 'Tell that to your friends out there. And remember this: the Soviets have just detonated their own atomic bomb, which means we are in an arms race that—'

'No, no.' My brother shook a fierce finger at me. 'It was not a true H-bomb, not like America's explosion at Enewetak in the Pacific last year. That one was a monster. A thousand times more powerful than the one dropped on Hiroshima. The Soviet bomb didn't have a staged fusion device.'

I stared at him. My little brother used to be always

skiving off to sail his dinghy on the lagoon instead of doing his maths homework, yet here he was talking about staged fusion devices.

'How on earth do you know that?' I asked. 'About the fusion device.'

'So you still think that because I didn't go to university like you and André, I have shit for brains.'

'No! Of course not.'

'Just because I work on the waterfront in Marseille and spend my days loading and unloading bloody great ships, doesn't make me a dumb knucklehead, you know.'

'I know that, Isaac.'

His voice grew louder and I threw a quick glance around the church. Nothing moved in the shadowy confession box or the gilded pulpit with its carved-eagle lectern. But still I checked out the Our Lady chapel with the blue-draped Madonna stained-glass window and the grand altar space with its candles burning steadily. Even the gilt box in the wall that displayed the service hymn number. We were alone.

'Wearing a docker's vest and dungarees,' Isaac could not let it go, 'doesn't mean I can't read or listen. Yes, I wield a docker's hook. That doesn't mean I don't know what questions to ask. Education of the masses lies at the heart of Stalin's Communism.'

There we had it.

My brother Isaac was a fully signed-up member of the French Communist Party, yet here he was in the house of God with me. The irony did not escape me. I slid an arm along his shoulder and pulled him closer. He might have been thin but I could feel the dense muscles of him, the sinews and tendons, the strength of him. But the strength of his convictions was what made me nervous.

'How is life in Marseille treating you?' I asked with an affectionate squeeze.

But he was too fired up. 'You don't realise, Eloïse, in your Paris bubble, that the country is seething with rage and frustration at Laniel's right-wing policies that are bringing industry to its knees and failing the workers of France. He cannot continue with the government's austerity programme. Cutting jobs. Refusing pay demands. We are about to go on strike because he is crippling the country.'

'Who is *we*? Your dockers' union?'

'All of the Socialist and Communist trade union groups are about to stop work and walk out. A general strike. No rail network. No gas or electricity. No postal system. Even miners and hospitals on strike.' His face glowed the way I've seen an evangelical preacher's glow. 'We will paralyse France and force Laniel out of office. Replace him and his greedy pigs who keep their snouts in the trough with—'

'Isaac.'

'. . . a left-wing coalition. With the PCF – the Parti Communiste Français under Maurice Thorez – holding it together. They will immediately kick the fascist Americans out of our country. This time for good. No air bases. No nuclear bombs to—'

'Isaac!'

He came back to me from his soap box.

'Would your protesters out there kill Goliath to make their point?'

He laughed. The sound of it was shocking after his angry tirade. 'Of course not. These men and women have been born and bred in the gutters of Marseille. They'd run like rabbits if they came face to face with a bull.' He rubbed my shoulder. 'Poor old Goliath, the cantankerous bastard.' He rubbed his own shoulder, which bore a telltale scar. 'They would attack air bases and face rifles. But not bulls.'

'A man would need a horse to get anywhere near Goliath. Even with axes there would need to be at least two or three men on horseback.'

'*Pauvre* Papa.'

'And stables? Would they burn stables with horses inside?'

'Probably. Oh, Eloïse, I wish you would come and fight on our side. We need people like you.'

I took my brother's hand in mine. 'Isaac, I miss you.'

'Not nearly as much as I missed you when you ran off to Paris to follow André, leaving me here with a father who couldn't stand the sight of me.'

'No, Isaac, Papa loves you.'

'He cannot bear to be in the same room with me.'

'You're wrong. It is because every time he looks at you, he misses Maman's beautiful face, you are so like her. You remind him how much he lost when she died, but underneath it all, he still loves you.'

'And André?'

I chafed the back of his hand with my fingers. 'André is André. A law unto himself. But Isaac, I didn't run away to follow in his footsteps, I went to university at the Sorbonne because it is the best in the country. I didn't go to Paris just because André was there.'

Liar. Liar.

'Anyway, you were never at home,' I added. 'You were only fifteen but always off at your political meetings and rallies. You had no interest in the farm.'

He stood up, breaking free from me. 'Why are you here, Eloïse? What is it that has brought you back to the Camargue?'

I smiled. To make him stay. 'Papa summoned me. He thinks that when the family is in trouble it needs to work together.' I felt such a yearning to sit him back down beside me, to wrap an arm around his thin waist as lovingly as my mother had done to me in the exact same pew nineteen years ago. 'Isaac, Papa doesn't make it obvious, I know, but I'm certain he would value it if you would come out to the farm. Share a meal with us . . .'

He drew a hand through the air, cutting me off. 'I know you mean well, but it's too late. I'm sorry, Eloïse. Can't you see?' He tipped his head on one side as if he could somehow find another me, another Papa, hiding behind the pew. 'Tell Papa from me that anyone who hands over his land to the American Air Force for nuclear weapons and a fleet of aircraft designed to destroy the Soviet Union is no father of mine. It is treachery.' His young mouth twisted. 'Treachery against France.'

'No, Isaac, no.' I stood to face him. 'Don't.'

But he retreated into the aisle. 'Listen to me, Eloïse, don't fall for all their blatant capitalist propaganda. The American bastards will destroy Europe if we don't put a stop to their godforsaken plans.'

'Isaac Caussade!' A deep voice boomed out at us from the altar like the voice of God himself. 'I will not suffer such profanity in the house of God.'

Father Jerome came sweeping down on us, his long Bible-black soutane flowing around him, and I thought as always of the wings of a crow descending to peck our eyes out. That flash of childhood fear came and went, a hangover from schooldays when the edge of a ruler would rap knuckles if their owner was found wanting in Latin.

'Father Jerome,' I said to divert his attention, 'the town is all stirred up out there today.'

Father Jerome was the kind of man who believed in castigation and praise in equal measure, depending on whether it was before or after his midday cognac. He had a drinker's bulbous nose, large and intimidating, but Isaac was no longer the gangly youth who used to mess about in the back row. He was a fully fledged docker.

'I'll curse when and where I like,' Isaac said, 'without a by-your-leave from God.'

'Did I not teach you not to take our Holy Father's name in vain?' the priest demanded.

'I have one unforgiving father already. I don't need another.' Isaac started walking towards the door, but he swung round to look over his shoulder with an unexpected half-smile for me. 'I will ask,' he said. 'About the stables.'

'Thank you. Goodbye, Isaac.'

I let my brother take his anger back out on the street.

'Eloïse, wait one moment.'

Father Jerome held up his hand as though stopping traffic. He blended in with the church as naturally as the pews or the organ.

'What is it, Father?'

'A word about your brother.'

'He meant no offence when he spoke.'

'Of course he meant offence. Offence to God.'

I let it pass.

'But I didn't mean that brother,' he continued. 'Your other one.'

'André?'

'Yes.'

'What about him?'

'How is he?'

'He has crippled legs. How do you think he is?' I drew a steadying breath. 'I'm sorry. I didn't mean to sound rude. I am shaken by . . .' I waved a hand towards the great arch of the door. Let him work out whether it meant Isaac or the vehemence of the demonstrators, whichever he chose. 'André is as well as can be expected.'

There. Better.

'He wasn't at Mass this morning, so I was concerned.'

186

My mouth dropped open. I shut it quickly. 'Does he usually come to church on a Sunday?'

'Oh yes.' His eyes grew gentle. 'God would welcome you here too, Eloïse. It might bring you the comfort you seek.'

I stared at him. My mind jammed. Still trying to absorb what he was saying. 'You mean my brother André comes to church here in Serriac every Sunday.'

'Yes, he does.'

I remembered the hymn book at his bedside. The midnight cry for help in the darkness.

'How does he get here?' I asked.

He looked at me perplexed. 'Your father drives him.'

I bit down on my tongue to stop it from telling him he was lying.

'My father comes to church as well?'

'No. Not Aristide Caussade. He drops André here and picks him up when Mass is finished. But he will always be welcome too.'

I nodded. I had no words. I made quickly for the door, blinking away tears. More than anything in the world I wanted André to find his own peace of soul.

CHAPTER TWENTY-FOUR

I stood with my back to the wall. It was warm on my shoulder blades. The air was fizzing, energy-snapping. Nerves tight. I watched it closely, the mass demonstration in the street. The mass thoughts. The mass mind. Drawing power to itself with every shout. The placards with their messages of hate and the voices hitched together like horses in a yoke by their chants of rage.

'Yankee bastards! Out! Out! Out!'

'No nukes here! No nukes here!'

I took a few quick snaps of the crowd with my camera, but I found it hard to keep my eyes off Léon in his uniform, coolly efficient as he went about his job. Prowling at the edges of the crowd, watching, digging out the troublemakers like weeds. Isaac had vanished. And the crowd was growing quieter because on the steps of the town hall Mayor Durand stood and addressed them, his powerful tones carrying over their heads as he sought to beguile them down the path of negotiation and debate.

He spoke well, but I did not stop to listen. I had work to do. The grey clouds had lowered a tin lid above our heads, trapping the anger in the town.

The back door of the town hall was locked, of course it was. But this was Serriac. It wasn't Paris, was it? So it was nothing more than an old brass warded lock, a simple basic design that was begging to be picked. They'd spent more money on the ornate brass door-knocker with its floral festoon than on the security lock itself.

I extracted two L-shaped picks from the pouch of tools in my bag, inserted one to slide the bolt across and one to raise the single lever. And *voilà*. A knife through butter. Job done. I slipped inside the building, quietly closed the door behind me and took a look around. I was in a rear vestibule of some sort, closed doors leading off it, a corridor straight ahead. High ceilings and fancy cornices even back here, and a woodblock floor of a silky pale oak that Papa would have loved. I made no sound.

I listened hard.

Silence. Except for the thump of blood through my veins. I could hear no voices, no sound of any kind, because everyone would be crowded out on the street to watch and listen to the events unfolding on their front steps.

Behind them lay an open goal.

Foolish Mayor Durand.

I thought he would know better. He hadn't stopped to

lock his office door. I could picture it. The sudden alarm, blood pressure shooting up to danger zone, a flight-or-fight response. He stayed to fight, needless to say, because that was his job and that was the kind of man Durand was. But he would have heard the shouts and angry chants of the protesters coming closer and experienced a flicker of panic. A door left unlocked.

I pulled on a pair of finest silk gloves, opened it and slipped quickly into the beautiful room once more. The tall windows were half-shuttered to keep out the heat and looked out on to a gravelled garden at the back of the building. It meant the light was low but I would be unobserved.

I moved fast. His black desk was my starting point. I snapped open drawers, one after the other, working at speed, delving, sifting and skip-reading each item. Pushing aside packets of Gitanes, notepads neatly stacked, a wooden ruler, an address book, a list of telephone numbers with no names or indication who they might be, and a shaving kit. A framed photograph of his daughter Marianne, sitting smiling on the back of a carousel horse.

A manila folder of letters. I flipped through them. Letters of complaint about the air base. About the noise of the aircraft. About the *hell-cursed* nuclear bombs. About the American airmen. About the chain-link fences stealing French land. About their guard dogs. About damage to the environment. About the night lights. About the smell.

What smell?

Complaints about complaints.

It was a fat file.

I replaced it and tried the last drawer, bottom right. It was locked. I felt a kick of expectation. He had something to hide. I dropped to my knees on the floor and tweaked the lock with a couple of picks until it obliged, but my expectation hit the dirt because inside lay nothing more exciting than a pistol. Behind it sat a small box of ammunition. I didn't linger but relocked the drawer and sat back on my heels.

Mayor Durand was not a man with nothing to hide, of that I was certain.

The sound of footsteps hurrying down the hall outside sent me leaping to my feet and my pulse hammering in my throat, but they shot past and in the silence that followed I checked the diary on his desk. His secretary was right. He was a busy man. Meetings. Lunches. Telephone calls. All scheduled. But there was nothing that caught my eye. In my time working for the Clarisse Favre Detective Agency in Paris I had come across more than one man with secrets to hide and I wasn't about to give up on this one.

'Think the impossible, Eloïse,' André had told me in his room, his crutches splayed on the floor between us. 'Use your imagination. Think one step beyond.'

One step beyond.

I dropped to my knees again and peered into the well of the desk. The underside was black, tucked away in the dark, unaccustomed to scrutiny by anyone. But I wasn't anyone. I snatched a small torch from my bag, squirmed under the desk and flicked on the beam. I scanned each centimetre of the smooth black surface above my head, craning my neck round to . . .

Smooth?

Not there. That spot. I ran a finger over it and found a small round indentation under my fingertip. I pressed it.

A click. A faint shift above me.

I scrabbled back out, shut down the torch and found that the beaded length of decoration along the top edge of the desk-well had slid forward a fraction. I tugged at it. It glided towards me to reveal a shallow secret drawer the width of the gap. A grin stole on to my face. Secrets, Monsieur le Maire? A man like you always has secrets.

Inside lay four large envelopes. And a thick bundle of American dollars.

I swept the envelopes on to the desk surface, opened each one and removed the sheets of paper from inside. It felt like stepping on a landmine and I trod with care, but one exploded in my face. What I was holding in my hand were the detailed architectural drawings of the American air base, complete with underground tunnels and chambers. And the nuclear silos.

How? How did Durand get his hands on this piece of dynamite?

I laid them flat on the desk and risked popping on the desk-lamp. From my bag I pulled out my camera — a sub-miniature 9mm Minox that fitted into the palm of my hand. Little more than the length of a cigarette and the width of a matchbox, it was a brilliant piece of German technology in a shiny aluminium case. I pulled the ends to extend the case-body and reveal the lens and viewfinder, then got down to business.

Quickly I fired the shutter button. Snapped the camera shut and reopened it ready for the next frame. Simple and efficient, it was expert at photographing documents. The perfect spy camera.

Don't leave home without one.

It took a conscious effort to keep my hand steady. I moved on to the other envelopes, all the time one eye on the door, ears alert for footfalls in the corridor. One envelope contained a bank document from the Banque Nationale pour le Commerce et l'Industrie, but I had no time to stop to read it. I clicked the button on the camera. The next envelope spilled out a glossy photograph of a beautiful naked young woman. I didn't recognise her, but sure as hell she wasn't his wife.

Voices seeped in from the corridor. A man and a woman in urgent conversation, the click of high heels approaching fast.

I snatched the contents from the final envelope, hurrying, fumbling, and out slid a newspaper cutting, yellowing with age and soft as feathers between my fingers. I wanted to stop. To sit. To cradle it in my hands. A picture of two young men in uniforms of the First World War, shoulder to shoulder, rigid. As though waiting to be shot. Above them ran the headline: MURDERERS OR HEROES? 53 MEN DEAD.

The man on the left was a young Father Jerome. The one on the right was my father.

Murderers or heroes? The words swelled inside my head.

I took the photograph just as the high heels stopped right outside the door. I snapped off the lamp, threw three of the envelopes containing their contents back into the secret drawer, the fourth one I pushed into my bag as I watched the door handle start to turn. I ran across the room for the blind spot behind the door so I would be hidden when it opened, but at the last moment the handle was abandoned and Captain Léon Roussel's voice shouted out, '*Vite!* Call Nîmes for more reinforcements.'

Their feet ran down the hallway. I could taste the fear in the building.

The main street of Serriac had lost its mind. Its usual quiet sense of decency and discipline had been steamrollered by a crowd that was out of control. Havoc held sway. The demonstrators had cut loose. Breaking windows. Hurling stones and battling with police.

Whatever it was that Mayor Durand had said to them in his address had failed miserably to hold them and when two fighter jets streaked through the sky like a taunt to the demonstrators they set fire to a street bench in the middle of the road. Two cars were overturned, more shop windows shattered. As if the town were to blame for the nuclear warheads on its doorstep.

Locals struck back. Fights broke out with café seats for weapons, and rage rolled at me like a wave, setting fire to something dark within me that made me want to strike back.

To defend my home. To protect my people. Something tribal and gut-wrenching. I helped a middle-aged woman back on to her feet, her head gashed, and tucked her into a shop for safety, but when I emerged I heard someone shout my name above the noise.

'Eloïse!'

Léon was further down the road by the bank, working with five other officers to corral a section of the crowd. I raised a hand.

'Go home,' he shouted at me, 'get out of here before . . .'

But I didn't hear before what. He moved his group of demonstrators away, slicing them from the body of the crowd. Systematically weakening the collective rage. He looked calm as he issued orders, but I wanted to shout, 'Be careful.'

And Isaac? Where was he?

I searched for his blond head and clambered up on a chair in a shop doorway where an old woman had been dozing before she fled inside. No sign of Isaac. But further down the road was a sight that jerked a moan from my lips. Six men in a circle. Big men, muscles like stevedores, heads thrust forward, threatening a lone figure at the centre of the circle. Wolves on a boar. The figure was no weakling, ready to defend himself with fists up, but he didn't stand a chance.

'No!' I screamed, and threw myself into the crowd, elbows flying.

The lone figure was Mickey, my mechanic from Chicago.

*

I reached Mickey just after the first blow had been thrown. His lip was split, blood spooling down on to his white shirt. At least he'd had the sense not to wear uniform, but he oozed American-ness with his crew-cut and his aftershave and his strong American teeth. His sense of owning the space he stood in. He blended into Serriac's ancient streets as well as a giraffe would.

'Leave him,' I said, and waved an arm around the circle to keep the Marseille men at bay.

A man doesn't hit a woman in public, though the biggest one with fists like meat-cleavers and dense black whiskers looked ready to do so.

'Eloïse!' Mickey exclaimed.

He tried to push me behind him but I stood firm at his side. Mouth dry.

'He has done nothing wrong, nothing to hurt you,' I said to the whiskers.

'He's a fucking Yank. Bringing nuclear bombs to French soil. And you call that *nothing wrong*? Get out of my way, stupid bitch.' He pulled a short metal bar from under his jacket and the circle grew tighter.

The gun at the bottom of my bag was itching to come out.

'Run, Eloïse,' Mickey shouted.

A hand grabbed my shoulder. It was one of the wolves behind me, and I smacked his arm away, but right at that moment a great wave of people came charging into us all, crushing and pushing and pressing us back, as they rushed to escape whatever it was that was coming up the street.

A jet of high-pressure water hit us. Soaking and battering us. Knocking some off their feet. I held tight against Mickey to keep us both upright, but more people backed into us, jostling shoulders, scrabbling to get away, when a great red truck barged its way along the centre of the road. The *brigade des sapeurs-pompiers*. Léon had called in the fire brigade.

Shouts of protest surged around me and I heard Mickey's voice let loose a piercing cry. His arm abruptly clamped around my neck with a harsh grip and I felt his weight drag on me.

'Mickey, let's get out of . . .'

My words jammed on each other. Mickey had released his hold on me and was slowly sliding down to the ground, the fingers of one hand splayed out as they clawed at my sodden dress.

'Mickey.' My voice scraped against my teeth.

The US airman lay sprawled on the slick road on his side, as though he'd had enough of all the fuss and decided to sleep. Eyes closed, mouth slack. I dropped to my knees, hands shuddering as I brushed his wet cheek.

The back of his white shirt was covered in blood.

I think of that moment as a dividing wall. There is what came before. And there is what came after. With that moment standing between them, a wall with death dancing upon it.

I sat in Léon Roussel's office, aware of a dull ache pulsing in me. I'd made a statement. Included the stevedores. Described the one with the black whiskers and the metal bar.

'But you saw nothing?' Léon pressed me.

'No.'

'No one who came too close? Who might have stabbed him?'

'We were all too close. All falling over each other to escape the water.'

'Eloïse, did you see a knife in anyone's hand?'

'No.'

'Are you sure?'

'I'm sure.'

He rose from his seat and came to sit on the front edge of the desk, less than arm's length from me. I could touch his thigh if I reached out. I wanted to touch him to make sure he was real. I had lost faith in my version of reality right now.

'Eloïse.' His voice was gentle but his eyes were a policeman's eyes locked on mine. 'Do you have a knife?'

'No. I have no knife. Mickey was murdered with a knife. Léon, I am not a murderer.'

He seemed to hold his breath and when he finally released it I was aware that in some way we had crossed a line.

'Then let's look at the alternatives,' he said calmly. 'Either he was stabbed by some random attacker just because he was American and anger had spilled over.' He ticked the point off on his fingers. 'Or . . .'

'Or he was targeted for some other reason. By someone who wants to create more serious ill-feeling between the American airmen and locals.'

My voice shocked me. So steady. So controlled. Thick

black shadows were shifting at the back of my mind, edging forward, and it took an effort to think straight.

'I want you to go home, Eloïse. The first time you watch a man die, part of you goes with him.' He eased forward and ran a hand softly down my wet hair. 'Go home to your horses.'

I let the weight of my head rest for a moment in his palm. 'We are at war,' I said, 'but the people of France don't know it.'

'Let's keep it that way. The turmoil and unrest in the factories and on the streets is already more than they can bear. It will take more time than we have to straighten out this chaos.'

'Léon, Serriac is lucky to have you to watch over it.'

'Hah! The American investigators will be down here like a shot, crawling all over the town like locusts to find the attacker. They also know how to look after their own.'

I felt the darkness edge forward. 'Léon.' It came out as a whisper. 'Léon, what if the knife was meant for me, not Mickey? What if in the confusion and chaos the blade found the wrong target?'

He stepped away from the desk and knelt on the floor in front of my chair. 'What if you go back to Paris today? I'll put you on the next train.'

I leaned forward, lowered my head to his shoulder, and felt his arms wrap around my back. He held me tight.

CHAPTER TWENTY-FIVE

I walked into my father's house. I say walked, but what I mean is ran. Out of my car and into the coolness of the gloomy hallway as if my heels were on fire. I'd spent more time looking in my rear-view mirror than at the road ahead on the drive back home.

From outside came the rattle and bang of hammers and shovels and the stink of ash stirred up in the humid air. Men were dismantling the incinerated remains of the stables but inside all was silent. The house felt empty. I headed straight to the dark sideboard in the living room and poured myself a healthy shot of Papa's cognac. I drank it down in two swigs, feeling it burn its way through the ice-cold rage inside me. I was grieving for Mickey, a man I scarcely knew, and I didn't know how to cradle the grief to me, how to rock it in my arms, because it didn't belong to me.

I heard a noise and swung round to find Papa standing in the doorway, his usual black felt hat on his head, black shirt stretched across his bull-chest. His boots were filthy but still on his feet. More floors for Mathilde to clean up.

'Are you all right, Eloïse?'

My father had not asked me if I was all right since Goliath had taken a chunk out of my shoulder blade with his horn when I was running from him at the age of seven. I'd sneaked into his pasture to rescue a fox cub caught in a snare but nothing ever got past that mean sharp-eyed bull. I suddenly recalled that Léon had been the one to patch me up and mop my tears. I'd forgotten that. It was a moment of failure in my father's eyes that I had not cared to dwell on till now.

'I'm okay,' I said.

'You look . . .'

He didn't go further, but his thick brows hunched together and his gaze travelled from the empty glass in my hand to the bottle in my other. In the end it was my clothing he remarked on.

'Is that blood on your dress?'

I looked down. My dress had dried, but the stain that darkened the front of it was unmistakable. He strode into the room, filling up the space, and I could smell the sweet scent of hay on him. Had he been feeding Cosette?

'Where is André?' I asked.

'He has gone to the doctor in Nîmes. For x-rays.'

'Is he worse?'

'He says not. I have to believe him. He tells me little.' His head swayed from side to side, a habit he'd picked up from his bulls. 'Louis drove him in my truck.'

'Papa, I saw a man die today.'

A low curse. 'Who?'

I put down the glass and brandy bottle. 'An American airman in the street in Serriac. There was an anti-nuclear demonstration of workers from Marseille and fights broke out. It was like a . . .' I paused. '. . . a war.'

He turned away. 'You know nothing of war, girl.'

'Papa, please.' I went to him, close enough to see that the sinews at the side of his neck were taut as bowstrings. 'I know about fifty-three people,' I said softly, 'shot in a barn during the First World War.'

He made a sound. A cough. As though he'd been punched in the chest.

'Please, Papa, tell me about it. Tell me what happened and why it's important to Mayor Durand.'

'One of these days I'll kill that bastard,' he growled into his beard.

'Papa, everything is twisted in a maze of lies and secrets that lead me in all the wrong directions. Please, Papa. Talk to me. I need to know what happened.'

'Eloïse, you *need* to know nothing.'

I delved into my bag, pulled out the envelope from Mayor Durand's desk and held it out to my father. For a fleeting second I thought he was not going to take it, but he did and eased out the yellowed newspaper cutting from inside. I heard him inhale, a gust of air. That was all. For two minutes we stood without a word until slowly his voice rumbled up from somewhere deep in his chest.

'It was in the filthy winter at the end of the battle of the Somme in northern France where there was mud in our boots, mud on our teeth, mud in our souls. Jerome and I had got separated from our company one night. We found ourselves on the edge of a village, just a pile of burnt-out ruins, but there was a stone barn still standing. It was full of Boche soldiers in German grey, asleep in the hay, even the guard. Jerome and I shot them all. Fifty-three of them. We counted each one.'

Papa was breathing heavily, mouth open to drag in air. I listened to him in silence, imagining the rifle hot in his hands.

'We were kids,' he said. 'Barely seventeen. We'd watched all our friends slaughtered at our sides, brains or guts blown into the mud by German guns and bombs. When we started shooting in the barn, we couldn't stop. Our fingers kept pulling the trigger, and then we hurled grenades. The smell was terrible.'

He halted, shook his head and looked at me as if he'd never seen me before.

'Somehow Charles Durand got his hands on a cutting from a local newspaper up there. He has been using it for years to blackmail me.'

'Why would anyone blackmail you for shooting the enemy?'

'They weren't the enemy. The bastard Germans had dressed up a bunch of their French prisoners in German army uniforms to make us think that they had more troops in that area.'

My heart tightened for him. 'They were French?'

'Yes.'

'Oh, Papa, how terrible. For you and for Father Jerome. No wonder he turned to the church to find forgiveness.'

He turned his back to me. He rested his hands heavily on the ancient sideboard, still clutching the piece of newspaper between his fingers, and hung his head, reminding me so much of a wounded bull in the arena. 'Jerome was lucky,' he muttered. 'Forgiveness is not easy to come by.'

I moved closer. 'I know,' I said softly.

'Fifty-three Frenchmen's lives.' He stared down at his hands, at his thick-knuckled fingers and the thin gold wedding band as though seeing blood on them.

'It wasn't your fault, Papa.'

'Of course it was my fault. Just like André's injuries are your fault. Facts don't change just because we wish them to.'

'I know,' I said again.

He uttered a guttural sigh, his hefty ribs rising and falling again and again, and said, 'I've never told anyone. Not even your mother. Jerome and I never speak of it. It is my own cross to bear.'

I put out a hand and touched his back, rested my palm gently on his muscular shoulder blade, offering a scrap of comfort. I wanted, this one time, for him to accept my love and not spurn it. Just this once. He didn't move, didn't pull away.

'Did Mayor Durand extract payments from you?' I asked.

'Yes, he did. He knew that I would be tried and sentenced, probably to death if the truth were known.'

I could feel the tremor that shook him. 'Is that why you sold part of our land to the Americans? Because Durand insisted?'

'It is. He was getting a rake-off from them for persuading me to agree to it.'

'Papa, I am so sorry. You should have told me before.'

I stepped right up to my father but still he didn't turn to look me in the face. I leaned my forehead against his broad back and I could smell the bulls and the horses and the rich earth of Mas Caussade on him, not just on his shirt but deep in the marrow of his bones.

'I love you, Papa,' I whispered.

Neither of us moved. For this brief moment we were father and daughter, and I felt a warmth flood into somewhere inside me that had been ice cold.

'Thank you for the newspaper cutting, Eloïse. We will never speak of this again.'

He straightened up and without a glance at me he strode out into the yard where his faithful Juno was waiting to greet him, snuffling her muzzle into his hand. I watched him scratch her slender neck, light one of his filthy cheroots that stained his beard, and take a long look up at André's bedroom window before making for the ruins of the stables.

It is a joy to hold something beautiful in your hands. It possesses a strange power to bring comfort. Is that what Father Jerome feels when he holds the Bible?

In my room – a bare, unloved kind of place – I sat holding two things of beauty. My subminiature camera. And my developing tank. Both created to perfection by the German-Latvian genius called Walter Zapp and marketed under the name Minox. I lined the equipment up neatly on the dressing-table surface and set to work at once. I planned to have the 9mm film developed and dried by the time André returned from the doctor.

I snicked open the elegant little silver camera, removed the tiny cassette of thirty-six frames and placed it in the recess in the glossy black developing tank. The tank itself was a cylinder about half the size of a wine bottle with a screw interior that made it simple to use. Which was just as well, because my hands disengaged from my brain and took over the job smoothly and efficiently. My mind went into freefall. Ripping through my day.

Isaac. My skinny little brother Isaac.

Father Jerome in his black soutane, yearning for Papa's soul.

My fingers turned the drum to engage the film-keyhole, then inverted the tank, pressing firmly into the sealing ring. The tank, with the cassette of film inside, was now sealed and lightproof.

Mayor Durand's office.

The busy clicks of the camera.

The secrets of the US air base laid out like cherries for me to pick.

They flashed bright as fireworks in my head.

Slowly, precisely, my hands screwed the drum anticlockwise down into the black tank.

Papa and Father Jerome in grainy black-and-white. Young soldiers.

Always another war. A Cold War now.

I thought about what that meant for my family as I picked

up the bottle of developing liquid, poured it through a hole in the top and agitated it gently with the thermometer.

Fifty-three bodies in a barn.

What terrible deeds did a war make you do? I thought of the gun in my bag today. What was I capable of to help my country?

To protect my family.

My hands knew what they were doing, even if I didn't. They pumped, they emptied, they washed the film again and again with clean water inside the tank to rid it of all trace of film emulsion.

The placards in the street. A ravenous creature with a thousand legs.

Pouring in fixer. Waiting. Waiting. And while I'm waiting, voices fill my head.

Out! Out! Out!

An iron bar.

Mickey, poor tragic Mickey. You were here to help protect us.

My fingers poured in the wetting agent to prevent drying streaks, while words rose to the surface of my mind like bubbles that had been trapped in my developing tank. Words I'd heard years ago in the mouth of Father Jerome.

'An eye for an eye, and a tooth for a tooth.'

My hand removed the cassette. Unspooled it. Hung the negative up to dry.

Mickey asleep on the wet flagstones with a circular crimson stain like a target drawn on his back.

Léon on his knees. My wet head resting on his shoulder.

Was the knife blade meant for me?

The fireworks in my brain abruptly blacked out. All I saw now was the blood on my dress, and I seized its hem, tore it over my head and threw it in a corner.

There was more to Father Jerome's New Testament quotation that echoed quietly like a distant church bell.

'*Resist not evil.*'

I dialled a Paris number. Let it ring twice, hung up and dialled again. That way she would know it was me.

'*Chérie!*' It was like a gust of Parisian smoke in my ear. 'I was going to ring you this evening.'

Clarisse's silky voice blunted a sharp edge within me. It sounded so real and ordinary that it made me smile, though she couldn't see it. Never did I think I would ever call my boss ordinary.

'Any news on Gilles Bertin?' I asked.

'Some.'

'Good or bad?'

'A mix.'

'Stop sitting on the fence.'

She chuckled, warm, throaty and infectious, so that I laughed too. A sound unfamiliar in my father's house. I stood in the dim light of the hallway, alone in the house, and I hadn't decided whether to be worried or relieved.

'Come on, Clarisse, what have you found out?'

'He's a hard nut to crack, your Gilles.'

'He's not *my* Gilles. And anyway, you are always an expert with the nut-crackers.'

Again the low chuckle. I heard her light a cigarette, and I could almost smell the whisky on her breath though it was only mid-afternoon.

'What have you got?'

She kept me waiting just long enough to start to annoy, then she slipped into professional investigator mode. 'All right. Gilles Bertin was born and raised in Brittany. In Concarneau. Parents were strict Jesuits. Dead now.'

'Jesuits.'

'I know. It fits with Intelligence work.'

'I agree. Both systems of thought can be fanatical about an idea. Anything more?'

'He lives in a smart apartment near the Trocadéro. Keeps a low profile. Works at the Ministry of Defence as an analyst and has a weakness for opera.'

'You're good, Clarisse. I'm impressed.'

She exhaled smoke with satisfaction. 'There's more.'

'Let's have it.'

'He is down in Arles on an assignment to liaise with the USAF at the air base.'

'Liaise on what?'

Another soft chuckle. 'Ah, there you have me, *chérie*. That is for you to find out.'

I frowned at the telephone in my hand. I was disappointed. Clarisse had given me nothing new, despite all her good work. I already knew from André that the MGB Soviets had him embedded in the Ministry of Defence.

'Thanks, Clarisse.'

'I haven't finished.'

I heard a secretive smile in her voice. 'What else?' I asked quickly.

'Gilles Bertin is cousin to your mayor, Charles Durand.'

I let out a whoop of relief that echoed through the empty house.

'Clarisse, I love you.'

I dialled again. This time a local call. It was picked up immediately at the other end.

'Good afternoon. Dumoulin Air Base. Airman Starkey speaking. How may I help you?'

Americans were very polite.

'I wish to speak with Major Joel Dirke, please.'

'That's not possible right now, I'm sorry, ma'am. Would you care to leave a message?'

'Yes, I would. Could you please ask him to telephone Eloïse Caussade.'

I supplied my father's telephone number and was assured my message would be placed in the mail box in the orderly room.

'Thank you very much.'

'My pleasure, ma'am.'

I hung up. Wheels were turning.

Outside, the stink of charred wood had settled in the yard and the air hung thick with grey ash. Papa and four *gardians* were shovelling the blackened remains of the stables into a large trailer, their movements etched with anger as they worked. I donned a scarf over the lower half of my face and picked up a shovel. I laboured alongside them, the work heavy, my muscles protesting. I had grown lazy. Not much call for spadework in Paris, unless it was of the digging-up-dirt-for-clients kind.

When the trailer was piled high with burned debris and hauled away, I brought us all a jug of cold lemonade and just for a fleeting moment it was like old times. Sharing a drink and a joke. The sense of a job done. The fond camaraderie that is the mark of Camargue farmers. I had missed it. I cleaned up, changed into fresh shirt and trousers, then went to tend to Cosette.

I was exercising her inside the large barn, leading her on a rein at a slow pace to ease her back into action and watching how much weight she could place on her right foreleg, when I heard the engine. Cosette whickered a greeting and pricked her snowy ears. She knew the sound as well as I did. Papa's truck.

I gave him fifteen minutes. That was all.

Enough time to get himself inside the house on his crutches. I didn't watch. Enough time to settle himself. Then I kissed Cosette's cheek and crossed the yard to the house.

'Hello, André. How did it go at the hospital?'

'All good, thanks.'

He didn't look good. He looked as if the doctors had drained the blood out of him. Pale, white-lipped, and a sheen on his skin that sent a chill through me. He was stretched out on his bed and I wanted to straighten out his legs for him but knew he would hate it. Every time I looked at his crooked legs, every single time, I saw the van slamming into us in Paris. I saw strings of blood.

But the moment I walked into the room, his eyes brightened, gleaming with expectation. I was his eyes and ears. I was his legs.

'What did the doctors say?' I asked, taking up my usual place on the chair. The very fact that I now had a *usual* place in his room made me smile.

'To hell with the x-rays.' He saw my expression and added, 'Okay, they were fine. No change.'

'Will they operate again?'

He mumbled something.

'Will they, André?'

'Maybe.'

'What does that mean?'

'You don't give up, do you?'

'No. I learned from a master.'

He laughed. I'd made him laugh.

'So, will they?' I asked again.

'They want to. They think they can improve my mobility.'

'That is wonderful news, André. Why don't you agree to it straight away?'

He gave me a long look from his perceptive amber eyes and we both knew why. If he underwent the operation he'd be out of action for weeks.

'André, have the operation,' I urged quietly. 'I'll do your running for you.'

He grinned at me. 'Run and get me a glass of something, will you?'

'Don't change the subject.'

'Please. Then tell me your day.'

'On condition.'

'On condition of what?'

'You have the operation.'

He laughed again, flashing his lion teeth at me.

CHAPTER TWENTY-SIX

'Who? Who?'

I listened to André murmuring that one word over and over.

'Who leaked this material from Dumoulin Air Base?'

He was holding my Minox magnifying viewfinder close to his eye and hovering over the strip of tiny negative film I'd developed.

'What if,' I said when he'd studied every frame in detail, 'what if it was Mickey?'

'Mickey the murdered airman? You mean he might be the leak?'

'It's possible, isn't it? And it would explain why someone might have wanted him dead. And why he came into town.'

'What was his work in the air force?'

'A mechanic. His full name was Michael Ashton. Senior Master Sergeant Michael Ashton. I admit I don't know how he'd have got hold of the detailed drawing of the airfield.'

André was intense now. Focused on work in a way I hadn't

seen before, but finally he placed the film and viewfinder down on the bedside table, picked up his wine glass and raised it to me.

'You did well, Eloïse.'

How many times had I wanted to hear those words, but now that he said them, I felt no warm glow, no sense of success. I hadn't done well. Mickey had died. I wanted to believe he was the Intelligence leak because it gave a reason for his murder. Clanging like a death-knell at the back of my mind was the fear that he'd died because he'd been with me at the dance last night. Just as André almost died when he was with me in Paris.

I'd sat in the bedside chair and described to him my day in Serriac. Kept it brief, and emotionless, and at the end I'd endured his scrutiny without a flicker.

'Is that all of it?' he asked.

'Yes. Isn't that enough for one day?'

He nodded. I don't know whether he believed me. I don't know whether he knew I was lying. I had made no mention of my talk in the church with Father Jerome. That was André's business, not mine, if he chose to seek strength from God on a Sunday. But neither had I mentioned the old newspaper cutting of Papa. I'm not sure why. In some way I didn't totally understand, I felt it was private business between Papa and me, but I offered something else to keep André's nose from sniffing out my lie.

'I've discovered that Gilles Bertin is Mayor Durand's cousin.'

He made no sound. But he threw back the rest of his wine

and a streak of crimson flared on his cheek. 'Is that a fact? You surprise me.'

'It could be that Mayor Durand is being fed information by someone from the air base which he passes on to his cousin – who just happens to be an MGB agent – for a big fat fee.'

Again no sound from André.

I pressed on. 'Which explains the nice little mountain of American dollars in his secret drawer.'

Very slowly my brother nodded.

'André, we have to report this to the police.'

'What?' He stared at me as if I had suggested drowning Juno, my father's dog.

'We cannot allow a traitor to France to continue as Mayor of Serriac. We must inform Léon Roussel at once.'

He reached over and took my hand in his. 'No.'

'Yes, André. We can't turn a blind eye to—'

He squeezed my hand. 'Listen to me, Eloïse, listen hard. My network is acutely aware that there is an agent inside the air base, feeding information to the MGB. Some of it is critical Intelligence information like the technical details of the Nike Ajax missile system which they are thinking of installing at Dumoulin. It's the world's first surface-to-air missile. An invention of technical genius. Designed to attack subsonic aircraft at high altitude and intended to defend key strategic points against Soviet bombers.'

'How do you know all this?'

He sighed, impatient. 'It's my job to know all this. The

point is that someone has been leaking top-secret information from that air base for some time. It's why I used to come back here from Paris every weekend. To dig around. To listen to rumours. To mix with the American airmen in the bars and cafés on a Saturday night. You and I have to find out who that leak is.'

'Not Mickey. Surely not Mickey. He was too . . .'

'Ordinary?'

I nodded.

André released my hand. 'I've told you before, Eloïse. In this business you must think the impossible.'

I heard the sound of footsteps crossing the yard. Approaching through the semi-darkness. It was twilight, the sky a peony-pink in the west, wisps of chalky mist creeping into corners. The cicadas were in full voice and an owl was calling from the tree under which Goliath lay, a soft ghostly echo of his voice.

I was jumpy. For good reason. A man next to me got knifed today. I was in the barn now grooming Cosette with sweeping strokes along the length of her withers and back, and over the powerful white curve of her well-muscled flank. I rested my forehead against her stocky neck and inhaled the strong sweet scent of her hide. She was a horse who loved to be groomed and lifted her leg obligingly, huffing contentedly. I was checking her wound and looking for any cuts or nicks on her knees and pasterns when I caught the sound of boots on the cobbles. But it was a footfall I knew well.

'Eloïse!'

'Papa?'

'Telephone call for you.'

I put down my brush, gentled Cosette's soft muzzle and raced indoors.

'Hello?' I could feel a pulse ticking at my throat.

'Eloïse? It's Major Joel Dirke here. You left a message for me to call.'

'Thank you for calling back, Major. Sorry to disturb your Sunday evening.'

'Not at all. What can I do for you? Things are a bit crazy round here at the moment because of . . .' He paused awkwardly. 'I don't know if you've heard.'

'About Mickey Ashton.' It hurt to say his name. 'Yes, I was in Serriac today.'

'Really? Maybe you're one of the people we should be interviewing.'

A ripple of alarm shot through me. 'I have already been interviewed by the police and made a statement.'

'Good. Thank you. We'll be taking over the investigation and going through them all.' Another pause. I didn't jump into it. 'I'm sorry,' he continued with his soft Southern voice, 'it must have been . . . harrowing.'

'Harrowing. Yes, you've found exactly the right word.' I placed a hand hard on my throat to stop the pulse. 'But that's not why I rang you. I was feeding my horse earlier and remembered what you said about missing the horses on your father's ranch.' I ran my tongue over my dry teeth.

'I wondered whether you'd like to come over and go for a horse-ride some time. It's beautiful scenery round here.'

'I'd love to, thank you. That would be mighty fine.'

'Good.'

'When were you thinking of?'

'Tomorrow?'

'I'm on duty tomorrow, I'm sorry. The day after? I have the afternoon off.'

'That suits me. About three o'clock when it won't be so hot?'

'Perfect. Thanks for the invitation. I look forward to it.'

'See you then.'

I put down the phone, the black Bakelite covered in my sweat. Horses are better than people. They don't lie. They don't pretend. They just kick you in the teeth if they don't like you.

CHAPTER TWENTY-SEVEN

LÉON ROUSSEL

The American captain left. At last. At long bloody last.

Léon immediately dumped the mountain of Lucky Strike butts spilling out of his ashtray into the trash and yelled to Feroulet in the outer office for coffee. He threw himself back into his desk chair, fighting the urge to grab a paintbrush and daub a sign on the outside of his door: AMERICANS ENTER HERE AT THEIR PERIL.

Maybe not. Given that one just got murdered in his town.

But Captain Doug Prendergast from the 1606th Air Group of the USAF was not the easiest of investigators to work with. Léon set about pile-driving his way through more of the hundreds of witness statements stacked in front of him. Despite the late hour – 21:40 – he still felt the pulse of raw energy through his veins.

He took it personally. This murder. It was his job to protect the inhabitants of Serriac from any marauding criminals, a job he loved with a passion and which he viewed as a trust. Even if it only meant digging into who had been stealing the fruit from Madame Daudier's orchard of apricot trees or smacking a few heads together in a dispute over tractors. Settling a drunken brawl or tracking down a burglar. These were his people and he had failed them today. When he thought about how easily that knife could have slid between Eloïse Caussard's slender ribs a shudder wracked him.

Adjutant Feroulet hurried in with coffee, black and bitter as the murderer's heart. The way Léon liked it.

'Go,' Léon said, and waved a dismissive hand. 'Get your jacket and go home. It's been a long day.'

'Sir, I can check through more of the statements before I leave.'

'Go home. You have a new baby. Get back there before your pretty wife runs off with her lover.'

Feroulet was young and his wife was very beautiful. For five seconds he looked alarmed, but then laughed and shook his head. 'She likes my uniform.'

'And your gun, no doubt.'

His coffee-carrier was a good officer but still green enough to flush at the tease. He muttered a quick 'Goodnight, sir,' and shot out of the door. For the next hour Léon buried himself in paperwork until he suddenly picked up yet again Eloïse Caussade's statement. He read it through three times, picturing her saying the words, and then reached for his car keys.

*

221

There were still lights on downstairs in the Mas Caussade. That didn't surprise him. What did surprise him was the lone figure that his Citroën's headlights picked out in the yard. Even in the darkness, he knew it was Eloïse.

He recognised her slight figure in the way she cocked her head like a cat listening intently. She had clambered up on top of an empty flatbed trailer and seemed to be sitting cross-legged, staring out towards the marshes. As his car approached, exposing her in its yellow beam, she jumped to her feet and looked ready to flee. But at the last moment she changed her mind and raised a hand in greeting. Léon felt a dull ache that made him want to wrap his arms around her and run for the hills. The Caussade men had always carved out a rough path for Eloïse Caussade.

When he turned off the engine, darkness came down like a blackout curtain and he reached into his glove compartment for a torch. By the time he climbed out of the car she was at his side.

'Léon, what are you doing here?' she asked. 'Is something wrong?'

He flicked on his torch, directing it on to the cobbles. Her dark hair was tied back off her face and the light skidded along her scar, shiny as a cat's eyes.

'I came to make sure you're okay. Today was tough on you and I was worried. I realise it's late.'

'You still working?'

'I was, but I needed a drive to clear the fog from my mind.'

'Thank you, Léon.'

He didn't want thanks.

'Shouldn't you be safe indoors?'

'I'm thinking about Mickey, the airman. Does his family know?'

'Yes. They've been informed.'

She slid her arm through his, her shoulder brushing close, and led him over to the flatbed. She swung up on to it with ease, and he joined her. They sat down side by side, her knees tucked under her chin, and for some time they sat in silence, listening to the chirrups and rustles of the night, feeling the flutter of moths' wings and a breeze fingering their skin.

'How are you?' he asked when their heartbeats were quiet. The torch was switched off.

She laughed softly. 'Probably not as bad as you.' For no more than a breath or two she dropped her cheek on his shoulder. 'Now, Léon, tell me why you're really here. I'm certain you've had a terrible time in town, clearing up the mess and keeping a polite tongue in your head for the American investigator. Fending off irate residents and inter-viewing angry demonstrators must have taken its toll.'

'It's my job, Eloïse. That's what I'm paid to do.'

'I know. But I can see it's much more than a job to you.' He felt her lean close, sensed her warm lips barely brush his cheek, her breath silky on his neck, sending its nerves into a frenzy. 'So why have you dropped whatever it was you were doing to come out and sit on a trailer on a starless night with me?' Her lips touched his ear, then vanished.

She was right, of course. She could read him so well even in the dark. He edged his shoulder away from hers, because if he didn't he would stay sitting like that all night and never tell her.

'I interviewed Isaac.'

Her face snapped round to face him, a paler oval of darkness. 'What did he say?'

'The usual. The end of the world is nigh and only the Communist Party can save it. The American capitalist system is designed by the rich for the rich. You know the party line.'

He felt rather than saw her nod. 'Come on, Léon, let me hear whatever it is you've come to tell me. I promise I won't swoon or bite your head off.'

'He tells me there are Intelligence leaks coming from the air base.'

She didn't react.

'And that there are rumours flying around.'

'What kind of rumours?'

'The kind your MGB friend might be here for.'

'He's not my friend.'

Léon waited for her feathers to settle. 'Rumours that are coming from a leak at the Dumoulin base and are getting the Communist devotees all hot under the collar.'

She smacked his knee. 'Tell me.'

'That the American aircraft industry is developing a nuclear plane. Not one that just carries nuclear attack weaponry. One that is powered by nuclear energy. One that Isaac claims is being rushed through its top-secret prototype stage in America far too quickly because they want to bring it to Europe. To our base here at Dumoulin. And if one ever crashes on landing or is shot down, God help us all.'

She gave a low whistle that seemed to attract some wild creature because an instant bark responded from the darkness. She slapped away a mosquito with more vehemence than necessary.

'So that's why he's here,' she muttered under her breath.

'Isaac?'

'No. My MGB Soviet agent *friend*.'

'Mickey Ashton could have been his contact.' Her intake of breath was so soft he almost missed it. 'But we have no proof that he was the leak.'

'None at all. And I didn't spot Gilles Bertin in Serriac today. Oh, Léon, so many secrets. So many things I wish I could tell you.'

'Then do so.'

'I can't.'

Fear for her uncurled in Léon's guts. 'That's the trouble with espionage, Eloïse. It builds barriers around you, it cages you alone with only your secrets for company. Is that what you want?'

Hell, he didn't want to hurt her. But neither did he want her locked in a cage of André's making. She was too wild for that. Yet she had spent her life helping her brother to knock in the bars that surrounded her. He wrapped his arm around her shoulders, aware of each slender bone of her, of the night sounds shuffling closer, snuffling and whispering.

She raised a hand to his face, her fingertips brushing, touching, exploring each of his features in the darkness and lingering on his lips. He felt desire for her burn through him as he kissed her soft mouth, heard her whispered moan. She tasted of salt marshes and raw nerves and a hunger so strong it stopped his heartbeat.

'Eloïse,' he murmured.

'What?'

She eased back a fraction, but he was still conscious of her breath on his skin.

'Don't do this,' he said.

She picked up the torch and flicked it on. By the patchy light of its beam he could see her eyes were huge and her mouth was curved on the edge of a laugh.

'Don't do *this*?' She brushed the back of her hand along his jaw.

Stop.

But the word refused to come out of his mouth. He took hold of her wrist and drew her hand away, but his fingers wouldn't release it.

'Don't continue your involvement in André's secrets. It's dangerous and you are not trained for it.' The thought tightened a hard knot in him. 'I worry about you.'

She grew still. She didn't remove her hand but used it to raise his hand to her lips. She kissed his knuckle. 'I owe André,' she said in a low tone. 'I owe André his legs. And I won't rest till I find the person who did this to him.'

There it was. Nothing he could say would change it.

He knew her. Knew that tone. Whether she was hanging from a tree branch or hunting down a murderer, she would never let go.

Léon drew her to him, holding her close. 'Then let me help you.'

CHAPTER TWENTY-EIGHT

'You know what a DLD is?'

'Of course. A dead letter drop.' I looked at André. He was wound up. I'd felt the tension the moment he'd pushed open my door.

'That's right.' He smiled approvingly, assessing my mood. 'I want you to execute one today.'

It was early morning and yesterday's clouds had sloped off to the west, leaving a naked blue sky that promised the heat would build fast. André was propped against the door-frame, wearing his workman's clothes, a rough collarless shirt and neckerchief, though he was no longer a workman. I noticed he was wearing boots for the first time instead of soft shoes. Was he planning on going somewhere? Or was he just clinging to the world he'd lost?

'Ready?' he asked.

'Of course. Where is it to take place?'

'In Arles. I've drawn you a map. Memorise it, then burn it.'

'What am I dropping?'

'The film you developed.'

'And who will pick it up?'

'No need for you to know anything other than it will be a CIA agent pick-up. When you've completed the DLD, don't hang about. Keep walking.'

'But why would the CIA want that film? Surely they already possess that information.'

He smiled with a small tolerant sigh. 'Because they need to know exactly which document was copied. They will narrow the field by working out how many on the air base had access to it.'

I nodded. Of course. André took hold of his crutches and swung himself across the room to stand right in front of me.

'Eloïse.'

He ducked his head to peer at my face more closely with a gentle expression. 'What's the matter? Are you nervous?'

'No,' I lied.

He took one arm off a crutch, leaving it tucked under his armpit, and rested a hand on my shoulder, the way he used to do with all our gang of followers as children, marking each one of us as his own. Like a brand on a bull calf. I could feel the strength of him through the thin material of my blouse.

'You'll complete the DLD with ease,' he said generously. 'Take care. Keep your eyes open. Come back home immediately. I'll be waiting.' He placed a sheet of paper and a brown envelope in my hands, and patted my shoulder. 'Don't let me down, will you?'

'No.'

'I'm trusting you.'

I never thought to hear those words again from my brother.

He smiled and shook his mane of hair from his eyes. 'You are my legs.'

I placed my hand on top of his on my shoulder and for a moment our Caussade bones fused. 'I won't let you down, don't worry.'

He turned and swung himself to the door. He manoeuvred the crutches like an extension of himself now and I could see the muscles of his back bunching under his shirt. At the door he threw me a look that I couldn't read and issued one final instruction.

'Take the gun. Just in case.'

As soon as André was gone, I inspected the envelope. It was sealed. Plain, brown, and with no writing on the front. It looked like one of Papa's envelopes from his bureau downstairs.

The sheet of paper he'd handed me was an instruction sheet telling me where and what the drop location was in Arles. I memorised it and then did as André ordered, burned it. In a glass trinket dish that used to belong to my mother.

So far, so obedient.

I crushed the warm ash with my finger tip, so that none of it was readable if someone tried. When it was nothing but powder, I hurried downstairs to Papa's bureau in the dining room that we rarely used, preferring to eat in the sprawling kitchen most days. The bureau was locked. It was a heavy mahogany piece with fancy brass handles and a brass lock that looked more forbidding than it was. It took me all of two minutes to make it oblige and no more than another minute to remove a brown envelope from the pile inside and lock it once more. By the time I entered my room again I'd been gone five minutes maximum.

I shot the bolt. Yes, I'd screwed on a bolt. Two in fact, top and bottom. They wouldn't keep out an axe murderer but they might gain me vital minutes to escape. In this case, they gained me the privacy I required.

I ripped open the sealed envelope André had given me and removed its contents. Two items tipped on to my bed. The developed film in a clear protective film wallet was one, a half-sheet of paper folded over tight was the other. Without a qualm I unfolded the paper to read its contents and felt a rush of exhilaration when I saw what was printed there in André's black ink. The thrill of the chase sent a bolt of excitement scrambling up my spine. It was like old times. Except I had far more to lose now.

359 20 10	229 13 4	1261 14 14	828 17 5
378 5 11	8 3 8	1261 1 5	1117 14 7
55 20 6		216 19 2	1261 7 11
784 9 1		48 1 8	289 16 5
1117 20 2		213 5 1	145 2 3
		571 32 3	358 35 6
		671 1 8	

853 5 1	299 5 1	25 6 4
1093 30 8	8 6 8	175 1 1
1093 35 9	75 33 13	415 24 2
69 3 3	303 5 5	1063 3 1
	774 35 1	1192 3 11
	471 3 7	

It was a code.

I smiled as I ran my finger along the columns of numbers. My old friends. The days when you can outwit me at this, André, are long gone. I dived under my bed, drew out my smart Parisian suitcase, unlocked it and removed from under a copy of *Paris Match* my battered old copy of Victor Hugo's *Les Misérables*. I flipped through the book, tracking down each page number, followed by the line number, followed by the word number. The first one was page 359, line 20, 10th word along. This turned out to be 'fields'. I wrote down its first letter in my notebook – F.

A simple code, if you possess the book that is the key to it. I possessed it, of course I did. With one ear cocked for any sound of André's crutches, I continued along every row of numbers until I had tracked down each of the first letters of the words and I ended up with thirty-five letters. When laid out in order they made up seven words:

FOUND IN DURANDS OFFICE

NEED HIGHER PRICE

I read it through twice and twice more, my brain latching tight as a leech on to the last three words. 'Need Higher Price'.

For whom?

For Durand?

For the source of the leak?

I made myself think the impossible, just as my brother had told me.

A higher price for André?

I reached under my bed a second time, pulled out my suitcase again and sat down beside it. From inside I extracted my magnifying viewfinder. I felt foolish, not quite sure why I was doing this. Both André and I had examined the film negative minutely, but there was something stuck in my mind, something that I couldn't shake off.

I laid out the strip of film, bent over it with the viewfinder screwed to my eye and started again scouring each face in the pictures I'd taken of the street in Serriac yesterday. A jumble of heads. Of backs and arms. Faces with mouths open, frozen into silence.

Where? Where was it?

The something that had caught like a fishhook in my mind.

It took me ten minutes to find it, and when I did, I knew who had killed Mickey. I felt my next breath catch in my throat and I wanted to reach into the tiny square of celluloid and tear out the person in it. Put a match to it. Watch him burn in hell.

I peered closer, my mouth dry. The face was obscured by

a placard declaring NO TO NUCLEAR BOMBS. But his thick head of hair showed clearly, white as snow in the negative. And the eyebrows were evident. Spiky and unmistakable.

The last time I'd seen him was at the hospital in Paris and he'd almost ripped my face off. It was Gilles Bertin's sidekick. Maurice Piquet. The one who liked to hurt.

The heart of the town of Arles is marked with blood. Today I could almost smell it on the hot and humid air that drifted up from the river. Violence and slaughter are etched into its stones, because towering over the twisting narrow street and casting a great shadow of darkness is one of France's most magnificent Roman amphitheatres, where men, women, children and animals were killed for sport.

This was where I was headed. I parked up on the main road, the Boulevard des Lices. On a Saturday it would be heaving with the finest open-air market in all of Provence, the scents of exotic spices and local cheeses and live poultry drawing crowds to pick and poke among the colourful stalls. But today it was quiet, just the usual Monday morning workers and delivery vans. The summer's tourists were still taking it easy over coffee and croissants, not interested in one extra grey Citroën 2CV nipping into the shade under one of the placid trees that lined the road.

I took a roundabout route on foot. Now and again I stopped and lingered in a shop doorway, seemingly to examine some item of interest. But the only interest I had was in watching who or what was moving in the street. A woman weighted down by bulging hessian shopping bags. A waiter scurrying with a bottle of champagne in his hand. A black-robed priest and nun deep in conversation. A child who regarded my scar with interest. An old dog already too hot to growl at a stranger.

No one whose face I knew.

André was right. I was nervous. No reason to be. Was there? I was just delivering a letter, but my heart didn't get that message. It was kicking against my ribs like a jackhammer, until the moment when I spilled out of the maze of cramped streets and emerged from the Rue des Arènes into the wide-open space where the ancient Roman amphitheatre reared up in all its monolithic glory. Every time – every single time – it had the power to reduce me to tears.

I strolled along the raised road opposite the arena and slid into a seat in one of the pavement cafés as if I had no particular aim and all the time in the world. A few tourists ambled past, popping in and out of the souvenir shops, but no one glanced my way. The amphitheatre was the main attraction.

I ordered a pastis, despite the early hour. I liked the milky soft yellow liquid and sipped it slowly while I inspected my surroundings. I had a good view from up here on the raised road. It ran alongside a section of the amphitheatre and I watched every person who strolled past or who stood gawping at the massive stone construction opposite. I studied them. Committed their details to memory. So I would know them again.

I was calm now. The jitters gone. This was the kind of work I'd done a hundred times for Clarisse in Paris. Observation. Patience. Timing. Action. Retreat. But when I worked for Clarisse a life was not at stake. It was the Roman amphitheatre that had brought a sense of perspective into my mind. Each time I came near it I felt the hairs on my arms rise, it was so awe-inspiring. It was a two-tiered gigantic stone construction 140 metres long, with seating for over twenty thousand screaming spectators, adorned by one hundred and twenty exquisite arches, plus three towers as a medieval add-on.

It was a place built for death. Death and chariot races. And now used for bull 'games'. Was it all the dead souls within its arena that gave it its power? Was it sitting there in the sun, waiting for more?

I lingered over my pastis. An hour later when I was ready, I stood, tossed a few coins on the table and proceeded to circle around the outer wall of the amphitheatre until I was satisfied no one was on my tail. When I came to the opening of an insignificant little street with a stone urn at its entrance and a metal grille over the first window, I knew I was on the right track. The street was in deep shade and shutters were closed. No eyes to see what they shouldn't see, no tongues to tell what they shouldn't tell.

Halfway down on the right-hand side stood a wide drain-pipe, black and rusty. Its upper part had been hacked off, so that it ended at waist height, capped off with a metal lid. As I passed it, I lifted the lid – it needed a good yank – and dropped the brown envelope containing the negative inside the pipe. I caught a glimpse of a cylinder within.

Lid back on, I was off down the street. It had taken precisely five seconds.

I was tempted to stay. To watch. To see who came. But I was certain that I would wait in vain. Nobody would come while I was anywhere near the DLD and it was a spot well chosen, because I didn't stand a chance of watching over the small street without being observed myself.

I walked in circles through the streets of Arles, switching back on myself, at times darting off at odd angles, or taking back alleyways that led me past waste bins and under strings of washing. When I was sure that no one was following me, absolutely hand-on-Bible certain, I picked up my pace and swung back to the Place du Forum. From there I dodged through the little crowd of tourists that always hung around the cafés with their yellow awnings and turned the corner, down towards the river.

No mist today. Except the mist of deceit.

I found the street with no problem. And the house. The one where the green and white Chevrolet had parked on a patch of dirt and I'd watched my brother under cover of darkness. André claimed he had persuaded the MGB agent that he was more use to them alive than dead.

More use to them how? What did you agree to do, André?

And how come I got a gun in my face each time I entered your room unannounced? But not Gilles Bertin. How come you didn't pull the trigger instead of riding off in his car? Tell me, André.

A scrawny ginger cat was lounging in a shady spot, seeking refuge from the relentless heat, and as I reached the doorway where I'd hidden that night, my body reacted. With a mind of its own. It recalled the person who had sheltered there with me, the feel of his shoulder under my cheek and his whispered breath on my ear. His concern for me like a third person squeezed in there with us. And as I passed the innocuous-looking doorway an unexpected heat rose in my chest.

Let me help you.

Léon's words last night. The night sky was witness to them. In the dark I had wrapped an arm around his neck and kissed his warm mouth.

The street was not as quiet as I'd expected now, so to gain time I bent and stroked the mangy little fleabag of a cat, which set it purring as loud as a tank. But as soon as there was a brief lull in activity in the street I moved over to the door of the house into which André and his companion had disappeared.

I knocked on the door, only once. No response. Part of me was disappointed. That part of me wanted a good long talk with Monsieur MGB. But the other part was pleased. It wanted a private snoop while the coast was clear.

I pulled out my lock-picks.

CHAPTER TWENTY-NINE

I slid a hand into the side pocket of the man's jacket hanging in the wardrobe.

A small cry of pain escaped me. I swore and snatched it back out fast. It felt as though my fingertips had been ripped by a ferret's teeth and when I looked I saw blood.

'Bastard,' I hissed at the suit.

It was charcoal grey with a faint stripe, exquisitely tailored, with a transparent cover over the shoulders to keep off the dust. This was a meticulous man. I twisted a handkerchief around my scarlet fingertips and with the other hand opened up the pocket so that I could peer inside. With care I extracted the contents. It was a wine cork with two razor blades embedded in it. What kind of person carried a weapon like that around? Or was it just to deter pickpockets?

Or perhaps ... I licked my lips ... perhaps he knew I was coming.

*

Opening drawers and cupboards, unlocking his suitcase and sticking a suspicious finger into cigarette packets.

'Come on, Gilles Bertin, you can't hide forever.'

I rummaged through a waste bin. I stirred the contents of his sugar packet and prodded his coffee beans for anything hidden inside. I upended the seat cushions on his sofa. I crawled under his bed. I peeled back the inner soles of his shoes.

Nothing.

Oh so careful, Gilles Bertin.

That was when I put my fingers in his jacket pocket. The tips of two were neatly slit open. Yet when I searched the rest of the suit, it had nothing to hide. A nasty trick, Gilles Bertin.

The house was pleasant enough, two storeys, tiled floors, plain unobtrusive furniture. But the wardrobe scared me because alongside the jacket with its secret weapon hung four Galeries Lafayette shirts, two black, two white, identical size and style, all normal enough so far. And then one navy-blue shirt. Cheap cotton. Two sizes larger.

It belonged to someone else. And I could only think of one someone else. A man with pale skin and spiky black eyebrows in a straight line above a large nose. Eyes cold as stone. A man whose name was Maurice Piquet, the bastard who'd wanted to rip my cheek off in the hospital. I slammed shut the wardrobe door.

Hurry.

I raced through the rest of my search. Under the mattress,

inside the pillowcase. Behind two boring pictures on the wall. A quick check on the underside of seats and tables. In the oven. The bathroom cabinet. Inside the high lavatory cistern and at full stretch I managed to squeeze a hand behind it.

An envelope slid into my hand.

Dislodged from its hiding place behind the cistern. For a second I stared at it, stupefied. Caught by surprise. Like I was caught by surprise by a grey van one night in Paris. I had a bright red flashback of memory to the strings of blood smacking me in the face as I spun upside down in my car. I blinked hard and wished that just for once my memory would tell me lies.

I slumped down on the closed toilet seat and with no warning my body suddenly ached for Léon. To have him here. Beside me. His grey eyes calm. I murmured his name, like honey on my tongue, and then I removed the contents of the envelope.

A bunch of photographs fell on to my lap. Images of aircraft. Landing. Taking off. Taxiing. Fighters parked on the apron. All at Dumoulin Air Base and I had to stifle a whoop of success. On the back of each was written the date and the name of the aircraft: Boeing B-50, F-84 Thunderjet, C-47 Skytrain. Singly and in formation. All taken in the last week with a long lens. I scooped out my Minox camera from my bag and as I set about photographing each one I had a sense of a suffocating fog starting to lift. A light flickered ahead for the first time because in my hand I was cradling proof that

Gilles Bertin was gathering Intelligence information for his Soviet masters.

I would go to Léon with it. He would know who to contact. Gilles Bertin would go to prison, where he would be guillotined as a traitor. André would be safe. It would be the end.

My mind clutched on tight to that thought and a bubble of relief began to rise in my chest. I thrust the photographs back in their hiding place and took one last look in each room to see if I'd missed anything.

Afterwards, I wished I hadn't.

His bed was not flat against the wall. I'd not noticed it before. The wooden bedhead was at a slight angle as though someone had reached behind it. I could have walked out. I should have walked out. Bertin – or, worse, Piquet – might return at any moment and I needed to get away from there fast.

But it was too tempting. I hurried over and yanked the bed away from the wall to see behind it. Taped to the back of the bedhead was a black leather-zipped pouch. A voice in my head told me to back off, to leave it there. *Walk away. Don't touch.*

Don't jump that fence.

Don't climb that roof.

Don't take that risk.

Don't break into a mayor's desk.

Since when had I listened to that voice?

I snatched the pouch from its position and unzipped it. I

felt a twinge of disappointment. Inside lay more photographs and I lifted them out. At least fifty. But these were not of bombers and fighters or anti–aircraft guns.

These were all of me.

I stared at myself spread out on the floor. Fifty of me. Time took an odd lurch and I wanted to rewind it, to put it back where it belonged. I couldn't tell whether it was fear or anger that curdled in my stomach.

There were pictures of me going about my life unawares. Images of me entering the police station with a basket of eggs for Léon, of me perched on the fountain watching the protest march in Serriac, of me striding out of the church with a keen sense of purpose. Me with a scarf over the lower half of my face shovelling the burnt remains of the stables. Me walking Cosette across the yard. And worst of all: me kneeling with blood on my hands and a face twisted by grief beside the body of Mickey in the street.

Me. Again and again.

A darkness spread across the back of my mind. How dare he? How dare Gilles Bertin invade every moment of my life?

The close-ups were the worst. My eyes. My scar. My hair. My mouth. I wanted to tear them into a thousand pieces. Too intimate. Too private. Too intense.

Why? Why all these images of me?

Time abruptly clicked back into place and I bundled up

all the photographs into a neat pile, hands jittering. I swore long and loud, then put everything back the way I'd found it and left the house with a sense of relief. Like coming up for air.

Outside, the sky loomed huge and spectacularly blue over the town of Arles, but in my head lay a darkness I couldn't shift.

'Eloïse.'

The voice stunned me. I whipped round.

'Clarisse!'

My boss was sitting, legs elegantly crossed, at a pavement café I had just passed, wearing a stylish lilac dress and very dark sunglasses. Cigarette in one hand, glass in the other, she looked like an exotic bird of paradise in a chicken coop. She was beaming at me, looking pleased with herself.

'Clarisse, what on earth are you doing in Arles?'

'I've been worried about you, so I popped down. God, you look grim, *chérie*, and what is that gruesome peasant attire you are wearing?'

I laughed and kissed her on both cheeks. 'It's so good to see you, boss.'

She swept me on to a chair next to hers and demanded an immediate coffee and cognac from an overawed waiter.

'What the devil have you been doing down here, *chérie*? You look as if you haven't slept since you left Paris.'

'That's because I'm missing being bossed around by you.'

She chuckled and a corner of it trickled into me, slowing my pulse.

'You, on the other hand,' I said, 'are a treat to look at and I hope you aren't rushing back to Paris. You can stay at the farm if you like.'

She pulled a horrified face, the kind of face that showed her age. 'Eloïse, I would rather tear out my eyelashes than sleep with bulls.' She fanned her cheeks with diva distress. 'No, my sweet, I am booked into the Hôtel Jules César on Boulevard des Lices, so that I don't have to step over cowpats at breakfast.'

My drink arrived. I skipped the coffee and went straight for the cognac. Clarisse watched me. When I replaced the empty glass, she nodded.

'You needed that.'

'I did.'

The heat inside helped. It steadied my hand. The amber liquid was melting the frozen image of the photographs spread out on the floor. My eyes scoured the street for a camera, but I saw none. That meant nothing.

'A bit jumpy, *chérie*?'

'What have you found out, Clarisse, that brings you scuttling down to the land of bulls and mosquitoes the size of a hand-grenade?'

She gave a mock shudder and drew hard on her cigarette. 'I came to help you.'

'I know,' I said softly. 'I'm grateful.' I squeezed her hand because I knew she wouldn't welcome the bear hug I was tempted to give her.

I rose to my feet as she stubbed out her cigarette. 'Not here in the street,' I said. 'Let's go to your hotel.'

'I've done more digging,' Clarisse announced.

'By the look of that grin on your face, you hit paydirt.'

'I don't grin, *chérie*. I smile graciously.'

'Tell me what you found.'

Clarisse ran a satisfied hand over her light-brown hair that was twisted into a sleek coil at her nape. Her green eyes were fierce in a way that belied her indolent manner and I wondered what was coming.

'It's your mayor,' she said. 'Cousin to Gilles Bertin.'

'Charles Durand?'

'Yes. He's not what he seems.'

'A smooth-talking money-maker who stands for election on a moderate Socialist ticket.' I didn't mention the word 'blackmailer'.

'Exactly.' She sipped her coffee and glanced approvingly around the elegant room with its handsome scrollwork and polished mahogany. 'Nice hotel. What's its history?'

'It used to be a Carmelite convent.' I shook my head at her. 'Don't tease. What is Charles Durand hiding?'

'It seems he used to be a rabid Communist in his youth and early adulthood.'

'Really? I've never heard that before. He keeps it very quiet.'

Clarisse smiled slyly. 'Clearly he had a change of heart, a Road-to-Damascus moment, and became a dedicated businessman instead.'

'Who lends money to farmers at exorbitant rates and when they can't repay, he repossesses their land and builds on it.'

'Which he would never do if he were a Communist, would he?' She paused to blow softly on her coffee. 'Unless . . .'

Our gazes locked on each other. 'Unless,' I finished, 'he is a sleeper.'

CHAPTER THIRTY

Mas Caussade never looked more welcoming.

I'd shot home from Arles as fast as my tin-can car would go. If anyone was following me, I didn't spot them, but I saw no point in anyone following me as it was obvious where I was heading. I had run home.

There was a flurry of activity around the house, with new stables going up already, hammers and saws and the clean fresh scent of new wood. My father was among the builders, banging in nails and giving orders. I stood and observed him for a few minutes. He looked happy to be making a new home for his beloved white horses, more cheerful than around me or André. Someone had trimmed his beard.

The dogs lazed in the shade, eyes never leaving Papa, and a handful of hens and ducks scratched in the dirt, bickering with one another. A row of crows sat on the barn roof like grubby urchins on a wall, waiting for a chance to snatch at any beetles fool enough to make a run from the stable. The sight of it all stirred something in me, the part of me I'd long forgotten that was moulded out of Camarguais black earth.

I turned my back on it and hurried into the house. I closed the door behind me with a resounding slam and in the gloomy hallway I leaned my cheek against the wall. I could hear the house breathe and gradually my own breathing slowed to its pace. I felt Mas Caussade wrap itself around me once more.

It was my home whether I wanted it or not. It offered me security. It offered me shelter. It offered me somewhere to lick my wounds, and for a blind moment I let myself believe it.

But I pushed myself away from the wall, brushing its touch from my cheek. It was all lies. It hadn't saved Goliath and it hadn't protected Cosette. So why should I believe for one second that it would save me from what was coming?

André didn't look pleased to see me. His room was stifling hot. There was a milky sheen of sweat on his skin that made me guess he had been exercising too strenuously again. I wished he would go outdoors and let the sun and the smells and the sight of the bulls get to work on him.

Or was I wrong? Had he been doing something he didn't wish me to know? He'd told me he trusted me. Was he lying? One more lie shuffled unseen among all the others. How could I help my brother if he wouldn't help me?

'The drop went smoothly,' I told him.

'I was sure it would.'

He was standing at the window, reluctant to take his eyes from it. What was he watching? My father and the *gardians* rebuilding the stables?

Or something else? Someone else?

I came forward to stand beside him. 'I found the drop site easily,' I said, 'inserted the envelope and left immediately, as instructed.' I followed his line of sight out into the courtyard and beyond into the fields. A pushy group of young bulls were shoulder-barging each other, testing their strength.

Their strength. So effortless. Is that what he stood here and hungered for?

'Thank you, Eloïse. You did well.'

'When will it be picked up?'

'That's not your business.' He softened his words with an apologetic smile, but it didn't stretch far. 'You've performed extremely professionally. Finding the plans. Photographing them. The DLD. I can rely on my "legs" to do their job.'

'I am going riding with one of the airmen tomorrow.'

'Good. The more we can become familiar with the air base the better. Of course, they have their own internal security but even that is compromised until we find the source of the leak.'

'What are we going to do about the mayor?'

'Nothing at the moment. First we find where the leak of information is coming from. Mayor Durand will be of use to us in doing that.' André stopped speaking and studied me thoughtfully from head to toe. I suffered the scrutiny uneasily.

'What's wrong?' he asked.

'Nothing. It went well.'

'Did anything else happen?'

'No.'

'Are you certain?'

I looked him straight in the eye. 'Yes.'

'Good. So you can relax.'

'One thing did occur to me while I was driving home.'

His teeth showed. 'I knew there was something.'

'I was running through the film negative again in my head.'

'And?'

'And I think there was someone in the street crowd that I recognise.'

'Who?'

'The man from the hospital. The one with eyes of stone. Maurice Piquet.'

I might as well have stuck the knife in him there and then. I wished I could take the words back because his already pale skin turned paper-white. His hand encircled my wrist.

'How am I going to save you, Eloïse?' he whispered.

He released his hold and stared out of the window once more, but this time his gaze was directed towards the huge tamarisk tree with its dense mass of pink flowers that grew just beyond the courtyard. Was he expecting someone to be hiding behind its trunk?

'André, do you mean that it was Piquet who was driving the van?'

There was no need to say which van. For us there was only one.

Without shifting his gaze he replied, 'If Piquet is down here, you must go back to Paris.'

'I'm not leaving you.'

Slowly, thoughtfully, he turned to face me. 'Then one of us is going to have to kill Maurice Piquet.'

CHAPTER THIRTY-ONE

Major Joel Dirke rode well. He rode like a man who was born in the saddle. I watched him come alive on horseback, the military stiffness washing out of his backbone with every kilometre we rode deeper into the Camargue wetlands.

I chose Tonnerre for him. He is one of Papa's largest riding stallions, a fine proud animal of immense stamina, but picky about whom he likes on his back. He liked Joel Dirke. That was obvious from the start, and they made a good pairing, both handsome and intelligent and with a way of looking at you that made you think twice about cutting any corners.

'I'm glad to see you ride Western-style down here,' he said. 'Like back home in Texas.'

'It's the only way to work livestock, using heavy-duty stirrups and both reins in one hand. Our horses,' I patted the strong neck of my horse Achille, 'are trained to neck-reining. He may be small but he has the heart of a lion when cutting a bull out of the herd, and can turn on a centime.'

'Smart too, I can tell.' He tapped the side of his head to emphasise the point. This was a man who valued intelligence even in his animals.

'Oh yes, you don't want to mess with these horses or they'll have you on the ground before you can say *merde*.'

He laughed and squeezed Tonnerre into a trot as we crossed a wide-open expanse of land lined with dogwood and a small waterway. Our approach sent a cloud of dragonflies and damselflies teeming up into the air, brilliant emperors and scarlet darters that shimmered brighter than jewels in the sunlight. The marshlands were wild and raw, stretching unchecked all the way to the sea where they turned into salt-flats from which salt had been harvested since Roman times. But the landscape was not the only thing round here that was wild and raw. Its bulls. Its horses. Its people.

We may look tame. But don't be fooled by looks.

I didn't question him. Didn't pester him. I let the peace and the quiet soak into him, waited for it to blur his mental sharpness and steal all trace of wariness from this alert military man. In his denim shirt, cowboy hat and pointed cowboy boots he was putting on a show for me. But that was fine. Because I was putting on a show for him.

After a long and exhilarating canter along a trail through the marsh, broad hooves flinging spray up over us in a kaleidoscope of rainbows, Joel Dirke gently reined in his horse and brought it to a halt. He was gazing ahead, transfixed. I experienced a quick pulse of alarm. What had caught his attention? I squinted against the sun as it dipped lower in the flat blue sky and released a laugh of relief. It was the sea lavender. Ahead of us it stretched in a great swathe of flowers, as if Van Gogh had taken his paintbrush and daubed the landscape purple.

'It's beautiful,' he murmured, his Southern drawl extending the word. 'Right now in Texas the land is yellow and parched.' A gleaming white egret swept into view, skimming the lavender, perfecting the painting. 'Is this why you brought me here?'

'I brought you here because I thought you'd like to see the flamingos in the lagoons. It must be tough living in camp all the time.'

He laughed. 'Yes, those Thunderjet flights setting off on patrol early morning sure blast us right out of bed every day.'

I smiled. 'And you said you missed your horses. I know that feeling. When I'm in Paris I miss them.'

'It was mighty kind of you to invite me.'

There was a pause, a small crack in time into which a sudden stillness seemed to slide. The birds fell silent. The only sound was the creak of leather as Joel Dirke swivelled in his saddle to get a better look at me.

'Well, Eloïse, as one horse-lover to another, let's talk straight, shall we? Why did you invite me out here?'

I didn't for one minute think this question would not arise at some point. 'Tell me first' – I smiled and eased Achille a few steps closer – 'why you accepted the invitation, if you thought it was something more than a local Camarguais native offering friendship.'

'You're an awkward cuss to pin down,' he laughed.

But by then I'd slid out of the stirrups, swung my leg over Achille's broad haunches and vaulted to the ground.

'Let's give them a break,' I suggested.

He nodded but didn't move. For a moment I thought he might gallop off. It didn't worry me. If I whistled Tonnerre would come. But he jumped down and together we ambled towards one of the pools where the water glared bright as a searchlight in the harsh sunlight. Shadows were lengthening and bees darted in and out of the purple flowers heavy with pollen. The horses lowered their heads to graze and the major asked his question again.

'Why did you invite me out here?'

Joel Dirke was a man used to getting answers.

'I have a suggestion to make,' I said. 'I thought you might pass it on to your CO.'

It didn't go down well. He flipped off his hat, his dark hair still springy but edged with a line of sweat, and fanned himself with its brim.

'My CO has plenty on his hands right now, dealing with the murder of Senior Master Sergeant Michael Ashton. In Serriac. In broad daylight.'

I couldn't blame him for the flash of anger.

'I understand,' I said quietly. 'It was terrible. Everyone is in shock in the town. But my point is that even though it was the protesters who did the damage, there is a sense that the air base is to blame. Emotions are ready to overflow.'

His dark eyes never left my face.

'So,' I continued, 'I am suggesting that Dumoulin Air Base sets up a public relations exercise to calm everyone down.'

Still no comment. Just the stare. The waiting.

'I believe that it would improve the situation by calming nerves.'

A pair of wading birds, black and white pied avocets, glided down to the pool and their long stiletto beaks started jabbing in the shallows. I thought of the knife jabbing into Mickey's back.

'You could issue an invitation to a select group of town dignitaries to visit the base. A kind of inspection. To reassure them. To explain how safely the nuclear element is stored.' I ran a hand down Achille's warm flank to give my words time to settle. 'To impress them not only by your American expertise but by your hand of friendship.'

I didn't look at him. I busied myself pulling out some tangles and burrs from my horse's white coat and giving him a good scratch behind his ears.

'Eloïse.'

I glanced over my shoulder at him. His hat was back on and he was gathering Tonnerre's reins in his hand.

'I will think about it,' he said with formal politeness, and swung up into the saddle.

'Do you think you'll ever go back to ranching?'

I was making conversation. Coaxing my companion out of his silence, though the silence was not unpleasant. I'd led him along a low ridge to a more wooded area to show him where in the shade of a copse of ash and feathery willow a fierce young stallion was guarding his pretty-faced mares. As Joel Dirke observed them, the stiff lines of his face softened and I began to think he had horse-blood in his veins.

'No, never,' he said with a smile. 'It's too much like hard work and brutal in the winter. No, there was never any question of it. As children my brother and I were obsessed with airplanes. We ate, slept, dreamed of aircraft at all times. Both of us trained as pilots and flew P-51 Mustangs during the war,' he tipped back his hat awkwardly, 'but my brother got shot down over Germany. Don't look so pained, he survived, thank God, but had the good sense to give up flying and find himself a cosy desk job in San Diego instead, while I'm still hurtling through the skies at over six hundred miles per hour.'

'I hope for his sake that his job is still with aircraft though. It's important to work at something you love doing.'

He paused and ran a hand fondly over his mount's neck, and eventually nodded. 'Yes.'

Whether that was yes to his brother's job or yes to working with what you love, I couldn't tell.

'It must be nice to have a brother with good sense,' I laughed.

'I met your brother the same night I met you. André, isn't it? He came to a meeting at the air base. He didn't speak much but what he did say seemed eminently sensible to me.' He tightened the reins a fraction and flicked some flies from around Tonnerre's ears. 'I'm very sorry about the accident. Godawful for him.'

'What was the meeting about?'

He shook his head at me with amusement. 'Allow me to retain at least some professional integrity.'

'If André was there, it must have been about Intelligence security.'

'Why don't you ask André?'

I skipped over that. 'So why was Gilles Bertin there?'

'You ask a whole heap of questions, Eloïse. Why are you so interested?' He cocked a dark eyebrow at me. 'A bit too interested, perhaps.'

'Of course I'm interested. You come down here, take over a chunk of my father's land and immediately the Caussade champion bull is slaughtered and our stables burned down. Wouldn't you be interested?'

'You have a point, I admit.'

He turned his head away to inspect the reed beds on our right from where I could hear the high-pitched *jeet* of a yellow wagtail. I wanted him to look back at me. I wanted him to say – yes, I can see that the United States Air Force has messed up your life right now, though it's all for the good of France, and in return you can ask me any questions you like and I'll answer them to the best of my ability, as well as arranging an open day for visitors to the Dumoulin Air Base. That's what I wanted him to say.

But it doesn't work like that.

'That's a lot of reeds,' he commented. 'Are they ever harvested?'

'Yes, it's called *sagne*. We grow it throughout the region for thatching, mainly on the old traditional cottages that some of the *gardians* still live in. There is a disused one a couple of kilometres away. Come on, I'll show you.'

I pushed Achille into a canter. I wanted this American to understand the kind of life we lead here, to feel connected to our community. So that he would fight for us.

The motorcycle screamed past us. Ripping up the dirt road. Shattering the stillness. A terrifying blast of sound that sent both horses into a blind panic, and it took all our skill to stop them bolting. I hated it. To see the animals spooked. To smell their fear. Their ears back, eyes rolling, muscles taut, adrenaline pumping. A horse is a prey animal and its instinct is to flee. I steered Achille round in a tight circle on one rein to keep control, but Tonnerre was stronger and gave Joel a hard time, fighting to throw his head. By the time we had them calmed down, still huffing heavily, the motorcycle had roared into the distance, vanishing from sight.

'Crazy son-of-a-bitch bastard!' Joel shouted into the cloud of dust that hung like smoke in the motorcycle's wake. 'He could have killed the horses or us if they'd bolted. Did you get a look at him?'

I soothed Achille's neck. 'No, the bike was past before I saw it coming. A flash of black. Maybe a flying helmet. I don't know for sure.'

'Crazy loon! I thought people round here knew better when it comes to animals.'

'They do,' I insisted. 'That idiot was not a local man.'

'Let's hope he breaks his infernal neck.'

I edged Achille up close to Tonnerre to reassure and calm the stallion and felt like doing exactly the same with my military friend.

'Joel, relax. After you've seen the thatched cottage we'll ride over to the lagoon to take a look at the flamingos. They are breathtaking.'

I had been keeping an eye on the horses, checking their jitters, so didn't see that Joel was smiling at me until I glanced up.

'May I say, they are not the only things round here that are breathtaking?' he commented courteously, and eased his horse into a gentle canter.

Dammit. I didn't mean him to get *that* connected.

Joel Dirke spotted it first. Sharp pilot's eyes.

'Look!' he pointed up ahead.

A thin rope of smoke was rising straight into the air from the roof of the single-storey thatched cottage. It lay set back from the dirt road some way to the north of us, surrounded by flat open grazing land. A row of ash trees and poplars offered shade, but the place had a dilapidated and deserted air.

The smoke was not rising from the chimney, but from the thatch itself, and a flicker of red bled into the smoke as we galloped over the springy green glasswort. Another fire. Another malicious act of wanton destruction. Out here, in the middle of nowhere. What was the point? As we approached, the horses were snorting sharply and twitching ears rapidly back and forth, anxious and nervy. The instinct to flee was kicking in. Joel jumped off Tonnerre and threw me his reins, just as the red flicker became a crackling snapping sheet of flame.

'Lead them away,' he ordered. 'I'll make certain the interior is empty. Stay clear.'

He ran into the burning building, terrifying the life out of me, though the downstairs seemed free of flames so far. I turned the horses and moved them back, calming them.

'Come out,' I yelled as the flames started to slide down the thatch, but there was no sign of Joel.

A sudden movement startled the horses. It was in the garden off to one side of the cottage where a shed was struggling to stay upright. From inside it stepped a figure.

I felt a thud, inside my head. As though someone had taken a hammer to me, but it was only my thoughts slamming into each other. The figure was Maurice Piquet. Even in a heavy leather jacket and from a distance, I knew him. As if his image was branded on to my retina. I knew his thick black hair and eyebrows that met in the middle and the way he held himself like a boxer ready for the ring. A leather helmet was pushed back off his head.

He looked straight at me and for a moment I thought he was coming for me. He made a dart forward as though coming to finish the job of ripping my cheek off, but then halted when I swung back up into the saddle. Instead he ducked behind the shed. Instantly I heard an engine kick into life and a black motorcycle shot out with Piquet astride it. It raced up on to the dirt road and shot off at speed, making me think with a shudder of the one that had followed me out of Serriac the day I visited the mayor.

'No one inside,' Joel called out as he emerged from the building, bent over, coughing smoke from his lungs.

I dismounted quickly, tethered both horses to a tree and ran over. By now half the thatch was aflame.

'Let's try to rake it,' I shouted above the noise of the flames.

I raced to the shed and from inside I seized a rake and long-handled hoe. Together we started to rake off as much of the blazing reed thatch as we could reach. Yanking and tearing at it, stripping swathes of it to the ground. Ash and soot swirled around us, making the air too hot to breathe, but in the end we were forced to retreat as the flames took hold of the roof timbers.

'Enough,' Joel said, 'enough.' He put a restraining hand on my wrist.

But it wasn't enough to save the cottage, and the heat burned inside me as much as inside the building. Why had Piquet done this? Set fire to a deserted old house. I could see no sense in it.

'We must report it to the police at once,' I said. Léon would know how to handle it. 'I'll return the tools to the shed and then we'll ride home and drive into town.'

'Eloïse, was that a motorbike I heard when I was in the cottage?' Joel frowned and glanced down the road. 'Did you see one?'

'Yes, I did. It shot off in that direction. I'll be quick.'

I hurried off towards the shed and replaced the tools. The shed was draped with heavy cobwebs and grime, a retreat for spiders and rats. So why was Piquet tucked away here? What was he up to?

I scanned the dirty shelves and tugged at a piece of sacking on one. Dust swam through the air and I found myself staring at an almost new tan leather suitcase. Not large, but big enough to hide something. I snapped open the lock and lifted the lid. Inside lay a black metal two-way radio with headphones. And folded up neatly beside it was a red Communist flag.

CHAPTER THIRTY-TWO

LÉON ROUSSEL

Léon closed the door firmly, thankful to see the back of Major Dirke. He didn't want anyone walking in on this new find. Too many rumours were flying around town already and sure as hell he didn't want another one starting up with more conspiracy theories. The leather case sat on his desk. He had inspected it closely for identifying labels, but anything that showed its maker or the shop where it was purchased had been well and truly removed. Good quality. Fairly new. It contained only the radio – a Motorola – and the flag of the Union of Soviet Socialist Republics, the USSR.

Eloïse had unfurled it and spread it across his desk to examine, but he had snatched it off. He would not tolerate it there. The violently red rectangle with its gold hammer and sickle and its star carried too much blood woven into its fibres for him to want to touch it.

Eloïse had folded the flag away and tucked it out of sight in the case, snapping the lid shut with a sharp click.

'Better?' she said, and perched on the chair in front of his desk.

He nodded. She was good at spotting his weaknesses, as well as making them seem perfectly reasonable. What she wasn't so good at was lying to him. Major Joel Dirke had come in with her at first, but had left after he'd given his statement and Eloïse had assured him that she was in no need of an escort back home as she had driven from the farm in her own car. Léon had noticed the American's reluctance to leave her, his hand on her shoulder. His look of concern.

'Thank you for your help, Major,' Léon had said briskly, then opened his office door and almost pushed him out. You can have too much of American boots, even cowboy ones. The team of investigators from the USAF, who were getting precisely nowhere in digging into Mickey Ashton's murder, had been a thorn in his side all afternoon and anyway he needed to speak to Eloïse alone.

'Are you all right?' he asked. She didn't look all right.

'Of course. I'm fine.'

Her eyes were wide, too wide, the silky skin of one cheekbone smudged with dirt. An acrid smell rose from her clothes and hair, where the fire had left its mark on her again. But that wasn't it. There was something more. Léon leaned forward, elbows on his desk, so that he could attempt to see what was making her give a quick toss of her head as if trying to shake something out of it.

'Eloïse, I've been receiving reports this week of unaccustomed activity out on the marshes. More vehicles passing through than normal. I took a look around, but found nothing except tyre tracks on the dirt trails. Far more numerous than I would expect.'

Her dark eyes studied him intently. Her tongue flashed across dry lips but she made no comment. Waited for more.

'What you found and brought in today is crucial evidence.'

'Evidence of what?'

'It backs up what I suspect is happening. It seems we have a group of people meeting somewhere where they won't be disturbed. To plan something. I believe those people could well be Communists preparing action of some sort, the way they planned their protest march in Serriac. The flag in the suitcase would indicate that Communists are involved.'

'Why on earth would they carry a flag around if it's meant to be secret?'

'Oh, they can't resist it. The symbolism. The field of blood. The hammer and sickle for the workman and the peasantry. Workers unite. Destroy the hated oppressor. They would pin up the flag at their meetings the way your father pins up his champion bull rosettes. To remind them why they're there.'

She stood up abruptly, scraping back her chair and catching Léon by surprise. She prowled back and forth across the small office, then threw herself back into her chair with a sibilant hiss.

'A Communist cell, you think?' she said.

'It's a strong possibility, yes.'

'And the radio?'

'To communicate with other members. Other cells and sections.'

She sat stiff and awkward in the chair, her scar bone-white. 'Isaac,' she whispered.

'It's possible he's involved, yes. He knows the area very well.'

'You think they've been meeting in the cottage that was burned?'

Léon leaned back and pulled open the cupboard behind his desk. From inside he extracted an opened bottle of wine and two glasses. Without a word he poured the rich burgundy wine and placed a glass in front of her.

'Now, Eloïse, time for the truth. Tell me why you lied in your statement. Why you lied to the American.'

She lowered her eyes, dark lashes shutting him out, so he sipped his wine to hide his impatience and let her think. *Whatever it is that has you scared, you must tell me. Don't you know that? Let me help. Remember?* But he sat in silence while she remembered.

When she raised her eyes again, something had shifted. Her full lips curved in a smile of sorts. 'You are too sharp, Léon.'

He raised his glass to her. 'To sharpness.'

She lifted her wine and drank almost half of it. 'To staying alive.'

'Who was on the motorcycle? You stated that you didn't recognise him, but you did, didn't you?'

'Yes.'

'Who was he?'

'A man called Maurice Piquet.'

Léon frowned, trawling through his prodigious memory for names. It rang no bells.

'He is Gilles Bertin's sidekick,' she explained. 'Another Soviet agent. This one likes to play rough. He was inside the garden shed.'

She said it calmly, as if saying the colour of his eyes. No mention of the fact that she clearly believed he was here to kill her, but her hand flicked across her forehead as if to ward off a bullet. Léon rose to his feet to rid himself of the desk between them. He stood by the window instead – any closer to her and he would have found himself plucking the strand of charred straw from the back of her hair or brushing the smudge of soot from her neck.

'We'll do this together, Eloïse. Tell me how you know Maurice Piquet.'

She told him in quick short sentences. To the point.

The hospital in Paris. When Piquet came close to ripping her cheek off. The sight of his bristly head in a photograph on the day of the demonstration. His role as Bertin's muscle man and the way he'd darted at her on the marshes. The killer look on his face before he'd raced off on the motorcycle, aware of the American military man in the burning cottage.

Léon listened, his gut cold as ice. How close had she come to death? First in the street alongside Mickey Ashton, then at the fire with the officer who was too busy playing intrepid hero to look after Eloïse. When she'd finished, he anchored himself to the window, one hand on the latch as if thinking of opening it. But it was to stop him from running over there and shaking her, to stop him from throwing her in his car right this minute and driving her to Paris without stopping.

'Eloïse, I am asking you again. Please will you return to Paris? It is not safe for you here.'

'The question is,' she was staring not at him, but at a streak of soot on her hand, 'why would an MGB agent who works for Soviet Russia choose to burn down a meeting place for Communist activists? Surely they would work together.'

'Eloïse, are you listening to me?'

'Why would he burn it?'

'The French Communist Party is made up of many factions and they are always falling out.'

'Or had they been disobeying orders from Gilles Bertin?'

'Now can we talk about you?'

'There's no need,' she said, her voice low. She shook her head at him but with a slow smile that drew him forward. 'You know I will not go back to Paris.'

The room seemed to peel away until there was just her, and he could taste the danger around her, like grit between his teeth. Outside his office there was the tread of police boots and a knock sounded on the door.

'Not now,' he called out curtly, but the sharpness of his tone was to do with her, not the man on the other side of the door.

'You're busy,' she said, and rose. She moved quickly to leave but he reached the door before her.

'Your friend from Paris is here, you said.'

'Yes. Clarisse Favre.'

Her gaze was quick, examining each part of his face. He reached up and at last plucked the stub of charred straw from her hair, which was tied back from her face. He let his fingers run to the ends of it, and it felt dusty, but thick and warm.

'Stay at Mas Caussade. I will go hunting for this Maurice Piquet. Stay at home with André.' He gave her a wry smile. 'The pair of you together should be a match for anyone.'

She nodded. For the first time he saw her hand quiver as it reached for the door and he had no idea whether it was fear or rage, but he drew her close and wrapped his arms around her so tight he could make out each ridge of her spine and feel the softness of her breasts pressed to his chest. Her body moulded to his, melting into his bones, and he heard her breath, rapid and hot. The smell of the smoke in her hair flooded his senses.

'If you must leave the farm at any time I want you to ring your friend, Clarisse Favre, and ask her to accompany you at all times. Do you still have the gun?'

She nodded. 'Yes.'

His arm curled around her narrow waist and she leaned back against the wall, drawing him with her. His lips found hers, hard and urgent, and her hand twisted round the back of his neck, her nails digging in, one leg twining around his. Pinning him to her. They remained like that, tangled

271

together for a long time, not even a hair's breadth between them, the clock on his desk ticking off the minutes till the heat began to recede and their breathing flowed together.

'Your father should be proud of you,' he murmured into her hair.

She gave a small snort of derision.

'It's true,' he insisted. 'Proud of all three of his offspring – you, André and, yes, even troublesome Isaac. You are all working so hard to change the world. Not all in the same way, but with heart and soul.'

She lifted her head. 'Thank you, Léon.' Her dark eyes glittered. 'I will tell Papa to make a note of that.'

'Will you please make a note of what I am going to say next?'

She kissed his chin. 'Try me.'

'Make a note of not going riding with good-looking Americans in future.'

She laughed, a rich sound that lapped around them, and she put a finger to his lips, silencing him. 'I'll just choose the ugly ones from now on.'

But the thought of how close she'd come to death while in the company of Major Dirke in the wetlands swept over him. He felt a spike of anger spring at him. He released his hold on Eloïse and walked over to the telephone on his desk. He held out the receiver to her.

'Call Clarisse Favre.'

CHAPTER THIRTY-THREE

'You don't have to do this,' I stated.

'Yes, I do, *chérie*. I promised that gorgeous policeman.' Clarisse swept an elegant hand, weighted by its heavy square emerald that rippled with the light from the window, in a careless arc. But there was nothing careless about her eyes. They were stern. 'I don't break my promises, Eloïse. I came down from Paris because I was worried about you.' She switched on her radiant smile. 'It seems I was right to be.'

We were seated in Serriac's smartest hotel, Le Karur. It was constructed by an adventurer who made his fortune from mining gemstones in India and possessed a tall crenellated viewing tower. That's where we sat. Sipping our coffee, surrounded by ruby-red cushions and looking down like eagles on the town spread out below us. Only Father Jerome's church tower rivalled ours.

I was overwhelmed by Clarisse's kindness. I had not always been the easiest of employees to handle, I admit, especially since the crash that ripped my life to shreds last winter. She had been generous to me then. Keeping me on full pay while I hid, wounded, in my lair and waited for my bones to knit. I'd once asked when we were drunk together in Les Deux Magots whether she was married and she'd snarled a *'Non'* at me, as if I'd asked was she a child-killer. And now this. This kindness.

'You have a business to run in Paris,' I pointed out.

'Rubbish! I'm on holiday. Monique is handling it.'

I raised an eyebrow. 'Monique couldn't handle her way out of a paper bag.'

'You are wicked, *chérie.*'

'I don't need baby-sitting.'

'Monsieur le Capitaine thinks you do.' She took her time lighting a cigarette and I could see her mind ticking over as she squinted at me through the fog of smoke. 'Captain Léon Roussel believes you are in danger. So do you, or you wouldn't be sitting here now. These thugs, Bertin and Piquet, need to be tracked down and thrown into prison. While the police try to find them, you must go into hiding. So I have decided we will go back to Paris.'

'No.'

'For God's sake, Eloïse.' She threw her hand in the air leaving a trail of smoke. 'Have some sense. I don't want you in danger. What are we going to do?'

André's words whipped through my mind. *One of us is going to have to kill Maurice Piquet.* André was not exactly in a position to do so.

'I am not returning to Paris until this is over,' I said. Calm and quiet.

Her green eyes narrowed further, her lipstick staining her cigarette. 'You stubborn little bastard,' she muttered. 'So get back to your horse-shit farm if you must and stay there. From all you've told me, it sounds as if you will be safest there. Stick tight to your brother and his hunting rifle. When you want to go anywhere, telephone me and I'll come for you. Got that?'

'Yes, boss.'

'Now I will escort you back to your piggery.'

'We don't have pigs.'

'Pigs, bulls, chickens. What's the difference? All the same.' She shuddered melodramatically. 'None of them smell of Chanel.'

'Do you know what I love about you, boss?'

'What's that?'

'Your perceptive mind.' I grinned.

But she didn't even crack a smile. 'Don't ever doubt it, Eloïse.'

I dismantled, cleaned and reassembled my gun. Even though it hadn't been fired. It made me feel better. I told André about the fire on the marshes, about the radio, about Léon's theory that it was a Communist cell.

I didn't mention Piquet. I'm not sure why. I didn't want him to jump at every shadow in the yard or at every creak of a stair the way I did.

I worked on the farm the next day. I rose at five o'clock in the morning, took a silent breakfast with my father, then did the job of a *gardian*. I worked all day till the sun was exhausted and spilled out of the sky and my limbs ached from the unaccustomed hours in the saddle. If anyone was watching – with or without a camera – they would see nothing but me with the bulls, me with my father, me with the *gardians*. Never me on my own. All day I stuck to my companions, as Clarisse would say, like horse-shit.

That evening when I rode into the yard, stinking of sweat and bulls, I was surprised and pleased to find André sitting outside. A stiff breeze was blowing that had shifted the mosquitoes and scoured the sky to a blue that was so vivid it hurt the eyes.

André was tucked out of the wind in a nook between barn and house. Seated in an ancient chair of woven reeds, a book on his lap, with one of the feral cats regarding the world with suspicion from under his seat. I dismounted, trying not to look too stiff and sore, and nuzzled my face against Achille's velvety muzzle, his long tongue licking the salt off my cheek. Around me Papa and three other *gardians* were swinging easily out of the saddle and leading their horses over to the stone trough for water.

As I flipped the reins over Achille's head I saw André watching me with an odd expression on his face. I waved. He waved back and called out, 'You look happy.'

It startled me. Happiness was not something I associated

with Mas Caussade these days. Yet when I let his words settle in my mind, I knew that he was right. This ache and sweat. These men and horses. This smell of salt marshes in my nostrils and taste of the Camargue wind on my lips. This was a brief spike of happiness.

The telephone call came late that evening; I was reading. My father put down the piece of dogwood he'd been whittling into the shape of an owl and answered it in the hall, his voice a low rumble, brief and polite in tone. His footsteps returned across the tiles.

'Who was it, Papa?'

The telephone rang infrequently, never in the evenings. I hoped it wasn't Clarisse.

'It was some slick Yank from Dumoulin Air Base. A Sergeant Wilkinson, who thinks you get a man to like you by calling him "sir" ten times in three sentences.'

'What did he want?'

'I told him it is too late for calls.'

'It's only nine o'clock, Papa.'

'Americans think the world is ready to jump to do their bidding.'

'Why did he ring?'

'It seems they are running scared.'

'What makes you say that?'

Papa had lowered himself into his chair and took his knife to the wooden owl's eye, scratching out a groove. I watched him for a full minute. I'd spent my childhood winters

277

fascinated by the flick and twist of the knife in his skilled hand and had tried myself but with no success.

At the end of the minute I prompted, 'What makes you think they're scared?'

'The Yanks have invited a bunch of what he called "dignitaries" over there on Saturday. Some kind of goodwill occasion, he called it.'

That was it.

I waited for more. None came. I stood up, walked over to the cupboard, poured out two glasses of wine and placed one at Papa's elbow. I took the other one back to my seat with me.

'Have you been invited, Papa?'

'I have.'

I sipped my wine and was tempted to take a bite out of the glass. Papa's leathery face was totally focused on one of the owl's feathers.

'Which other dignitaries?'

He didn't look up. 'No idea.'

'Will you go?'

A huff, like one of his horses, came out of his wide nostrils. 'I will.'

I swilled wine around my mouth.

'Am I invited?'

'You are. Though I don't know why.'

I exhaled very quietly so that he would not hear my relief. *Thank you, Major Dirke.*

*

How could I make such a mistake?

I was being so careful. I'd drawn in my claws. Talking to no one. Upsetting no one. Stirring up no trouble. I was determined that nothing should go wrong before the visit to the air base, no risk of any calamities that would cause it to be cancelled. I kept my head down. My mouth shut.

The next two days were spent in a blur of bridles and leather, herding black mean-eyed four-legged creatures of solid muscle and cleaning out hooves. Scrubbing my horse's muddy coat. Falling into bed with aching bones, still wet from a shower. And eating, always eating alongside the men. When did I last eat like this? Not since a child. As if there were a gigantic hole inside me. Léon had laughed when I'd complained I would end up as fat as Madame Cazal who ran the bakery, and he wrapped his arms around me.

'It's all the physical activity.' He'd smiled and kissed my mouth. 'You taste and feel more like a Camargue girl again.' He took a gentle bite of my good cheek as though eating an apple straight off the tree.

But I liked it. I liked feeling my arms stronger and my legs more muscular. It made me feel safer.

'Don't go to the air base on Saturday,' he said.

I leaned my head on his shoulder and lifted his hand to kiss its palm. It was warm and robust under the touch of my lips and smelled of ink. I didn't want to argue. We had little time.

Each day, late in the evening, Léon turned up at Mas Caussade under cover of darkness. A dark shadow in the night and each time my heart stopped. I had not expected this. This pain when we were apart. This sense of something tearing inside me when he left. He didn't drive out to the farm, he walked the five miles, or rather, ran, so that there would be no sound of a car for someone to track. I waited for him in the barn with Cosette and each time the heat of him engulfed me.

'Don't go to the air base,' he said again. But he knew me too well. 'I'm trying to protect you.'

'I know.'

'So why do you make it so . . .'

'Difficult?'

'Yes. So damn difficult. We aren't talking about breaking a limb or grazing a knee falling from a tree. We are talking about a knife in the back or a bullet in the throat. Take care. Oh, my love, take care.'

We did not know then. About the bullet that was about to strike. Just when I thought I was safe.

I had laid down rules for myself. To do as Léon asked, to take care. My mistake – my fatal mistake – lay in ignoring one of them. It was Friday morning and the clouds had drifted in, obscuring the sun. They were ragged and untidy, as if someone had tried to shred them the way Bertin and Piquet shredded my nerves. My rule was – never stand still outdoors. Don't give them an easy target. A simple rule that can save your life the way not stepping off a cliff is a simple rule that can save your life. Easy to put into practice.

So why did I break it? Why did I pause outside the barn

on my way to tend Cosette and bend to pet the feral cat? It was automatic, unthinking, a triggered response when the little striped animal curled itself around my ankles. As I straightened up, the crack of a rifle shot ripped through the silence. I felt the bullet lift my loose hair as it whistled past the side of my neck and heard it smack into the side of the barn. I stood a finger's breadth away from death.

A second shot from somewhere in the distant fields followed in less than a heartbeat. The cat fell limp and lifeless at my feet. I leaped into the barn, mind spinning, my heart clattering in my chest, and snatched at a billhook lying against a pile of wood.

If you've never been shot at, you don't know what it does to you. Believe me. It alters who you are. It cuts you loose from the things that bind you to being a civilised human being. If the person wielding the rifle had walked into the barn right then, I would have cleaved his skull in two with the billhook. I know that sounds inhuman. But it's not. It is the essence of humanity. It is what makes the human race survive, that white fear, that naked panic, that burning desire to live.

I pressed myself tight to the inside of the barn wall. Peered around the edge of the door, scanning the horizon, searching the fields for the position of the rifle. For any sign of a figure. Approaching. Or fleeing.

A third shot crashed through the yard. But this time it came from the house. I jerked round to look. André was in his upstairs bedroom, window wide open, a rifle levelled at his shoulder and aimed at a spot where a clump of tamarisk trees had spread into each other like a dense fortress. He pulled the trigger again. The shot ripped into the small copse, sending up a grey wave of wood pigeons that wheeled around the sky, their wings heavy with alarm.

'There,' André shouted, 'there, beyond the stream.'

I tightened my grip on the billhook and ran.

Blood glistened on the slender leaves of a mimosa. A ladybird had dragged its feet through it, leaving threads of scarlet cotton, and the glasswort was trampled underfoot. But there was no sign of the gunman. The murdering bastard had fled.

I widened my search, billhook at the ready.

But I found no one, no trace. Except a few spots of blood leading in a zigzag direction away from the house. From here the Mas Caussade yard looked far away, at least five hundred metres, so whoever fired at me was good. Very good. A shudder clawed its way through me and my breath raced in and out of my throat.

As I hurried back to the house, I wondered how often André stood there with his rifle at the ready.

That night when Léon came to the farm, I didn't tell him. I intended to, I wanted to, but the words hooked themselves to the roof of my mouth and wouldn't leave. When he walked into the barn in the darkness, I stepped into the circle of his arms and felt the aches and pains and the dull shame of my earlier mistake vanish. He was still breathing hard from his run and I could feel the damp fabric of his shirt and smell the weariness of his day on him.

'Bad day?' I asked.

'Still ploughing my way down the names on my list for interview. The thrill of being a gendarme knows no bounds.'

With my thumb I soothed a crease from between his brows and drew him over to our seat of hay bales where I poured him wine and fed him cheese and olives until finally a stillness returned to him.

'I've been trying to track Maurice Piquet,' he said.

'Any success?'

'I found one of the demonstrators in Serriac who remembers a man who answers to his description. He has good reason to remember him.'

'Why? What happened?'

'The man who sounds like he might be Piquet wrenched the docker's wooden protest placard from his hands and slammed it into his face. Broke his nose.'

'*Merde!* Why did he do that?'

'The docker claims it was unprovoked. Just a desire for violence. But the point is that if I can find him, I can lock him up for assault.' Slowly he brushed a fingertip along my scar. 'You would be safer with one of them off the streets until we have proof that he is involved in the murder of Mickey.'

An image of a striped cat lying dead at my feet flashed through my mind. 'We would all be safer.' I wrapped both my palms around his hand to keep it safe. 'I worry about you. Asking so many questions.'

He smiled and scooped me closer to him. 'It's my job, Eloïse. But it's not yours. So I want you to stop. Remain on the farm but don't go out on your own. You're safe here.'

'I am a sitting duck here, Léon. Both André and I. We might as well have a "come and get me" sign on the door.'

He knew me too well. He didn't let that pass.

'What happened?'

'You should check the hospitals in the area. To see if Piquet has registered with any.'

He cupped the back of my head in the palm of his hand, preventing me from turning away. 'What happened?' he asked again.

I closed my eyes. He leaned forward and softly kissed each eyelid.

'What happened?' he asked for the third time.

The words unhooked from the roof of my mouth and slid out for Léon to hear. Leaving the taste of blood on my tongue.

CHAPTER THIRTY-FOUR

The Dumoulin Air Base rolled out the red carpet for us. A line of fifty crisp young men from the mighty United States Air Force stood to attention as a welcome guard and we were greeted by the commanding officer himself, Colonel Masson. Smart, sharp and smiling.

There is something about a large number of men in uniform that is immediately intimidating. They have the better of you without moving a muscle. In identical uniform, shoulder to shoulder, they are no longer individuals, but merge into one superhuman being. They belittle you. They reduce you. Even when standing there doing nothing except staring straight in front of them like wooden soldiers, you know – and they know – that they are a highly efficient killing force. And parked behind them are their highly efficient killing machines.

Only Mayor Durand with his impressive gold chain of office around his neck and Captain Léon Roussel in his authoritative dark uniform and braid could have stood toe to toe with them. There were more than a hundred of us, some I recognised, some were new to me. We had been herded into a large soulless reception room where we were presented with indifferent wine and what they called potato chips.

Our party was mainly male, of course – the president of the Chamber of Commerce, the heads of the major businesses, a number of landowners like Papa, and a big-bellied hotel owner. Among the few women present, all done up in their Sunday best, were the town's well-respected chief librarian, as well as my old loud-voiced headmistress who oozed disapproval of the whole event and kept lifting her hand to wipe a sheen of sweat from her forehead as though the nearness of so much nuclear power made her nervous. And in a dress designed to have the military eyes out on stalks, Clarisse Favre. Léon had insisted she accompany me.

'Papa will be with me,' I'd pointed out. 'He can be my guard dog.'

'Your papa,' Léon said in his best stern-policeman voice, 'will have his eyes on the aeroplanes and his ears on the facts and figures. Not on you.'

I knew he was right. So here she was. Glued to my side. In a Chanel dress of moss-green linen, the exact colour of her eyes, skimming her slender hips. The plunging neckline was not disguised in any way by the addition of a tiny chiffon scarf at her neck. With her hair swept up in an elaborate knot she looked a million dollars, but this was not her usual style. When I asked her who she thought she was dressing for, she slid me a satisfied smile.

'For the Americans, *chérie*. They're men, aren't they?'

I laughed. Usually she prided herself on dressing only to please herself.

It was odd. The way the mood in the room changed. On the arrival of the visitors I was conscious of an awkward suspicious edge to them that was not well hidden behind the polite smiles and handshakes. But the air base had rolled out its most personable officers to mingle with us and answer our questions, and there was something about these American airmen with their clean-cut faces and their can-do attitude. There was something that was ... I struggled to put a word to it ... that was *inspiring*.

Highly skilled. Highly trained. And passionate about what they were doing here. Saving the free world. A few of them spoke a little French but the CO had laid on interpreters to mingle with them. I could feel the hostility drain away like sand running through my fingers. Across the room I caught the eye of Major Joel Dirke and we exchanged smiles, but he was caught in the grip of a local chicken farmer who was looking irate. Maybe the overflying aircraft were disturbing his hens' laying pattern. I'd heard one man claim the noise of the jets had made his dog so nervy it would not go boar-hunting anymore. What was Joel Dirke saying? That it's all part of saving the world?

It was Léon my eyes sought out. Again and again, scanning the heads, but he had not arrived yet and I felt a stirring of concern. What police business had detained him?

'Mr Caussade, I am pleased to see you came.'

Colonel Masson was standing in front of us, looking uncertain of his welcome. My father shook the CO's hand but grunted his response in Provençal, which made me want to pour my wine over him.

'I am Eloïse Caussade,' I offered, 'and this is my colleague from Paris, Mademoiselle Favre.'

He greeted us with military courtesy. 'It's good to see so many here,' he said, looking around the room. He was half a head taller than most, with eyes that drilled into you, seeking out your weak spot. 'I intend today, by the grace of God, to bring a spark of enlightenment to the subject of nuclear power and its force for doing the Lord's work. To purge the land of the evil of Communism which seeks to rid the world of His churches.'

Ah. So it was personal. I found myself liking this man who believed in the godliness of America's purpose in Europe.

'I look forward to hearing more,' I said. 'That's why we're here.' And before he could move on to the next group, I asked silkily, 'Is it true that you are planning on flying nuclear-powered aircraft over here from America, even though it is still in the early stages of testing?'

His surprise was so fleeting, I barely saw it. His military training kicked in. He knew exactly how to deal with an ambush. Shoot it down.

'Miss Caussade, you are mistaken.'

'About the aircraft being powered by nuclear energy? Or about it coming to Dumoulin Air Base?'

'Both.'

'Colonel, there are rumours about this prototype aircraft that are coming out of this air base. It clearly means you have an Intelligence leak. Are you aware of it?' I kept my voice low and private. 'The local Communists are using this information as yet more propaganda to turn people against American interference in our country. Rumours like this add fuel to the Communist fire.'

My father watched the colonel. Clarisse watched me. But I looked past them. I looked across the room, past the smart military khaki uniforms and the freshly pressed suits to the ornate gold mayoral chain of office with the horned head of a *taureau noir* at its heart, the symbol of Serriac. Its wearer, Mayor Charles Durand, brandished a glass in one hand and a cigar in the other, a fine-looking man in his grand regalia. Around him stood an attentive group. One man was voicing his opinions with a dramatic dance of his hands, but the mayor was not listening. He was staring at me. Not casually. Not out of boredom. He was staring straight at me like one of the USAF's anti-aircraft rockets. As if he would shoot me down.

A hand cupped my elbow. I looked round. It was Léon. Firmly he steered me away from the CO to a quiet corner and said, 'I have news.'

CHAPTER THIRTY-FIVE

LÉON ROUSSEL

Léon did not let go of Eloïse's arm. He stood close to her, holding on to it, because for some inexplicable reason he clung to the belief that while his hand was locked around her arm, she would be safe from rifle bullets and from knives sliding between ribs. It was self-delusional of course, he knew that. But right now it was all he had.

'What news?' she asked quickly.

She had a fire in her dark eyes today. It seemed to be consuming her. He recognised it at once. It was exactly how he felt when working on a crime case and knowing that the answers were close. The heat builds in your chest. A fire in there that never goes away. That's what he saw reflected in her eyes and it made him want to whisk her away from here. He glanced quickly around the noisy reception room, assessing the mood the way he would a rowdy street gathering on a Saturday night. Across the room both Colonel Masson and Mayor Durand still had their eyes on her.

Léon put a small smile on his face for their benefit. 'What the hell were you saying to Masson about the leak at the air base?'

She shook her head. 'Tell me, what news?'

'This morning I've been over at the burned cottage again with a couple of men, digging around. Literally.'

She was good. Her expression didn't change, just the faintest hiss escaped through her teeth. 'What did you find?'

'Nothing pleasant, I'm afraid, Eloïse.' He had thought about not telling her, but she deserved to know. 'We dug around in the garden and around the shed, and in the end we unearthed something of interest.'

'What?'

'A pair of bull's horns. They'd been hacked off very roughly.'

She didn't flinch. 'Goliath's?'

'It seems probable. We will have to unearth his head to make sure.'

She nodded. Her neck stiff. 'You must tell Papa.'

'Of course.'

He didn't mention the dried blood on the horns, indicating that the poor creature may have still been alive when they were removed.

'You think it was this Communist cell that committed the crime?'

'It looks that way but we need proof. I will bring Isaac in for questioning again.'

'But he told me the city-dwellers of Marseille would be too frightened to face a bull.'

'That's probably true.'

'So who would have the nerve to enter a field with a black bull like Goliath?' She paused and the sound of chatter buzzed in their ears. He wanted her to come to it herself.

'Isaac,' she whispered.

'It's possible. Again, we have no proof yet.'

'No, I don't believe it. Not Isaac. He would never do that. But we both know that there are many farmworkers who went off to earn more money in the factories and docks of Marseille, so they would have had experience of how to take on a bull.'

'It's possible.'

'Did you find anything else?'

'Tyre tracks. If we can trace Piquet's motorcycle, if we can make a match . . .'

'So many ifs. He could be anywhere.'

Léon tightened his grip on her arm. He could see the mayor heading their way. 'You have set yourself up here,' he murmured, 'as bait. In full view of anyone who might be interested.'

He saw her swallow, her long slender throat struggling as if something was caught there.

'I thought Gilles Bertin might have been among the guests, but I can't see him,' she said.

Léon thought about what it took for her to come here, believing Bertin might turn up. 'No, Eloïse. I contacted Colonel Masson and checked every name on the list. I would never let him anywhere near you. Or near André, for that matter.'

'Louis is playing guard-dog at home today. I sat him down at the bottom of the stairs with Papa's hunting rifle with instructions to shoot the balls off anyone who comes barging through the door.'

'For God's sake, Eloïse, you know that is—'

But he was interrupted by the smooth tones of the mayor. 'Captain Roussel, I think we are in for a treat today,' he said with a bonhomie that didn't quite match his face. He switched to Eloïse. '*Bonjour*, Eloïse.'

'*Bonjour*, Monsieur le Maire,' she said coolly, and walked stiffly away to join her father. Léon saw the good-looking major with whom she had gone riding immediately materialise at her side.

Dammit. What was that about?

Léon sat himself down next to the headmistress, Mademoiselle Madeleine Caron. She was a straight-backed woman in her fifties whose sharp features and equally sharp reprimands he recalled only too well from his schooldays. She was wearing a brown felt hat set at a precise right angle on her head and maintained a blinkered focus on the colonel. Léon listened to the colonel's talk on the necessity of establishing the Dumoulin base here, but he listened with only one ear, drifting in and out. Most of his attention was focused on the audience. They had all been shepherded into a lecture theatre with tiered seats and a podium up front for the speaker and the interpreter. There was lots of rustling and expectation in the room.

Colonel Masson had welcomed the visitors and run through the history of Dumoulin Air Base from a small grass airfield during the war to the efficient cog that it was now in the military machine that was fighting against the Soviet threat. The United States had already poured millions of American dollars into the air base, building full and extensive facilities for the airmen and aircraft deployed here. However, the runways were not long enough or sufficiently reinforced to accommodate the new larger and heavier aircraft coming into service. Masson spoke well. Just the right touch of military arrogance and paternalistic concern. His pride in the base and in his men shone through.

The colonel swept a hand in the direction of the front row. 'We are particularly pleased to welcome Monsieur Aristide Caussade and his daughter here today because we owe Monsieur Caussade a debt of thanks. By allowing us to take possession of a stretch of his land, it will enable us to extend our main runway from seven thousand feet to the ten thousand feet required for larger aircraft. *Merci*, Monsieur Caussade.'

He led a ripple of applause, though there was an awkwardness about it. People were not sure they wanted 10,000ft runways, and definitely not larger aircraft. Léon noticed that the mayor played it safe, giving token applause but no more and the woman beside Léon gave a grunt of anger. There was a stir of interest when Colonel Masson commenced a slide-show of the base's facilities and of the different types of aircraft on its apron. The images displayed up on screen paraded the sleek miracles of technology and Léon could not deny the thrill of viewing the aircraft roaring into action.

'Here we have the Republic F-84 Thunderjet, Strategic Air Command's primary strike aircraft. A turbojet fighter-bomber armed with six M3 Browning machine guns, plus of course a considerable weight of bombs and rockets.'

In a series of still shots the plane flashed across the screen, up into its take-off, black smoke billowing behind.

'Now the Boeing B-50 Superfortress.'

A large four-engine bomber loomed up on screen and a murmur ran through the crowd. Léon caught a quick movement by the headmistress next to him. She took out a camera from her bag on the floor at her feet, but before it got anywhere near her eye, it was removed by a polite young sergeant with a firm shake of the head.

'Handsome beasts, aren't they?' The colonel smiled with pride. 'And as soon as the extended runways are constructed, the new B-47 Stratojet will be deployed here. Designed by Boeing with thirty-five-degree swept-wings to fly at high speed and high altitude ...'

The CO's voice rumbled on but Léon's focus was on the faces around him. Seeking out any flash-point. One man with a deep scowl and his bottom teeth clenched on his moustache, locking in any words. The bank manager in his pin-striped suit, his head pulled back as far as it would go. An angry hooded pair of eyes at the end of the next row of seats. Elsewhere a shake of a head. And a blank expression nearby, except for a tight click of back teeth over and over.

'. . . six turbojets . . .'

The headmistress was sitting on her hands as though to keep them from striking out.

'. . . primary mission is as a nuclear bomber capable of striking the Soviet Union . . .'

On the other side of Léon sat five eager young men who ran the local football club. Mouths open. Eyes shining. Hanging on Colonel Masson's every word.

'. . . altitude of thirty-five thousand feet . . . mainstay of Strategic Air Command's bomber strength . . .'

Léon couldn't see Eloïse's face, though he'd tried. She was seated at the front beside her father. Clarisse on her right. Around the edge of the room stood a phalanx of American airmen, observing their French visitors with an attitude that Léon could only describe as professional but condescending, like the investigator into Mickey Ashton's murder. Léon was well aware that in American minds the French were inefficient, impolite and still had public lavatories that were little more than a hole in the ground. Americans were obsessed with plumbing. Plumbing and weapons. They were good at both.

'Now the big one,' Colonel Masson announced before pressing the button for the next slide. 'Our giant of the skies.'

He paused for dramatic effect. Léon saw Eloïse turn her head and say something to Clarisse, who smiled in response. Eloïse's profile looked tense and her hand brushed across her scar, just as the image of a gigantic aircraft burst on to the screen. Immediately the man in front of Léon cheered and a smattering of applause followed it.

'Ladies and gentlemen, I present to you the B-36 Peacemaker. We call it our "long rifle" because it will keep the peace for France and for all of Western Europe from as far away as America.'

More applause. It was hard for Léon to gaze at the Peacemaker and not feel grateful to it for the protection it offered. He could sense the conflicting emotions rampaging through the room, but no one looked ready to cause trouble. Not yet.

'Built by Convair in San Diego in California, the Peacemaker is the largest mass-produced piston-engined aircraft ever built.'

The headmistress muttered something sharply under her breath, pressed her hands to her breasts, then twitched her head to stare at Léon to see whether he'd noticed. In her way she reminded him of the colonel, tall and commanding, accustomed to giving orders.

'... with a wingspan of two hundred and thirty feet and with four bomb bays capable of delivering ...'

Something had happened. Eloïse was sitting bolt upright, shoulders stiff. Neck taut. What the hell had occurred while his attention was on Madeleine Caron at his side?

'. . . a phenomenal cruising altitude that puts it out of reach of most enemy interceptors and anti-aircraft guns . . .'

Léon checked the image on screen. What was there to upset Eloïse? Nothing. Just the plane. He scanned the room. Nothing out of place.

'. . . with a range of ten thousand miles . . .'

Eloïse turned. Eyes huge. They sought him out. He threw her a what's-gone-wrong expression but she abruptly got a grip on herself, shook her head at him and turned back to the colonel.

'. . . can stay aloft for forty hours . . .'

Léon rose to his feet, excused himself as he made his way to the end of the row of seats, and moved quietly forward, keeping against the side wall. One of the airmen positioned at the edges of the room politely asked him to remain still until the colonel had finished.

Colonel Masson was wrapping it up. 'But these are just pictures. No substitute for the real thing.' He smiled at his audience, then waved a hand towards the door. 'We will now take you outside and escort you around the base to show you the facilities and, more to the point, the aircraft up close. I'm sure you'd all enjoy . . .'

Mayor Durand stood, waiting until all eyes turned to him, then he interrupted the colonel. He ran a hand down his gold chain of office, fingering the bull's head at the centre.

'Colonel Masson, I speak on behalf of all the people of Serriac when I say it is the nuclear weapons that you store here that causes us greatest concern.'

There was a chorus of murmurs but the colonel quelled any rising unrest with a firm nod of agreement. 'That is why, Monsieur le Maire, as part of the tour, we will be taking you over to the concrete igloos where the nuclear bombs are stored and we will be explaining a certain number of safety measures that are in place.' He reintroduced the smile. 'Don't worry, none of the bombs is armed. That process only takes place once a bomb is onboard the aircraft. And now,' he indicated the door, 'before the tour, let us demonstrate the awesome power that the Soviet Union is up against. It so happens that one of America's mighty Convair B-36 aircraft is overflying France today, so we are fortunate that it will be performing a fly-past for us here at Dumoulin Air Base. Ladies and gentlemen, I give you the Peacemaker.'

A USAF airman, wearing uniform trousers so crisp they looked to Léon like they might snap if he bent a leg, whisked open the door and from outside rolled the sound of thunder, but louder, longer, stronger than any thunder they had ever heard. A mighty growing roar. For a moment it felt to Léon as if the end of the world was coming.

CHAPTER THIRTY-SIX

I am outside. Staring up at the sky. For a split second I couldn't think straight. The noise pummelled my brain. Six 28-cylinder engines roared past just over my head and all I could feel was the power of the great Peacemaker on its fly-past, the ferocious mind-bending power. Called the Peacemaker because you only needed to take one look at it coming for you and you would go down on bended knees to make peace immediately.

But I wasn't ready to make peace. Not now. Not while these men of war were gazing with such devotion up into the skies that they were missing what was right under their noses.

We had all been herded outside and divided into four groups for the tour, ready to view the camp recreational facilities – the gym, swimming pool, cinema, bars, games room, library, boxing ring, as well as the church, hospital and technical control centre. It struck me as a bad idea. Like showing starving kids the steak and chips you get to eat every night.

'First,' announced Major Joel Dirke, 'we will show you the stars of the show today – the aircraft themselves. But don't go too close. I wouldn't want any VIP guests to get sucked up by a jet or pulverised by a propeller.' He waved his hand like a magician producing them out of a hat and we all turned to inspect the large group of planes at the start of the runway, engines already fired up. 'Thunderjet fighters at the front. The B-50 bombers at the rear.'

I saw the way he looked at them. The way a parent looks at a beloved child singing on stage, pride and joy gleaming on his face. Clarisse had been swept into a different group but I'd made straight for this one the moment I saw he was to be its escort. Interestingly, so did the mayor. He came to stand right next to me.

'You have been asking too many questions, Eloïse,' he said, leaning too close, checking my reactions. 'Getting in the way.'

No preamble. No charm. No, 'Nice to see you here, Eloïse.' I didn't back away.

'Getting in the way of what?' I asked.

'In the way of things you don't understand. Of people you don't know.' He added with emphasis, 'People you don't want to know.'

His eyes were hard and leaden. If he thought he could frighten me, he was right. Blood pounded in my chest.

I gave him a smile. 'I'm surprised you don't have your camera with you today.'

'What's that supposed to mean?'

'Well, I know how you like to keep photographs in your desk.'

I was stirring. Stirring hard.

His teeth bit down on his lower lip, so fiercely he must have tasted blood. It effectively stopped any words rushing out, but the expression in his eyes made the pounding rise to my throat.

'Now, ladies and gentlemen,' Major Dirke said, raising his voice over the increasing noise of the aircraft engines, 'let me introduce you to the elephant walk.'

Several people laughed.

'Elephant walk is a USAF term for when a number of aircraft taxi in close formation down the runway for minimum interval take-off.' He smiled at me. I didn't smile back.

Twelve silver planes were rolling towards us. In the lead came six fighters in pairs, with six huge bombers tight behind them, with 'U.S. AIR FORCE' emblazoned in huge letters on their sides in case we should forget who was laying on this show for us today. I glanced round for Léon, wanting him at my side, but he was standing behind the four groups, deep in conversation with Colonel Masson. Discussing the Mickey Ashton murder, I guessed, but all talk was forced to cease as the brain-drilling whine of the jets grew louder.

A phalanx of raw power roared past us as the first two fighters surged up into the air together with such unimaginable force that I could feel it pressing down on my body. Rattling my lungs and pushing against my eyeballs. Vibrating the ground under my feet. Shaking me up.

Adrenaline pulsing. As the next pair of fighters accelerated with a blast at our eardrums, I looked around at the faces in the crowd, all transfixed. Except one.

Time seemed to slow to little more than a crawl as I registered a face with eyes blinking in slow motion, a hand with no rings undoing a jacket's top button, reaching inside, under an oyster-coloured blouse to bring out . . .

Time sped up. It cartwheeled forward and I started to move. To open my mouth. To shout a warning. To drag my feet from the concrete in which they had sunk and hurl myself forwards.

Too late. My hand reached out but found . . . nothing. The headmistress was gone. Mademoiselle Madeleine Caron was charging across the gap that lay between the visitors and the runway as fast as her long legs would carry her and in each hand she gripped what looked like a large khaki egg. Her loose skirt was billowing around her legs with every stride and her hat flew off, so that her long greying hair streamed out behind her.

A collective cry rose from the onlookers, a shout of warning from the airmen. All drowned out by the deafening sound of the jet engines. She was jinking from side to side as she ran, quick and agile. The crack of a rifle ripped through the air but the bullet spat harmlessly into the ground at her feet. She sent one of the grenades spinning through the air with all the grace and speed of a fast bowler in English cricket.

Time paused. We all saw it. The grenade arcing through

the air. Hitting the concrete runway. Rolling. Over and over. No one breathed. Then time was off again at top speed. The explosion. The crater. The undercarriage of a plane blown apart, the wing crashing on to the concrete. The noise a dull thump, a screech of metal.

Madeleine Caron spun to face us, bullets dancing around her as she took off once more, dodging and darting, coming right at us. A red stain flowered on the shoulder of her jacket but she kept running, drawing back her other arm to throw what was clutched in her hand.

All around me people turned to run, screaming. Everything happening fast, feet tumbling over each other. I saw her face now. Drained of colour. As if all her blood had flowed into her rage. Two more bullets thudded into her side but she stumbled on until one keen marksman sent a shot right through her thigh. She dropped to her knees. Hauled back her arm and launched the last grenade. Straight at me.

I jerked back. Tried to run. An elbow thudded into my back, a foot hooked around my ankle. I stumbled, scrabbling on all fours, fingernails clawing at the concrete to find a hold. My body braced itself for limbs to be blown apart but, when the explosion came, it wasn't what I expected. I heard the boom all right. But then it felt like being hit by a truck from behind. I crashed to the ground face-first and crimson pain seemed to scorch right up inside my head. I knew I must be standing at the mouth of hell.

CHAPTER THIRTY-SEVEN

I risked opening one eye a crack. The light was dim and I could taste blood on my teeth. I opened my other eye. Not a good move. Pain turned into blinding light inside my head. I closed my eyes, waited till I could catch hold of a few ricocheting thoughts and attach them together, then opened my eyes again.

A sense of grief sat heavy on my chest, crushing my ribs, but I didn't know why. It took me a full minute to work out that I was in my own bed in my own bedroom and that the grunting noise I could hear was my own breathing. I tried to pull together the images spinning through my mind but they kept splintering apart again and again until the only one I was left with was Mademoiselle Madeleine Caron on her knees, blood darkening her blouse and seeping from her mouth. Her eyes huge with rage. And hate.

I raised a hand to my face and found a bandage on my forehead, a dressing on my nose, and as I touched it with cautious fingertips I swore under my breath.

Léon? Where was Léon? Was he hurt? An image of him lying bleeding on the ground tore through my mind, but surely he'd been too far back with the colonel. Dimly I dragged forward the memory of him in conversation. He *must* be safe. But . . . I could still see a blurred image . . . of a dark uniform shredded.

'Please.' I whispered the word out loud to give it strength. 'Please let him be safe.'

'Who do you mean, Eloïse?'

My head rolled to the side. A man's face broke into a thousand pieces and slowly re-formed. Amber eyes. Sandy hair. A look of concern softening his features.

'André,' I murmured.

André was seated in a chair beside my bed. He was smoking a cigarette and had a book open on his lap. Even though I couldn't see its cover, I knew by the extreme thickness of it that it was *Les Misérables*. He reached out, slotted my hand in his and closed his fingers around mine. His were warm, mine were cold.

'That was close, little sister.' He squeezed my hand. 'Too close.' He leaned forward and kissed my head.

That was all. But I could feel a jumpiness in his fingers that had not been there before.

'What happened? After she threw the grenade. Who was hurt?'

'Two guests died.'

My heart stopped. 'Who?'

'Two men from the bank. No one you know.'

No one you know. Four words that pieced my world back together.

'I'm sorry,' I said. 'For their families.' Guilt soured my stomach. 'If I hadn't suggested this open day on the base, they would still be alive.'

'No, that's nonsense. It would have happened eventually. When the USAF got round to inviting locals over in an attempt to build bridges, Mademoiselle Caron would have done exactly the same. It seems she was hell-bent on causing mayhem from what I heard.'

'Is she dead?'

'Yes, she is.'

'Was the mayor hurt?'

'No, unfortunately.'

'And Léon?'

There. The question was out.

'Don't look so worried. You can't get rid of Léon so easily.'

'He's okay?'

'He took a hit but not serious.'

I pushed myself to sit up straight and wanted to seize the words from his tongue. 'How bad? Where is he? What happened to him?'

'Calm down, you'll only start bleeding again. Lie back. He's doing okay, that's what the ambulance men said when they brought you home. He's in the military hospital at the air base. His back got a bit cut up, but he'll survive.' He stubbed out his cigarette and smiled at me. 'Léon is made of solid steel, you should know that.'

I nodded, just once. Lights darted across my eyes, making André's face sparkle. 'Tell me what happened at the end.'

'You don't remember?'

'I was hit from behind. Was it the blast from the grenade? It felt like a truck.'

The truck in Paris slammed into her mind . . . the strings of blood hurling themselves across the car.

'No, no truck. It was Léon. It seems he threw himself over you to protect you, but the blast hit him so hard that he smacked you into the ground. Concussion and a broken nose, but you'll live.'

The silence grew loud in the room while we both considered whether that last statement was true or not.

'A hero,' André muttered softly.

Was he happy for Léon? Proud of his friend? Or jealous? I couldn't tell. He released my hand, folded his arms and looked serious.

'Now,' he said, 'down to business. Let's hear everything that occurred at the air base.'

I lay back against the pillow and talked him through it, step by step. When I say 'talked him through it', that's not quite true. There were several times when I found my eyes shut and my talking was all inside my head, so I had to backtrack. But he was patient. Gentle. Kinder than he'd been since the crash. We talked about Madeleine Caron. Deceased. Shot dead. 'She was a raving Communist,' he said, 'and she certainly made her point. That will be millions of dollars worth of damage she caused to the planes and the runway.

I don't think Colonel Masson will be inviting locals around again in a hurry.'

I told him about my conversation with Mayor Durand. I left it till last because I knew he would be angry.

'You told him you knew about the copied documents in his desk? Are you crazy, Eloïse? Why the hell did you do that?'

'Because I am sick to death of having my life threatened. Can't you see that? I am sick of having people hiding in shadows, stalking my movements and making my mind spiral down into black holes. I want to drag them out of the shadows. To hold them up to the light where I can get a good look at the bastards.'

I was shaking. Not with fear this time. Not with shock. I was shaking with gut-wrenching rage. 'I'm not like you, André,' I said fiercely. 'I thought I was. But too many people are getting hurt. Including you. I can't accept it as a necessary part of the job, I can't live with them hovering round my bed at night. I thought I could but I was wrong.'

'Eloïse, hush, let it go.' He stroked my arm where the blisters from the stable fire had left their mark. 'Rest now. It's almost morning, it will be light soon and then the shadows will melt away and you'll feel like my brave Eloïse again.'

But it wasn't true, I knew that. I would never feel like that Eloïse again. I'd lost something in that blast yesterday that I wouldn't be getting back.

'I told Mayor Durand that I knew about the top-secret documents in his desk because I wanted to frighten him, to panic him into making a mistake. It's the only way he'll ever reveal his source of Intelligence at the air base.'

'They are scared of you, Eloïse.'

'That's good. Because I'm scared of them.'

He studied me by the dim light of the lamp. 'But they don't know you,' he said softly, 'like I know you.' He patted my hand. 'Now go to sleep. It won't feel so bad when you wake up.'

I let myself believe him.

'I'll read you to sleep.'

When I was a child he always read me a bedtime story, always, in which good triumphed over evil. Books, I've learned since, do not tell the truth. He sat back in his chair with what came close to a contented sigh and opened the book.

'I may not be here when you wake up,' he told me as he turned to the first page.

'Where will you be?' I asked, anxious.

'At church.'

I blinked with shock. Even that hurt.

André started to read aloud the story of man's attempt to make amends in life for something he did wrong, his voice smooth and comforting. I closed my eyes.

I was woken by shouting. Somewhere downstairs in the house.

'Get out of my way, you piece of pig-shit.'

'*Non.*'

'Don't you point your rifle at me.'

'*Allez-vous en.*'

'I'm going nowhere, so get off the stairs.'

'Clarisse!' I called out.

'There, you see?' Clarisse's voice spiralled up to me, triumphant. 'She wants me to go up there.'

I heard Louis' belligerent tone on the stairs and I realised André must have set him there to guard me, the way I'd done for him yesterday. I liked that. Not just the extra safety, but the fact that my brother cared enough to do so.

'Louis,' I yelled, 'let her come up.'

I heard his grunt in response. And her delighted laugh.

Clarisse swept into my bedroom with all the ferocity of the mistral, except that the mistral is a cold wind whereas Clarisse was brimming with warmth and flowers.

'*Chérie,*' she said, throwing open the shutters, '*ma pauvre chérie.*'

The day was overcast, the sky a dirty white and the air cooler, which made my pounding head easier to ignore. 'Clarisse, what are you doing here on a stinking farm? I never thought to see you step foot in a bull-yard.' I grinned at her and felt my nose pop painfully.

'Only for you, Eloïse, only for you.' She rolled her eyes in disgust and dumped a vast bouquet of flowers on my bedcover.

'Thank you. You are kind to me.'

'I am. And don't you forget it when you get back to work.'

I skipped over that thought. She bent close and kissed my

311

cheek so lightly that I barely felt it. She smelled even better than the flowers.

'You look a terrible mess,' she declared bluntly.

'Have you heard anything more? About Madeleine Caron, the woman who did the attack?'

'I've been asking around and everyone says the same, just that she was a headmistress with strong anti-American views. One old gossip smacked her toothless gums with pleasure in telling me that Madeleine Caron had an affair with Mayor Durand in their younger days, but that might just be the old crone sticking the knife in. It seems that Colonel Masson wanted some people like her to come to the open day because he had the messianic belief he could convert them.'

'Such hubris would be funny if it weren't so tragic. What about the others who were killed in the blast?'

'Unlucky bastards.'

She reached into her bag, pulled out a silver hip-flask and unscrewed the top. She tipped it to her lips and took a long swig, before offering it to me.

'Breakfast,' she said. 'Good for sore heads.'

I took the flask, drank and felt a small fire spring into life in my gut. Cognac.

'Thanks. Now, one more favour, please?'

She rolled her eyes. 'I can guess.'

The military hospital on Dumoulin Air Base was sterile. The building was newly constructed, white painted, perfectly clean and run with military precision. If I were sick, I mean really sick, I'd rather burrow into the warm straw in our barn next to Cosette and the rats than be pinned between pristine sheets in this soulless sterile USAF box. But I was grateful to them. When I saw Léon lying on his side swathed in bandages and bruises, I wanted to kneel down and kiss their shiny germ-free floor in thanks for taking good care of him.

'Hello, Captain. How are you feeling?'

He opened his grey eyes. Bloodshot, I admit, but open and looking at me with the kind of expression that made me want to strip my clothes off and climb right in there with him. To wrap myself around him and hold him till his injuries were forgotten.

'Oh, Eloïse,' he said with an ache in his voice, 'look at you.'

'You're not doing so good yourself,' I said with a smile. It hurt to smile, so I kept it for when it was needed.

I kissed his unshaven cheek and then his lips, a gentle brush, but he wrapped an arm around me and pulled me to him. I buried my battered face in his neck and we stayed like that, breathing each other in, letting our skin grow together again. When a nurse came to re-dress the wounds on his back, Léon said, 'Not now,' in a tone that sent her scurrying further down the ward. She was accustomed to obeying the voice of authority. I sat down on the chair next to his bed, a stiff military seat not designed for comfort. He continued to lie on his side to ease any pressure on his back, but he held my hand as if he might slide down somewhere dark if he let go.

'Now,' he said, 'tell me. Broken nose?'

I nodded. Carefully.

'I'm sorry.' He pulled a face. 'Concussion?'

'Better now.'

I had stripped the bandaging off my face and I thought I didn't look too bad. Clearly I was wrong. My forehead was bruised from one side to the other, with a wide scrape of skin removed, nose swollen, cheekbones puffy, eyes blackened. I still wore a small dressing on my nose to keep it straight. Compared to the Paris crash, this was nothing.

'And you?' I asked.

'Just a few holes in my back.'

'Just?'

'That's it. Now let's talk about what went on there yesterday.' Even in bed he had his policeman's face on. 'There was more news that I wanted to tell you, not just about the bull's horns we found at the burned cottage.'

'What?'

'It's about Gilles Bertin.'

'You've found him?'

'No. But I found something of interest.'

I wrapped his fingers tight in mine. A snake of fear shifted position inside me. 'Tell me.'

'I finally got my hands on a search warrant. On suspicion of criminal activities.'

'To search what place?'

'Guess.'

I took a deep breath. 'Gilles Bertin's house. You've searched it?'

'Bullseye.'

CHAPTER THIRTY-EIGHT

LÉON ROUSSEL

Her face.

Hadn't it been through enough? Léon wanted to take it in his hands and kiss each rip and bruise and break. There was black blood in her nostrils, panda rings around her eyes. Yet she seemed indifferent to it and unselfconscious when a passing patient stared openly.

Her fingers touched his lips, as if to pull the words from behind them. 'Tell me,' she said again.

He described the search of Gilles Bertin's house in Arles, just the way he'd written it up in his report. The house was rented, so he'd looked up the owner on the town's register and acquired a key from her. On Friday the premises were empty, so he and his two officers proceeded to search every cupboard and drawer, as well as all possible places of concealment.

'I did that too,' she whispered.

'What? How did you get in?'

She gave him a hint of a smile. 'I have hidden skills. I didn't tell you because I knew it was illegal and I didn't dig up anything that helped us.' She paused, cupped his chin in her hand and gave it a sharp shake. 'Did you?'

He imagined her finding the photographs of herself hidden behind the bedhead and the sickness that must have welled up in her when she shuffled through them.

'Yes, I think we did.'

'You found the photographs? Of me.'

He nodded and a dull flush seeped up her neck.

'And the aircraft ones as well?' she asked.

'Yes.'

'What else?'

'Guns and a rifle.'

Her eyes widened and her scabbed eyebrows shot up. 'Where? I searched but didn't find them.'

'They were under the floorboards.'

She gave a low-key whoop of delight. In the next bed a pleasant young crew-cut airman with his leg in plaster looked across but quickly went back to his *Life* magazine.

'Did you take the guns away?'

'Of course. We are now searching for Bertin himself.'

She sat back in her chair. She looked a small figure in this large impersonal ward but there was something in her that filled the space, something like those nuclear bombs out there on the base. Something unstoppable. She narrowed her eyes and smacked her hand on his wrist.

'Stop teasing me,' she said.

But he hesitated a moment longer. This was police business. He shouldn't be telling her.

'I found a small diary. Under the linoleum in the bathroom.'

'You are very thorough.'

'It's my job to be.' But he hesitated once more.

'Come on, Léon,' she said softly with the sideways look she gave when she knew he was uncertain how she would take something. 'Let me hear it.'

'In the diary was a list of your movements each day, what you do and where you go.'

To his surprise she shrugged. 'I have got used to the idea that I am being watched. I don't know why. Gilles Bertin seems,' again the dull flush, 'obsessed.'

'Obsessed, maybe. Or reporting to someone.'

This time he felt a tremor ripple through her fingers, though her expression didn't change.

She thought for a minute and then pointed out, 'But none of that helps us.' She moved closer, her voice a whisper. 'Which means there must be something else you found.'

His fears for her safety were growing stronger. 'I hope you came here with Clarisse, not alone,' he said. 'Where is she?'

'Outside in the car.' She waved a hand dismissively. 'What is the something else?'

'It's a photograph of two men. Drinking in a bar together somewhere, laughing as if they know each other well.'

'Who are they?'

'A man who I believe, from your description, to be Gilles Bertin. Pencil moustache and deep chin cleft.'

'And the other?'

'Colonel Frank Masson.'

CHAPTER THIRTY-NINE

Clarisse drove me home. She wouldn't come into the house, so we sat in silence listening to the ticking of the engine of her cream Ford Vedette. One of the dogs wandered over and cocked a leg on the front wheel, but to my surprise she laughed.

'Thank you,' I said, 'for all you've done. It has meant a lot to have you here.'

I stretched across the seat and enfolded my fragrant friend in my arms, and she stayed there, her head against mine, far longer than I expected. 'Go back to Paris,' I said with an affectionate hug. 'It's safer there.'

She drew back with a wince. Her poor ribs had taken a bad knock in the general panic to escape the grenade yesterday. 'I'll go if you come with me,' she said. 'Come with me now. Right now. Before things get worse.'

She was smiling her usual sleek smile but I could see in her eyes how earnestly she meant it.

'I can't. Not until I've found the driver of the van. André will not be safe till I do.'

'Oh Eloïse,' she sighed. 'And what will you do when you find him? Kill him?'

It wasn't said as a joke. She was deadly serious.

'Of course not,' I said lightly. 'That's what the police are for.'

She stared at me, examining my battered face, completely unconvinced. 'I worry about you,' she muttered.

Four simple words that squeezed my heart. I was so touched, so tempted to shout, 'Drive, Clarisse, drive. To Paris. To safety. To a life without bullets whistling through my hair or grenades hurtling at my face.'

To a life without Léon?

'Don't worry,' I said. 'I intend to come out of this in one piece. But thank you, I'm grateful, I truly am.' I opened the car door. 'Now go back to Paris.' I climbed out.

'Damn you,' she laughed, and smacked the cream fascia with her palm, 'you'll be the death of me.' She roared off in a cloud of dust.

I gave her half an hour head start and then I drove to Arles.

I took my time. On foot in the old part of town. Using window reflections to check behind me, dodging down shortcuts, twisting through alleyways only fit for cats. The ancient stone walls wrapped around me and I kept in their deep shadow as I doubled back on myself in the maze of tiny narrow streets where the sun rarely reached. The strips of sky overhead were thin and grey as the cobbles. I liked it that way. Trapped. No escape.

This time I would wait in his house till he came home. However long it took. Days. Weeks. I'd be there to greet him. I touched the canvas bag at my side, felt the weight of the gun and the weight of my decision. Both took me to the edge.

Clarisse's words whispered in my ear. *What will you do when you find him? Kill him?*

To my surprise, the door of Bertin's house was unlocked. I stood in the tiled entrance hall and listened. No sound, no movement except the movement of the thoughts in my head. They were crashing into each other until I drew out the gun and curled my hand around its metal grip. That silenced them.

I removed my shoes and edged my way on silent feet through the rooms. The place felt different. Less serene, more jumpy. Or was that me? The image of Léon in his dark police uniform and with a legal warrant in his pocket searching each room slid into my mind and loosened my breathing. I didn't expect to find Gilles Bertin here this morning but I was willing to wait. And wait. But first I checked the downstairs rooms and the kitchen. No hint of him in the living room or dining room, but the kitchen bore his imprint.

A cup of coffee sat half-drunk on the table alongside the flaky remains of a croissant and a small glass dish of apricot jam. A jacket hung on the chair. The window at the back looked out on to a miniature courtyard with a slatted bench and a limp climbing rose. No sunlight, just the dirty lid of the grey sky. On the table lay an open newspaper and a pair of heavy-rimmed spectacles. The yard was empty.

I stepped back against the wall just inside the kitchen door and stood there immobile, my ears straining to catch the faintest scratch or whisper. After a further two minutes I shifted to the bottom of the stairs. Out in the open, I moved quickly, racing on tiptoe to the upper floor. I stopped, listened. With fingers cold as ice on the gun grip I edged to the first door and stepped inside.

No one. Nothing. An empty bedroom with no wardrobe to hide in. Musty and unused.

Yet I was convinced Gilles Bertin was here. Somewhere. Unless he'd left in such a hurry he'd had to abandon his coffee and spectacles. He didn't strike me as a man that careless, so I made my way silently across the landing towards what I remembered to be the main bedroom. The door was part-open. With my foot I pushed it further, gun out in front of me.

I saw him at once, Gilles Bertin himself, and I resisted the urge to back away. Smart dark suit trousers, Ronald Colman moustache, hair slicked down. The distinctive shaded cleft in his chin. Stupidly it occurred to me that it must be hard to shave in there. Not that he'd be shaving anymore. Gilles Bertin was sprawled flat on his back and the front of his white shirt had been decorated with a scarlet sunburst.

Something shut down in my head. First Mickey. Now Bertin. My legs wanted to rush me to his side, but I clung on to my sense of caution and I entered slowly. Eyes and gun barrel darting over every corner of the room. Skin prickling. Finger itching to pull the trigger.

No one else was in the room. I stood at Bertin's side, staring down at the dead body of the man who had struck such fear in me, and I hated the feel of tears on my cheeks. I turned away. He wasn't worth my tears. Quickly I searched the rest of the house, creeping on tiptoe, jumping at the slightest shadow, but I forced myself into every room.

Reluctantly I returned to the main bedroom. Neat, tidy, dark furniture, damask bedcover. I recalled only too well what was hiding behind the bedhead, so I went over, located the photographs in the pouch and dropped it into my bag. I forced my gaze back to the bloody shirt on the body on the floor.

I must go and telephone the police. Léon won't be there. But still. Go. Telephone.

Instead I dropped to my knees on the hard wooden floor that Léon had torn up. This close, Bertin's face was slack and without menace, eyes closed, specks of blood glistening in his moustache.

Glistening? Not dried to black flecks?

It had only just happened. *Get out. Get out now. Run.*

A noise behind me. I spun round still on my knees and found myself nose to nose with the wrong end of a gun.

*

'Eloïse! *Merde!* I almost shot you.'

I looked up. My mother's face stared back at me.

'Isaac!' He'd been behind the door. I jumped to my feet. 'Isaac, what are you doing here?' My words came to a halt as I took in the gun in his fist. The blood on his fingers. The smear of scarlet streaked across his shirt-front. My hand grasped at his arm and clenched it tight. 'What have you done?'

My brother's wide eyes clouded with panic. 'No, Eloïse, no, no. It wasn't me. I didn't do it.'

He opened his fingers and released the gun as though it burned his skin. It clattered to the floor and both of us jumped back from it. I stared at its blued metal. I knew the weapon, a Smith & Wesson revolver, Chief's Special. Small, compact, a five-round cylinder, American manufacture. Somewhere my brain registered these facts. As if they were more important than the fact of a man lying dead at my feet with a sticky hole blasted through his chest. That fact got pushed away to somewhere dark. Somewhere I didn't want to touch.

'What the hell happened to your face?' Isaac demanded.

I swung back to him, suddenly angry. I didn't know whether the anger was at my brother or at the man on the floor. 'What the hell happened to your hands?'

Our gaze fixed on the blood on them. It was daubed over his palms in a spider's web of scarlet runnels, but how do you get blood on your hands if you shoot someone with a gun? It doesn't happen. Unless you put a hand on them. To check that they're dead.

'What happened here, Isaac?'

'I didn't shoot him. I swear I didn't, Eloïse.' He pushed his hands away from him as if he couldn't bear to have them near. He was shaking his head back and forth, denying their existence.

I had to get him out of this room. I took hold of his arm and propelled him out the door. The bathroom was at the end of the landing and I swept him inside, turned on the washbasin taps and pushed his hands into the flow of water. The basin turned pink.

'Tell me exactly why you are here,' I said. 'We have to be quick. The police will be on their way.'

In the mirror I could see his face as white as the wall tiles, his lips unsteady. I leaned my body against him to offer comfort.

'Please, Isaac.'

He kept his eyes down, his pale lashes shutting out the world and me with it. 'I was given instructions to come here,' he said. 'To come to this house. I was told the door would be unlocked and I must go upstairs to wait for a message from someone.' His gaze flicked briefly to my face in the mirror. 'It's not you, is it?'

'No, Isaac. It's not.'

'I came here and found . . .' The words dried up.

'Was anyone else here?'

'No. I felt the man's chest to see if he was breathing but . . .' He shook his head.

'Do you know who he is?'

'No.'

'What happened next?'

'I heard the front door open. I snatched up the gun because I thought it was . . .'

I turned off the tap. 'You thought it was the killer returning? For you?'

He nodded, one sharp terrified jerk of his head. I lifted my skirt, it was a full circular navy-blue one, and I dried his hands on the underside of it. I didn't want any sign of him left on the towel.

'So you saw no one?'

'No.'

I wiped the taps and washbasin with my skirt. 'Tell me who gave you the instructions to come here.'

For the first time he looked at me, blue eyes dark with confusion. 'I can't.'

'Isaac,' I raised my voice, 'this is not the time to be secretive about your Communist affiliations. You've been set up. Someone wants you accused of murder. Can't you see that? The police will be here any moment. You have to get out. But first,' I buttoned up his jacket to hide the smear of blood on his shirt, 'first, tell me who sent you here?'

'I can't.' I opened my mouth to object but he stepped away. The initial shock was passing. He was gathering himself together, his limbs stiffening, his mouth firmer. 'I can't tell you, Eloïse, because I don't know. The leader of our action group within the Parti Communiste Français contacts our controller by telephone. We have no idea who it is. It's safer that way.'

'So you do the bidding of someone you don't know.'

'It is not as blind as you make it sound.'

'Isn't it?'

Now was not the time to argue the point. I steered him out the door on to the landing.

'Run,' I said urgently.

He blinked hard. Realisation was dawning on him. 'Eloïse, you must leave with me. Right now.'

'Go, Isaac, go. After what happened at the air base, the police will be looking to show the Americans how they treat violent Communists.'

Abruptly he wrapped an arm around my shoulders. 'Thank you.' He kissed my cheek. 'Come too.'

'First I must deal with the gun.'

He'd forgotten the gun. His fingerprints all over it.

'Go now,' I urged. 'I'll follow.' I pushed him to the stairs. 'I promise.'

With a last nervous look back at me, my brother raced down the stairs and out the front door. I lifted my skirt, snatched off my waist-petticoat, wet it under the tap and wiped every surface either of us might have touched, including the gun. When I'd finished, I stood over Bertin. I wasn't sorry. I couldn't find it within myself to wish him back into his life. The cleft like the mark of Cain on his chin. But he held no power over me now.

Who was responsible?

I hurried down the stairs and out into the street, ears straining for the sound of police boots. When I turned the

327

corner at the end I heard a car's engine come roaring into the street behind me. We'd made it out only just in time. As I wove my way through the old streets of Arles back to my car, I thought about the gun lying on the floor back in the house. I hated the knowledge of what it had done. I hated the hand that had held it. When I said I knew the weapon, the Smith & Wesson revolver, I didn't mean I knew the make of it. I meant I knew the gun. The *actual* gun. I knew it because I'd last seen it in the drawer of Mayor Durand's desk.

CHAPTER FORTY

I wanted to get the dust of Arles off my feet and the stink of its air out of my lungs. Worse, much worse, I wanted to get the image of a man with a hole in his chest out of my head. But I was so worried about Isaac and about Léon in his hospital bed that for one foolish slippery moment I forgot to be worried about me.

I'd parked on the wide main road again, not far from Clarisse's hotel on the south side of the old town. My thinking had been this: it would make for a quick getaway. If I needed it. Today was Sunday, so the town was in a lazy mood under the overcast skies, quietly catching its breath after the bartering and trading and shouting of yesterday's street market. On Sundays Arlesians stretched out their legs under a café's small zinc table, sipped their wine and shuffled cards in a game of belote.

Sunday in Arles was not a day for holes in chests.

My 2CV was still where I'd left it under a mottled scaly plane tree, a pavement café murmuring contentedly nearby.

My only thought was to get to Serriac as fast as possible. To confront the mayor. To speak to the police. To start laying out the facts in an order that made sense inside my pounding head.

That's why I didn't see it, not until I reached my Citroën, one hand on its door. The flat tyre. I walked around the car, inspecting it, and felt my gut twist. Not one flat tyre, but four flat tyres. I groaned and looked around me in a quick but thorough sweep. He was here somewhere, I was sure of it. I reached into my boot and removed the tyre iron.

'Can I help you, mademoiselle?'

Each word was steeped in irony. They seemed to come from the shadow of a grey van parked in the side street next to the café, so I walked over, the metal bar tight in my fist at my side.

'*Bonjour,*' I said. 'I've been looking for you.'

Maurice Piquet stepped forward into the light. I didn't run. I *didn't* run. Instead I did look to see if he had a knife, but he was holding nothing in his meat-cleaver hands. He was wearing a dark fedora over his spiky hair; a lightweight suit covered up his bulk and made him almost blend in among the tourists. Almost. How can you blend in when you have the eyes of a killer?

'You've been restyling my car, I see,' I said.

'And you've been restyling your face. Pick a battle with a brick wall, did you?'

'Something like that.' I didn't dare look away from his square face, not for a second.

Without turning my back, I moved over to the café and sat down at one of the pavement tables under a striped sun umbrella, the tyre iron discreetly across my lap.

'Won't you join me, Monsieur Piquet?'

He'd have joined me anyway. He was more alert now, as if his brain had ground through its gears, and he sat down heavily opposite me. I signalled the waiter.

'Two brandies, *s'il vous plaît.*'

'What the shit are you playing at, lady?' Piquet demanded.

'I'm not playing. I'm serious.'

'I don't like games, especially bitch games.'

I let it pass. Insults were harmless, knives were not. Ask Mickey. Piquet's voice was deep, the kind that seems to rise up from somewhere underground, which was exactly where I wished he was right now. He lit a cigarette. I waited till I had his full attention.

'Why have you and Bertin been trying to kill me?'

He looked surprised by the question; his bristly black eyebrows shot up, but he looked tired too, as if hadn't had it easy either and I was just one more annoyance to his day. 'Because you and that bastard crippled brother of yours are filthy traitors to France.'

That wasn't the reply I was expecting. The waiter brought our drinks and I reached for mine a little too fast. I felt the warm liquid burn the roof of my mouth and I gripped my glass to keep my hand steady. At the table to one side of us a young couple gazed at each other like new lovers and I sat back stiffly in my chair. I didn't want anyone, even someone I didn't know, to think Piquet and I were lovers.

'André and I are not traitors,' I stated. 'You and Bertin are the ones betraying France, you and your Communist comrades in Moscow.'

He laughed and there was something in it that made my skin crawl. 'Listen, bitch, get your facts straight. You and your Commie brother André are the ones stirring up shit here. He's been working for the MGB for years as a double agent, thinking that we haven't pegged him, and now he has dragged his baby sister into it too. Don't think we don't know what you're doing, because we do. You're as bad as he is.'

This didn't make sense. Who was this man?

He knocked back his brandy and his stone-grey eyes observed me with disgust. 'First he comes down here, sucking information out of the Yank airmen every weekend, and then you join him and take over his job.'

My teeth clamped down on my tongue. My hands kept clear of the metal bar on my lap. I didn't trust myself with either of them.

'You start shaking your tail at every American who comes near,' he continued, 'with the intention of milking them for new data – the airmen in the bar and at the dance, the major you took riding. Don't look at me like you don't know what the fuck I'm talking about, lady.'

He had a tongue in his head full of venom. I leaned forward, hands flat on the table.

'You're wrong,' I said. '*You* are the Communist. *You* and

Bertin are both MGB Soviet agents. You are the one who chased me out of Serriac on your motorcycle, aren't you? Admit it.'

'You're right, lady, I did.'

'And the note. You put the note on my windscreen to scare me into running back to Paris, didn't you?'

'That was Bertin. He wanted you gone from anywhere near the air base. But you've got it all upside down, lady. Think about it. *You* are the interfering bitch who set up the visitor session at the air base, so don't even bother denying it. I heard that you were the one who made it happen.'

I nodded.

'You arranged it,' he said, 'so that your Commie hardliner comrade – the headmistress – could damage the US aircraft and runway.'

Fear circled inside me, fear of what his words meant.

'No,' I said. I could hear the jagged edge to my voice. 'It's not true. You're lying.'

Let him be lying. Please. Let this hard-muscled murderer be a lying bastard as well.

'Was it you or Bertin who drove the van in Paris that smashed into my car?' I demanded. 'The one that crippled my brother?'

This time he laughed long and loud, turning heads. 'No. Is that what he's told you?'

'Did you shoot at me on the farm?'

'Listen, bitch, if I'd shot at you, you'd be dead.'

Silence sat between us on the table. Just the grind of traffic and the clink of glasses chafed at it. I kept my face still, eyes flat and expressionless.

'You,' I said again, 'are an MGB Soviet agent.'

He pushed his big square face close up to mine. To a passing glance we might look like lovers.

'Lady,' he hissed at me, 'I am CIA.'

He had to be lying. Had to be. This time I was certain of it. Because if he wasn't lying it meant that André was and I couldn't bear that. But even as I told myself that Piquet was a lying bastard, something started to unravel in my head. Things started to make more sense.

'And Bertin?' I asked.

'CIA.' He flashed a vicious smile at me and I wanted to reach across the table and rip it off his face.

'The pair of you? Both CIA?'

He nodded, grinning at me.

'Why should I believe you?'

'Believe what the fuck you want, lady.'

I didn't want to believe this. I would sell my soul before I believed it, I would let Cosette gallop back into the fire before I believed it. I would have to walk away from André if I believed it, so no, no, I rejected his lies. To believe him would be like tearing out of me all that made me a Caussade.

'Gilles Bertin is dead,' I announced.

'Now who's lying?' he sneered.

'He has a bullet in his chest. Inside his own house.'

It was in my voice, the small voice of truth that rings clear as a bell, and he heard it. His face became rigid and his heavy lips drew back to bare his teeth. I felt nothing but grim pleasure to see the shockwave ripple through him and I threw what was left of my brandy in his face. He stumbled to his feet, cursing me.

'That's for Mickey Ashton,' I told him.

'That piece of Yankee shit deserved to die. He was feeding technical information to the Russians. So when I was ordered to put an end to him, the protest march was the perfect cover. Bertin's idea.' The mention of Bertin stopped him in his tracks. 'Start counting the fucking hours, lady, because you haven't got many left, I promise you.'

I watched him go, pounding down the crooked side road back into the old town where Bertin's house lay. And with every footstep I heard the last few links that held the Caussade family together snap apart.

Clarisse placed a glass of cognac in my hand and wrapped my fingers around it, but it was going to take more than that to shift the chill inside me.

'What has happened, *chérie*? You look sick.'

'I'm not sick.'

We were seated on a dainty chaise longue in Clarisse's hotel room. A magazine lay open on the bed, her shoes had been kicked off under the coffee table, her reading glasses abandoned on a satinwood chest. The normality of it gave me something to cling on to in a world that had been spun upside down.

'You were meant to stay at home, Eloïse, not to knock

yourself out running around Arles on your own. I promised your policeman, remember?'

I laid a grateful hand on her shoulder. 'Don't lecture me, please, Clarisse.'

'Bad day?'

'As bad as it gets.'

'Are you going to tell me what happened?'

Her green eyes watched me over her glass with such affection that I came close to telling her it all. Everything. Needing to pour the poison out of me. Instead I swigged down the cognac and rose to my feet.

'It's too dangerous, Clarisse. I don't want you to get hurt, which is what happens to people I am seen with. So go. Leave Arles. I couldn't bear to see you ...' *Dead* was the word that so nearly tumbled from my tongue. '... in danger.'

She studied me through half-closed eyes, the way I'd seen her study surveillance photographs that I'd brought her in Paris, assessing their value. 'Very well,' she conceded, 'I'll go home to Paris.' She gave an elegant shrug. 'I've had enough of the stink of bullshit anyway.'

In return I found her a smile. 'Good. At last you are seeing sense.'

But I would miss my boss, miss her a lot. I hugged her, but she had become stiff and unyielding, hurt by my desire to drive her out.

'Can I do anything for you before I go?' she asked.

'I need four new tyres.'

'On a Sunday? What happened?'

'They've been stabbed.'

'*Merde!*'

'Exactly.'

She walked over to the telephone beside the bed. 'I'll work my charm on the manager.'

I was sure she would too.

'Clarisse.'

She heard something in my voice that made her lift her head and look at me. 'What is it, *chérie*?'

'Does the CIA kill people?'

'Yes, all the time, I imagine. This may be a Cold War, but it's still a war.'

He was coming for me. Whichever side he was on.

CHAPTER FORTY-ONE

When wounded, human instinct is to hide. Or to fly to those we love to take care of us. I was wounded. I don't mean my face. I mean inside. I could feel the drip, drip, drip of blood and I could hear the soft sobs of pain deep within my head.

I drove fast on my four new tyres, I drove to the only place on earth I wanted to be. I kept the car windows down so that the wind that whipped across the marshes could lay the taste of salt on my lips to replace the taste of betrayal. Every field, every stream, every stretch of woodland, they all held memories of André and now it all meant nothing. He had handed me to his enemies on a plate.

I tried to hate him, my own brother, whom I'd trusted with my life, but I wasn't capable of it. If he was working for Soviet Russia, if it were true, then what was I? A cover story? Was I the smoke and mirrors? Was I supposed to distract the CIA watchers, the Bertins and Piquets of this world, while André got on with whatever it was he was doing?

And what about the drop I'd made in Arles? The negative film I'd taken. Who picked that up? I slammed the heel of my hand on the steering wheel and felt a dull shame flush through me. My broken nose throbbed, but the pain of it didn't come close to the pain of knowing.

He'd fed me to them. Piece by piece.

Did you think, André, that I would never notice that bits of me were missing? And what about Mickey Ashton? You led me to believe he was the source of the leak from the air base and Piquet says the same, but what if he was murdered because he'd danced with your sister? The sister that the CIA believes is a Soviet agent.

There are too many what ifs, André. What if you hadn't lied to me? What if you hadn't told me that Bertin and Piquet were enemy agents? I was seeing it all from the wrong end of the telescope, wasn't I?

'André!'

I screamed his name at the top of my lungs to get it out of me, to let it be snatched away by the wind and torn to shreds. Tears were streaming down my face, but I dashed them away with the back of my hand. I wanted no part of them. No part of his name. No trace of it in my lungs. If I could have taken my father's garden shears and sliced through the bond that bound me to him and him to me, I would have.

When I reached the turn-off that led towards Mas Caussade I put my foot down and shot past. I had to speak to him. Of course I did, of course I needed to. So bad the need made me ache. But first I drove to the only place on earth I wanted to be.

I was allowed in only because I was a Caussade and the colonel was grateful for Caussade land. A smart salute and a polite greeting, but I was escorted at all times. The Dumoulin Air Base was on high alert. It made sense, because three townspeople had died here yesterday and, whatever the rights and wrongs, the Americans now saw us all as a threat.

I walked down the long corridor lined with oil paintings of aircraft into the white-painted ward with its men and beds that I didn't even see. It was as if the paint had white-washed them all out as well and only left one bed in shiny military grey. I walked over. Léon was engrossed in a thick pile of paperwork, seated in the chair beside the bed and wearing a navy-blue dressing gown made of some silky material that made him look faintly dissolute. I never thought I would ever say that Léon Roussel looked dissolute. They were two words that didn't fit together.

Despite the facts and figures that were occupying his mind, he seemed to sense me, as though he could smell the scent of my skin before I'd even reached his bed. He raised his head and instantly threw his paperwork on the blankets, pushing himself awkwardly to his feet. He opened his arms, murmuring my name, and I walked into them.

We stood there holding each other close and not a sound entered our world. Not a cough nor the clatter of a mug nor the shout of 'Cheat!' in a game of cards on the next bed.

Nothing touched us. At one point he pulled back his head and studied my face, his grey eyes gleaming, the way the evening sun hits the flat steeliness of the marsh pools on a summer's evening and sets fire to them.

We stood there holding each other close for a long time.

CHAPTER FORTY-TWO

LÉON ROUSSEL

'André is a double agent.'

'Slow down, Eloïse. Piquet might be lying,' Léon pointed out. 'We don't know for certain yet. We have only one man's word.'

'Spoken like a true policeman.'

Léon knew she was right, of course, and he was proud to be one, but it was also spoken like someone who didn't want to see her hurt. Or to wrong his boyhood friend.

'We have to guard against their lies or we lose our grasp of the truth,' he told her. 'They buy control with their lies, these people who live in the shadows with their secrets and their threats and their guns.'

Eloïse leaned against him, her arm warm through his shirt. They were seated on the edge of his hospital bed. He'd managed to dress himself in a hurry but his shoes and socks on the floor might as well have been in the Caussade bull-yard for all the hope he had of picking them up. His back felt as if it had been ripped into by one of Goliath's horns again.

'That's not what André has been telling me, Léon.'

He kissed the side of her head. 'So which one is lying?'

A faint moan escaped her and she lowered herself to the floor on her knees. Her hand gently lifted one of his feet. 'I must speak to André,' she said.

But he could hear the reluctance in her words, spoken in an undertone, her head down, her silky curtain of hair swinging forward across her cheek. He understood. She didn't want her love for her brother blown apart, and he didn't blame her, but she'd have to do it. If she didn't, he would. She handled his feet as though they were fragile and carefully eased on first one sock, then the other, smoothing them with tender touches while he looked down on the sheen of her dark head.

'Do you think your father is involved?'

She looked up sharply. 'Why do you ask that?'

'Because if André has been continuing to work from home for whichever side he is on, before you came home he will have needed help.'

She nodded but looked away and picked up a shoe. 'The other day I found something written on the leather of André's wallet.' She opened up the shoe and slid it on to his foot. He couldn't see her face but he could feel the tension in her fingers. 'It was a message. It said, "Take Me Out". At the time I didn't understand it.' Her breathing paused.

'Now you do?'

She tied the shoelace. 'Now I think the wallet was intended to be passed to his Soviet handler if ever he thought he was in such danger that he needed to be taken out immediately.'

'Taken where?'

'To a Soviet safe house.' Her voice was as soft as her hands. 'It makes sense. It also makes sense for Piquet to burn down the cottage where the Communist activists met if he really is a CIA agent.'

She slipped on the second shoe and tied its lace, but when it was done she didn't move. She sat staring at her hands.

'Will I go to prison?' she asked.

'No, I won't let that happen. We'll go together to the police station, you make your statement about how you found the body of Bertin lying dead in his house and we will get you a lawyer. I know a good one. But why did the gunman leave the gun there?'

Still she didn't move. 'I entered his house illegally,' she admitted. 'It will look to the police as if Bertin might have surprised me while I was skulking around, believed I was a burglar and I shot him to silence him. That's what it looks like, doesn't it?'

'No, Eloïse. There's no reason to think that.'

She lifted her head. 'You should be in bed, not running round the town.' She attached a small smile to the end of it, though he could not imagine where she'd got it from.

He stood up but his movements were unsteady and she rose to her feet to balance him with a hand under his elbow.

'Thanks for doing my shoes.'

'You're welcome.'

He lightly kissed her mouth and together they walked out to the air base car park. There was something she wasn't telling him. He could see it in her smile, hear it in the whisper behind her words. As they walked side by side he wondered which vital piece of information she was keeping from him. And why?

They drove both cars, his black Citroën saloon tucked in just behind her 2CV. The sky was the same colour as the earth and the white horses in the fields could smell what was coming, so gathered close and sought shelter under the trees. Léon knew that what lay ahead was about to hit hard, and he didn't mean the rain.

They drove into the yard and he sat for a moment after the jolting of the rough roads to give his back a break. But Eloïse jumped out of her driving seat the second the handbrake was on and scooted over to his open window. The wind was stronger now, snatching her hair into long threads and tugging at her skirt, so that she had to hold it down. She glanced up at André's window and his tall figure was silhouetted there, watching them. She bent quickly to Léon's car window, her hands on the door and her face on a level with his. He could see a jewel of fresh blood glistening inside her nostril.

'Don't come in the house, Léon. Please.'

A wave of despair swept over him. She was in no fit state

to cope with a man like André when cornered. To confront him on her own was asking too much of herself, if it was true that he was an MGB agent. But Léon knew Eloïse. He'd seen her stand up to a boar with no more than a long stick in her hand and that same expression on her face. She was looking at André's window again.

'You shouldn't let André shape your life,' he said. 'You must make your own choices without needing his good opinion. You need to step away, and whether he is CIA or MGB shouldn't prevent that. He doesn't deserve you as a sister.' If André Caussade turned out to be a traitor, it would tear her apart if she didn't protect herself.

Her head snapped round. 'No, Léon, don't say that. You know it's not true.' She shook her head, a dark trail of her hair clinging to the sweat at her throat. 'My mother died when I was four years old and I did everything I could to help look after my tiny new brother, Isaac. Papa hid away with his bulls, grieving. Mathilde was there, but for no more than a few hours each day.'

'Don't be hard on yourself, Eloïse. You did what you could, but you were young.'

'It was André who stepped up. Only ten years old. But André took care of us, he made us a family again, he held us together. He dealt with dirty nappies, he patched up our scrapes, read us books, taught us to swim and climb and to fight our own battles. He taught us loyalty. He sat up at night when we were sick and rocked us in his arms when we had screaming nightmares.'

She put a hand through the open window and curled it into Léon's hair, gripping tight.

'It's not how you think, Léon. Papa taught us manners and how to sweat out hard labour on the farm and Mathilde taught us to laugh and cook. But it was André who put big ideas into our heads. He gave us ambition. He made us self-reliant.'

'By throwing you in the river or abandoning you alone in the marshes to find your own way home.'

To his surprise, she laughed, delighted to recall that dangerous method of education, and he found himself smiling.

'Yes, André made me who I am today.'

'No, Eloïse. *You* made you who you are today, and you may not know André as well as you think you do. So please be careful.'

She scrubbed her hand through his hair, as if to rearrange his thoughts, and then released it. Her brown eyes in their bruised sockets fixed on his.

'What is it, Eloïse?'

'I recognised the gun on the floor in Bertin's bedroom. It belongs to Mayor Durand.'

'Are you sure?'

'Yes, I've seen it in his desk.'

Léon's sense of foreboding deepened as he tried to slot that piece of information into its place in his mind without making things worse for her. He didn't ask how or when she'd seen it in the desk.

'Eloïse, Durand reported his gun as stolen last week.'

'He's lying,' she said fiercely and walked away towards the house.

Léon watched her, each step, each determined swing of her arms. She kept shaking her head as though there was something inside that she was trying to dislodge. From the wide doorway of the new stables, still under construction to the right of the yard, Aristide Caussade stood with a claw hammer in his hand. He watched her enter the house.

CHAPTER FORTY-THREE

I knocked this time, though I knew André had seen me coming. He opened the door and stood back to permit me to enter. The air in the room was too stifling and stale to breathe and I headed quickly to the window to open it.

'No, Eloïse,' he said sharply. 'Don't open it. Don't make it easier for them than we have to.'

I stepped back from the window. Whoever *they* were, I didn't want any of their bullets lodged in my skull. I was angry. I'd marched in to confront André, ready to hurl my anger at my brother, but when I took a good look at him in the confines of his room, the light soured by the darkening sky as charcoal-grey clouds lowered over Mas Caussade, I felt the sharp edge of my rage grow blunt.

His skin was looking grey and had acquired the papery texture of someone who lives indoors. He'd lost weight. His cheekbones were stark in his face, but his body had gained more solid muscle, the result of hours of working at it. What else was he to do up here? A couple of booklets lay on his bed – 'If an A-Bomb Falls: Will you know what to do?' – with a lurid red cover image of a mushroom-cloud explosion. The second one displayed a more muted black-and-white mushroom cloud with the title 'Survival under Atomic Attack' and was an official US government civil defence publication.

He saw me staring.

'I believe in being prepared,' he commented.

'If that's true, why didn't you prepare *me*? Why lie to me? Why keep me in the dark? Why let me take unnecessary risks that could have got me killed?' I couldn't keep the anger out of my words but I kept the hurt locked away. I didn't let him see that. 'I am your sister, yet you threw me to the wolves.'

His face remained still. Not even a frown, just a thin veil of wariness. It dawned on me that he was frightened of what I might do. Other parts of him might have changed, but not his amber eyes, they were the same. Locked on to me.

'Sit down,' he said. 'Tell me what has triggered this out-burst.' His manner was calm, unruffled by my accusations. 'Is it your friend in the car outside?'

'No.' I didn't sit. 'Léon is your friend as well.'

He raised an eyebrow in dispute, but let it pass.

'This has nothing to do with Léon,' I insisted. 'It has to do with sharing a drink with Maurice Piquet and finding Gilles Bertin's dead body.'

That shook him. A flicker when his eyes blanked out, then nothing. 'Poor Eloïse, I'm sorry. Stumbling over dead bodies is never pleasant.'

'Did you kill him?'

'No. Did you?'

'No.'

Neither of us knew whether to believe the other. Léon was wrong. I was no longer the sister I'd been in Paris, ready to follow my brother blindly to the ends of the earth. I'd changed. As André looked at me now, I realised he knew it. The gap between us was far greater than the two metres of pine flooring.

'How did you find his body?' he asked. 'Where was he killed?'

'At his house. Shot in the chest.' She didn't mention Isaac, not even to him.

He thought quietly about that. 'And Piquet?' he asked eventually. 'You spoke to him and lived to tell the tale?'

'Piquet informed me that he is a CIA agent. He doesn't work for masters in Moscow, as you claimed. He works for Washington. He insists that you are the one in the pay of the Soviet MGB Intelligence agency.'

'Did he now?'

'Why don't you deny it?'

He uttered a short impatient sigh. 'Do I need to, Eloïse? With you of all people.'

'Tell me the truth, André. Just tell me the bloody truth.' My voice was rising. 'For once, be honest with me.'

He sat down on the edge of the bed and stretched out one leg as if it ached. 'Very well,' he said, so calm I wanted to shake him. 'Ask me something.'

'Are you spying for the Russians?'

'No.'

'Piquet claims you are.'

He leaned forward, hands on his knees. 'Who are you going to believe? A murdering lying bastard who would slice your tongue out as soon as swill wine with you?' He paused. We both knew what was coming next. 'Or me? Your brother.'

I stepped forward, closer to him, and peeled my tongue from the back of my teeth.

'Are you a double agent? Working for the CIA but pretending to have turned to the MGB?'

'No. I am a CIA agent, pure and simple.' He shrugged his shoulders. 'Sorry to disappoint you.'

'Why would Piquet tell me he works for the CIA if he doesn't?'

'You're going to have to ask him that.'

'André, why should I believe you?'

'Why should you disbelieve me?'

'Because nothing makes sense anymore.'

He laughed and it smacked me right between the eyes because it was his old laugh, his Paris laugh that I had missed so much.

'Welcome to the world of spies, Eloïse.'

'I want to trust you but . . . I don't know who to believe . . . or who to trust anymore.'

He tried to stand but I pushed him back down and leaned over him, my hands on his shoulders. 'No more games,

André, no more lies. Tell me the truth and then I will trust you. Not before.'

His eyes narrowed to a thin amber gleam. 'I think you give your trust too easily. Too cheaply.'

I frowned. 'What do you mean?'

'In exchange for a kiss. From your friend in the car outside.'

I didn't move. But the rage was back and I didn't trust myself. 'Léon has nothing to do with this.'

'Can you be sure? Ever since you came back Léon Roussel has been hanging round here, manipulating you. At Goliath's burial was he the one who set the fire to make you think you were in danger? To make you turn to him for help. Don't think that I don't know he's been turning up here every evening, beguiling you with his mask of uprightness and trustworthiness. Even now when he should be in a hospital bed he is here with you, trying to find out more.'

'No!' I smacked both my hands down hard on to his shoulders. 'No, you are lying again, André.'

He smiled softly. 'Can you trust him?'

'Yes.' I moved away and wiped my palms on my skirt. 'Yes, I trust him with my life.'

I walked to the door, slammed it behind me and flew down the stairs. In the yard I walked over to the open window of Léon's car, bent down and kissed him full on the mouth. When I pulled away, André was watching from his window, as I'd known he would be. I climbed into my own car and sped away from Mas Caussade.

*

353

The mayor's house befitted his position. It was grand but not ostentatiously so, a fine square stone-built mansion with beautiful proportions and an elegant portico. I rang the old-fashioned bell and hoped Mayor Durand wasn't taking a Sunday afternoon nap.

His daughter opened the door, my glass-blowing friend, Marianne.

'Eloïse, this is a surprise.'

She smiled with her usual warmth and I felt sick at the thought of hurting her family.

'I've come to see your father, actually. Is he around? I know it's Sunday but this is kind of urgent.'

'Your poor face.' She leaned close and kissed me delicately on one cheek. 'I heard you'd been at the air base. What a hideous tragedy. I never did like that vile headmistress but I'd never have expected her to do such a thing.'

'Is your father home?' I interrupted. Marianne could talk for five minutes without drawing breath.

She laughed. 'Yes, he's in the garden at the back. I'm in the middle of baking,' she wiggled floury fingers at me,' so just go round the house and you'll find him there.'

I kissed her. 'Thanks, Marianne.'

How did a man like Charles Durand produce a gem like Marianne?

'Good afternoon, Monsieur le Maire.'

Charles Durand leaped out of his skin. He hadn't heard me approaching across the grass and I was now standing right behind him. He'd been bent over his roses, dead-heading them with a pair of secateurs, humming quietly to himself, and a thorn tore a trail across his thumb when he jumped.

'Eloïse, for God's sake, girl, that's no way to ...' He stopped as he took in my face. 'Well, you certainly look a mess, don't you?'

I ignored that. 'We didn't finish our conversation at the air base yesterday, did we?'

All pretence of politeness dropped from his face and he threw an uncomfortable glance towards the house to ensure no one else was within earshot. Almost touching the roof, the clouds looked bruised and blackened. I could feel the first spit of rain.

'I don't want you here at my house,' he hissed at me. 'I don't want you anywhere near my office either. So say what you've come to say and then get out of my garden.'

I didn't blame him for being protective of it. The garden was extensive and well stocked, the kind of sweet-scented haven that could lull you into thinking all was well in the world, as bees murmured among the heavy blossoms that lined the gravel paths and yellow-plumed serins dropped in for a drink at the Roman stone fountain.

'I wouldn't be in such a hurry to throw me out, if I were you, monsieur.' I omitted his title.

'You have nothing to say that I want to hear. You Caussades have always been difficult.'

I could hear an undercurrent in his voice and I realised

this man was afraid of me. Of what I knew. 'Let's talk about blackmail,' I said coldly. 'About you and blackmail. And then we can get round to you and treason.'

He was a tall man and he used his height well. He stood too close, an intimidating presence, and looked down his handsome nose at me. I was forced to look up.

'I don't know what the hell you're talking about,' he said. But he didn't walk away.

'Your blackmailing of my father is finished.'

His eyes donned a mask of innocence. 'What lies has the old fool been telling you?'

'My father is not old. And he is certainly no fool. He has the newspaper article in his possession now and intends to burn it, so you will get no more money out of him. The chances of an obscure local newspaper in northern France being still in possession of a copy of an edition printed thirty-five years ago are nil. Especially after being caught in the middle of two world wars. I doubt that the newspaper even exists anymore. This is the end of it for you.'

He wanted to hit me. I could see it in his face, the flicker of physical rage, but I was accustomed to bulls. I stood my ground. In one hand he still held the dead head of a coral-pink rose, its petals soft and defenceless, and slowly his fist tightened on them.

'You are talking nonsense, girl. I know nothing about any blackmail.'

He was cool. I had to give him that. Anyone else would have believed him. I could see how this corrupt man so easily manoeuvred himself into the role of mayor, but his coolness drove me to strike harder, to light a fire under him.

The rain started to fall more heavily.

'Monsieur Durand, you are a traitor and the punishment for treason in this country is execution by guillotine.'

This time he raised the secateurs to within a hand's breadth of my scar. I felt my gut lurch but I didn't drop my gaze from his.

'Get off my land,' he said in no more than a whisper.

'I photographed them all,' I told him, matching my tone to his. 'Each one of them. All those documents in your secret drawer.'

This time I had him. His pupils narrowed to pinpoints and he glanced again for a split second over to the house. Was his wife there? Or Marianne at a window? Watching us in the rain.

'You have no proof they were mine,' he said.

'I took pictures of them next to your desk diary, your name embossed on it in full view. So don't let's play games, monsieur.'

'In which case you must have brought the documents into my office yourself to incriminate me. Illegal entry as well. No one is going to believe you, not even your tame police-man. They'll take my word over yours.'

He was right. Of course he was right.

'Are you prepared to risk it?' I asked. 'To have the stink of a scandal before your next election? Do you want to take that chance? We both know the truth – that you are a lying treacherous bastard.'

'*Merde*, you're even more trouble than your brother.'

'I know you are gathering top-secret information and selling it at a high price to Russia. That is treason. That's why the Soviets are building their own nuclear bombs far faster than expected. They're using stolen American technology passed on by people like you.'

'Don't lecture me, girl.' He uttered a short sharp laugh like the bark of a dog. 'I am not a Communist. I am not a capitalist. I am an opportunist. I support both, so that whether it's the Russkies or the Yanks who win this Cold War eventually, I will come out on top.' He smiled a thin smile. 'Whereas you will be thrown in prison by both sides.'

The rain was soaking us now, blurring our outlines. I had no wish to talk with a man who had sold his soul for American dollars.

'A name,' I demanded. 'Give me a name.'

'What name?'

'The name of your source of information at Dumoulin Air Base, the person passing you documents.'

'Or what?'

'Or I will go to the police. Your Smith & Wesson gun has just been found beside the dead body of Gilles Bertin in Arles, so they will be interested in talking to you anyway. Even though you reported your gun stolen, they will be aware that it could be a set-up for using it in a crime. The police and the voters of Serriac are going to be crawling all over everything you've ever done. I hope your tracks are well covered.'

Rain ran in rivulets down his cheeks, his carefully groomed hair flattened to his head, but he made no attempt to move away. His lips were bone white. I wanted to hate this man who had put my father through such hell but all I felt was disgust. I felt dirty just sharing the same sodden air with him.

'A name?' I repeated.

But I'd underestimated this man. A crack of thunder rolled above our heads and though I saw his lips move, I heard nothing. I thought he was about to take his secateurs to me, then bury me in his sodden rose bed.

'Do you know, Eloïse, what I did a few years ago to teach your father a lesson when he refused to pay up any more?'

I wouldn't play his game. I said nothing. But I felt the cold rain seeping much deeper than my bones.

'When he refused to pay,' the mayor continued, slowly lowering the secateurs and dropping the crushed petals on the wet grass, 'I told your brother André about what your father did. He refused to believe me at first, so I showed him the newspaper cutting.' Durand's lips pulled into a thin smile. 'It seems he went home, had a blazing row with your father and left immediately for Paris.'

That is when the hate came. A cold wave of it crashed down on me. 'I will make you regret that,' I spat at him through the rain.

I spun away and hurried back to the pathway. He let me get almost as far as the house, my skirts plastered to my legs, the raindrops landing like small bullets on my broken nose.

'Wait,' he called.

I waited, but looked over my shoulder, eyes screwed up against the rain.

He hadn't moved. 'Mickey Ashton,' he shouted. 'He was my source.' Another crack of thunder almost drowned out his next words. 'Now it's your friend, Major Dirke.'

A chasm seemed to open up inside me. Was Durand telling the truth? Or was this another lie to add to the pile in my pocket?

CHAPTER FORTY-FOUR

LÉON ROUSSEL

Léon wrapped Eloïse's wet figure in a rug from the boot of his car and bundled her into her 2CV with instructions to drive slowly. Her windscreen wipers in a storm like this would be of little use, so he stuck close to her bumper all the way from Serriac to Mas Caussade. He wanted her to leave her car behind and travel in his black Citroën but she insisted on driving herself. She drove slowly, especially when they came to the tight bend where tyres had dug deep into the dirt and gouged a crater that stretched right across the road and which was now filling up with muddy rainwater. Her car limped through it until another thunderclap made her jump, her foot plunging down on the accelerator so that she kangaroo-hopped forward.

What the hell had gone on with the mayor? She'd shot out of his gate, a low moan coming from her, but his first concern had been to get her home and dry until she was ready to talk.

He planned to do his own kind of talking with Monsieur le Maire tomorrow at the gendarmerie.

The sky was almost dark, so he switched his lights on, though it wasn't yet evening, and the rain was lashing down. It was time to have a talk with André too, but not the gendarmerie kind. Not yet. A bottle of wine and a handful of fat olives might oil the wheels, but he was well aware that his boyhood friend knew how to hold his tongue when he chose.

Whatever it was that André had said to his sister up in that room of his had damaged her. She'd come out and kissed him in front of André to prove a point, but what that point was, he could only guess at. Léon flexed his shoulder blades to try to unstick the dressings on his back that chafed from too much driving, but he was still upright and still moving from A to B, which was about as much as he could hope for right now. The Arles police were dealing with the body in Bertin's rented house in the old town, but there was still the matter of the mayor's gun. And why the hell it was left lying there.

The wind was fierce when they reached the farm, tearing the blossom off the tamarisk tree and shifting some of the timbers of the half-constructed roof on the new stables. Yet a dozen *gardians* were milling around in the yard in the rain, crouched inside their rainproofs and soothing their horses as they prepared to ride out.

What was going on?

Before he and Eloïse had even shut off their engines Aristide Caussade came barrelling out of the house in a sou'wester and shiny cape of olive green. He wrenched open Eloïse's door and almost lifted her out of her seat.

'Thank God, you're back.'

'What is it, Papa?'

'André has gone missing.'

Léon could feel a pressure the moment he stepped inside the house. As though something was ready to blow. Years ago, under a willow tree on a river bank, he and André had heated up an unopened can of beans over a campfire to see what would happen. They'd watched transfixed as the metal sides bulged and then the whole thing exploded with a thrump, beans ripping high up into the foliage. That's what it felt like in the Caussade house. That kind of pressure.

Eloïse shot up the stairs in front of him two at a time and he followed, his back protesting, but she halted in the doorway of André's room with a cry. The room was in chaos. Only the bed and wardrobe stood in place. Everything else had been thrown or smashed or trampled and the smell of violence was overwhelming.

'Don't touch anything,' Léon said. 'This looks like a crime scene.'

But Eloïse didn't enter. She pinned herself to the door-frame and watched him pick his way carefully around the debris on the floor. The chair and cabinet lay on their sides, broken, books strewn, lamp in pieces, and even the mattress was on end on the floor, resting against the wardrobe.

Had André used it as a shield? A battering ram? How many

had come for him? It sickened Léon to his core to imagine what had gone on here but he did a rapid check for weapons or blood. He found neither. Outside, the high wind was rattling the window and the rain battered at the glass, but the catch was firmly locked, so no forced entry that way.

He looked up and saw Aristide Caussade standing behind his daughter. He looked stricken, his shoulders were hunched under the oilskin, head low and thrust forward.

'What happened?' Léon asked.

'I came back from the fields,' Caussade rumbled, his mind on the devastation of the room rather than on his words. 'The front door was banging open in the wind and Louis lay unconscious at the bottom of the stairs.'

'No rifle?' Eloïse asked. Her voice was stiff and awkward. 'How is he?'

'No, no rifle. Louis will survive. His head is made of solid bull hide, he says.'

'How many men?' Léon asked.

'Three.'

'Did they come in a car?'

'Yes.'

'Did he see them leave with André?'

'No. He saw and heard nothing. He was out cold.'

Aristide Caussade shook himself, spraying water from his oilskin like a dog. He was a man of action, not words. 'Enough questions. We have to search. The men have scoured the outbuildings and the nearby area, but this fucking rain is washing away all tracks.'

He gripped his daughter's shoulder, knuckles white with the force of it, as if to ensure this child was not snatched away from him.

'You're the policeman,' he said. 'Where do we start?'

'We start by asking Louis for a description of the attackers.'

'Big hard-fisted thugs, he says.' Caussade looked down at his daughter and his dark eyes, so like hers, were fierce with hatred. 'The bastards were speaking Russian, he says.'

CHAPTER FORTY-FIVE

They shut the front door of the farmhouse when they left and told me to bolt it on the inside. They told me to stay here in case André turned up. They told me to wait. Because that's what they expected women to do. Wait.

'I'll get my men out searching, despite the filthy night,' Léon said. 'Louis remembers that the three Russians drove up in a black Peugeot 203. We'll put out an immediate search for any in the area.' He paused and chafed my hand between his, the conviction in his eyes giving me a thin thread of hope when he added, 'We'll find André, I promise.' He pressed his lips to my forehead. 'Stay safe.' He set two of Papa's *gardians* to sit in the kitchen with me.

But the moment I heard their cars drive off into the wet evening, I picked up the telephone in the hall. The receiver shook in my hand and only then did I realise that I was still in wet clothes, cold and shivering. But I barely noticed. Like I barely noticed the darkness creeping across the hallway tiles as night started to settle on the farm.

Guilt was eating into me. I had broken my promise. I had not kept my brother safe. I put down the receiver, walked into the living room and opened Papa's wine cupboard. I poured myself a shot of brandy and knocked it straight back, feeling it kick some warmth into my veins. I returned to the telephone, dialled a number and did not let the images of André fighting for his life in that stifling room upstairs rob me of words.

'Hello.' My voice came out rough. 'May I speak to Major Dirke, please?'

I sat in my car outside the gates, engine rattling like a wheezy lawnmower, while I waited for the guards on duty to decide to open them. The wind had dropped as the worst of the storm passed out to sea, but the rain was still coming down in sheets, trickles of it sneaking under my canvas roof and dripping on to my shoulder.

'Come on,' I muttered. I was frightened they wouldn't let me in again.

But Major Joel Dirke was as good as his word. He was waiting beside the guard-kiosk, raised a hand in greeting and jumped into my passenger seat. The gates swung open and the guard waved us through as I peered through my drenched windscreen into the black night. The streetlights on the air base blurred and starred as if they were swimming underwater, but I followed Joel Dirke's instruction and pulled up outside a building that was marked 'Recreation Hall'. I wasn't here for recreation.

'We'll make a run for it through the rain,' he laughed. 'Ready?' He had his fingers on the door handle.

'Joel, will you sit here a moment first, please?' I rested my hand lightly on the arm of his wet raincoat and swivelled to face him. 'There's something I want to talk to you about.'

He looked at me, surprised.

Say yes, Joel, say yes. I am staking everything on you.

I smiled at him encouragingly. The outside lights from the building shone into the interior of my car, turning us both an odd shade of green.

'Well now,' he said, his Southern drawl more pronounced, 'what's this all about? No more thatched-roof arson, I hope, or hand-grenade attacks. It's getting increasingly dangerous around here.' He laughed again and I thought how easily it came from him.

'Joel, my brother has been taken.'

'Taken? What do you mean by that?'

'I mean he was abducted this afternoon.'

He was a military man, so his jaw didn't drop open, but it came close. 'You're talking about André Caussade?'

'Yes.'

'Hell, Eloïse, that's terrible, what happened? Have you informed the police?'

'Yes. Three men came to the house. They attacked the man who was with him and seem to have driven off with André in their car. He put up quite a struggle.' I kept my voice calm, my tone factual. 'I thought you might know where they've taken him.'

'Me?' The laugh didn't come this time. 'Why me?'

'Because I believe you are in touch with Communist agents down here.'

'What? Why the blazes would you think that?' he demanded.

I placed my hand on his arm but he snatched it away. 'Listen, Joel, you told me that your brother is in the aircraft industry in San Diego, California.'

He nodded warily. 'So?'

'Colonel Masson told us yesterday in his speech that the aircraft company Convair is located there. They build the Peacemaker and are developing the version of it that will be powered by nuclear energy. Is that right?'

'Yes it is.' He was shifting uneasily in his seat. 'What's this about?'

'Answer me this, Joel. Does your brother work at Convair? Quite a coincidence if he does.'

Silence. Just the rain battering the roof of my car and turning the windows opaque.

'Does he?'

He nodded. He watched me the way you watch a snake.

'I believe that he has been passing information to you about aircraft development, which you have been passing on to Soviet agents here.'

'No.'

'I am informed that that's exactly what you've been doing.'

His hand shot out to the door handle.

'Wait, Joel, please. I am not interested right now in

369

whether or not you are the leak at this camp. Or in the identity of the person to whom you passed any information. All I'm interested in is finding my brother.'

It took him a full minute to think about that.

'Help me,' I said, and even I could hear in my voice how much it meant to me, 'and I will say nothing to anybody about your involvement.'

Did he believe me? Would he trust me?

'You have no proof,' he pointed out. He sat back in his seat and considered my offer.

'No, but I have an informant. I could start them investigating you. I realise that there are two distinct factions of Communist allegiances in this country. There are the French Communist Party activists like my brother, Isaac, who cause trouble with strikes and industrial demands but who are not actual traitors.'

He turned his face away at the word traitor.

'Then there are the Communists who are agents of the MGB and report directly to Moscow, feeding them stolen technical, military and political secrets.' I paused. His gaze did not return to my face. We both knew which one he was. 'There must be somewhere down here, some house or barn, where at times the agents and their handler meet together to plan their next move. Somewhere they might have taken André. A safe house.'

I took a deep breath and hung my heart on my next words. 'Do you know of one?'

He brushed a hand across his mouth. I felt the minutes

ticking away and André's life ticking with them. Finally he nodded.

'If you swear to keep your mouth shut, I'll drive you there. I don't want your brother to be killed.' He looked at me in the dark and I could feel his sadness. 'I am not a bad man, Eloïse, but I believe Communism is the only decent way forward for mankind.'

I quickly sidestepped that issue. 'I'll follow you in my car,' I said.

He opened the door, turned up his raincoat collar and ran through the pouring rain to his car, which was parked further down the street. But instead of slipping into the driving seat he seemed to have opened the boot and was bent over it, rummaging inside for something. What was he doing? It was hard to see. I peered ahead through the rain, the windscreen awash with the downpour, the noise hammering on the roof and I felt panic rising in me. Something was wrong.

I was suddenly overwhelmed by the certainty that Joel was searching for a gun hidden in the boot with the intention of returning to my car and putting a bullet in me. No one would hear anything. Not in this torrential rain. He'd drive my car back out into the flooded marshes and abandon my body out there for the wild boar to find.

No. I told myself that was the panic talking. Out of control. The darkness and the rain were getting inside my head and the loss of André was pushing me over the edge. Joel was a decent person, even though he was handing information over to the enemy. Don't lose your grip, not now when André's life was at stake. I snatched up my shoulder bag, pulled up my oilskin hood and raced over to Joel's car, splashing through puddles. When I reached his Chrysler through the dense curtain of rain he stopped rummaging in the boot and straightened up.

'I can't find the damn thing,' he shouted over the drumming on the metal roof. 'I'm looking for a map.'

A map? I experienced a rush of relief and felt foolish. Of course, a map to the safe house.

He stood back, ducking away from the rain. Before I could turn and run back to my car, his strong arms swept me right off my feet and threw me sideways into the boot. I screamed and shouted and kicked out viciously, but the thunder came again, rolling down the valley with a vengeance just as a hand wrenched my bag from my shoulder and slammed down the boot lid.

My world turned black.

Fear spread itself out in the cramped dark boot. It took up nearly all the space, leaving little room for me. I kicked and screamed. I called down the fires of hell on Joel Dirke's head. I smashed my fists against the metal cage until they were raw, but it got me nowhere and drove out my power to think.

So I went quiet. My limbs ceased their thrashing. I forced my lungs to breathe deeply. Be silent. Be still. Be clever.

I curled in a ball but he was driving fast, so I was thrown back and forth. I banged my head when the car streaked over a pothole. A sharp bend in the road slammed my shoulder against a metal ridge. I was shaken. Juddered. Jarred. Jolted till my bones felt as if they were disconnecting.

But slowly, slowly, my mind started to function again. One by one small facts slotted into place.

Fact 1: I had pegged Joel for an information-carrier, that's all. Passing documents from one person to another. I was wrong. He was dangerous.

Fact 2: the road was uneven and winding. So it was not the route to Serriac or Arles.

Fact 3: he was driving at high speed, too fast on flooded road surfaces. At night. In rain. In bad visibility. He was asking for trouble.

Fact 4: he hadn't pulled over to the side of the road and shot me.

Fact 5: he hadn't dumped my body in the marshes.

Fact 6: the guards at Dumoulin Air Base knew I drove in to meet him. My car was still there.

Fact 7: he now had no choice but to kill me.

My mind jammed on Fact 7. *No choice but to kill me.*

I smacked my thoughts back into action and the obvious question reared up: where was he taking me?

Where?

I didn't know. I was blind in a box.

I felt around but there was only the cardboard carton with papers in it. Nothing else. My fingers found the boot lock and I cursed Major Dirke for having the sense to snatch my bag from me. To snatch my gun.

I lay as still as I could despite the jolting, with the rain hammering down on the boot lid. I had lost.

The car halted. Dimly I heard male voices. My heart was racing, fear playing tricks on me, jumbling my thoughts, but I readied myself. I had twisted round so that I was lying on my back with my knees scrunched up to my chin and my feet by the boot lock. It would be dark outside, so Dirke wouldn't be able to see clearly when he opened the boot.

If he opened the boot. My mind circled round and round that *if* and my breath got all caught up on it, coming in gasps. He might drive the car into the water on the coast and leave me to drown in it. Because that would be my guess, that we'd driven half an hour south to the sea. If I were him, that's what I'd do.

But the voices?

I tensed my muscles. The boot lifted up. The moment I saw Joel Dirke I lashed out with my feet like a jack-in-the-box springing up. Yes, I felt my feet connect. With his face. I knocked him backwards into the rain, and he lost his footing on the muddy ground with a scream. I scrambled out to run but I was seized by strong arms on both sides and swung off my feet, hanging there like a ragdoll.

'Don't give us trouble, bitch,' a deep voice shouted in Russian.

'Get her on board,' urged another Russian on my other side. '*Bystro.*'

I struggled like a wildcat, kicking and biting and screaming at the top of my lungs but it was pointless. They were big heavy men with close-cropped heads and no interest in me except as a package to deliver. As they hauled me along a short jetty I realised I was right. It was a shoreline. Through the driving rain I saw the yawning blackness of the sea and could make out off to my left the flickering lights of a fishing village. It had to be Saintes-Maries-de-la-Mer, where the Camargue meets the Mediterranean.

I was dragged aboard a motor boat and dumped on its slippery wet deck, sobbing and soaked, a male hand knotted into my hair to stop me jumping overboard. The engine started up and I could feel fear wrap itself around my spine as we slid out into the darkness.

CHAPTER FORTY-SIX

I was tipped down the companionway. No ceremony. No consideration for broken bones. I caught my nose on the way down as I tumbled into the saloon, but at least I could stand on my own two feet now without being shaken like a ragdoll. I braced myself against the roll of the boat.

Do you know what it's like when the worst that can happen finally happens? The relief it brings is enormous. Because you no longer have to carry the weight of fear. That's what I experienced now as I hit the floor in the saloon, the freedom that comes with having nothing to lose. The pounding in my head ceased and somewhere deep inside me strings were being cut that had tied me in knots.

'Hello, André,' I said.

'Eloïse!'

'You're not looking so good.' I smiled to show him I'd reached that point of freedom.

The boat's saloon was all highly varnished wood and gleaming brass with red velvet benches on which sat three other people. Only one I didn't know, and I think I can safely call him a heavy. Another big man, wearing a black waistcoat with silver buttons and a tattoo on the side of his neck. Russian, I'm guessing. He carried a gun in his hand.

On the other bench sat André and Joel Dirke. The difference between them was that whereas Joel was wearing a smart uniform, drinking out of a bottle of beer, and had a face unmarked by anything more than a few raindrops, André's face bore signs of his recent struggles. Cuts and bruises marked his skin, and his hands were bound tightly together at the wrist. Worse, his wrists were attached by rope to a concrete block between his feet, the rope looped around a metal staple in the block. It was not hard to guess its purpose. Big enough to drag him to the seabed. I was certain I'd have one of my own very soon.

'André, I'm sorry.' I spoke as if no one else were in the room. 'I'm sorry I didn't protect you well enough.'

'Eloïse.' He said my name the way he used to when we were children, with the emphasis on the first syllable. 'You did everything you possibly could.' He smiled a sad smile at me. 'Considering I tied one hand behind your back.'

The Russian who had dumped me down the companionway descended behind me and pushed me over to the bench beside his fellow countryman.

'Sit!' he shouted.

I sat and felt the boat rock under me in a sudden swell. 'Major Dirke.' The American officer didn't look at me. 'You are not the kind of man I thought you were.'

'You and your brother are fighting for the wrong cause,' he responded angrily, though it seemed to me that I was the one with cause to be angry. 'The only way we can maintain peace in this world is by keeping an equal balance of power, so yes, you may rant and rage about treachery but I am passing technical information to the Russians for a very good reason. Otherwise America will ride roughshod over the whole world with its commercialism, backed up by its H-bombs.'

I wasn't here to argue; it was too late for that.

'You don't understand,' he said, 'what terrible forces you are unleashing on the Western world by enabling American expansionism to spread unchecked. You haven't experienced it close up the way I have.'

I turned away from him with a shudder and spoke to my brother. 'I lost you, André, I no longer know where your allegiance lies. Are you working for Russia? Or for America? Judging by that concrete block at your feet it seems the Communists have already made up their minds to that question.'

'I told you to trust me, didn't I? But I didn't make it easy for you, I know. The only reason I told you that Bertin and Piquet were MGB Soviet agents was to keep you away from them. To ensure you stayed safe, Eloïse. I couldn't bear for you to get hurt.'

'But why? Why keep me away from them if they were CIA agents and no danger to me?'

'Because I didn't want you killed, my courageous little sister.'

I frowned in confusion. 'Who would want to kill me?'

'Me, of course, *chérie*.'

At the top of the companionway stood Clarisse.

'How many times, *chérie*, did I ask you to return to Paris? To get away from here?'

Clarisse had raised her voice to compete with the rain thundering down on the cabin roof and shrugged off her bright orange oilskin. She was dressed in black, black for grief. That is what she said to me. 'I don't want to watch you die. It breaks my heart,' she murmured.

I had no words. No recriminations. No rage at the woman who now freely admitted she was one of the Soviet handlers of MGB agents, not even when she confessed she had fired a rifle bullet into my hair and into my cat to warn me off staying down here in the Camargue. What good was rage to me now?

'Why are you doing this, Clarisse?'

'Didn't your brother tell you? The CIA suspected I was working for the Soviets but they could find no proof. They were always sniffing around and getting nowhere, so your brother used you. To spy on me. When you were at my detective agency in Paris the CIA agents believed you were working for me in every sense – as a detective and as an espionage operative. You see, Eloïse, you were so damn good at the detective jobs that it enabled me to extract large amounts of cash from some of the richest men in Paris.'

'What? How do you mean?'

'Through blackmail, of course. To finance the Communist Party activists in France. All those dirty little secrets you were so adept at digging up for me and yet you never suspected a thing. You helped a lot.' She smiled but I was not fooled by it this time.

I shook my head vehemently. 'No! No, that's not why I did my job for you. Not so you could blackmail them.'

'Hush, *chérie*, calm down. I know that, but your charming CIA thugs – Bertin and Piquet – didn't. I'd recruited your brother to defect to my side and they believed you had defected too. André is a double agent, yes. Handled by us. And yes, he used you. He got his little sister to work for me in Paris, so she could report back to the CIA on what I was doing. But he was very selective. He only gave them sufficient snippets to stop them getting suspicious that he had turned. Oh, *chérie*, don't look like that. He was the one who suggested I recruit you that day when you sat in the café with your friend like a little flower waiting to be picked.'

I felt sick. And it was nothing to do with the rolling sea.

'André? Is it true? I remember you were always asking what cases I was working on.'

André edged forward on his seat to be closer to me. 'Yes, it's true. I realise now that I should never have got you involved, but you were so eager and you could be so useful. But after the van crash, I knew the only way I could keep you alive was through ignorance. I tried to send you back to Paris so many times for your own safety but you wouldn't go. You just kept digging to find out who the informants were at

Dumoulin Air Base. When that airman was stabbed, you just had to find out what other leaks were coming out of there, didn't you? You sank your teeth in and wouldn't let go.'

I turned away from him. It hurt too much to look at him.

'Listen to me, Eloïse,' he insisted. 'I had to keep you away from the CIA men because if *she*,' the word was filled with disgust, 'thought for one second that you were in contact with them, she'd have killed you without hesitation.' He raised tormented eyes to her. 'Isn't that so, Clarisse?'

She smiled at me with such sorrow. 'Yes, it's true.'

Something bad wrenched loose inside me. 'So it was all about maintaining your network to get top-secret information out of Dumoulin?'

'Of course it was,' snapped Joel Dirke. 'And you came and started tearing it apart.'

'You are betraying your country,' I said to Clarisse. 'You are a traitor and you *will* be executed.'

She came over, sat on the bench next to me and draped an affectionate arm around my shoulders. I shook it off roughly. She winced and rubbed her ribs, pulling a face at André. 'Your bloody bullet at the farm came close to ending it for me after I shot the wretched cat. You scraped my ribs raw. Don't shudder, *chérie*.' She kissed my cheek. 'It was all working so well till you came.'

'Do you really think no one else will realise what you are doing?' I said. 'I've already found out that you' – I pointed at Joel – 'and Mickey Ashton were handing stolen secret documents to my brother in the bars of Serriac on a Saturday night. He then took them to Paris. With Mayor Durand playing middleman.'

'That foolish mayor,' Clarisse said with a sigh of annoyance, 'was getting too greedy. Always wanting more and more money for every scrap of information, however small. I had to teach him a lesson.'

'A lesson?'

A lesson? Abruptly I made the connection and it sent a chill through me. What kind of evil person was she, this woman who'd been my friend? 'You killed Bertin,' I said. 'With the mayor's gun.'

'Exactly, *chérie*. Bertin was becoming too troublesome.' She gave me a slow smile intended to provoke. 'You're not the only one who knows how to pick a lock.' She turned to André but my brother wouldn't even look at her. 'A lesson for you too, *mon ami*. I stole Durand's gun and set your baby brother up to take the fall for that job, so that you'd know not to step out of line in future. Especially when your lovely sister was in such danger now. But somehow the little Houdini got out of there before the police arrived.' She switched her attention back to me with sharp suspicion. 'Did you have anything to do with that, Eloïse?'

'No.'

Clarisse was a killer. A cold-blooded killer. This woman who had helped me and cared for me and brought flowers when I was ill. Who was she? It was only extraordinary good fortune and lucky timing that had saved my younger brother Isaac from rotting in a gaol cell right now. The pain of it cut too deep and left too many parts of me in tatters. Oh André, what have you done to me?

'After the accident—' Joel started to say.

'It wasn't an accident.'

'Okay, after your brother was injured, we had to change to doing the handover in church on a Sunday and Clarisse came down to set up a new courier to Paris.'

'So now you know,' Clarisse said. 'Satisfied?'

'No,' I said. I wished André would speak. He sat silent, eyes on the concrete block. 'Who killed Goliath and burnt down our stables? Was it you, Clarisse, giving more of your "lessons" to my brother?'

She looked surprised. 'No, I had nothing to do with it. But I know who did it. Don't you?'

I shook my head, but André looked up, his face part dead already. I could not bear to see him so defeated.

'I can guess,' he said.

'Who?' I asked quickly. 'Who?'

'Mademoiselle Madeleine Caron.'

'The headmistress? Why would she do that?'

Clarisse nodded. 'You always were a good guesser, André. Yes, it was Madeleine Caron. She loathed you Caussades. Claimed you represent everything that is unequal in Western society and wanted your farm broken up and distributed among the *gardians*.'

André groaned. 'Her four nephews are *gardians*, aren't they? They will be the bastards who killed Goliath. You and your Communist principles are evil, Clarisse.'

Clarisse's tone suddenly flipped into one of cold anger. 'You think your cosy world down here with your horses and your bulls is so safe, don't you? But you're wrong. A new world is coming, one we are fighting for, dying for. At war for. We have cells like this one in every American base in the country, with people passionate about our cause. Don't you understand that? Communism will bring justice and equality to the people of France at last, it will bring freedom from the crippling yoke of capitalism – even your brother Isaac understands. He is one of us. This is just the start.'

She took my chin in her hand and turned my battered face towards hers. 'You could still be a part of it, Eloïse.'

I spat in her face.

She leaned closer and kissed my mouth. 'I never wanted to kill you, *chérie*,' she whispered.

'You drove the van, didn't you?' I said bleakly.

There was a silence in the saloon. The boat's engine rumbled in the background while the rain continued its incessant hammering, and the waves slapped at the hull outside, but no one spoke inside.

Slowly Clarisse nodded. Her face was sad and suddenly looked older. 'This job is not easy, *chérie*. I didn't know you were in the car, I swear. I thought André was driving. I didn't trust him anymore, I suspected he was feeding more and more details of my organisation back to the CIA, so he had to go.' Her hand reached for mine. 'I didn't mean to hurt you.'

I leaped at her. My hands closed on her throat before the Russian could make a move, but Joel was the first to react.

He slammed his beer bottle against the side of my head, but the American was a gentleman by nature and would never hit a woman hard. I rolled to the floor and backed up towards André, who nudged his leg against me. It was like old times. I knew immediately what he was telling me.

Clarisse glared at me as she clutched her throat. Her mouth was a tight hard line.

'Throw them overboard,' she ordered.

CHAPTER FORTY-SEVEN

It was cold on deck but the air scoured my lungs clean after the filth in the saloon. The rain was falling hard and I was grateful because it washed her kiss from my lips as I emerged from below. The wind had eased and the night wrapped around us like a barrel of pitch, except for the thin gleam of lights from the fishing village still within sight on the shoreline.

My senses absorbed these things. But my mind was sharp and clear and focused on André coming up the short companionway behind me. He was stumbling. Making it awkward for the Russian behind him. In his arms he clutched the concrete block to which he was attached and the other Russian, who had followed me, leaned down to yank him up. In that moment I shrugged off my oilskin and kicked off my shoes, ready for what was coming.

André struggled out into the open, battered by the rain and releasing the block on to the deck with obvious relief.

His eyes found mine. What did I see there? In that brief flash I saw the same look he'd given me when we would hurl ourselves off the bridge into the mighty Rhône. The certainty that we were immortal. And just as I did back then, I believed him.

One of the Russians came at me with a rope to tie my hands, and I fought him off so savagely that the second one, clearly not a good sailor, lurched over and grabbed my arm. That was his mistake. He thought he could take his eyes off my brother for even one moment.

I saw André brace his feet against the wet deck, lean back and start to turn. Within seconds he was yanking the concrete block at the end of the rope up into the air. Spinning like a hammer-thrower. Using his body as a fulcrum, he swung the block, whirling it through the pouring rain like Thor wielding his hammer and slammed it into the back of the Russian who was trying to break my arm. I heard ribs crack. He dropped like a sack of shit. The second one abandoned the rope he was holding and was reaching for his gun when the block came round for a second swing. Lower this time. It took out his legs. He went down with a scream.

The third Russian came charging up the companion-way and fired wildly into the night, but he had the sense to stay within the safety of the hatch to avoid the swinging block. Balancing himself against the pitching of the boat he squinted against the rain and tried to take more careful aim.

Now. It was now. Or it was never. I jumped up on to the side of the boat. André scooped up his block in the cradle of his strong arms, took a grip on the wrist I offered him and we pushed off. Down into the blackness.

He was trusting me.

Shock numbs the brain. Cold numbs the limbs.

For a heartbeat I froze. But instincts are strong. I kicked frantically to try to slow our descent but the block was like an anchor dragging us down. I could see nothing. The blackness as dark as a tomb, but I kept my grip on my brother. I would drown before I let go of him.

We fought the weight of the concrete, though our lungs were starting to beg for air. It should only have taken a second for me to seize the sheath knife strapped to my brother's shin under his trousers, the one I'd felt when he'd nudged his leg against me in the saloon. He'd often worn one as a boy in the wilds of the marshes, to skin a snake or build a thatch. It should have taken me a second to extract it. It took me five.

My muscles were slowing. My brain was sluggish. The cold water stealing their strength. Bright lights were sparking behind my eyelids, my brain fighting for oxygen. Blackness curling in at the edges.

I started to cut the rope with the knife. Laborious aching movements. Jerky. Blind. Lungs burning and thoughts losing track as we descended deeper. But I should have known that any blade of André's would be sharper than a scalpel and before I'd realised what I'd done, it had sliced right through. Suddenly we were flying up. An illusion. Of course. We had stopped descending, that was all. I told my legs to kick for the surface, but they didn't hear. A hand wrapped itself around my arm and we started to rise.

CHAPTER FORTY-EIGHT

We lay on the muddy shore. Stretched out on our backs, gazing up into the murky blackness of the night sky as if it were the most beautiful sight on earth. Rain was pouring down on our faces and it brought my skin and my thoughts back to life. André had proved it again – the Caussades are immortal.

We were both breathing hard from the swim but one thing struck me. 'Your legs did well,' I said. 'They didn't seem to slow you up.'

A chuckle at my side startled me. 'Oh, Eloïse, I thought you'd have guessed. I have been working them hard for months and regaining use of them steadily.'

'But the wheelchair? The stumbling?'

'A front. To make others believe I was finished, washed up.'

Always a pretence. Always hiding something. As if he was frightened to let anyone see him, really see the person he was. Did this brother of mine even know himself who he was?

'You could have told *me*,' I pointed out.

'No, I couldn't. You of all people had to believe I was crippled to convince others it was true.'

'You were using me again.' It was an accusation.

He turned his head. In the darkness I could just make out his gentle smile. 'Yes, I was. Thank you, Eloïse. Thank you for everything you did to help me. I'm glad I trusted you. I never stopped working for the CIA. The rest – all the passing information to Clarisse – was a front, like the stumbling I did to confuse others. Bertin and Piquet always believed I had been completely turned and gone over to the MGB, but it wasn't true. I want you to believe me, Eloïse.'

It sounded like a goodbye.

But he didn't wait for a response from me. He sat up quickly. 'Now,' he said, 'let's go find that boat.'

The rain turned to drizzle as I ran barefoot along the coastal path that led to the lights of Saintes-Maries-de-la-Mer. André raced ahead of me and though his legs might not yet be quite what they used to be, his eyes certainly were. He could pick his way at night as sharp as a fox and he led me across the long soft stretch of sand to the jetties where the boats were moored.

No one was about in this filthy weather, the small village hunkered down till the morning. Under cover of darkness we padded silently in wet clothes down the jetty where the smaller boats bobbed quietly, pulling at their ropes. The creak of masts like old bones and the rattle of sheets and mooring rings murmured around us, but nobody came to challenge us. André selected one boat. Small, neat, but fast-looking. He jumped on board, put his foot straight through the hatch lock and slipped down to the engine room.

I stood on the jetty, tense, keeping watch. Now that the dense veil of rain had thinned, I could see a light out in the distance on the black expanse of water, so fiercely black tonight it looked like a hole in the earth's crust. The light came and went, flickering in and out of my vision, and my heart tightened in my chest as the conviction grew inside me that it was the boat from which we'd jumped. Returning to its mooring. Clarisse was coming back for me.

At my feet an engine barked into life. André had managed to get it going and was untying its ropes. I hopped down on to its deck.

'No,' André said immediately. 'You're not coming.'

'Of course I am. You can't think that at this stage I'm backing out when—'

He didn't argue. He came over to me. Gave me a smile and pushed me overboard.

I stood on the beach, sand cold between my toes, the surf swirling around my ankles, turning them numb. I didn't notice. My eyes were locked on the light in the distance, nearer now, growing larger, my ears straining for the sound of its engine.

Don't, André, don't. I beg you.

I didn't know whether the words were inside or outside

my head. If I'd known how to start a boat I would have gone hurtling after him, but I didn't. So I waited, gaze fixed, mind churning, and felt fear again slink its way under my skin.

The night had swallowed André's boat because he was running it with no lights, but I knew precisely where it was headed. If he tried to climb back on board Clarisse's boat he would be torn to shreds by her three Russian bears. He had no gun. Only a knife. A knife against a Tokarev gun.

But she was a traitor to France. My brother was not a man to walk away from that.

The low boom of the waves, churning and growling like a live animal, merged with my thoughts, pounding inside my head.

'André!' I shouted out to sea. 'Don't! Please don't.'

But my words were lost, it was too late. A vein of lightning ripped the night sky apart and I saw clearly the two boats. The smaller one was racing towards the larger one, almost there, so close now. The white glare of the lightning flash vanished, robbing me of my night vision, but I blinked and found the boat's light again. My toes dug deep into the wet sand.

Then an explosion shattered the night. A violent sheet of flame roared up into the black sky as André's boat slammed at full speed into Clarisse's vessel. I couldn't hear the noise of it. I couldn't hear the waves at my feet. I couldn't hear the beat of my own heart. All I could hear was the scream from hell spilling out of my mouth.

*

393

Dawn trickled over the horizon, grey and soulless. I'd stood on the beach all night, waiting for my brother. But he didn't come. Dimly I was aware of movement around me, of people, of uniforms, of voices. Some spoke to me, some left me alone as if I looked like a leper. They all merged in my mind, all lost in the mists of my grief.

Only Léon was real. Only his voice reached me and only his tender grey eyes brought a flare of warmth to the cold sorrow that lay behind my ribs. He wrapped a warm blanket around me and stood at my side hour after hour while his men questioned local inhabitants and trawled the sea for wreckage.

And for bodies.

'How many?' I asked.

'Five.'

'Are they recognisable?'

'Some. One, sad to say, is Major Dirke.'

I nodded. 'I'm sorry.'

I watched a seagull stalk the surf with its feet like yellow plates that it slapped on the sand till a tiny pink crab emerged. The orange beak devoured it.

'The other four men I don't recognise.'

'Do three have tattoos?'

'Yes, they do.'

'They're Russian. They were on Clarisse's boat.'

'That is important to know.'

'No women's bodies? No sign of Clarisse?'

'No. The fourth man is in marine clothes, so he might have been the pilot.'

I licked my dry lips three times before I got the words out. 'No sign of André?'

'No, Eloïse, I'm sorry.' He curled his arms around me, drawing me close, rubbing his hands up and down my back to build some heat within me. His breath was soft on my ear. 'He might have jumped.'

I jerked back my head. 'What?'

'André might have jumped from his boat just before it hit Clarisse's.' He gave me a smile and my heart started to beat steadily. 'He might be alive.'

I breathed deeply, the early morning air scented with the salty tang of the sea and I caught a glimpse of the first glimmer of hope.

CHAPTER FORTY-NINE

Two months later

The blush of pink wings filled the sky, skinny legs trailing behind, long necks thrust forward like rosy walking sticks. The flamingos were lifting off the water in the last rays of the setting sun, when the lagoon looked on fire and the shadows lengthened. We were all caught on the cusp between night and day.

I sat astride Cosette and ambled peacefully around the dense beds of reed that fringed the lagoon. A lurid green tree-frog crossed our trail and Cosette whinnied softly to tell me about it. We took this track every evening, sometimes with Léon at our side on Achille, to watch the thousands of flamingos leaving their feeding grounds to fly to their roosting sites for the night. I watched the scene with infinite pleasure and each time I saw the birds leave, I thought of how I had left for Paris because I thought my world lay there.

Foolishly, I'd thought I could live without the place that

formed the bedrock of who I am. I gave Cosette's neck a pat and with no direction from me she stepped off the trail into a dense knot of tamarisks and undergrowth where a silvery white egret was preening its feathers on the roof of a dilapidated hut. It was draped in sea-green moss and silvery lichen, leaning back into the foliage behind it as though trying to hide. Exactly like the person who built it.

I dismounted and loosened Cosette's girth, so that she could graze in comfort.

Inside the hut lay some lengths of timber and a box of nails. I took a hammer off the rickety windowsill and continued the task I had started yesterday, replacing the rotten planks at the back. It was not my hut. It was André's. He had built it in the days when he ran free on the marshes, but it had slowly shed its sturdiness over the years.

I hadn't heard from André. I didn't expect to.

It had taken me a long time but I had finally learned what manner of man he is. A man of blind devotion to his country. I won't say what manner of man André *was* because I choose to think of him as alive. Still on the prowl out there. Of course I know I could be mistaken. But he is still a fundamental part of my family, and I hold on to that.

I continued to bang in nails contentedly and looked out through the grimy window at the first clouds bunched on the horizon, moody and gold-tipped. Dark political clouds were rolling from the east too that would test France to the limit, but I had faith in my country. In my country and in my fellow countrymen and women.

Traitors like Clarisse will not succeed in dragging France into servitude under the yoke of Communism, because we will root them out, every last one of them. I hit the shiny head of the nail with my hammer, driving it into place, just as we will drive people like Clarisse into the place they deserve.

I was wrong when I thought I could be a part of that world, but it took a person like Léon to show me that a world of lies and secrets and deceit is not a world I want to be a part of. So I work on the farm now. I have great ideas for it and sit at night with Léon drawing up plans and schemes that Papa will agree to. The world is changing and we will be changing with it.

And when André comes, the hut will be ready.

Acknowledgements

A book is a complex animal and it takes a complex process, which involves many very clever people, for it to end up looking so smart and sassy on a bookshelf. I am always in awe of the wondrous and dedicated team at Simon & Schuster UK who work such miracles for me and my book. Thank you a million times over to each and every one of you.

I am profoundly grateful to my superb editor Jo Dickinson for her wisdom and insight and for her calmness when I am in urgent need of it. Thank you, Jo, for everything you do. It is a privilege to work with you, the best of the best.

Huge thanks also to my awesome agent Teresa Chris for all the support and kindness, and yes, for all the whip-cracking when required too. You help make my job a joy.

I am greatly indebted to Lieutenant Scott Dyson of the RCN for being a constant source of information concerning all things military and for his generosity in giving time and expertise. However much research info I gleaned from military books, it was invaluable to have a military voice at my side to guide me away from pitfalls. Any errors are definitely mine, not his.

Thank you to Steve Sharam for – well, just for being his inimitable self, listening to my bookish woes and for introducing me to Scott Dyson. My warm thanks also to David Gilman for his daily shot in the digital-arm to keep me going.

Thanks yet again to my fabulous buddies in Brixham Writers. Always full of wise advice and noisy laughter. I raise a cup of tea and a choccie biscuit to you!

For her friendship and her speedy fingers my huge thanks to Marian Churchward. You make it fun as always.

Lastly my love and thanks to Norman for his encouragement and belief in my story throughout all the crazy ups and downs and sleepless nights, for his ingenious ideas when I'd tied myself in a knot and for sharing his impressive knowledge of aircraft.

Kate Furnivall

The Survivors

'Directly I saw him, I knew he had to die.'

Germany, 1945.

Klara Janowska and her daughter Alicja have walked for weeks to get to Graufeld Displaced Persons camp. In the cramped, dirty, dangerous conditions they, along with 3,200 others, are the lucky ones. They have survived and will do anything to find a way back home.

But when Klara recognises a man in the camp from her past, a deadly game of cat and mouse begins.

He knows exactly what she did during the war to save her daughter. She knows his real identity.

What will be the price of silence? And will either make it out of the camp alive?

AVAILABLE NOW IN PAPERBACK, EBOOK AND AUDIOBOOK

SIMON & SCHUSTER

Kate Furnivall

The Betrayal

Could you kill someone? Someone you love?

Paris, 1938.

Twin sisters are divided by fierce loyalties and by a
terrible secret. The drums of war are beating and France is poised,
ready to fall. One sister is an aviatrix, the other is a socialite
and they both have something to prove and something to hide.

The Betrayal is an unforgettably powerful, epic story
of love, loss and the long shadow of war, perfect for
readers of Santa Montefiore and Victoria Hislop.

**'Exquisitely heart-wrenching and utterly
engrossing. *The Betrayal* is an absolute gem'
Penny Parkes, author of *Best Practice***

**AVAILABLE NOW IN PAPERBACK,
EBOOK AND AUDIOBOOK**

**SIMON &
SCHUSTER**

Kate Furnivall
The Liberation

A country in turmoil.
A woman with one chance to save herself.

Italy, 1945.

Caterina Lombardi is desperate – her father is dead, her mother has disappeared and her brother is being drawn towards danger. One morning, among the ruins of the bombed Naples streets, Caterina is forced to go to extreme lengths to protect her own life and in doing so forges a future in which she must clear her father's name.

An Allied Army officer accuses her father of treason and Caterina discovers a plot against her family. Who can she trust and who is the real enemy now? And will the secrets of the past be her downfall?

This epic novel is an unforgettably powerful story of love, loss and the long shadow of war.

'A thrilling roller-coaster of a read, seductive, mysterious and edgy. I LOVED it'
Dinah Jefferies, author of *The Tea Planter's Wife*

AVAILABLE NOW IN PAPERBACK,
EBOOK AND AUDIOBOOK

SIMON &
SCHUSTER